RUN TIME

CATHERINE
RYAN HOWARD

CORVUS

First published in Great Britain in 2022 by Corvus, an imprint of
Atlantic Books Ltd.

10 9 8 7 6 5 4 3 2 1

A CIP catalogue record for this book is available from the British Library.

Hardback ISBN: 978 1 83895 166 5
Trade paperback ISBN: 978 1 83895 167 2
E-book ISBN: 978 1 83895 168 9

Corvus
An imprint of Atlantic Books Ltd
Ormond House
26–27 Boswell Street
London
WC1N 3JZ

www.corvus-books.co.uk

Printed and bound by CPI Group (UK) Ltd, Croydon CR0 4YY

RUN TIME

The road is narrow, the edges of it crumbling, as if losing its battle to hold the treeline back.

Donal is tense behind the wheel. Grip tight, back ramrod-straight, eyes fixed on the road surface illuminated by the beam of the headlights. The rental is a seven-seater Volvo that gave him pause when he saw it first and made him sweat nervously when he found he had to step *up* into it. He's only ever driven his own succession of second-hand Nissan Micras, and only around and between cities on smooth, well-lit streets. This car is far bigger and more powerful, and this road is basically a boreen with ambition.

Underneath the wheels, he feels the surface start to gently rise. It's cutting through dense, gloomy forest, steadily thickening with darkness on either side of the car. Donal knows this is because it's gone six on an overcast, late-January evening, but it feels like it's because the forest is absorbing the light, sucking it in, swallowing it up whole.

Feeding on it.

'It's so creepy out here,' he says.

Steve, sitting in the passenger seat, snorts and says, 'That's, like, the whole idea?' in a tone that adds a silent *you idiot* on to the sentence's end.

A heat flares across Donal's face.

He's already downsized his goals from *Do such an amazing job that you and Steve Dade cement a years-long professional partnership that will culminate in you both on stage at the Dolby*

1

Theatre holding a pair of little gold men to *Don't get fired before shooting starts*. Donal has never held an assistant director position before. Not even close unless you counted the word *assistant*. His most recent job was glorified receptionist-slash-dogsbody at a casting agency. Getting a gig as Steve Dade's AD on this was an incredibly lucky break and Donal can*not* blow it.

The problem is that he's intensely aware of that and has been a ball of acute anxiety ever since he reported to set. He can only hope that when shooting starts tomorrow, he'll be better at his job than he's been at making conversation.

'This is such a waste of time,' Steve says. 'They're probably not even there.'

'We can leave a note.'

'Can't we just leave a note anyway?'

'Joanne asked that we speak to them,' Donal says, 'as a courtesy. That you do.'

Joanne is the owner of Cedarwood House, their set, and also this other, smaller property, Cedarwood Lodge. Steve had refused to spend the money to book out the lodge as well, so here they are, driving to warn the Airbnb-ers who *did* book it this weekend about the shoot.

Steve groans like a teenager who's just been ordered to go do his homework.

'What are they even *doing* out here?'

'Mini-break,' Donal says. 'A last-minute booking.'

'Who books a house in a place like this in *January*? Wait.' Steve twists in his seat to look back down the road. 'Did you miss the turn? She said the gates were a mile apart. We should have— *There!*'

This exclamation coincides with him jutting an arm across Donal's face to point at something on the driver's side, obstructing Donal's view and making him slam a foot on the brake in panic.

The car screeches and shudders to a violent stop that jerks both men forward against their seatbelts before shoving them back against them again.

'*Dude*,' Steve says. 'What the fuck?'

Donal mumbles an apology even though it was clearly Steve's fault, then looks for what Steve was pointing at.

The right headlight has found a wooden sign, hand-painted and peeling, nailed to a tree trunk at the edge of the road: CEDARWOOD LODGE, above a black arrow. In the gloom beyond, Donal can just about make out that the arrow is pointing to a pair of wrought-iron gates hung between two stone pillars. One stands open, inviting them to turn on to what looks like a dirt track through the trees that immediately disappears into a dense, inky blackness.

'Cedarwood,' Steve scoffs. 'Where did they get the name? Aren't these – what are Christmas trees?'

'Firs,' Donal answers. 'And maybe they're U2 fans.' He turns to find Steve looking at him blankly. 'That's where Bono grew up. Cedarwood Road. In Glasnevin. They have a song about it. On *Songs of Innocence*.'

The blankness is morphing into bemusement, so Donal clears his throat and looks back at the gates, hoping the gloom in the car will hide his blushing cheeks. He just should stop talking to Steve entirely. Become mute. Stop the stupidity that is apparently intent on constantly leaking out of his mouth in the presence of this man.

'Go on, then,' Steve says, pointing. 'Let's go.'

Donal eyes the narrow entrance. 'I should hop out and open the second gate, shouldn't I?'

'Don't be daft. You've *loads* of room.'

'Are you sure? I don't think—'

'It's not a bloody *bus* you're driving.'

It's not a bus, no, but the gap made by the single open gate does not look as wide as the vehicle Donal actually *is* driving.

He bites his lip to stop himself from saying this out loud and lowers his window in the futile hope that this will somehow help him see in this dark. He swaps the brake for the accelerator and begins to turn the wheel, his grip slipping a little on a surface made moist by his own sweat. Tentatively he noses the car through the gap inch by inch, barely breathing, braced for the horror sound of a scrape.

Once he sees the rear of the vehicle has cleared the second, closed gate, he lets his muscles relax with warm relief and, accidentally, breathes a sigh of one too.

'All right, *Granny*,' Steve says.

It is indeed a dirt track beyond the gates, narrower than the road they've just left and dotted with unexpected mounds and water-filled potholes. The chassis bounces over and into every one, while Donal winces in time. Every cent on this shoot counts – because there's so few of them – so of course they opted for the cheapest insurance cover on the car, the policy that probably says if you do any damage at all, you'll have to pay for it out of your own pocket.

'This is *so* pointless,' Steve says. 'They're not even going to hear anything. Not all the way out here.'

And then, as if on cue, they hear something: a high-pitched, otherworldly, testicle-retracting shriek. Loud and getting louder, because whatever is making it is heading right for them.

A set of red glowing brake lights appear on the track up ahead. Except they're not brake lights, because they can't be, because they're too high up off the ground.

Not lights, but *eyes*. Glowing red, in the middle of two enormous wings.

On something that's *flying*.

At high speed.

Directly at them.

At the windshield.

The shrieking takes on a kind of raw, guttural sound that reminds Donal of the demons that get exorcised from dead-eyed, white-haired children in the kind of seventies horror movies he doesn't have the stomach to watch. He jams on the brakes just as he hears Steve say, 'What the——' and then the shrieking reaches a fever-pitch that makes Donal's eardrums thrum with pain, and then there's yelling too, and then a *whooshing* sound, as the … the *thing*, this huge, black, feathered *thing* with a pair of glowing red eyes swoops past them and over the car and disappears into the night.

Silence.

Utter silence. As if, all around them, the dark is holding its breath.

Donal is holding his, *has* been holding his for way too long to be healthy, and now he starts gasping and coughing and trying to swallow down lungfuls of air, while also trying *not* to do this because he's pretty sure he just made a fool of himself and nearly crashed the car and almost wet his pants because of an owl.

An *owl*.

Who, flying directly into their headlights, looked surprisingly large and like he – she? – had red eyes.

'*What*,' Steve says. 'The fuck. Was *that*?'

'An owl.' Donal thinks he's redeeming himself by saying this. Yes, he reacted like it was some kind of monster coming at them, but now he's realised the error of his ways and can offer an informed explanation. 'Barn owls make those kinds of weird screeching noises. That's one of the explanations for banshees, actually. Owls and foxes. Foxes, especially, at this time of year. They're mating calls, but they sound human. Well, human-like. That's what people were actually hear—'

'Foxes don't fly,' Steve snaps, 'and that was way too big to be an owl. Did you not see the *size* of it?'

'Yeah, but it's just a perspective thing. It looked bigger because it was flying right at us.'

'Or because it *was* bigger. That thing was as big as a man. The wingspan must have been, what? Five metres across?'

Donal would've gone with more like one, but he doesn't say this.

'Hey,' Steve says then, 'did you ever hear of the Mothman?'

A chill travels down Donal's spine and into his bladder because, unfortunately, he has. The Mothman was a ghoulish, winged creature, larger than a man, with black feathers and burning red eyes, who was said to stalk the town of Point Pleasant, West Virginia. If you saw him it meant that some kind of awful tragedy was about to happen, or that you were watching a generally mediocre but occasionally terrifying early-noughties movie starring Richard Gere.

Donal had first seen *The Mothman Prophecies* as an impressionable eleven-year-old thanks to an irresponsible babysitter (his older brother) and for years had been convinced that its most disturbing sequence involved the Mothman walking on his wings, like a pterodactyl. But re-watching it (just once) as an adult, he'd discovered there was no such scene.

It must have come from one of the many nightmares he'd had in the weeks after his first viewing.

'Because it looked just like that,' Steve is saying. 'The red eyes, the massive wingspan, the swooping down on to the road ...'

'It was just an owl.'

Donal is telling Steve this, but he's also telling himself.

'Like hell it was,' Steve mutters. 'But hey, did we pick the right place to make a horror movie or what?'

Final Draft is due to start shooting in twenty-four hours, on a secluded set, in the dead of winter. This first week will be all night shoots, in a week that Met Éireann promises will be plagued by violent storms and freezing temperatures. Donal hasn't yet mastered talking to the director, let alone helping him achieve his vision and doing everything that an AD should do, which is basically holding the whole show together. If something goes wrong, the blame will almost certainly land squarely at his feet.

And mothmen, banshees ...

They didn't come to tell you that everything was going to work out just great, don't worry, all good.

It was just an owl, Donal says silently, before releasing the brake and taking them onwards down the dirt track.

The track twists and turns through the trees, hiding the house until the very last moment. It's a small, square, red-brick bungalow sitting in a puddle of gravel that crunches under the wheels as Donal pulls up, parallel to the muddy Ford Fiesta already parked there. Smoke billows from the chimney but only one of the windows – the nearest one to them, to the left of the front door – suggests there's a light on inside. When the headlights disappear, the window transforms into a rectangle of buttery yellow glow.

'Looks like a gatekeeper's lodge,' Donal says. 'Only it's a bit too far from the gate to do any keeping.'

Steve snorts. 'Looks like a shithole to me.'

They get out, their breath clouding in the freezing air. The surrounding trees block what little is left of the daylight. The only way to know there is any is to look straight up, between the trees, into the patch of the blue-grey sky directly above their heads. In a few minutes' time, it will be completely dark.

It's deathly quiet. As they make their way to the lodge's door, the only sound is the crunch of gravel underfoot, and then Steve's firm double-knock seems to ricochet off the trees, dangerously loud.

'They won't be expecting anyone,' Donal whispers. 'Not out here. So let's just hope no one has a gun.'

'Or is a screenwriter.'

'Or worse, thinks they're one.'

Steve makes a *humph* noise that Donal chooses to interpret as a lazy laugh because, bloody hell, he needs the win.

They hear a rustling noise from inside and then the door,

creaking open – just a few inches, enough to reveal a rusting safety-chain pulled taut and, beyond it, half the face of a man eyeing them coldly.

'Hey there,' Steve says, holding up a hand to signal that they come in peace. 'Joanne asked us to call round – the owner?'

The only eyebrow they can see rises in question.

'My name is Steve Dade.' Steve pauses here to, Donal presumes, allow the man the opportunity to say something like, 'Wow! Really? *You're* Steve Dade?' When it doesn't happen, he pushes on. 'I'm directing a movie that we're shooting down at the main house—'

The door abruptly slams shut.

Steve is muttering a, 'What the …?' when the safety-chain rattles and the door re-opens, wide enough now to reveal the whole of the man.

'Sorry,' the man says. 'Say again?'

The man is a little older than Steve, Donal would guess, so late thirties, early forties, but not trying as hard as Steve to look like he hasn't had to start ticking the next box along on the form. He's wearing jeans and an old T-shirt and his feet are in thick, woollen socks, the kind you wear inside hiking boots. Strong jaw, bright blue eyes. He's holding a stemless wine glass, half-filled with red, and something smells good in the air that's wafting out into the night from the space behind him.

They've interrupted his dinner, Donal thinks.

'We're shooting a feature,' Steve says, 'down at the main house.' He points into the woods, pointlessly; the main house is at least a mile away through the trees, so there's nothing to see. 'A horror movie. Starting tomorrow evening. So if

9

you hear any strange noises ... We'll mostly be shooting at night, you see, and there's going to be a bit of screaming. You shouldn't hear anything from here but just in case you do, we wanted to give you a heads-up. So you don't, you know, think someone's getting murdered and call the Gardaí.' Steve laughs here. The man does not. 'We've, ah, spoken to them too, so they should know to tell you anyway. The lads in the station in Durrus, I mean. But Joanne insisted we—'

'We wanted to tell you ourselves,' Donal interrupts, before Steve can suggest they're only here because they were forced to come, or casually deploy any more phrases like *shooting a feature*, or refer to members of An Garda Síochána as *the lads* another time. 'And to give you this, just in case.' He hands over one of his business cards.

It's a very simple affair: plain white, the thinnest paper-stock, Arial in black. All it says is CROSS CUT FILMS above his name, email address and mobile phone number. Donal made them himself, on the inkjet in the production office, just this morning, because Steve said printing professional ones was an unnecessary cost.

'This is Donal,' Steve says. 'My assistant.'

Assistant director, Donal corrects silently. His official credit, but not one Steve has thus far acknowledged in real life.

But then, everyone is wearing many hats on this project. Donal is also, effectively, the line producer *and* production manager. He's his own assistant and an assistant to Steve – who is directing *and* producing – as well as acting as the assistant director. *Assistant* is probably just the easiest catch-all thing to call him, really, when you think about it. That's all it is.

Donal *hopes* that's all it is.

The man is frowning at the business card.

'Don't worry,' Donal says quickly. 'At this distance, with the trees, it's very unlikely you'll hear anything.'

The man opens his mouth to respond – to argue, Donal worries, and he'd be right to because if they're not going to hear anything, why are he and Steve here to warn them not to call the Gardaí if they do? – but before he can, a new hand appears from behind the door.

This one has delicate fingers, pale skin, and tapered nails painted in a high-gloss red. It curls around the edge of the door and pulls it open wider, revealing a second occupant: a woman in a bathrobe. Her long, dark hair is dripping wet.

She takes the business card out of the man's hands and asks Steve, 'What did you say your name was?'

'This is ridiculous,' the man says to her, snatching it back. Then he turns and disappears into the gloom beyond the door.

A moment later, an internal door slams like a thunderclap.

The air swirls and shifts, infused with a new tension. Steve clears his throat and looks off to his left, into the black of the forest, which Donal instinctively knows, after just a few hours in this man's presence, is a signal that his boss is done with this situation and now it's up to him to extricate them from it.

'Don't mind him,' the woman says, managing to pull her eyes off Steve long enough to roll them. 'He's been in a mood since we got here. Says he was told something about a sea view and of course he just can*not* allow for the fact that maybe he looked at a few places and got two of them mixed up. He wants to move to somewhere else, but pickings are pretty slim around here. I guess it's the time of year.' She sighs. Eyes back to Steve. 'Did you say you were the *director*?'

Donal thinks he recognises the tone, the accompanying expression on the woman's face. This conversation is about to go one of three ways. One: she'll ask Steve a bunch of stupid questions, starting with the classic, 'I've always wondered … what does a director actually *do*?' Two: she'll pitch an idea she's convinced would make a great film that in reality barely amounts to an anecdote. Three: she'll say she's always dreamed of being, or is, or thinks she could be, an actor.

Steve knows this too, because he says a curt, 'Yep,' and then, without leaving a pause, 'Anyway, we should be getting back.'

'Sorry to disturb your evening,' Donal says. Steve is already turning to go, collecting Donal at his elbow, turning him around too just as Donal adds an excruciatingly cheerful, 'Have a good night!'

They crunch their way across the gravel, back to the car. The woman stays standing in the open doorway, watching them, until Donal revs the engine and starts reversing. Only then does she turn and go back inside.

'I think we should make as much noise as we possibly can,' Steve mutters. 'Make *sure* they leave.'

ACT I

FINAL DRAFT

Based on a terrifying true story.
That hasn't happened — yet.

Written by
Daniel O'Leary

January 2022

Cross Cut Films
Temple Bar, Dublin 2
danielod@crosscutfilms.ie

FADE IN:

EXT. TRINITY COLLEGE DUBLIN - DAY

Granite university buildings form an imposing
U-shape around an expansive cobbled square in
the heart of Dublin's city centre. At the mouth
of the 'U' sits the emblem of Trinity College
Dublin: the 100ft campanile.

Hundreds of students mill about in early-
morning sunshine, dressed for cold weather.

INT. CLASSROOM - DAY

A vast room with a vaulted ceiling, overlooking
Front Square. Oil paintings of old white men
hang from the walls in antique frames.

A dozen twenty-somethings sit around a table,
listening intently to OLDER MAN 1 (50s,
distinguished looking, designer knitwear)
who is seated at the head of it. Beside him
is OLDER MAN 2 (50s, distracted professor
vibes, tweed blazer with scuffed leather elbow
patches).

> OLDER MAN 1
> So if your characters don't surprise
> *you*, how on earth do you expect them
> to surprise your *readers*?

Heads nod, sounds of agreement are made.

At the opposite end of the table sit KATE
(20s, fresh-faced beauty, bookish) and
GUS (20s, gangly, floppy-haired and badly
dressed).

                    GUS
            (whispering to Kate)
    If your characters are genuinely
    surprising you, you should probably
    seek the services of a mental health
    professional.

                    KATE
                  (to Gus)
    Ssshhh.

                 OLDER MAN 2
    Unfortunately that's all the time
    we have today. Round of applause,
    please, for our distinguished guest,
    who has been so generous with both
    his time and his expertise.

The students comply. Gus does a slow handclap.

              OLDER MAN 2 (CONT'D)
    And all the best with the Booker
    announcement. But of course, whatever
    happens, it truly is an honour just
    to be nominated, isn't it?

Older Man 1 smiles tightly.

                 OLDER MAN 1
    So they say.

The students collect themselves, stand to go.
The room grows noisy with their leaving.

                    GUS
                  (To Kate)
    It might be an honour but it's not
    fifty grand, is it?

Kate slaps his arm in playful reprimand.

EXT. TRINITY COLLEGE DUBLIN - DAY

Kate and Gus make their way across Front
Square, joining the flow of other students
disappearing into the tunnel beneath the thick
concrete and grimy windows of the Brutalist
Arts Block.

EXT. BOOKSHOP - DAY

They emerge into chilly, midday sunlight and
make a beeline for a bookshop housed in a
distinctive, red-brick building with a pair of
large bay windows at the front. The sign over
the entrance reads 'HODGES FIGGIS'.

One window displays multiple copies of the same
book: *Evenings* by George Weston. Hanging behind
them is a large photo of the author posing
behind a chesterfield desk in a book-lined
office, no computer in sight. George Weston is
Older Man 1.

A small, handwritten note on paper torn from
a pad and hastily taped to the glass at elbow-
rather than eye-line says that Joel Jackson will
be signing copies of his new book *Inside* in-
store today.

Kate and Gus disappear inside …

INT. BOOKSHOP - DAY [CONTINUOUS]

… and enter an expansive bookstore, full
of nooks and crannies. Customers browse in
respectful quiet, as if in a library.

Kate goes to shelves marked 'Fiction A-Z' and starts reading the spines.

> GUS
>
> What are you looking for?

> KATE
>
> That book George mentioned. The one about the British butler during World War II.

> GUS
> (scoffing)
> *George?* You two are BFFs now, are you?

> KATE
>
> That's what he said to call him.

> GUS
>
> He didn't mean it.

> KATE
>
> Help me look or be quiet.

> GUS
>
> I'll be quiet in Crime.

He leaves Kate to her search, which ultimately proves fruitless. Kate spots a man stacking books on a table nearby and approaches him.

This is JOEL (30s, handsome, wearing trendy trainers and trendy frames).

> KATE
>
> Sorry to bother you, but do you have *The Remains of the Day*?

                    JOEL
          Oh - I don't work here. Sorry.

Kate looks down at the table, confused.

                JOEL (CONT'D)
          These are mine. I mean, I wrote them.
          It.

An acrylic sign is sitting on top of the books.
He turns it around so Kate can see it. It's a
picture of Joel holding a copy of *Inside*.

                    KATE
          Oh God. I'm so sorry.

                    JOEL
          Don't be. Happens all the time. And
          at least you asked me about a book.
          Usually people are looking for the
          toilets.

                    KATE
          Sounds glamorous.

                    JOEL
          Hey, it gets me out of the house.

                    KATE
          Are you here to do a signing?

                    JOEL
          I am, but alas no one is here to get
          their book signed.

                    KATE
          That's not true. I'm here.

JOEL

You're looking for Ishiguro.

KATE

Not any more. I've changed my mind.

JOEL

You shouldn't. Trust me.

KATE

Do they teach you how to promote your
own books or are you just a natural
at it?
          (pointing to the books)
Will you sign one for me?

JOEL

Are you *sure*?

KATE

I have enough points on my loyalty
card to cover it, so I don't really
need to be, do I?

JOEL

Well, God knows I need the sale.

He picks up a copy and takes a pen from a
pocket.

JOEL (CONT'D)

Who should I make it out to?

KATE

Kate. Spelled the usual way.

Joel signs the book.

                         JOEL
          Nice to meet you, Kate spelled the
          usual way. I'm Joel.

                         KATE
          I should hope so. Otherwise you're
          just desecrating that book.

Joel laughs.

                         JOEL
          So what do you do, Kate? Besides take
          pity on unpopular authors.

He hands the signed book back to her.

                         KATE
          I dream of being an unpopular author
          someone else takes pity on one
          day. I'm a student. On the Creative
          Writing MA, across the street.

                         JOEL
          So you're a writer.

                         KATE
          Trying to be.

Gus reappears, clutching a couple of blood-
spattered true-crime books.

                      KATE (CONT'D)
                        (to Joel)
          This is my friend, Gus. He's trying
          to be a writer, too.
                        (to Gus)
          This is Joel. And this is his book.

Gus and Joel exchange silent nods. Gus looks
down at the table of books, makes a face.

> GUS
> Looks like it's flying off the
> shelves.

> KATE
> (warningly)
> Gus.

> GUS
> (faking innocence)
> What?

A beat of awkward silence.

> KATE
> (to Joel)
> Well, we better go. We have a seminar
> starting soon.

> JOEL
> And I have a very busy afternoon of
> standing here alone to get to.

> KATE
> Can I ask you something?

> JOEL
> Sure.

> KATE
> What's the best writing advice you
> ever got?

Gus rolls his eyes while Joel considers the
question.

                         JOEL
        I'd have to say … Write the book you
        want to read but can't find on the
        shelf.

                         KATE
        Oh, that's good.

                         JOEL
        Isn't it? Unfortunately I didn't take
        it, so now no one else wants to read
        it either.

                         KATE
        That's not true. I do.

                         JOEL
        Get back to me in fifty pages.

                         KATE
        I will.

                         JOEL
        I hope so.

His gaze lingers on Kate until she looks away,
blushing.

A cranky Gus pulls her away by the elbow. They
join the queue for the cash registers.

While awaiting her turn, Kate opens her copy
of *Inside* and sees that Joel hasn't just
signed it - he's written his number in it too.
She looks back towards the table where Joel is
standing, meets his eye and smiles.

                                    DISSOLVE TO:

ONE

It all started the day of the audition.

A TV commercial, for Neutraxium, a headache pill that sounded like something that would *give* you a headache. I was auditioning for the role of ROLLERBLADER (female, 20–22, Caucasian), a 'natural beachy beauty, subtly sexy, with a gym-toned body and California-cool, Gwyneth vibes', who simply *refused* to let headache pain get in her way.

I was none of those things, but I guess that's why they call it acting.

The hallway outside the audition room was lined with the usual suspects: young, fair-haired, willowy white women who had grown up in towns where their beauty was considered exceptional – who had then moved to LA to discover the same face just helped them fade into the crowd.

I took an empty seat and surveyed the competition while pretending to read over my lines – *line*. About half of the other auditionees were actually in rollerblades or sitting with a pair of them lined up on the floor by their feet. No one was wearing clothes that extended beyond the shoulder or below the knee, even though it was a January day and, for LA, a cold one. Most were lightly tanned and sporting beachy waves. Nearly everyone was sipping continuously from a water bottle bigger than their head. A reusable one, of course.

My beach waves were frizz; my skin was the pasty, bluish pallor of someone who spent most of the daylight hours inside under fluorescents; and my single-use plastic cup was filled with a sickly sweet, artificially flavoured iced-coffee concoction. But casting directors weren't looking for perfect. They didn't know *what* they were looking for, especially when it came to commercials. Every time I auditioned for one, I saved the description to a note in my phone just so I could compare it to the actor in the finished product. To date, I'd failed to find a good match.

And I had a *lot* of those notes.

'They're running behind,' the woman sitting opposite me said – *to* me, I realised after a beat. She was one of the rollerbladed, absently slicing alternate feet beneath her chair, making a repetitive scraping noise that was already annoying. 'Ninety minutes, the assistant said a half-hour ago.'

I nodded and smiled because I had never been to a single audition where things weren't running behind and because I wanted to discourage a longer conversation.

That was when the first call came in.

I felt my phone ringing before I heard it, buzzing against my thigh through the fake leather of my fast-fashion handbag. The other eyes in the corridor turned towards me; several signs were stuck along its length, warning NO PHONES.

I rooted for mine, wondering who was calling me. The pool of potentials was embarrassingly small. I hadn't been at all good at making friends in LA, but I'd excelled at losing touch with the ones I had back home. My guess was that it was someone from work, wondering if I'd swap a shift. They all knew I was good for it because I was never going anywhere and never doing anything.

But the number on screen started with the country code for Ireland, and the numbers that followed it told me the call was coming from a mobile. The fact that I was looking at numbers at all and not a name told me that the mobile belonged to someone who wasn't in my contacts, someone I didn't know.

Or didn't *want* to know.

I kept my breath steady, told myself not to overreact. Auditions were bad enough for me these days without adding extra, unrelated anxiety to the mix right before I got in the room. I stared at the phone until it cut off mid-ring.

Either the caller had hung up or they were leaving a voicemail. I hoped for a voicemail, ideally one that would leave no doubt that the person thought they were calling someone else, that this was just an innocent wrong number. I counted off the seconds, imagining the length of a standard message, but the phone's screen dimmed, then went black.

No new voicemail notification.

I copied the number and pasted it into Google on the off-chance it appeared on someone's professional website or a forum warning about scams, but there was no match for it on the internet.

In my hand, the phone had grown slick with sweat.

'Everything all right?' Rollerblade Girl asked me, and I immediately rearranged my face into a smile and looked up at her and said yes.

But even then, it already wasn't.

Nearly two hours passed before I got in the room.

It almost always looks the same. A hotel meeting space with no windows, basement level, cheap to rent. A trestle table at one end with a quartet of bored-looking people sitting behind it, side by side and facing you. One has a clipboard and at least one other one is looking down at their phone, ignoring you. No one is ever introduced and their roles are never made clear, but you can safely assume that the one who talks to you is the casting director. Off to one side will be a person operating a camera who won't acknowledge your presence in any way except to point it at you, and there's a bit of red tape on the floor showing you where to stand.

Once upon a time, in another life, this had been my domain. I'd enter these sad little rented rooms and meet their stone-faced occupants feeling like an undefeated boxer entering the arena who knows her opponent would do well to avoid a KO in the first round. Outwardly I was charming and always just on the right side of the confident versus cocky line. I'd often walked out of these rooms *knowing* that in a few hours' time, I'd get a call to say I'd been offered the job.

I used to be great at auditions, but now I just hoped to get through them.

I took my spot on the tape and flashed a smile at each of the blank faces in turn. Only the red-haired woman on the end returned it.

Casting director: identified.

'We'll just get you to do a quick ID to camera,' she said.

My palms were clammy; I tried to wipe them discreetly off my jeans. Then I turned to face the lens and said, 'I'm Adele Rafferty, auditioning for the role of Rollerblader, and I'm self-represented,' as confidently as I could, which wasn't very confidently at all seeing as the very first thing I was telling them was that I was agentless, that I couldn't *get* an agent.

If there was any flash of recognition at my name, I missed it.

That ship had sailed.

And then sunk.

And anyway, I didn't *want* to be recognised these days. That was the whole reason I'd come out here, to LA.

'Are you American?' Red Hair had an iPad in front of her on which I thought I could just about make out my headshot in matchbox size, upside down: my CV. She was zooming in on the text with two fingers.

'Irish,' I said. 'I moved here six months ago.' It was important to say the second bit because otherwise they thought you were saying you were Irish-American, because American people with Irish relatives inexplicably said *they* were Irish too, and you, the actual Irish person, were forced into doing your own differentiating.

Red Hair frowned, so I jumped straight in with the answer to the question I knew was forming on her tongue.

'I have dual citizenship,' I said quickly, 'because of my mother.'

Translation: *I can work here legally, it's okay.*

'And you're' – Red Hair's eyes flicked to the iPad – 'twenty-two?'

I nodded. 'Yes.'

And indeed I had been, four years ago.

'Can you rollerblade?'

'Yes.'

I couldn't *not* rollerblade. I'd never tried. I was the Schrödinger's Cat of rollerbladers: until I put a pair on, I both could *and* couldn't do it. Both were equally true until the attempt. If I managed to not only get through an audition but also do well enough to be offered the job, I could certainly figure out how to rollerblade before the shoot started.

One obstacle at a time.

'Have you appeared in any pharmaceutical campaigns in the past?' the casting director asked, her eyes still on the iPad.

'No,' I said.

'Have you appeared in any campaign in the last year?'

'No.'

'Whenever you're ready then,' Red Hair said, finally looking up at me. A little smile. 'In your own time.'

I smiled back. I tried to push the phone call from home out of my mind. I tried to trick myself into thinking I was myself from a year ago, when everything was different. When *I* was different. The Before me. I hoped I was only imagining a sheen of sweat at my temples, my hairline, across my upper lip.

I took a deep breath.

Then I stared down the barrel of the lens and said, with the theatrical defiance of a woman climbing up something in tiny white shorts who Tampax would have you believe has her period, 'I refuse to let headache pain get in *my* way!'

Count to two, turn back to Red Hair. She was nodding thoughtfully, like she was tasting a food she'd never tried before and the jury was still out on whether she liked it or not.

The other three continued to look like they were waiting for the valet guy to reappear with their car outside a restaurant that had just served them an expensive lunch they hadn't enjoyed.

'Great,' Red Hair said in a tone that suggested this was, at the very least, a gross exaggeration. 'Now I just want to try a couple of things, okay?'

I nodded vigorously to show I was willing. This movement pushed a trickle of sweat out of my hairline and down the side of my face.

'Great.' The word was losing all meaning. 'Let's take it again, but with a different emphasis. Let's say ... On "refuse".'

'Sure.' I counted to five. I took a breath. I stared down the lens which I knew was picking up every single bead of moisture on my face, which only made more rush to join them. 'I *refuse* to let headache pain get in my way!'

'Hmm.' Red Hair did some more imaginary food-chewing. 'Let me hear it with the double emphasis.'

'I *refuse* to let headache pain get in *my* way!'

'Bring it down a little ...'

'I *refuse* to let headache pain get in *my* way.'

'Slow it down ...'

'I *refuse*' – pause – 'to let headache pain' – pause – 'get in *my* way.'

I was sure now that my face was not only shiny with sweat but blood-red beneath it, too.

'Not that slow,' Red Hair said, frowning.

'I *refuse* to let headache pain' – pause – 'get in *my* way.'

'Can we just do one where you refer to it as a "little headache pain"? Like you're minimising it. It doesn't affect you. It's trivial.'

'I *refuse* to let a little headache pain' – pause – 'get in *my* way.'

The heat on my cheeks felt like it had developed its own pulse.

'Now bring it back up for me ...'

'I *refuse* to let a little headache pain' – pause – 'get in *my* way!'

My right eye started to sting; sweat had dripped into it. Red Hair was wearing a wool cardigan over a white button-down shirt with a silk scarf draped around her neck, which meant it wasn't warm in this room at all, which meant *my* being warm would be even more noticeable and definitely not mistaken for anything other than nerves.

As I thought this, the man sitting at the far end of the table finally looked up, looked at me and wrinkled his nose in disgust.

I knew then I wasn't getting this job. I wasn't even getting *called* for any job involving this casting agency ever again. Right now, I was less *natural beachy beauty with California-cool, Gwyneth vibes* and more *Have you or someone you love suffered adverse side-effects of Neutraxium?*

If this commercial ended up going in a different direction, as they so often did, and that direction was ambulance-chasing law firm canvassing for more plaintiffs in a class-action lawsuit against the headache pill's manufacturers, then *maybe* I had a chance.

A small one.

But otherwise ...

'Great,' Red Hair said. 'Let's just try one more thing. This woman is beautiful and confident and strong, but she's also not *too* any of those things, an everywoman. She's aspirational, but also relatable. You want to be her, but you're also *already* her. Do you know what I mean?'

I knew better than to say that *nobody* could know what that meant, that I didn't even believe Red Hair did.

'Think about that,' she said. 'Then take it again.'

I did what she asked. Or tried to.

'Thanks,' she said then. 'Ah – she glanced back down at her iPad – 'Adele.'

I mumbled something that hopefully sounded like, 'Thank you for the opportunity,' and then an assistant was suddenly there, to my right, as if she had materialised silently from the wall.

I knew I was supposed to follow her out of the room, so I did.

'They'll be in touch,' the assistant said to me once we were in the hallway, which was what every assistant had said to me at this point in every other audition. But then she added something unexpected. 'I loved *Winter Snow*, by the way. Is it true they're making a sequel?'

This comment set off a torrent of contradictory feelings. Elation because she'd loved the movie. Insult because she was asking about a sequel when my character had died at the midpoint. Shame because this conversation was happening at an audition for a one-line part in a headache-pill commercial I definitely wasn't getting. Fear that she'd recognised me, and that she'd heard what had happened the last day I'd been on a set, that the whispers had not only managed to cross the Atlantic after me but the continent of America too.

The day I'd dreaded for months had finally arrived. My plan had failed. I couldn't escape.

My face must have fallen as I cycled through these emotions because the assistant frowned and said, 'Sorry. I saw it on your CV.'

'Oh— No.' I waved a hand. 'It's totally fine. Thank you for saying so. I appreciate it.'

What I really appreciated was that she *hadn't* recognised me, actually. She'd just seen *Winter Snow* on my CV. It was also cooler out here, in the corridor and, away from the Trestle

Table Quartet, the anxiety that had been seeping out of my skin during the audition was just an unsettled feeling in the pit of my stomach.

The invisible vice around my chest sprang open, allowing me to breathe again.

'It was such a fantastic role,' I said, smiling. Maybe I could salvage this now, here, with the assistant? There was no way I was getting the commercial, but if I could just avoid getting struck off the agency's list … 'Incredible writing.' No harm to redirect the glow of achievement on to the rest of the team. *The great thing about me is how humble I am.* 'And I don't know about the sequel, but I hope so.'

It was by far the best acting I'd done all day.

Out on the street, I held my arms away from my sides in a futile attempt to dry my armpits and hoped the Uber I couldn't afford but had to summon because I didn't drive – in LA, yes I *know* – would have ice-cold A/C on full blast.

That's when I saw I'd had a second call.

The same Irish mobile number had called my phone ten minutes before, when I'd been in the audition room, looking like I desperately needed to *take* a couple of Neutraxium.

But I still had no new voicemails. I hadn't replaced the Robot Lady greeting with one of my own and I wondered if that was why the caller wasn't leaving a message: they weren't sure if this number was actually me. If that was the case, I wouldn't do anything to confirm it for them.

I was still holding the phone when it rang again.

I know now what, let's be honest, I knew then: I shouldn't have answered it. But a little bit of misplaced hope can be a terrible thing. Because what if it was someone back home calling to give me the second chance I desperately needed? To offer me the role that would make everything better, that would carpet over the last horrendous year, that would make everything right and okay and good again, that would make *me* feel that way?

I pressed ACCEPT and put the phone to my ear.

I wasn't entirely reckless. There was only a minute chance this phone call was a good thing, and an overwhelming likelihood that whoever was on the other end of the line was bad news. So I would say nothing. Let them identify themselves before I confirmed this number belonged to me.

But there was only silence on the line.

They didn't say anything either.

They were waiting, too.

And the silence wasn't total. There was breathing. I put a finger in my other ear and turned away from the traffic to hear it better. Yes, there it was: steady, regular breaths. Louder than normal, if I could hear them down the phone while standing on a kerb on Sunset in the middle of the day. Masculine, maybe. Sort of ...

Patient.

There were five thousand miles between me and whoever was at the other end of the line, but in that moment, the sounds of exhalation in my ear might as well have been a breath on my neck.

And then—

Click.

Whoever they were, they'd ended the call.

TWO

I got the Uber to bring me straight to work.

I worked reception at the Goodnite Suites at Universal, a two-storey motel painted in Heartburn-Remedy Pink that had been used as the backdrop for at least half a dozen true-crime re-enactments. Our guests were mostly families making a pit stop at Universal Studios on their Californian adventure. I worked second shift so I met them minutes after they'd arrived, at check-in, when they were still excited and happy and hadn't yet realised that even though we had 'Universal' in our name, we were actually five miles away from it, in Burbank; the schedule of our complimentary shuttle bus was more aspirational than anything; and our rooms were very popular with the local cockroach community. All I had to do was smile, make sure they heard the accent and present them with a voucher for our dingy poolside bar in a way that made it seem special when actually we handed one out to every single guest.

Every hour I worked at the Goodnite dragged, but that afternoon it felt like the clocks were ticking backwards. I could only push the anonymous calls out of my mind long enough to wonder if I'd been too hard on myself, if things hadn't gone as badly as I'd feared and there was still a possibility, however minuscule, that I might get a call-back.

I'd be different at the call-back. I'd have my nerves under control. I'd bring some *Winter Snow* anecdotes to casually share with the assistant. I'd be the old me, the *real* Adele Rafferty.

The one who didn't think twice about answering her phone.

And then I heard a voice on the other side of the reception desk say, 'Oh, my God. It's *Wendy*!' and time came to a sudden, complete stop.

Female. Irish accent. Over-excited.

My stomach was sinking before I even raised my eyes.

Standing in front of me was a family of three: mother, father, lanky blonde girl of about nine or ten. The girl had a smartphone that had all her attention and the father was looking around, appraising the place with an expression that suggested he was finding it wanting. The woman was staring at me, smiling manically, eyes wide with excitement.

'Wendy!' she said again.

I was not Wendy, but I also *was* Wendy, and this was the nightmare scenario I'd been dreading ever since I moved to LA.

Or at least ever since, having moved to LA, I realised I was going to have to get a normal job here.

'I have to tell you,' the woman said, 'I am *such* a big fan!'

She didn't have to tell me that it wasn't of me, but of *These Are the Days*, Ireland's second-worst soap opera and my employer for some fourteen years.

'Great,' I said in the Red-haired Casting Director sense of the word.

I hadn't planned on becoming an actor and I'd certainly never planned on being the child version. But *These Are the Days* had had an open casting-call at a hotel in Cork that my best friend, Julia, had convinced her mother to bring her to. On the same day, *my* mother had needed a babysitter and had asked Julia's if I could tag along. The casting director spotted me on the sidelines and got me to parrot off some lines, and within weeks I had a part-time job playing Wendy Morgan, youngest daughter of the drama-attracting Morgan clan – and loving every single minute of it.

I was an actor before I ever wanted to be one, but once I was, I never wanted to be anything else even half as much. At sixteen, I quit school and went full time. At twenty-three, over the show's summer break, I played a supporting role in my first ever feature film and non-soapy-suds acting gig, *Winter Snow*. When it was released the following year, everyone who mattered said it was good and, more importantly, that *I* was good in it.

My phone started ringing. My agent realised I existed. Glossy magazines that came free inside the weekend papers started draping me across couches dressed in sequinned dresses I couldn't afford and printed interviews with me under headlines like PROMISING YOUNG WOMAN and OUR NEXT BIG THING and DON'T CALL ME THE NEXT SAOIRSE RONAN because I wasn't used to doing press and routinely made silly, off-the-cuff remarks to journalists that they gleefully seized upon and printed out of context. I even got an IFTA nod: (one of the) Best Supporting Actress (nominees) 2020, thank you very much.

All the while, my resentment towards *These Are the Days* grew – because whenever the phone rang, I had to say no to whatever was being offered to me by the person on the other end. We filmed six days a week for ten months of the year and with my stock rising, the powers-that-be weren't inclined to enrol Wendy in a faraway college she'd only come home from the odd weekend, or put her in a six-month coma following a pile-up on the motorway that – twist! – she'd wake up to remember *she'd* caused. (All ideas: actor's own.) So I quit the show.

The bosses at *These Are the Days*, not at all impressed with my abrupt and ungrateful departure, made sure it would be a permanent one and killed me off in a DART derailment that unfolded in primetime over five nights. It sent ratings through the roof, so I ended up leaving an even more popular show than the one I'd decided to leave. What I didn't understand was that I was getting offered all those other things *because* I was on a popular show. The directors who took me out to boozy lunches so they could talk to me about their 'vision' weren't doing it because they thought I was an exceptionally good actress, or even an okay one. They were doing it because they hoped I'd get the *These Are the Days* viewers off their couches and into the cinema, or at the very least forking out for a movie-on-demand.

When Wendy Morgan died, all my glittering opportunity went into the prop-grave with her. I hadn't booked a single paid acting-gig since, at home or here in LA where, like so many deluded Irish actors before me, I'd moved to *pursue new opportunities* six months after I'd left the show, six months ago.

Well, that wasn't strictly true. I had booked *one* paid acting-gig, back in Ireland. But I'd never actually got paid for it, because it was on that set that everything had gone so inexplicably, horribly wrong. My cheeks still burned at even the most fleeting thought of it and I mentally pushed the memory away now.

There were just as many opportunities in London. In New York, even, if I'd had more fight in me, if it wasn't taking everything I had back then just to put one foot in front of the other. But I picked the place that was furthest away, the city to which there were no direct flights from Dublin, in a time-zone whose morning was Ireland's night. Where I could walk into an audition room safe in the knowledge that none of the Trestle Table Quartet knew about what had happened.

It was just a bonus that that was also the city where almost everyone lived in the space between their dreams and reality, where it was okay to desperately want to be the thing you weren't yet, but the very fact you lived there still sounded like some kind of success to people back home.

Adele Rafferty? She's in LA these days. Yeah, things must be going well.

I smiled weakly at the woman on the other side of the reception desk because I didn't know what else to do.

No one back home knew I was working at the motel. I hadn't even told Julia, for God's sake; I couldn't bring myself to. Through a series of vague assertions and white lies, I was letting everyone think that I was getting enough acting work to keep me going. Was this woman about to ruin it all? Was her next move to ask for a selfie? Would my shame go *viral*?

The idea of there being a new picture of me online set off a wave of mild nausea. When I left the show, I deleted all my social media accounts. I started to feel, looking at them, the eyes of *everyone else* who was looking at them, the silent sea of strangers who – I was convinced – sat in judgement of me, who were waiting with bated breath to see me fall.

And I *had* fallen, so every time my phone dinged with a notification, I was terrified it was someone who'd found out about that, helping everyone *else* find out about it via a Twitter thread or an Instastory.

It was just a bonus that my lack of an online presence was now keeping evidence of my abject failure to achieve my life's primary goal off the phone of the people I knew, the faces I recognised. Family, friends, peers.

I didn't want that situation to change.

On the other side of the desk, the woman's smile had dimmed.

'What are you doing *here*?' she asked.

'Researching a role,' I said, the implication of my conspiratorial whisper being that no one else was supposed to know. And then, even though it was difficult, what with the full, crushing weight of my deep shame pressing against my chest, I said, at a normal volume, 'Welcome to Goodnite Suites. What name will help me find your reservation today?'

I pocketed my phone, mumbled something about cramps to my colleague and escaped back-of-house.

There was a housekeeping cart sitting outside the staff toilet with various partially consumed foodstuffs on top: a six-pack of Coke with three missing, an already-opened tube of Pringles, a half-full bag of miniature Snicker bars. Left behind by guests, collected by the housekeeper.

I grabbed a fistful of Snickers on the way in, went to the further of the two stalls, sat on the toilet lid and stuffed two of them, whole, into my mouth.

In the last few months I had really begun to understand why people overeat. It isn't what they eat, it's *why* they eat it: because when you feel literally full from food, it's a brief respite from feeling figuratively empty inside.

As I swallowed, I decided I was done: I was quitting acting.

No, that wasn't what I needed to do. There was no acting to quit. What I needed was to stop *wanting* it to happen.

And I was going to.

Right now.

To continue with this idiocy was to delude myself into ignoring the realities of the situation. I couldn't get work at home; what had happened had put paid to that. But I could *only* get work at home, where I was a tiny fish in a puddle of pond water. Out here, in LA, I was a flake of fish skin in the Pacific.

And if by some miracle I *did* get work here, and that work led to more work, and *that* work led to even more, proper, high-profile work … Well, eventually my past would catch up with me, like the spread of red dots on a map of the world in a Hollywood disaster movie, growing large enough to touch each other and merge into one.

I'd have to walk into a room or into a table-read or on to a set where I'd know what the eyes on me were thinking, what they were thinking of.

I wasn't ready for that yet.

I didn't know if I'd ever be.

Why the hell was I doing this to myself? Everything would be so much easier if I stopped trying to be an actor. Everything would be *better*.

So I was going to stop trying, starting now.

Then I took out my phone and saw I had a new email from the Neutraxium commercial casting agency, and a gold firework of hope exploded in my heart.

I'd never once got an email telling me I'd been unsuccessful at an audition. You were expected to deduce that from the fact that you hadn't got one after an unspecified number of exquisitely torturous days.

So if they *were* emailing me …

Oh, my God.

Had I just had The Moment, the one where the despairing actor convinces herself her dreams must die right before she gets the call that makes them happen?

I saw a flash of future-me sitting on a leather couch on *The Late Late Show*'s set, dressed in something expensive a stylist had borrowed, telling Ryan the huh-*larious* story of how I'd been sitting on a toilet, crying and stress-eating miniature Snickers, when I got the news that I hadn't booked the cheesy commercial that morning because the casting director had been *so* taken with me that she'd sent the video of my audition to David Fincher/Emerald Fennell/Jordan Peele (delete as appropriate) who'd cast me in the role for which I'd just collected an Oscar a few days before, and everyone would be far too busy being impressed with me to even remember that other business from some no-name movie set forever ago that they'd only heard vague, unsubstantiated rumours about. *All I can say about that, Ryan, is that it wouldn't have happened to a man.*

I opened the email.

Thank you for attending the audition this morning. Just to let you know our Neutraxium commercial has been cast. We look forward to seeing you for something else in the near future.

The words 'Neutraxium commercial' were in a different font, bigger and in colour; it had been inexpertly copied and pasted in.

I deleted it.

I leaned my head against the side of the stall, closed my eyes and envied all the people who didn't want things.

I was *really* done now. Really. Fully resolved to wake up a different Adele tomorrow. One who didn't want anything except not to want anything at all. I would just live my life. I would take some time to make new goals – small, normal, ordinary ones; *achievable* ones. *Dreams* would mean the things I saw while I slept. I would move somewhere where coffee shops were full of baristas and coffee-drinkers, not auditioning actors and wannabe screenwriters tinkering with their specs. Where people were happy with their lot, because they had the good sense to recognise that their lots *were* a lot. I would stop tying every knot of my self-worth to what I did for a living and start actually *living* instead.

I popped another Snickers.

This was a new feeling. I had never seriously considered giving up before. I imagined a different me who didn't care that she'd never had the acting career she'd dreamed of, and it made me feel a little light-headed, sorta floaty, like I was being untethered from the only driving force I'd ever known.

But I meant it, I really did. We'll never know now, but I think if I'd just had a chance to sleep through the night that night, everything would've been different. The problem is that successful actors' careers are hardly ever a steady graph of failing upwards. Read their biographies, watch their interviews. It's not that they put in the hard graft, time and dedication and then one day, after ten thousand hours or however much that shite supposedly is, they reached the next level and got The Call.

The Call can come at any time.

That's both the magic and the horror of it all. The teenager folding shirts at Forever 21 spotted by a casting assistant on her lunchbreak and the RADA-trained thespian who'd spent a decade with the Royal Shakespeare Company both have an equal chance of the next gig being the one that changes their life. Opportunities didn't necessarily come to those who had earned them. They ran up to the people who happened to be in the right time and place, which meant that no matter how badly things were going or what had happened in the past, the *very next thing* could turn everything around.

That's why it was so hard to truly give up, to turn off the wanting, no matter how resolved I was to leave it all behind.

Especially when, just after 4:00 a.m., my phone rang again.

EXT. WEST CORK COUNTRYSIDE - DAY

Super: Three months later

A lone car drives on a narrow road that cuts
through dense, expansive forest.

INT/EXT. JOEL'S CAR/WEST CORK COUNTRYSIDE - DAY

Joel is behind the wheel. Kate sits beside him
in the passenger seat.

Her phone beeps with a text message from Gus:
Have you told him yet? She glances at Joel.
His eyes are fixed on the road ahead. She
responds: *Not yet! Tonight!*, followed by the
champagne bottle emoji. Gus replies: *Here's
hoping he doesn't throw the bottle at you.*

                    JOEL
               (glancing over)
     Who's that? My number-one fan?

                    KATE
     The one and only.

                    JOEL
     What's he doing this weekend?

                    KATE
     Chairing a meeting of your fan club,
     as far as I know.

                    JOEL
     That or plotting to kill me.

                    KATE
     He's just jealous.

                    JOEL
So you agree? Finally.

                    KATE
Jealous of your *career*, not your
girlfriend.

                    JOEL
If he's jealous of my career, he's in
real trouble.

They turn off the road at a sign that says
'CHERRY COTTAGE' and on to a dirt track that
winds through the trees. The forest is dense
and gloomy, blocking out any view of the sky
from inside the car.

The track seems to go on for ever.

                    KATE
How did you even find this place?

                    JOEL
A friend recommended it to me. He
comes here to write.

EXT. CHERRY COTTAGE - DAY

The track delivers the car to a small gravel
clearing. In the middle of it sits a quaint
stone cottage, smoke rising from its chimney.

A woman waits in the doorway: MAGGIE (70s,
ruddy-cheeked, homely). She waves and smiles
when she sees the car.

After Joel has parked it, she hurries to meet
them.

                    MAGGIE
Welcome to Cherry Cottage!

                    JOEL
Maggie?

                    MAGGIE
Joel.

                    KATE
I'm Kate. Hi.

                    MAGGIE
Pleasure to meet you. No
trouble finding us, then? It's
straightforward but …

                    JOEL
A bit of a ways from everything,
isn't it?

                    MAGGIE
That's the idea. Come on inside and
I'll show you what's what.

Maggie goes inside.

Kate looks back at the treeline. It's barely
thirty feet from the house and the only gap in
it is the end of the track they just drove up.
She has to look straight up to see anything
that isn't forest - and that's darkening sky.

                    JOEL
Everything all right?

                                KATE
       Yeah. Just … Nothing. It's fine.
       I guess I was just picturing it
       differently.

Joel takes her hand, squeezes it reassuringly
and leads her inside to …

INT. LIVING SPACE - DAY [CONTINUOUS]

… the ground floor of the cottage, which has
an open-plan kitchen and living space with a
surprisingly trendy, modern look compared to the
cottage's exterior. Glossy kitchen cabinets,
marble countertops, sleek leather armchairs.

The windows at the front of the house are
original, but the wall at the rear has been
replaced with a pane of floor-to-ceiling glass
that shows only forest beyond.

                                KATE
                  (muttering to herself)
       More trees. Great.

                                JOEL
       Wow.

                                MAGGIE
       It's unexpected, isn't it? We
       renovated the whole place during
       lockdown. I let my son make all the
       decisions. His taste is far more
       modern than mine.

She points to a ring-binder on the kitchen
countertop with a picture of the cottage on
its cover. It sits next to a welcome basket

filled with wine, chocolate and cheese. A set
of keys is tied to the handle with ribbon.

>   MAGGIE (CONT'D)
>   Everything's pretty self-explanatory,
>   but all the info is in there. The
>   bedroom is at the end of the hall.
>   I've set a fire for you; all you
>   need to do is light it. And the keys
>   are there. So, unless you've any
>   questions …?

As Maggie talks, Joel removes the cottage keys
and attaches them to the car keys.

Kate wanders to the bookshelves in the corner
by the fireplace. One of them is packed
tightly with books - but multiple copies of
the same book: *First Draft* by Gary Sheridan.

>   JOEL (O.C.)
>   I think we're fine. Thank you.

>   MAGGIE (O.C.)
>   You have my number anyway. And I'm
>   only a mile away. If you'd kept
>   going, the next turn-off would've
>   been mine. If you need anything,
>   don't be shy.

>   JOEL (O.C.)
>   We won't.

Kate takes one of the books down, looks at the
cover. The image, font and dark colour-scheme
suggest it's a thriller. The terrible quality
suggests it's been badly self-published.

Maggie comes and stands beside her, smiling proudly at the books.

> MAGGIE
> That's our claim to fame. He wrote it here, in the cottage.

Kate opens the book to look at the author picture on the back flap. It's a silhouette of a man; he is unidentifiable. The author bio reads: *Gary Sheridan was born in Cork, Ireland. First Draft is his first novel.*

> MAGGIE (CONT'D)
> Feel free to take one, but a word of warning: you might want to wait until after you get home to give it a read. It's, ah, about a couple trying to survive a night of terror in a cottage not unlike this one.

Joel joins Kate and, over her shoulder, looks disdainfully at the book in her hands.

> JOEL
> (muttering)
> I think I'll be able to wait.

THREE

I was reaching for the device before I'd even fully surfaced from the depths of sleep, before my brain had a chance to form the conscious thought that my phone was the source of the electronic beeping.

The screen was glowing now with a *different* Irish mobile number and the clock display was telling me it was just gone 4:00 a.m. I put these two things together and came up with: *Whoever's been calling is someone legit, unrelated to acting, and they have the kind of news so bad you can't leave it in a voicemail.* I sat straight up in bed, alert now, having been hit by a wave of ice-cold dread. I tapped the green button on the screen.

'Hello?'

'Ah … Hi.' The voice was male. Irish. Uncertain. 'Sorry to call you so early but I'm looking to speak to Adele, ah …' A shuffle of papers. 'Rafferty?'

My mind's eye started a slideshow of images that could potentially match the voice. A doctor, wearing a white lab coat over those scrubs, standing in a hospital corridor lit by fluorescents. A member of An Garda Síochána in his navy blues, standing in the hallway of my parents' home with his hat in his hand. A tabloid journalist who'd heard something from a friend who'd heard something from another friend, trying to get a comment from me so he can whip up some clickbait.

Back to the doctor.

'This is Adele,' I said.

'Oh. Great. Hi. I got your number from Yvonne – Yvonne Stokes? At the Lindsey Ryan Agency?'

The slideshow flipped to an altogether less stressful image of the woman who sat behind the desk just outside my agent's office. Early twenties, always dressed in shapeless linen sacks printed with abstract shapes in primary colours, ice-blonde hair cut like Mia Farrow's in *Rosemary's Baby*.

My *former* agent's office. The one in Dublin who'd tried to persuade me not to leave there, not to run away.

'You're in the States, right?' he said. 'East coast, I hope?'

'Ah … West, actually.'

'Oh shit. Really? What's it there, like—'

'Four in the morning,' I finished.

'Is it? Oh God. I can call you back? Let me call you back.'

My, 'No!' came out sounding louder and firmer than I intended it to, so I forced a smile before I spoke again so he'd hear it in my voice. 'What I meant to say was, it's fine. I'm awake now.'

And I really wanted to know what he was calling to say. I had absolutely no idea what it could be. I didn't even really know what I *wanted* it to be.

'Well, this is probably a long shot, but my name is John. I work with Daniel O'Leary and Steve Dade at Cross Cut Films.'

The way he paused after he said that made me think I should know who they were and what that was, but I didn't so I said nothing.

'We're shooting a feature,' he pushed on. 'A psychological horror. In West Cork, starting tomorrow. Or we were supposed to be starting tomorrow. Our lead actress just dropped out. Our *only* actress, because it's just her onscreen for, like, seventy minutes of the thing, and we were doing all her solo stuff first. It's a family emergency, there's nothing she can do, but as you can imagine we're in a bit of a bind now. Postponing will cost a small fortune and this is an independent production. The crew is already on set. So.' He inhaled sharply. 'I know this is, like, literally last minute, but would you consider stepping in?'

My first thought was, *Stepping in what?*

'It's a big ask,' John said. 'I know. But do you think there's *any* way we could make this happen?'

I frantically replayed everything he'd said, looking for something to parrot back to him so I could buy my addled brain some time to process this.

I landed on, 'Tomorrow?'

'We have a little wiggle room,' he said, 'and we've had to take into consideration the time it would take to get you here from LA but ... Ideally, yeah. And we'd need you for two weeks.'

'Two weeks?'

'Skeleton crew and a tight schedule.' He laughed. 'I know. But we'll get it done. Steve loved *Winter Snow*, by the way. Is it true they're making a sequel?'

'I hope so,' I said automatically.

Was I being offered a job? And was that job the *lead* in a *movie*?

Wait – had he actually said my name at the start of this conversation? Did he know who he was talking to? Or was this the cruellest wrong number ever?

'And don't worry about prep,' John said. 'There's practically no dialogue until week two, so you'll have some time.' He cleared his throat. 'Look, we'd love to have you. We think this feature is going to create a lot of buzz, and we're all in agreement that you'd be perfect for Kate. In fact, don't quote me on this' – he lowered his voice – 'but we were just saying that Saoirse having to drop out might actually be a *good* thing.'

'Saoirse,' I repeated.

'You didn't hear that from me. But, yeah.'

And with that, everything suddenly made sense. Only one Saoirse had no last name and there was no way that *my* name was under hers on any list. I was, minimum, a dozen pages later, if the pages were in small type and the list was printed in two columns on both sides.

John had presumably name-dropped to impress me, but what he'd actually done was reveal that I wasn't his first phone call. If this role originally had an Oscar-nominated actress in it, it could be his fiftieth. He was ringing around, looking for someone – anyone – who looked right but wasn't successful enough to be on a job right now or due to start one. He knew damn well I was in LA and what time it was here, but he'd called anyway because he was desperate.

Maybe he even knew about what had happened on the set of *We Were Kings*.

But this was a good thing, because with my head out of the clouds and the stars wiped from my eyes, I could actually think straight. I was being offered a job. An *acting* job, back home.

'I have an offer ready to send through,' John said, 'but I've had no luck getting your agent on the phone. I wouldn't expect her to be answering on a Saturday, of course, but—'

'She's not my agent any more.'

'Sorry, I misunderstood. Who—'

'I don't have one.' I felt my cheeks burn. 'Here, I mean. Yet.'

A beat passed.

'Don't worry about it,' John said breezily. 'We can do this direct. And, ah, Adele, before we go any further, I should warn you. Steve and the, um, original actress were good friends, so she wasn't getting her usual fee. It was a favour. There *is* money, just not a lot. But we'll fly you here business class, if that makes up for it at all.'

There might have been more to that sentence but I was too busy thinking about the words *business class*.

Up until then, I hadn't been thinking about money at all.

'So, look,' John said, 'I know this is asking a lot, and I'm conscious of the time there, but if I sent over everything now ... Do you think you could give us an answer in, say, a couple of hours? Just because, you know, if you say no, we're under pressure to—'

I said that was fine and spelled out my email address.

Then he said, 'There's, ah, just one other thing.'

I braced myself for the words I was sure were coming.

Look, Adele, I can't pretend I didn't hear about what happened, and I wanted to check in with you about that because, you know, we'd like to avoid having a similar situation arise on our set ... How are you feeling, these days?

'We'd, ah, need you to sign an NDA,' John said. The blood rushing in my ears drowned out whatever came immediately after that, but I picked it back up at, '... in the public domain. We want it to stay that way until we release a trailer. Steve's done it that way since *Sundown*. It's how he likes it.'

They wanted me to sign an NDA. A non-disclosure agreement, a legally binding contract that said I couldn't tell anyone I was doing this film or, by extension, that I was back in Ireland to do it.

I resisted the urge to laugh.

This was too perfect. An NDA meant I could fly home, shoot the movie and get back here again without anyone ever knowing I'd left LA.

This wasn't just an opportunity, it was *exactly* the opportunity I'd been waiting for.

'Would that be a problem?' John asked. 'The NDA?'

'Not at all,' I said.

At this point, silly me thought it would solve a few.

FOUR

I got out of bed, stood and reached for the switch on the wall that turned on the light, a bare bulb hanging from the fan in the centre of a yellowing stucco ceiling that only ever showed me things I didn't want to see.

I'd found this place via Facebook. A studio apartment above the garage of a house on a leafy stretch of Beck Avenue in Studio City. The homes on both sides of it had already been torn down and rebuilt as gleaming Cape Cod-style McMansions, and God knows this one needed to be too. Everything seemed to be rotting or peeling or sinking. I rarely had the luxury of hot water but often enjoyed a sour smell whose origin I couldn't identify. The floorboards were loose, shifting and creaking beneath the terracotta shagpile, and I spent more on Raid than I did on deodorant. But it was the only listing I'd found within budget that didn't involve having roommates, was within Affordable Uber Ride range of work and whose owner didn't seem like the type to google me.

I collected my dented laptop from the floor and climbed back into bed with it, balancing the machine on my thighs. The email was already there, even though my call with John had ended less than a minute ago. It had three attachments.

The first was the non-disclosure agreement. Twelve pages of densely typed legalese that it was safe to assume was pretty standard. NDAs were common these days. Directors didn't want all the fanboys living in their mother's basements tweeting reviews of their as-yet unmade movies based on the casting choices alone, or something in the background of a Snapchat from set accidentally revealing a crucial plot point. Legally binding secrecy could serve another purpose, of course: giving the impression that whatever was going on behind it was worth trying to find out about. Maybe that was what this NDA was, really. The start of the marketing campaign.

If it was, it didn't bother me. Not when it was going to work in my favour.

The second attachment was the script. *Final Draft*. I didn't know at the time that that was also the name of the industry-standard software screenwriters used but if I had, it might have crossed my mind that the title of the script was decidedly lacking in imagination and that that didn't bode well for the rest of it.

From what John had said I'd gathered that Steve was the director and now, thanks to the script's title page, I knew the Daniel he'd mentioned was the writer.

I didn't read the script. Not then.

I read *some* of it.

Okay, I *scanned* some of it. Very quickly. Basically, I checked the first twenty pages for sex and the last ten for gratuitous violence, and then I flipped through the rest to see how often my character, Kate, appeared. She seemed to be on every page.

My character.

As if my decision was already made.

But it was opening the third attachment that did that. John hadn't sent an offer, he'd sent a contract, ready for me to sign. I scrolled until my eyes landed on a Euro sum: €849.00. A daily rate, based on a minimum of twenty-one days' pay. It was almost double what I'd earned per day on *These* and a lot more than the minimum suggested by Irish Equity, the actors' union, for feature films. I made $15 an hour at the hotel, so ... I did the sums on my phone's calculator app and saw that I'd make about a third of a year's Goodnite Suites salary from *Final Draft*.

Doing what I loved.

Which, just a few hours earlier, I'd decided I was definitely going to *stop* doing.

The Goodnite Suites would almost certainly fire me when I told them I was leaving for two weeks starting now, but I'd worry about that later. There was no way I was going to turn down *the lead in a feature film* because I was worried I wouldn't be able to pick up another job handing out keys in a roach motel.

And once the *Final Draft* trailer was released ...

Well, hopefully I wouldn't have to worry about getting another normal job anytime soon.

I opened a new browser window and searched for *Steve Dade Ireland director*. The top result was his IMDb page. His profile picture was a group shot that didn't say who was who, but underneath it was a reassuringly long list of credits. The most recent one was *Sundown*, a gloomy-sounding thing about a dying man looking for his lost son. It was just the sort of project that got generously funded in Ireland and then lauded with praise on its release, before failing spectacularly to find an audience because no one wanted to watch gloomy things about dying men and lost sons at the cinema on a Friday night.

Sundown had been released in March 2020 (ouch), two months after *Winter Snow*, and a year after Steve's previous outing, *Bring Me the Night*. That was a short film about a serial killer stalking a victim who turns out to be stalking him, and it had won things. Proper things, at festivals I had heard of. Before that, there was a long list of TV commercials and music videos. I had heard of the brands and the bands involved, too.

This business was full of people with bonus or inflated credits, carefully worded to make their skit in a retirement-village talent show sound like they'd trodden the boards at the Old Vic. But Steve Dade seemed like the real deal. Okay, so, he wasn't a *big* deal, but neither was he some tortured, moody film-school grad making incomprehensible shorts about inanimate objects who'd managed to wrangle funding out of some state-sponsored scheme because he was good at filling in application forms and he'd had the foresight to shoehorn a faery fort or an Ogham stone into the plot.

I did an image search for Steve but just found lots more group shots taken at warm-white-wine events: premieres, festival launches, award presentations. The same one appeared multiple times in the results: two men in their late twenties or early thirties, arms thrown around each other's shoulders, standing in front of a one-sheet for *Sundown*.

One of them was holding a trophy shaped to look like a film canister. He was prematurely grey with thick, dark eyebrows and wearing trendy tortoiseshell frames and Converse with a tuxedo. Not entirely unattractive. I figured he had to be Steve Dade.

This made sense because when I searched for Daniel O'Leary, the same picture came up – multiple versions of it, taken from slightly different angles, by multiple photographers. Daniel must be the *other* guy in it and, according to his LinkedIn page, a director of Cross Cut Films and also its Head of Production. He was using the same photo for his profile picture on there. I presumed whatever award they'd won must have been an important one that warranted this much showing off.

Even though I'd been told there was supposed to be nothing about *Final Draft* in the public domain, I searched for it anyway – and that's when I found out about the software. 7,270,000,000 results and all of them, seemingly, about getting it or using it. It crossed my mind that the title of the movie was going to present the publicity campaign with quite the challenge. Hopefully someone would get a clue and change it before release.

I went back to Steve's IMDb page to take a second look at his credits and that's when I spotted that, four years ago, he'd been an assistant director on *The Liar's Girl*, a four-part drama set in Dublin, based on the real-life Canal Killer case. I hadn't watched it; I didn't have the stomach for any true-crime stuff.

But I knew about this one because Julia had been in it.

My best friend Julia who, despite her having the bad luck of bringing me along to the audition for *These Are the Days,* had been undeterred from pursuing her childhood dream of becoming an actor. She was a proper one, though: she'd studied Drama at University College Cork and spent her time doing theatre, mostly in London so far but with her sights set on Broadway. TV was something she did only because it paid well and only if it fit neatly into a break in her schedule.

In the opening episode of *The Liar's Girl*, she'd been one of the Oh, She'll Definitely Be Dead Soon female characters – and then an actually dead one, lying on a slab in the morgue a few scenes later – but still, she must have met Steve Dade.

I checked the time and added eight hours: approaching lunchtime in Ireland, on a Saturday.

I decided to call her to ask about him.

My thinking was that I hadn't actually signed the NDA yet and I could ask Julia general questions without telling her the specifics of *Final Draft*. And wasn't I entitled to do some due diligence? I didn't know any of these people and I didn't have an agent to know them for me, so asking Julia was about the only option I had.

If mistakes felt like mistakes in the moment, we wouldn't make them, would we?

My apartment had a Juliet balcony cut into the slope of the roof that offered a view of next-door's pool. Well, sort of. During the day, it was obstructed by the eucalyptus trees the neighbour had planted *in order* to obstruct the view, but at night, the kidney-shaped water glowed a radioactive blue through the leaves. Sometimes, when I couldn't sleep, I went out there with a cheap beer and stared at it while I drank.

I went out there now to call Julia.

The skies above my head were clear, a mostly starless purple haze: as night as it ever got above the glowing streetscapes of LA. The house that owned the pool and the one my apartment was attached to were both dark and silent. Even at this hour, I could hear the distant hum of traffic on the freeway several blocks away.

I tapped Julia's name and put the phone to my ear.

She picked up after five rings with a, 'Hello?' that sounded both cautious and uncertain, as if anticipating the muffled audio of a butt-dial.

'Hey,' I said. 'It's me.'

'*Heyyyyyyy*. What's up? Long time, no chat.'

Our WhatsApp chat pinged with something new every other day at least, but I couldn't remember the last time we'd had a real-time conversation. I didn't need a therapist to tell me why that was. I didn't want to admit that things in LA weren't going to plan or talk about the reason I'd come to LA in the first place, and I was always worried that those were the *only* two topics Julia ever wanted to talk about.

'I know,' I said. 'It's been ages. Sorry. Can you talk now?'

'Ah … give me one sec.' I listened to the sounds of Julia moving from wherever she was to wherever she needed to be to carry on this conversation. Heels clacking on a wooden floor, a creaky door opening and closing. When she spoke again, she sounded echoey and amplified, like she'd gone into a bathroom. 'Isn't it, like, the middle of the night there?'

'Sort of.'

'What's going on? Is everything okay?'

'Everything's fine. But, listen. Do you by any chance remember Steve Dade?'

A painfully long beat of silence bloomed on the line, so long that it convinced me that Julia *did* have something to tell me about him and that none of it would be good.

But then she said, 'Who?'

'Steve Dade. He directed your episode of *The Liar's Girl*.'

'*Did* he?'

'According to IMDb he did, yeah.'

'Well, Slab of Dead Girl Number Two was second-unit stuff. I probably wouldn't have met him. I don't think I did … Why do you ask?'

'I can't say.'

But Julia and I had been best friends since we were kids. She knew me better than anyone. She knew that all she had to do was say nothing, to wait me out, and eventually I *would* say.

Eventually or, you know, half a second later.

'Okay so, you can*not* tell anyone this,' I said. 'There's an NDA, and I don't want to get fired before the ink is even dry. But I just got a call offering me the lead in a horror film Steve Dade is directing in West Cork, starting tomorrow. Or, well, as soon as I can get there. The original lead actress had some kind of family emergency. Low budget and skeleton crew, but still, an actual, proper movie. I've only flicked through the script but it looks like it's just my character on screen, by herself, for almost the entire thing. Reading some weird book and running around some woods. And there's actual money.'

'Wait,' Julia said. 'Are you talking about *Final Draft*?'

'Final … *what*?'

Not my best work, I know, and also a pointless denial in light of everything I'd already revealed, but for some reason confirming the project's title felt like crossing a line.

There was a thud on Julia's end then, followed by an indistinct male voice.

Away from her phone, she called out, 'I'll be out in a minute!' Back to me, at a normal volume, 'This sounds great, Adele, but are you sure about it? What if Martin finds out you're back in Ireland? Do you think he'd—'

Another thud, on Julia's end. Someone knocking on a door, I realised now.

Harder this time, more insistent.

'I *said*,' Julia shouted, 'I'll be *out* in a *minute*.' Back to me, after a loud sigh, 'Sorry. I'm in the final week of rehearsals for this thing and it's going to be shit no matter how many times we run it and everyone is just realising that today. Stress levels are high. Anyway. Where were we?'

I didn't want to go back to where we'd been, so I said, 'So you *don't* know Steve Dade then?'

'No, sorry. The name didn't even ring a bell. What else did he do?'

'Lots of things,' I said, a little more defensively than I'd intended.

'Have you asked Lindsey about him? Told her about this?'

'No ...' It hadn't occurred to me to do that. She wasn't my agent any more; it would feel a bit cheeky to call her up and ask for her time.

There was a third knock on the door at Julia's end then, this one louder and even more demanding than the previous two.

'All *right*,' she shouted, away from the phone. Then, into it: 'Sorry, but I have to go. They're screaming at me here. We're not supposed to take breaks.'

'No, I understand. But just before you go, do you ...' I bit my lip. 'Do you know where he is, at the moment? Martin, I mean.'

'No ...' Away from the phone: 'I said *all right*!' Back into it: 'I *really* have to go and slip someone' – her voice rose again – '*a fucking Xanax.*' Normal volume: 'Let me know what you decide. And let's meet up at the airport, okay? Before you fly back.'

'Yeah, I—'

'Bye.'

Julia had already hung up by the time I said, 'Bye,' back.

I stood looking at the radioactive pool and sipping my beer for a few minutes, and then I decided that I *would* send an email to Lindsey.

I opened my email app and quickly typed a message to her.

Hi Lindsey,

Hope all is well with you! Quick q and no worries whatsoever if you don't have time to answer. I can't say too much but I might have an opportunity to work with a director called Steve Dade (VERY hush hush – delete this email!), but all I know about him really is what's online. Do you know him? Any reason why I should be wary? Thanks in advance but like I said, no worries!

Thanks so much,

A

As soon as I pressed SEND I regretted all three exclamation marks.

Lindsey only had two email response speeds: immediately or so long after you'd sent it you'd forgotten you were waiting for her to reply. So I waited, sipping my watery beer and gazing at the pool some more, trying not to think about what I might wear to the premiere or, worse, start hoping that there would be *premieres*, plural, because we'd open internationally and smash the box office and win awards ...

My phone dinged with a new message.

I know Steve! Good friend of a good friend. Green light from me. Won't say a word although I think I know what it is. (So glad they finally got it over the line – although they REALLY

need to change the name!) Delighted for you — so happy
you're doing this! Lx

I read it three times to make sure I hadn't just hallucinated
the exact words I'd hoped I'd see. Then I typed Lindsey a short
but effusive thank-you message, and called John and told him
my answer was yes.

By then, I had made three assumptions.

One: the three calls I'd had within the last twenty-four hours
from the other Irish mobile were related to this, that they'd
been one of John's colleagues trying to confirm they'd the right
number or even John himself calling me from another phone.

Two: that Julia knew about *Final Draft* because actors
talked, and Lindsey knew about it because she was an agent
who had probably had clients audition for it or something *and*
she and the director had a mutual friend. An NDA wasn't an
invisibility cloak, it was just your bog-standard cloak that hid
whatever was underneath from prying eyes. It was enough
for me. It meant I could fly back to Ireland, shoot this movie
and leave again before anyone would know I was there.

Three: that this was it, the second chance I'd been dreaming
of. The role that would make everything okay again. The next
news anyone would hear about Adele Rafferty would be my
playing the lead role of Kate in Bright Young Thing™ Steve
Dade's *Final Draft*, and it would drown out that other stuff,
wash it all away, clean my slate. Give *me* the power. Give me
my power *back*.

I had no evidence for any of these assumptions and I'd be
proved wrong on at least two counts.

INT. LIVING SPACE - DAY

Joel enters carrying bags of groceries and
sets them on the kitchen counter. A small
suitcase and a weekender bag are already on
the floor by the door.

Kate is lighting the fire.

> JOEL
> That's everything, I think.

He joins her and they embrace, watching as the
flames take hold.

> JOEL (CONT'D)
> I finally get you alone.

> KATE
> I finally get *you* alone.

> JOEL
> I know things have been crazy, but
> now that the book is done, I'll have
> a lot more time.

> KATE
> When do I get to read it?

> JOEL
> As soon as Belinda assures me it's
> not a *complete* pile of shite.

> KATE
> (pretends to be offended)
> You trust your agent over me?

                    JOEL
I pay her to tell me the truth.

                    KATE
I'd tell you it for free.

                    JOEL
                (smiling)
I don't doubt it.

They kiss, until—

A mobile phone starts to ring. It's Joel's. He
frowns at the screen.

                JOEL (CONT'D)
Fuck. That woman has a sixth sense.

He runs a hand through his hair, suddenly
nervous.

                    KATE
Answer it.

                    JOEL
            (into the phone)
Hello?
                (pause)
Belinda? Hello?
                (to Kate)
All I can hear is static.

                    KATE
Maybe it'd be better outside?

                    JOEL
                (into the phone)
        Belinda, hang on. The reception is
        terrible here. I'm going to try
        outside.

Joel hurries out the front door.

Alone now, Kate's eyes drift to the other side
of the house, to the wall of glass that shows
nothing but a steadily darkening forest that
somehow seems even closer than it did before.
She shivers. She turns her back on it to go to
the kitchen, where she starts unpacking the
groceries.

INT. BEDROOM - DAY

A contemporary bedroom decorated in neutral
tones, made dim by the late-afternoon light.
Kate carries her weekender bag inside, turns on
the light and sees—

Her own reflection, staring back. And through
it, forest. There's another floor-to-ceiling
window here.

                    KATE
        You have *got* to be kidding me.

She spies a switch on the wall near the bed
and jabs it with a finger. A blind slowly
descends with an electronic hum.

                KATE (CONT'D)
        Thank fuck for that.

She unpacks some clothing, a make-up case, lacy lingerie. Hidden at the bottom of her bag is something wrapped in a sweatshirt: a bottle of Moët.

> JOEL (O.S.)
> I don't understand this, Belinda.
> What are you saying, exactly?

Kate goes to the smaller window overlooking the area to the front of the house. She sees Joel talking animatedly on the phone, pacing. When *he* sees Kate watching, he turns his back to her, rendering whatever he says next inaudible.

Kate watches for a beat more. Then she rewraps the champagne, returns it to the bag and slides the bag under the bed.

EXT. CHERRY COTTAGE - DUSK

Although there is still some light left in the late-afternoon sky, none of it seems to be penetrating the forest that surrounds Cherry Cottage. The lights on inside the house glow brightly against a backdrop of dense, dark trees.

INT. LIVING SPACE - NIGHT

Kate and Joel sit at opposite ends of the dining table, faces lit by candlelight, eating dinner in silence.

Kate is wearing a chic black dress and more make-up than before; she's made an effort. She is the only one. She watches as Joel tops up his wine glass from the bottle that was already within his reach. This action empties it. Kate glances at her own empty glass.

> JOEL
> Did you put the other bottle in the fridge?

> KATE
> Joel, before you drink any more, I have to tell you something. I have some news.

> JOEL
> *I* have some news too.

He gulps back half his wine in one go.

> KATE
> But I thought you said Belinda only rang to tell you it'd be next week before she could—

> JOEL
> (interrupting)
> I lied. I wasn't going to tell you until we were back in Dublin but … Fuck it.

He swallows the rest of his wine.

> JOEL (CONT'D)
> (muttering)
> Useless bitch. After all the money I've made her. I should demand it back.

> KATE
> What did she say?

                    JOEL
Did you put the other bottle in the
fridge?

                    KATE
I don't think you need any more.

                    JOEL
I promise you, darling, you've never
been more wrong about anything in
your entire life.

He tips his head back to drain the last few
drops of his wine.

                    JOEL (CONT'D)
You didn't see any whiskey around
here, did you?

                    KATE
What did she *say*?

                    JOEL
She's dumping me.

                    KATE
What?

                    JOEL
They had to pulp 5,000 copies of
Inside, did you know that? More
returns than sales. Oh, and she
thinks the new book is - how did
she put it again? I want to get it
exactly right, it was so succinct …
Ah yes: five pages of mediocrity and
395 pages of sophomoric wank.

Kate raises her eyebrows.

> JOEL (CONT'D)
> (frowning)
> Hang on. Maybe it was 395 pages of
> mediocrity and five pages of wank,
> but either way, not what you want to
> hear from your agent, now, is it?

> KATE
> *Belinda* said that?

> JOEL
> Those exact words. Right before she
> hung up on me.

> KATE
> And what words had *you* said by that
> point? Because that doesn't sound
> like B—

> JOEL
> (interrupting)
> Three years of my life, pissed away
> down the drain.

> KATE
> Is there any chance you're being a
> bit dramatic?

> JOEL
> Zero chance, according to Belinda.

> KATE
> It's just one person's opinion, Joel.

                    JOEL
                (voice rising)
        She's my *agent*. No one else will ever
        get to *have* an opinion on this book
        unless she sends it out.

                    KATE
        It's just a setback. You can write
        something else.

                    JOEL
        Kate, please. I know you're trying
        to help but you're not. You *can't*,
        because you have absolutely no
        fucking idea what you're talking
        about.

Kate bites her lip. She stands up.

                    KATE
        I think I'll open the other bottle.
        For *me*.

Joel suddenly bursts into tears. Kate is taken
aback and, for a moment, just stares at him
in shock. She quickly recovers and goes to
console him. He clings to her, all bravado
gone.

                    JOEL
        I just don't know what to do if I
        can't do this. What am I if I'm not a
        writer?

                    KATE
        You *are* a writer. A great one.

He pulls her on to his lap and she holds him as he cries.

INT. BEDROOM - NIGHT

The bedroom is dark, lit only by the light from the hall. Kate helps an unsteady, semi-conscious Joel into bed.

Once he's settled, evidently asleep, she stealthily retrieves the champagne from beneath the bed.

INT. LIVING SPACE - NIGHT

Kate uncorks the champagne over the kitchen sink and pours herself a generous glass of it. She raises it to her own reflection in the window.

> KATE
> Congratulations, Kate. Well done. I'm really proud of you and I'm sure this is just the start of very big things.

She clinks glasses with her reflection, swallows a mouthful, then sighs resignedly.

She flops down on one of the armchairs in front of the fire. The clock on the mantel tells her it's only 8:15 p.m. There's no television. She tries to stream something on her phone but it never gets past the buffering stage.

Her eyes wander to the shelf filled with copies of *First Draft*. She takes one down and settles in to read.

                    KATE (V.O.)
                    (reading)
The dense fir forest loomed above the
car, growing darker with every twist
and turn of the narrow, crumbling
road. Karen had jumped at the chance
of this last-minute getaway, her
first with Jack, who'd been so busy
with work lately, so consumed by it.
But the deeper they drove into the
forest, she wondered if they really
needed to get this far away …

                                    DISSOLVE TO:

FIVE

Dublin Airport was only just waking up when my flight landed at 5:20 a.m. local time.

It had been less than twenty-four hours since I'd taken John's call but I felt like I'd been travelling for days. I'd boarded my first flight, LAX to JFK, five hours after he'd woken me up, and boarded my second, transatlantic to Dublin, ninety minutes after the first one landed. Now, waiting at baggage claim, my hair felt greasy and limp and my skin had that awful tight and itchy feeling that meant it didn't just *look* splotchy and dull under the fluorescent lights in the airport bathroom, it actually was that.

I should've drunk more water on the plane. Or you know, some. Any.

I'd been too distracted by the nice wine and the swanky little bag of miniature lotions and soft socks, and then the ridiculous luxury of being on a plane overnight with a seat that folded flat and had a pillow and everything, and the voice in my head that, through it all, kept whispering, *I can't believe this is happening*.

The only people in the airport at that hour were the other passengers on my flight and however many ground staff and immigration officers were needed to get us landside. It made it easy to spot the grey-haired woman wearing a *Jurassic Park* sweatshirt waiting in Arrivals, holding up a handwritten sign that said CROSS CUT.

'Hi,' I said, pointing at the sign. 'I think that's me.'

'You're Adele?' After I nodded, she said, 'They told me I couldn't put your name on the sign,' and then she rolled her eyes, which felt like an indictment of me as a diva.

'Yes, it's all *very* secretive,' I said, rolling *my* eyes to convey that I agreed with her and that it was nothing to do with me, because Google Maps had said it was going to take nearly five hours to drive to set.

'I'm Peg.'

'Nice to meet you.' I could say that now that I was home. The habit in LA was to say *nice to see you* in case you had met the person before but they weren't important enough for you to remember, but they weren't *un*important enough for you to risk offending them because the power players in town subbed in and out constantly, and there was every chance that last month's cater-waiter would be next month's Spirit Awards nominee. I pointed at Peg's sweatshirt. 'I'm a big fan, too.'

She looked down as if seeing her own clothing for the first time and pinched some of the sweater material, pulled it away from her to look at it.

'Of *Jurassic Park*,' I clarified.

'Oh.' Peg shrugged. 'I've never been. This is my son's. You need to pick up anything to eat on the road or ...?'

As far as I could see, there was nowhere open to pick up anything from, but I wasn't hungry anyway. Somewhere over the Atlantic, my stomach had developed that empty, acidic feeling you get when you eat a dinner followed by a breakfast but don't go to sleep in between. The coffee they'd served us shortly before landing was now sloshing around in there, making things worse.

And then, remembering that I could use this phrase and not be misunderstood, that the most useful two words in all of the Irish-English language were once again available to me, I added, 'I'm grand.'

'Good.' Peg jerked her chin towards the exit. 'Then let's hit the road.'

I was in my dressing room at Ardmore Studios, locked inside it, and there was a face at the window that I recognised, but she shouldn't be here, she hadn't got the part—

'Wakey, wakey, love,' Peg called over her shoulder. 'We're almost there.'

I opened my eyes.

All I could see were trees. Christmas trees. Densely packed in a gloomy forest that seemed to entirely encircle the car. I turned to look up ahead, through the gap in the front seats: trees. I twisted around to look out the back window: trees. Out the window on the other side of the car: trees.

Where had the world gone?

I'd managed to stay awake until our pit stop at the services at Junction 14, but I'd spent most of the drive since dozing in the back of the car, my forehead resting against the window. The last time I'd woken up, a blink ago, we'd been leaving Cork City behind. When I'd called John back to tell him I'd do it – and to give him my passport details, dress size and dietary requirements – he'd said they were filming *Final Draft* at a house in the West Cork countryside. Those were his words: *West Cork countryside.* As he said them, I saw peninsulas of rolling green fields and, at their edges, rocky outcrops slicing into a steel-blue sea. Not this claustrophobic forest.

'Where are we?' I asked.

'Nearly there,' Peg said over her shoulder, as if that was different to *almost* there. She could be driving me to my death, for all I knew. The whole I've-never-heard-of-*Jurassic-Park* thing could be a ruse.

Suddenly, the car shot out of the trees and on to the grey-glass surface of the sea.

That's what it looked like to my sleep-deprived, jet-lagged brain, anyway. What had actually happened is that the road that had been cutting through dense forest was now stretching across an old stone bridge linking two land masses. To my right was either a large lake or the mouth of a wide river. To my left was a stretch of sea that had wedged itself between the land we were on and the land I could see to the south. The tide was high and the walls of the bridge low, making it seem, just for a moment, as if we were crossing the water itself. Even under cloudy winter skies, the effect was spectacular – and brief, because at the other end of the bridge, the road narrowed again and turned sharply to the right, hiding all views of the water unless you were prepared to twist around to an uncomfortable degree in your seat.

Now the landscape outside the car was rocky hill, barren and ancient, dotted here and there with tufts of whatever wild grass had fought to survive. The only thing I could see that I didn't believe had been here since the land had risen out of the ocean eons ago was the smooth, black tarmacadam of the road. It was starting to rise, carrying us up the hill, occasionally revealing a cap of more forest on the summit.

Peg's eyes met mine in the rear-view mirror.

'Not what you were expecting?' she said, smirking.

'It's a bit more …' She'd already told me she lived around here, so I had to choose my words carefully. '… remote.'

'Oh, it is that. You won't hear anything out here except the wind and herself, wailing.' Before I could ask who *herself* was supposed to refer to, she added, 'The banshee.' The smirk intensified. 'Bet they don't have *those* in Hollywood, now, do they?'

No, they didn't. I couldn't say that in my six months in California, I'd ever encountered a female spirit typically sporting a long mane of wild, white hair whose cry heralded the death of someone close to me. The banshee's bare feet were stuck firmly in Irish folklore. But like many people my age, my first thought whenever I heard the term was – and bear with me here – *crisps*.

When I was a child, Tayto had sold a brand of crisps called Banshee Bones. They were salt-and-vinegar flavoured puffs that in no way resembled bones, that came in a black bag with a banshee on the front. Tayto's banshee was a witch-like old woman with white hair, pointy teeth and skeletal hands, who you could easily imagine shrieking and wailing and generally scaring the shite out of people in the middle of the night. There had been more than one where I'd lain awake in bed until all hours imagining that I could hear her terrorising the three-bed-semi suburb of Cork City where I grew up. Most likely they were after days during which I'd consumed a bag of Banshee Bones.

'She's not the only one you might meet out here,' Peg continued. 'There's the hag, too. The Hag of Beara?' I frowned; I'd never heard of her. 'You can even go and see where she sits, if you've got time. And you must have heard about the White

Lady. Sure, everybody knows about her now, after poor Sophie.'
I knew she meant Sophie Toscan du Plantier, a Frenchwoman
whose unsolved murder in the area just before Christmas 1996
had been the subject of two true-crime documentaries recently,
both of which had recounted how Sophie reportedly 'saw' the
White Lady the day of her death. 'If you see her walking on
the water up by Three Castle Head, it'll be one of the last things
you'll ever see.' Peg paused. 'Or so they say.'

I wanted to point out that Peg was part of this *they* and that
telling people who were about to spend two weeks staying
out here this kind of information on arrival might not be the
best welcome, but I was distracted by a buzz in my pocket.

I hurried to dig out my phone, hoping it was Julia. I'd sent
her a WhatsApp yesterday, while I was waiting to board in
LAX, to tell her Steve Dade had got a thumbs-up from Lindsey
and so I'd taken the job. Julia had read the message but hadn't
responded, which was Normal Julia Behaviour. She regularly
sent replies hours or even days later apologising for forgetting
to. But I wanted her to say in writing that my secret was safe
with her. More than anyone, she knew how important it was
that my being back in Ireland remain a secret. And she already
knew something about *Final Draft*.

And, okay, yeah: I wanted someone to be happy for me. To
congratulate me. To tell me this was great and so exciting and
was definitely going to lead to even greater and more exciting
things, that it was going to make everything okay again. I
couldn't tell anyone else, so Julia had to play that role, too.

But this new message wasn't from Julia. It was an Irish
mobile I didn't recognise, one that wasn't stored in my phone.
A new one. This wasn't the number John had called me from,

or the number attached to the earlier calls.

Are you in Cork yet?

I assumed it belonged to someone on the production.

The car slipped back into dense forest, now with added gloom. The trees capping the summit seemed to be even closer together than their relatives at the foot of the hill and were holding a low mist in the air between their branches. I felt rather than saw the road begin to level out.

I started typing a response to the text but only got halfway through the word *almost* when Peg said, 'Here we are.'

She was turning the car before I saw the gap in the treeline on the right she was aiming for: a narrow, unpaved road between a set of wrought-iron gates, pushed all the way back. There was no sign, no house name or number or letterbox. Nothing at all that gave any indication as to what might be at the other end of the road, which, once she'd turned on to it, I saw – and felt – was more of a dirt track than a road, muddy and uneven.

Now I understood the wisdom of hiring a taxi driver from the local area to go all the way to Dublin Airport to collect me and bring me back. I couldn't imagine anyone who didn't already know this place ever finding it.

The track twisted and turned as the wheels of Peg's taxi bounced over potholes and former potholes that had been filled in without finesse. I started to feel vaguely carsick. I put my phone away, figuring I was moments away from meeting whoever had sent the text in person. There was no need to respond now.

As we rounded a corner, a pair of imposing stone pillars came into view. On either side of them were the crumbling remains of stone walls, overgrown with moss and other spreading green things. And through the gap between the pillars, perfectly framed by them, was Cedarwood House.

I knew that's what it was called because one pillar said CEDARWOOD and the other said HOUSE.

Cedarwood House was a structure made of age, strength and symmetry, and built of stone. Five sash windows to the front: three upstairs, and one on either side of the front door which itself was set dead centre. All the wood was painted a bright, glossy red. Two chimneys on a time-battered slate roof which, if you drew straight lines down from them, would land on the two little potted plants sitting like bookends on either side of the front step. The walls were mostly covered in a thick ivy that seemed to be both crawling up and cascading down. As the car passed through the pillars, the ground changed from uneven dirt to loose gravel, crunching beneath the wheels.

There were two vehicles parked outside the house already, a clunky SUV-type thing and a gleaming motorhome.

Peg pulled up alongside the SUV but kept her engine idling.

All the windows on the house's upper level had their curtains drawn, even though it was – I checked the clock on the dashboard – gone eleven.

'Doesn't look like there's anyone here,' I said.

'There's more buildings round the back.' Peg twisted around in her seat to hand me a business card. It was thin and cheaply printed, and matched the livery printed on the doors of her car. *Sheep's Head Transport*. 'I live at the bottom of the hill, just before the bridge. If you need me, I can be here in twenty minutes.'

'Great,' I said. 'Thanks.' I traded the card for the soft twenty-euro note that had been in my wallet since I'd moved to LA, and thanked her. The production would pay the fare but still, it felt like good manners to give Peg a tip.

'Ta, love,' she said, taking it. 'You're very good.' She turned back to face front just as I heard a *thunk* from somewhere behind me: Peg had opened the boot. 'Best of luck, then.'

I got the message. I pushed open the door and climbed out.

The air felt damp and icy and smelled like a pine air freshener that had been buried in mulch for a month. I walked to the rear of the car, feeling the sharp points of the gravel push through the thin soles of my ten-dollar ballet flats. I was dressed for seasonless LA, not the Irish countryside in January, and was immediately freezing.

As soon as I'd hoisted my dead-weight suitcase out of the boot and closed it after me, Peg took off, kicking up gravel behind her wheels. I listened until the noise of the engine faded and then there was no noise at all, except for a twig snapping somewhere in the treeline behind me.

Where the hell was everyone?

I took out my phone, thinking I'd call the number who had texted to ask me about my arrival. They'd probably done it so they could send someone out here to greet me, and since I hadn't responded—

I froze when I saw what was on the screen.

Another text message, from the same number, that had come in just a couple of minutes ago.

If you're not, don't go. Not safe. Trust me.

And then I heard someone shouting my name.

SIX

I stared at the words on my phone's screen and cycled through all the possible meanings, trying to find a scenario that made sense and wasn't also absolute worst-case.

Before I could, I saw that the door to the motorhome had opened and a guy was coming out of it – the same one who'd been calling my name. He was spindly and tall, with tufts of red hair shooting up in all directions, freckles on skin so pale it had a slightly bluish pallor. A little younger than I was, twenty-two or -three. As he hurried across the gravel, waving at me, I saw he had neon yellow laces in his hiking boots and a smartphone in one hand, which he slipped into a back pocket just as he reached me.

I waited for him to say, 'I was *just* texting you!' but instead he said, 'Sorry. I was on a call with the catering service, which is always quite the adventure around here. Reception is a moving target. Anyway' – he stuck out a hand – 'I'm Donal, the assistant director.' Big, wide smile. 'Welcome to the set of *Final Draft*.'

'Adele,' I said. My knuckles were white around my phone, but the only thing I knew for sure was that acting unhinged right out of the gate – or out of the cab – would not improve this situation. I dropped it down by my side and shook his hand with my free one. 'And, ah, thank you.'

'No, thank *you*,' Donal said. 'You saved all our arses.'

'Happy to.' I studied his face, searching for unease or suspicion, for signs that my reputation had preceded me, but found none. His niceness seemed genuine. 'And, um … where *are* all the other arses?'

'Sleeping.' Donal pointed behind him, at the house. 'Upstairs. Cedarwood House is our location *and* some of our accommodation. Space is at a bit of a premium around here so … The motorhome, for example, is my room, the production office *and* hair and make-up.'

'Did you text me just now?'

'No, why?'

I opted for a half-truth, my safest bet. 'It's just that I got a text message I thought must be from someone on the production, asking me if I was here yet. It's a bit weird because I didn't recognise the number, and obviously I haven't told anyone I was coming here, so …'

One half-truth and a big, fat lie.

'Call out the number to me.' Donal took out his phone. I did and watched as he tapped the digits on to the screen. 'Nope,' he said, then angled the phone so I could see for myself. Under the number was a line of blue text: *Add Number*. If there was a match for it in his contacts, that line would display the owner's name. 'But that's not to say it wasn't someone at Cross Cut. Back at the office, I mean. I have all the crew's numbers in here but not everyone in the company. Did you try calling the number?'

'I will,' I said. 'Later. To be honest, all I want to do right now is have a shower and go to sleep.'

There was no way I was calling that number back in front of him.

'Well, I'm delighted to tell you that you can do both of those things,' Donal said, smiling. 'So, it's night shoots this week. That's why everyone's asleep – they're already on that schedule. Which is breakfast at six p.m., lunch at midnight and dinner around seven o'clock in the morning. We're doing a half-day's shooting today, so your call-time is seven p.m. and we shoot at eight, but the aim is to be done by midnight.'

I was down a night's sleep, in the wrong time-zone and worried that my career-saving role on this production might be in jeopardy already, so I took almost none of that in. The only thing that stuck initially was that my call-time was 7:00 p.m. Even with an hour on either side for unpacking and getting ready, that meant I could fit in a good five unconscious hours right now.

If I *could* sleep.

If you're not, don't go. Not safe. Trust me.

'Wait,' I said. 'I'm shooting *tonight*?'

'It's nothing to worry about,' Donal said, waving a hand. 'We've moved some stuff around to account for you coming in last minute. We're just going to shoot the scene where Kate toasts herself in the window and then settles down to read the book.' I nodded like I'd totally read the script and knew exactly what Donal was referring to. Yep. *Sure.* 'There's, like, three lines of actual dialogue and the rest will be voice-over. You'll be grand.' He bent to lift my suitcase off the ground. 'You're in one of the cabins around the back. They're really nice. They're new. We're the first people to stay in them. Come on, I'll show you.'

He turned to go and I followed him, across the gravel to the far corner of the house and then around it.

Behind the house was a landscaped garden with a stone fountain at its centre and four gravel paths jutting out from it like spokes. There must have been a sale on gravel when they built this place. The ground had been levelled, cut into the gentle slope of the hill, so the forest that surrounded it on three sides sat just above it. The extra few feet made the trees not just loom overhead, but tower above. I had to look straight up to see sky.

I looked back at the house and saw that, just like in the script, the ground floor had a huge floor-to-ceiling window at the rear that stretched from wall to wall. Or maybe it was one of those snazzy bi-fold doors that completely disappeared and left a gaping hole at the back of the house. From this angle, there was nothing to see on the other side of the glass but darkness. Maybe things were better in summer or on sunny days, but the forest seemed to be completely blocking natural light from entering the house. It was as if the trees had been tasked with hiding it.

We walked up some stone steps and started following a beaten path through the trees. Donal asked about LA and my flights and the drive down in Peg's taxi, his breathing suggesting that my suitcase was growing heavier in his hand with every step.

Eventually, we emerged into a little clearing where three cabins sat, the kind that people took to panic-installing in their gardens during lockdown so they could have a few hours away from whoever was in the house instead of killing them. They looked to be about the same size as the motorhome. They were set side-on to the house and erected side by side on the rising ground, a bit like steps of a stairs. Each one had a strip of decking to the front, protected by the overhang of the roof, with two white plastic chairs sitting there, facing out.

It didn't pass me by that I was here to shoot a horror movie and I was *literally* staying in a cabin in the woods.

I glanced back at the house, or where I thought the house should be. I couldn't see anything now except trees.

If you're not, don't go. Not safe. Trust me.

Who would've sent me a text like that? And why? I felt a rush of anger towards them, whoever they were. Here I was, finally, getting the break that I not only needed but *deserved*. And this anonymous texter was ruining it for me.

'Here we are,' Donal said, going to the furthest cabin and setting my case on its decking. He was panting a little and there was a light sheen of sweat on his forehead despite the cold, having made a heroic effort to keep the wheels of the case off the muddy ground the whole way here. He opened the front door and stepped back.

'After you,' he said with a smile.

I looked from him to the opening, into the yawning gloom of the cabin beyond. Donal didn't strike me as a serial killer, but it did cross my mind that he was ushering me into a small, confined space in a forest in the middle of nowhere, on the quietest, emptiest, most deserted set I'd ever been on in my life. Apart from Peg – who'd already floored it out of here – no one actually knew where I was, geographically speaking.

No one knew that I was here in the woods on top of a mountain in the wilds of West Cork, with a guy I'd only met a few minutes ago and knew nothing about, after getting an anonymous text message that seemed to be warning me not to come here.

Donal was frowning now. 'Everything all right?'

But if I set the text message aside, nothing about this was in any way out of the ordinary. I didn't know anyone because I was a last-minute replacement and so hadn't had any meetings or auditions or been around for pre-production fittings or table-reads. The location was a gloomy, secluded house in the woods because the events in the script took place in a gloomy, secluded house in the woods. There was no one around because it was late morning and *Final Draft* was shooting at night, so everyone was asleep except for the person who had to get up to come and meet me.

And really, it was a *great* thing for me that no one knew I was here.

'Sorry,' I said. 'Yeah. Just a bit, you know, loopy from jet-lag.' I stepped on to the deck and went inside.

There wasn't much to see until Donal flipped a switch behind me, turning the lights on. The cabin's interior had both the gleaming appearance and fresh-out-of-the-box smell of a brand-new car.

It was a studio. The only interior door was one at the rear that I assumed led to a bathroom. In front of it was a double bed. Immediately in front of me was a kitchenette, a booth-style dining area and a two-seater couch facing a small TV attached to the wall opposite. Everything was decorated in calming, neutral tones.

Despite its small size, it felt spacious and airy – but also a little cold, as if no one had spent any length of time in here in the recent past.

When I turned around, I saw that Donal was nervously awaiting a verdict.

'It's great,' I said. 'Lovely.'

He didn't seem convinced. 'Are you sure?'

'It's nicer than the place I actually live in.'

Donal laughed at this and I resisted the urge to whip out my phone and show him photographic evidence.

He carried in my suitcase and set it down just inside the door.

'So,' he said. 'I'll just provide you with the pertinent information and leave you to sleep. As you saw on the way in, we're a ways from, well, *everything*. But we have a catering service delivering daily and if anyone wants anything else, I'm very happy to do a run to SuperValu in Bantry.'

'Bantry?' I knew Bantry as a bustling town with restaurants and bars and hotels and people, and I hadn't seen anything like that anywhere near here. 'How far away is that?'

'About twenty minutes' drive.'

'Really?'

This made me feel much less like I'd been dropped at the end of the world.

'I've put a few things in the fridge to hold you over for the day,' he said, 'but let me know if there's anything specific you want for tomorrow and onwards. It'll be a hot breakfast tonight. All meals will be served in the cabin next door. That's our designated cast and crew dining room. And coffee station, lounge, bar – whatever else it needs to be. It's fully stocked and there's plenty of snackage in there too, so, you know. Help yourself.'

I looked around. 'How is the entire crew going to fit into one of *these*?' I presumed they weren't and that Donal was about to tell me that meals would be served in multiple sittings.

But he said, 'Easy. There's only eight of us.'

I couldn't hide my surprise. I knew how many people it took to make twenty-three minutes of television. *Bad* television, at that. How could you possibly make an entire movie with *eight*?

Final Draft was beginning to sound a bit more no-budget than low-budget.

'We're a skeleton crew,' Donal explained. 'Steve is directing, obviously, but he's also sort of producing because Daniel can't come to set yet. His brother's getting married in France, so he's not available until next Monday. Mick is our DOP and Liam is second camera.' Since I'd moved to LA, I'd learned that 'DOP' was a distinctly Irish thing; everywhere else, the director of photography was the 'DP'. 'Mark is on sound. Neil is hair, make-up and a bit of wardrobe, too. Then we have Aaron, who's going to do whatever we need him to do as we need him to do it – driving, sorting the food, fixing the printer, that kind of thing. And we haven't actually put this to the test yet, but he says he can be Mick's gaffer too. The guy looks like Chris Evans at the start of *Captain America*, so we'll see about that ... And I'm assistant director but also kind of a line producer *and* a production assistant. And, most importantly, Chief Snackage Co-ordinator.' He winked at me as he said this and I thought, *That's the second time he's used that word, he must really like it*. 'And then there's you, which makes eight. At least until Simon Pearse arrives next week.' When my face didn't respond to this with anything resembling recognition, Donal added, 'Your co-star?'

I hadn't even thought to ask who *else* was going to be in this thing. As far as I was concerned, I already knew the most important bit of casting information: I was Kate and Kate was on screen by herself for most of this movie's run time.

'Oh,' I said. 'Yeah, of course.' I smiled. '*Simon*. Right.' I'd IMDb him as soon as I got the chance.

'Don't worry. Steve just wants to make this movie the same way he started out making them – back in college, when it was just him and Daniel and a few friends and a bit of beg, borrow and steal, you know? This was going to be a big studio thing for a while – with Primal Pictures – but Steve backed out when he realised it was going to be like making a movie by committee. *Creative differences*, officially.' Donal grinned as he said this. 'He managed to cobble together some private funds so he can make it his way, but that's also *this* way, because the budget is small. But I think the script lends itself to this kind of movie-making. If it was, I don't know, a period drama set in a palace with an ensemble cast, I'd be like, yeah, we're totally screwed.' He smiled. 'This is mostly your character, alone, in a place that looks exactly like this. I think the chances are good that we're going make something pretty cool here.'

I made a *hmm* noise.

'So,' I said, 'what you're telling me is that, back in college, Steve didn't have any female friends.'

Donal looked at me blankly.

'Am I the only woman on set?'

'Ah ...' His cheeks reddened. 'Yeah. I know. It's a bit of a testicle fest.' A flash of panic. 'I mean, not that you need testicles to be a man. Obviously you don't. If you get, like, cancer and you have to get your testicles removed, or if you're not born with ...' His face was splotchy now with patches the colour of beetroot. 'Sorry, I don't know why I keep saying testicles. And I just did it again, there.' He cleared his throat. 'I did raise the issue with Steve. He said he hadn't thought about that, that he just hired the best guys – um, *people* for the job.'

'And yet managed to confine all his picks to one half of the population,' I said. 'The *smaller* half, at that. What are the odds?'

Donal opened his mouth but no words came out of it.

'There's a reason they call it *unconscious* bias,' I went on. 'The men who say they don't even think about gender *are* the problem. It's so ingrained, if they don't think about it, they keep doing it.'

Now Donal was shifting his weight, cheeks aflame, unable to make eye contact with me. I suddenly felt sorry for him, and also that maybe this set wasn't the place to go full Feminist Warrior. I needed this job. The power was theirs in a very practical sense, before we ever got anywhere near the patriarchy.

'Anyway,' I said, 'it's not your fault.'

My eyes strayed to the lock on the inside of the cabin door. It looked like one of those ones that was easily jimmied open with a plastic keycard, the kind that belonged indoors, not serving as the only barrier between you and whatever might want to get at you from out there in the dark. The only consolation was that, since we were doing night shoots, I'd be sleeping in here during the day.

'Well,' Donal said, 'I'll, ah, leave you to get some sleep. Do you need anything else? A wake-up knock on the door?'

'No thanks, I'm grand. I'll just use my phone.'

'Oh – speaking of phones ...' He cleared his throat. 'The reception around here is truly diabolical. There isn't any, basically, except for a few mysterious pockets that come and go. Sometimes mid phone call, which is helpful. If you *do* need to make a call or check your messages or whatever, just let me know. We can hop in the car and drive down to the road. That's what I've been doing. And there's, ah, no wifi either. Steve didn't want it on set. Makes it easier to keep a secret if everyone's offline, you know? I think the lack of mobile phone service is partly why he picked this place, actually.'

I was tempted to gather the skin on the back of my hand and pinch it between my thumb and forefinger, just to make sure I wasn't actually dreaming up this whole thing. Patchy mobile phone reception? No *wifi*? I couldn't have designed this situation better myself.

All right, I would've omitted the ominous text message. But still, this meant my anonymous texter wouldn't be *able* to text me. That would make them much easier to ignore.

'Good to know,' I said.

Donal gave a little wave and then turned and went out the door, closing it carefully behind him. There was a window inset in it with a thin, gauze-like curtain over it; through it, I watched him disappear into the trees. Alone then, finally, for the first time since I'd got into the car that John had arranged to bring me to LAX, I felt exhaustion sweep over me in a drowning wave, rendering every limb twice as heavy and filling my brain with a fog.

I looked at the suitcase I should unpack, the fridge I should forage in for some late breakfast, the bathroom where I should shower before I did either of those things. I saw the call-sheet I should definitely look at on the dining table and, sitting next to it, a printed copy of the script it was imperative I finish reading. I swiped at the screen of my phone and looked at the anonymous text message I should respond to, from the number

I should at the very least try calling now. I didn't seem to have any service, but maybe if I went back outside I'd find one of the mysterious pockets of it Donal had mentioned.

But when my eyes landed on the bed, the only thing I actually wanted to do was slip out of my muddy ballet flats, shrug off my coat and crawl into it. So I did, burrowing under the weight of the winter duvet, luxuriating in the soft and fresh-smelling sheets. I didn't so much drift off to sleep as face-plant into it, having completely forgotten to set an alarm.

My mistakes were piling up like crashed cars on a freeway, each one smashing into the one that had smashed before in rapid succession, exponentially increasing the chance that we'd all soon be engulfed in a deadly fireball from which there'd be no escape.

But I didn't know it yet.

INT. LIVING SPACE - NIGHT

Kate is curled up on the armchair, reading,
with a blanket over her. The only sound is the
crackling of the fire, until—

A single, heavy THUMP on the front door.

Kate bolts upright. Her eyes go to the clock
on the mantel: it's just after 3:00 a.m. She
holds her breath, listens. The sound doesn't
come again.

Tentatively, she approaches the door. Steps up
to it. Turns her head to put her ear against
the wood.

A log in the fire collapses with a loud SNAP,
startling her.

She retreats, then turns and runs down the
hall and into the bedroom …

INT. BEDROOM - NIGHT [CONTINUOUS]

… where Kate aggressively rouses Joel from his
drunken sleep.

                    JOEL
                 (muffled)
        What? What is it?

                    KATE
        Someone's here.

                    JOEL
        What?

                    KATE
        Wake the fuck up, Joel. Someone's
        outside.

Joel hoists himself up on to his elbows.

                    JOEL
        What time is it?

                    KATE
        Too late for anybody to be knocking
        on our door all the way out here. Get
        up.

With an eye-roll, Joel relents.

INT. LIVING SPACE - NIGHT

Joel nonchalantly approaches the front door as
a nervous Kate follows closely behind.

                    JOEL
        Did you open it?

                    KATE
        No, I did not fucking open it, Joel.
        We're miles from anywhere, it's the
        middle of the night and I was by
        myself because you had a toddler
        tantrum.

                    JOEL
        Jesus Christ. Calm down. It's
        probably just a disorientated bird or
        something.

                            KATE
                        (incredulous)
        A disorientated *bird*?

Joel opens the front door.

EXT/INT. CHERRY COTTAGE/
LIVING SPACE - NIGHT

The only light outside is that which escapes
from behind Joel as he stands in the doorway.
Everything beyond it is dark and still. He scans
the area: from his POV, we see that there's no
one there.

                            JOEL
        Hello?

Kate stands inside, a few steps behind him,
shifting her weight from foot to foot.

                            KATE
                        (whispering)
        Do you see anything?

Joel moves away from the house to get a better
look. He surveys the treeline - nothing, no
one - then moves to check the car doors are
still locked. They are. Everything seems fine.

                            JOEL
                (shouting through the open door)
        There's no one here.

Kate watches Joel come back inside and lock
the door behind him.

                              KATE
          Do the deadbolt too.

With an eye-roll that Kate doesn't see, Joel
complies.

                         KATE (CONT'D)
          Someone was there. They knocked.

                              JOEL
          How many times?

                              KATE
          Just once. One knock.

                              JOEL
          One knock?
                         (sighs)
          Where were you when it happened?

                              KATE
          On the couch, reading.

                              JOEL
          So … You fell asleep.

                              KATE
          No, I didn't.

                              JOEL
          You fell asleep, Kate. There's no one
          out there. And why would there be?
          You said it yourself. We're miles
          from anywhere. And the only car out
          there is ours.

KATE

I know what I heard.

JOEL

Good for you. I'm going back to bed.

He turns and starts back towards the bedroom.
After a beat, Kate follows him.

INT. BEDROOM - NIGHT

Kate and Joel lie beside one another in bed.
Joel is on his side, turned away, snoring. Kate
lies on her back, staring at the ceiling. The
digital alarm clock on the bedside table glows
4:05 a.m.

Kate tosses and turns, then - resigned - gets
up again.

INT. LIVING SPACE - NIGHT

Kate makes herself a cup of tea. She checks
the front door is actually locked, the
deadbolt turned, the house secure. Then she
returns to the chair in front of the dying
embers of the fire.

She picks up *First Draft*, finds her place and
settles in to read on.

KATE (V.O.)

When his breathing had turned into
snores, Karen crept out of the warmth
of their shared bed and tiptoed
into the living room. She couldn't
sleep, the swings and punches of
their earlier argument replaying on

a loop inside her head. She selected
a paperback from the shelf beside the
fire and settled in to read. It was
a true story and she was immediately
enthralled; around her, the night
and the fire and the trees dissolved
away. The clock on the mantel had
just ticked into the witching hour
when she heard the first knock on the
door.

Kate stops. She looks towards the door,
frowns. She flips to the last page of the
book and starts scanning the text, touching an
index finger to the paper as she does.

> KATE (V.O.)
> *But, unbeknownst to Karen, it was*
> *already too late. It had been from*
> *the moment she'd arrived in the*
> *woods.*

INT. LIVING SPACE – NIGHT [DREAM SEQUENCE]

A man wearing a black ski mask and holding a
long, glinting knife slowly rises from behind
Kate's chair. He brings the knife down—

> KATE (V.O.)
> *She felt the knife go in a heartbeat*
> *after she sensed his presence.*

The knife plunges into the flesh of Kate's
neck, spilling glossy red blood over her pale
skin. She silently screams and squirms.

> KATE (V.O.)(CONT'D)
> *A tunnel of white-hot pain burning
> through her core.*

Kate looks up at her attacker, reaches for the
ski mask, pulls it down—

> KATE (V.O.)(CONT'D)
> *And as she looked up into the face of
> her killer, she realised ...*

—revealing Joel's face underneath.

> KATE (V.O.)(CONT'D)
> *... she knew him.*

Kate screams.

SMASH CUT TO:

INT. LIVING SPACE - DAY

Kate wakes up with a start.

The room has been transformed by a weak winter
sun. The wall of glass is now a vibrant
tapestry of lush greens. The clock on the
mantel says it's just gone eight o'clock.
A copy of *First Draft* is splayed on Kate's
chest; she fell asleep reading it. She yawns
and gets up, starts towards the kitchen—

But freezes when she sees that the cottage's
front door is standing wide open.

> KATE
> What the …?

Kate runs down the hall to the bedroom where she sees, from the doorway …

INT. BEDROOM - DAY [CONTINUOUS]

… Joel's sleeping form, still in bed and snoring heavily.

ACT II

SEVEN

Opening my eyes didn't turn off the dark.

For one heartbeat of total panic, I didn't know what was happening or where I was. But then a shape started to take form in the depths of the darkness: a rectangle of not-quite-as-dark. As my eyes adjusted, I put a name to it. *Window*. In this … *Cabin*. Behind Cedarwood House, the set of *Final Draft*.

I was in bed, in a warm cocoon of marshmallow softness, but if it was already dark outside then I really shouldn't—

A knock at the door.

And then someone on the other side of it, calling my name.

For the second time, I realised. The first was what had woken me up.

'Coming,' I called out, flinging back the duvet – gasping at the cold that it had been keeping away – and hurrying to the door in my bare feet. When I opened it, I saw Donal holding a plate covered with tinfoil and a takeaway cup of what smelled like burnt coffee. Well, I assumed it was him, because we were both standing in complete darkness.

'On the wall to your right,' the shadow's voice said.

I felt for the switch, then blinked in the glare of the light. It *was* Donal.

'Sorry,' I said to him. 'I slept in.'

He waved his free hand. 'It's completely fine. It's only a quarter past and everyone's had a bit of a sluggish start today, so you're grand. We're all still trying to adjust to the schedule. Some of us are having more success than others. Here.' He handed me the tinfoil-wrapped plate he was holding in his other hand, careful not to topple the takeaway cup resting on top. 'Room-service breakfast. That should save you a few minutes.' He grinned. 'Just don't get used to it, okay?'

'You're a lifesaver.'

The smell of whatever greasy meat was under the foil made my stomach rumble loudly, but Donal, ever the gentleman, didn't react.

'Since we don't have stand-ins,' he said, 'and you found out you were coming here about five minutes ago, we're not going to do a full rehearsal. We'll send you to Neil in the motorhome and then bring you to set for a quick rehearsal, then we'll shoot straightaway. That okay?'

'Okay.'

But I must have looked nervous because Donal said, 'You'll mostly just be sitting on a chair, reading.'

'Okay,' I said again, meaning it a bit more this time.

'And just so you know, Steve has a strict no-phones policy on set. He'll freak if he sees one. But feel free to bring it with you when you come down – you can leave it in the motorhome. That's where you'll be hanging out between takes.'

'Got it.'

'See you down there?'

'See you there,' I said with a smile.

I went back inside, closed the door behind me and collapsed back against it, exhaling a string of whispered swear words.

And then I said, '*Fuck*,' out loud.

I couldn't believe I'd forgotten to set an alarm. I'd been planning a leisurely shower and hair-wash followed by an in-depth read of the script, and then meeting everyone over breakfast in the crew cabin. Now I didn't have time to do any of that *and* I was going to meet the crew for the first time, quite literally, on set. I was even going to meet *my* director that way.

This job was off to a bloody great start.

I went to the bed and felt in the folds of the duvet for the hard smoothness of my phone. No missed calls, no new messages. But that could just be because I also didn't have any service. I held the phone aloft and walked it around the cabin, but no bars appeared on screen.

Maybe I'd have more luck in the motorhome. Hadn't Donal said he'd been on a call in there when I'd arrived?

My stomach rumbled again. The last thing I needed was to spoil every shot tonight with my digestive juices, so I sat at the little dining table and peeled the tinfoil off the plate.

This revealed the sweet greasy goodness of an Irish breakfast: rashers of bacon, scrambled egg, sausages, grilled tomato and little discs of both black and white pudding. The food looked delicious. I hadn't had anything even resembling it since I'd been in LA. Back there, my breakfast was invariably a bowl of soggy supermarket own-brand cereal. On the very rare occasion I went out for a breakfast or brunch I couldn't afford, alone, I found my options limited to pancake chain-restaurants and places where the menu listed ingredients such as *metabolic essential oils* (whatever those were supposed to be) and to order you had to say monstrously cringeworthy things to your server like, 'I am illuminated'.

But I thought my first Irish breakfast in six months could be even more delicious if I wasn't shivering with the cold, so I climbed back into bed and, with the plate carefully balanced on my lap and the cup within easy reach on the bedside table, resumed stuffing my face from under the blankets.

I was polishing off the second sausage when I became aware of something tiny and sharp sticking into the bare skin of my foot. When I moved it, I felt the sharp thing move with it, *roll* with it, underneath my heel.

There was something in the bed other than me.

My first thought was *bug* so I swiftly picked up the plate and hopped out, throwing back the covers to see what horror was hiding underneath. But what I found was an earring. A small, sparkly drop designed for pierced ears, missing the backing that would have kept it secured in one, caught in the threads of the fitted sheet.

I thought I knew exactly how it had got there. In fact, I thought I was especially qualified to know. Something very similar had happened at the Goodnite Suites, only that had involved a stick-on, leopard-print nail. The guest who'd discovered it had completely freaked out – we'd ended up having to fully comp them for a night at the Hilton Universal City just to get them to calm down – but all that had happened was that one of our room attendants had made a bad choice when it came to her nail glue and chosen a brand that just wasn't up to repeated bed-making.

I transferred the earring to the sill of the kitchen window, where I was sure whoever had prepped this place for my arrival would see it when they returned, and didn't give it another thought.

I brought my phone with me to the motorhome because I was hoping I'd have service there. As it turned out, I needed it just to get to the motorhome in the first place.

Like any Urban Dweller in the Countryside straight from Central Casting, I was discovering that *after dark* out here meant something different to *after dark* everywhere else. I could see the house now, or rather its lights, which were just about managing to filter through the trees. But when I looked down, I couldn't even see my own feet, let alone what gnarled roots and ankle-twisting boulders might be sitting in the way of them. I had to use my phone's torch app to help judge where and where not to step until, finally, I reached the stone steps that led down into the walled garden.

Now there was a *lot* of light. The wall of windows at the rear of the ground floor was a giant fluorescent strip, bathing the walled garden in a harsh white glow.

On the other side of the glass, I could see three – no, *four* – guys manoeuvring their bodies around reflectors and cameras and lights. One of the guys was Donal but none of the others looked like Steve Dade. Everything seemed to be angled towards an armchair at one end of the room, next to a fireplace, where Kate would sit and read the book she'd found in the house that she and Joel had rented for the weekend.

I knew that because, after eating and showering, I had quickly read the relevant pages of the script – or what I thought were the relevant pages because, for some reason, the scenes weren't numbered. They always were in a shooting script, which meant I'd been supplied with an earlier version, a script from before pre-production began in earnest. I'd made a mental note to ask Donal about it.

The scene through the glass looked like an actual, real movie set and, better yet, it was waiting for me. I felt what was either a frisson of excitement or the chill of a January night prickling the back of my neck.

I made my way around the side of the house and across the gravel to the motorhome. Its lights were ablaze and the door was wide open, but when I stepped up into it, I saw that no one was there yet.

The interior was pretty much what I'd been expecting, although the sum total of my motorhome knowledge came from watching re-runs of G-list celebrity road-trip shows on BBC America on the weekday mornings when I didn't have auditions to go to, which was most mornings. The main door was narrow and opened outwards, leaving a gaping hole of black night-time behind the passenger seat. Standing with my back to it, a little kitchenette was to my immediate right. At the opposite end was a U-shaped arrangement of built-in seating with a dining table in the middle; I assumed that was the spot that converted to a bed. On the wall opposite was a boxy cubicle with a concertina-style plastic door that I guessed was the bathroom, although the lack of any funky chemical smells suggested it wasn't being used as one. Beside it was a floor-to-ceiling cupboard and, next to that, a little couch. All the window blinds were down.

But this motorhome wasn't prepped to take a pair of vaguely familiar faces pretending to be friends on a hunt for worthless junk through the English countryside. Every square inch had been taken over with production-related paraphernalia. The entire rear wall was stuck with schedules, storyboards and Post-it Notes, and a laptop was open on the table at the back. A Hollywood mirror was propped on the couch with a folding plastic chair sitting in front of it. A tension rod had been strung behind the front seats to make a clothing rail, from which hung various garments in clear, plastic dry-cleaning bags that still had the tickets safety-pinned on.

I was happy to see the jeans and a huge, fluffy towelling robe, but not so happy to see strips of something black and sequinned that looked like a safety harness but was probably supposed to be a cocktail dress. I hung my coat from one of the bare hangers at the end of the rail. I checked my phone, but the situation was unchanged: no new messages, no missed calls, no service.

'You must be Adele.'

The new voice was male, smooth in what struck me – even in just four words – as a smarmy way, and so close I could smell the cigarette smoke on the speaker's breath.

When I turned, I found a man standing less than two feet of clear air in front of me. Forty-ish, well dressed in what looked like a pricey wool jumper over a white-collared shirt and jeans, with thick brown hair that was a little curly at the crown. He was pulling the door to the motorhome closed behind him.

I took a step back and said, 'That's me.'

'Neil,' he said, taking a step forward. He extended a hand. I hadn't done handshakes since March 2020 but everyone on this set seemed to be mad for them. The easiest option was to shake it, so I did, feeling the squeeze of his cold fingers around mine. 'I should tell you, I'm a special effects guy primarily. But Steve is on a tight budget here, so everyone's double-jobbing …' He added his other hand to our shake, covering mine with his, rubbing it like he was trying to warm me up. 'But we'll figure it out, won't we? Between the two of us.'

He was looking at me the way I'd looked at my breakfast.

I retracted my hand, which he only let go of on a delay, caressing my fingers as they left his grip.

'So, wardrobe first?' I asked briskly. I wanted to move things along, to get whatever needed doing done so I could get the hell out of this motorhome.

Because I knew this man.

I had encountered him many, many times before.

Ten years ago, he was my friend's dad who 'accidentally' walked in on me in the bathroom when I was staying over after a teen disco. Six years ago, he was the sound guy at a TV show with his hands down my dress, fitting a microphone pack to my bra strap, telling me about the time he had to fit one to a famously beautiful woman and how he'd had to rush off to take a cold shower afterwards. Two years ago, he was the man who sent me a message via Instagram to compliment me on my profile pic, and then abuse and insults when I didn't respond to it.

I didn't know Neil at all but I knew *exactly* who Neil was: a man who thought women were for him.

'Wardrobe first,' he confirmed. He reached for the clothes rack and – my heart sank – pulled out the sequinned safety harness/cocktail dress. 'This is you.'

I did my best confused face.

'Did I prep the wrong scene?' I asked. 'I thought this was the one where Kate curls up on the couch with a book?'

'It is, but that's right after the dinner scene.' Neil held the dress a bit higher, making it look even shorter. 'This is what she wears to that, so she still has it on. Minus the heels.'

The heels?

'For a home-made dinner, with her boyfriend, in a country house in a forest?'

'She's making an effort,' Neil said. 'It says so in the script.'

'An effort to do what? Catch pneumonia?'

I laughed lightly because that's what was demanded of me here. If I *actually* got mad, I'd immediately be labelled 'difficult'.

Neil's lips had set in a tight line. 'Is there a problem?'

'It just isn't what any woman I know would wear in these circumstances,' I said, trying to keep my tone casual. 'Are there any other options?'

'This is what we have.' He paused. 'Perhaps if you'd been the first choice for the role and we'd had a chance to do fittings ...'

The abominable dickhead.

Resigned, I took the dress from him.

'Now,' he said, 'you won't be able to wear a bra with that, but I can tape them. We'll see how good a job it does of keeping them in first.'

For added ick, his eyes dropped to my chest as he said this.

I wanted to ask him what life was like with a micro-penis, but what I wanted more was to get away from him. I turned towards the bathroom, the only space in the motorhome where there was some form of partition between me and him, and reached for its door.

'Oh, you can just get changed here,' Neil said from behind me. 'No one is going to see you out there and trust me, I've seen it all.'

But so had I. This was far from my first Lecherous Larry rodeo, which was sad, but what was sadder was that I knew there was very little I could do about it officially. Because what had he done, exactly? Made a decision a woman wouldn't have? That wasn't a crime. Looked at my body and said something about the fit of the dress across my chest? He was *supposed* to clothe me. It was impossible to convey to men how men like Neil could make women feel, let alone go to HR with it.

And the very last thing *I* wanted to do was go anywhere near HR.

Besides, what was the point? If I said something to Donal or Steve now, they'd most likely have a chat with Neil, he'd apologise to me, and the next time we met in this motorhome it'd be even worse. The second time I complained I'd be asked if maybe I was overreacting, if I was being too sensitive. *Come on, he didn't mean it like that. He was just joking. Christ, you really can't say* anything *these days, can you?*

But because female actors had been dealing with this shit for, quite literally, the entire history of motion pictures, I had developed my own tricks. I knew the magic words to say, the ones that never, ever failed. So now I turned around, looked Neil dead in the eye and said, 'Yeah ... but, you see, I *really* need to change my tampon.'

A flash of physical recoil, a quick recovery.

'Oh,' he said. 'Yeah. No, of course. Go ahead.'

I made a face. 'It's just that it's, like, an *actual* crime scene down there today.'

Neil looked away, nodded.

'I'll just be a sec,' I said, as I smiled sweetly and turned to enter the bathroom.

*

The motorhome's bathroom was a shade smaller than a telephone box and much more claustrophobic. It was wet-room style, with a shower head fixed to the wall and a toilet with a tiny sink on top of its cistern whose lid was shut with parcel tape and labelled with a handwritten sign saying DO NOT USE. There was a mirror on the wall to my right, and the only window was small, frosted and set high above the toilet.

I had about as much room to get out of my clothes and into Kate's outfit as variety-show magicians have inside quick-change curtains.

When I removed the dry-cleaning bag, I saw that the dress was even worse than I'd feared. No part was an immediately obvious skirt or front or sleeve – just figuring out how it went on and which way was a brain-teaser.

I didn't like the solution. The skirt was so short I wasn't sure it counted as one. There was no back to the dress and barely any material at all above the waistband. Instead, a series of criss-crossing straps travelled up the front, just about covering the parts that legally constituted *not naked*, before tying in a complicated configuration at the back of the neck.

You know, just the kind of thing you pack to wear to the dining table in a cottage in the country in the dead of winter.

I pulled and tugged and rearranged and did my best to stretch the dress across a *little* more skin before I took a deep breath and opened the bathroom door. Neil was standing with his back to me, looking at something on the kitchenette's countertop – but then he turned around and I saw it wasn't Neil, but Donal.

'Hey,' he started. 'How are—' He fell silent when he saw what I was wearing. 'That's ... *That's* what he gave you?'

'I know,' I said, still tugging at the hem. 'I thought I'd mixed up my scenes. By the way, my script doesn't have scene numbers on it, so I had to count.'

'Yeah ...' Donal was already reaching for the robe I'd seen on the clothes rail. It was in a dry-cleaning bag like the rest of the items hanging there, which made me think that it wasn't for me to wear between takes but on camera. I didn't care. I accepted it gratefully and was even more grateful that he averted his eyes while I pulled it on. 'Steve is still doing a bit of tinkering with the script, so the numbering is a work-in-progress. I'll get you an updated one as soon as I have it. And the ending, when he decides what it's going to be.'

I didn't know that my script didn't have an ending. I'd only scanned the pages and had assumed the ones at the end *were* the end.

'And I'll check with him on the dress,' Donal added.

'Please do. I mean, what am I running through the woods in? A bikini?'

Donal laughed, then stopped abruptly. 'Sorry. It's not funny.'

'It's so off-base it *is*, a little. It's just so obviously not what a woman would choose.'

'I'll talk to Steve,' he said. 'Leave it with me.'

'Where did Neil go?'

'He needed to grab something from the house, he said. He'll come straight back. Can I make you a coffee?'

Donal pointed at the little capsule-coffee machine on the kitchen counter. I didn't want a coffee, but I wanted him to stay so I wouldn't be alone with Neil when he returned, so I said I'd love one.

When he turned around to start playing with the machine, I wrapped the cord of the robe tight around my waist and tied a knot in it. I slipped my hands into the pockets – and felt something at the bottom of the one on the right side.

When I pulled it out, I saw it was a folded piece of white paper.

'Sugar?' Donal asked.

'Two, please.'

I unfolded it. It was immediately identifiable as a page of screenplay. This didn't strike me as strange. Wardrobe items were often rented, borrowed or re-used. As I scanned the text, it was to see if I could identify on which production this robe had had a former life.

But what I saw on the page didn't make any sense.

```
19     INT. LIVING SPACE - NIGHT                    19
```

Kate and Joel sit at opposite ends of the dining table, faces lit by candlelight, eating dinner in silence.
                     Did he notice this?
Kate is wearing a chic black dress and more make-up than before; she's made an effort. She is the only one. She watches as Joel tops up his wine glass from the bottle that was already within his reach. This action empties it. **Annoyed? Resigned?**

Kate glances at her own empty glass.

                        JOEL
    Did you put the other bottle in the
    fridge?

```
Joel, before you drink any more, I
have to tell you something. I have
some news.
```

It was a page from *our* script.

From *Final Draft*.

But a version of it that had scene numbers and handwritten notations.

The coffee machine began to whirr and hiss.

'Milk?' Donal asked.

'Yeah,' I said absently. I slipped the paper back into my pocket. 'Um, can I ask you something? The other actress. The one who had to drop out. How long was she on set for before she had to go?'

'Oh, she was never here,' he said over his shoulder. 'She didn't get that far.'

'What was her name again?'

I asked this in my best I've Already Been Told This Information, I've Just Forgotten It voice.

'Actually ...' Donal turned around, leaned against the counter. Behind him, the coffee machine had started spluttering drops of dark brown liquid into a tiny white cup. 'The truth is, I don't know. I didn't ask. She was before my time. You see, I'm a last-minute replacement, too. I was only hired on Tuesday.'

'*Tuesday?*'

'I know. I bet you feel downright *prepared* now, don't you? By comparison?' Donal grinned. 'I *told* you you'd nothing to worry about.'

I had never heard of an AD coming to a job so late. That meant Donal hadn't even been in his role for a whole week yet and today was the first day of principal photography. On a bigger production, it just wouldn't work. On this one, I didn't really see how one week of prep didn't automatically mean complete disaster.

'What happened to the first AD?'

Donal shrugged. 'Steve said there'd been some creative differences. But, again, I—'

'Didn't ask,' I finished.

'Yeah,' he said sheepishly. 'Look, I just *really* wanted this job.'

Just like I had really wanted mine.

On one hand, there was nothing unusual about personnel on a production chopping and changing at the last minute, and nearly every film had a long and winding road to being seen on screen. More often than not, sections of that road contained numerous zig-zagging sharp corners, dead-ends and looping bends.

But the only good reason I could think of for there being a sheet of annotated script in the pocket of a robe the production had supplied was that there had been an earlier iteration of this production and the original Kate, having come to set, had put it there.

And perhaps, before she'd left, she'd also lost an earring.

But why would they want to keep that from me? Try as I might, I couldn't come up with any good reason for *that*.

EIGHT

And then, finally, it was time to walk on to set.

I was entering the only place I've ever felt truly at home where I'd get to do the only thing I loved with my whole heart, for the first time in a long time. As I made my way across the gravel towards the front door of Cedarwood House, everything else, the whole last year, got its volume turned down. Each step in a pair of fur-lined wellington boots that Donal had given me pushed it a little deeper into the background until it was a distant hum, then barely there white noise, then practically nothing at all.

It was replaced by the buzz of glorious possibility.

Acting was fun. Even on a bad day, it beat doing almost any other job. On a good day, it felt like playing. On a *great* day, it felt like transformation. There was no high like those moments where not only did you become your character, but everything else around you – the words, the scene, the set – became that character's world. It was like time-travelling, having an out-of-body experience and taking a recreational drug for the first time, all rolled into one.

And better yet, it was *communal*. The path there was laid by numerous creative people dead-centre in their zone, in the midst of peak flow. The writer had written his or her best script. Set design had knocked it out of the park. Your co-star, like you, had transcended their skills and become *their* character, and it was almost certainly your director who'd managed to get those performances out of you both when it mattered.

But what I really loved about it was that, even on those magical days, the end of the day was only ever the beginning. When someone yelled, 'Cut,' all it did was put raw footage in the can. You never had any idea what that was going to end up looking like or sounding like or what kind of episode or movie it would make. Where people would end up watching it. *How* they would. Which people. What they would think.

When Sam Neill was falling over in a field while looking up at a pole with a cut-out of a dinosaur head on it on the set of *Jurassic Park*, he couldn't have known that he had just filmed one of the most game-changing scenes in cinematic history, in one of the most successful movies of all time *and*, a quarter of a century later, an incredibly popular gif. It was just another day on set for him. Maybe it was Taco Tuesday at craft services and he thought *that* was going to be the highlight.

Every moment on set was just a beginning. Anything could happen next, and that's what I loved about the job. That's what I was thinking when I crossed the threshold and walked face-first into a wall of hot, sticky tension.

Cedarwood House had no hallway. The front door opened directly into the living space, which was open plan. To my right was a sleek, severe kitchen, the kind that looked like it could double as a sterile operating theatre if the need arose. From outside, the wall of windows to the rear had been a beaming fluorescent light; inside, they were a yawning black hole. A staircase disappeared into the ceiling to my left, not far from two leather armchairs which were pointed towards a stone chimney breast.

Lights, equipment and men spread out in a semicircle from the fireplace like a blast-radius of debris after an explosion. The entire floor was covered in snake-like spools of coloured electrical cables. Every light seemed to be on and on full, and a fire was in the early stages in the hearth. The video village – the monitor where the relevant crew members, including Steve, could watch what the cameras were capturing in real-time – was in the kitchen, the three seats in front of it facing the inside of the breakfast bar. The air in the room had the oppressive, solid heat of a sauna.

My presence may as well have been a mute button; everyone stopped what they were doing, fell silent and turned to stare. But the two men engaged in a loud, finger-jabbing argument were the last to see me so Steve Dade's, 'How about because that's your fucking *job*, asshole!' rang out loud and lingered, as if hung from invisible hooks in the air.

I didn't know where to look, but I knew it wasn't into the faces of any of the men whose eyes I could feel crawling all over me. (Thank God for the robe. No – thank *Donal* for it.) I looked to Steve, whose facial expression was unreadable. When I said, 'Hi,' to him, raising one hand in a small, meek wave, he didn't react in any detectable way. I started to doubt the science that said you couldn't spontaneously combust from embarrassment.

Donal had left the motorhome at the same time as me but he only entered the room now, twenty seconds delayed. I turned to him, desperate for guidance.

He nodded slightly and then stepped a little in front of me to address the crew.

'Hey, everyone,' he said cheerily. 'Let me introduce you

to Adele, who's going to be our *amazing* Kate. She has really done us a *huge* favour by stepping in at the very last minute. She even flew in overnight from LA so we can start shooting this evening. Isn't that great?' Silence. The energy differential between Donal's voice and the atmosphere in the room put me in mind of a naïve substitute teacher who hasn't yet realised his class of sullen teenagers are about to eat him alive. 'Let's just all take a minute to say hello, shall we? We can go around the room.'

I dared to look at Steve again just in time to catch his eyes roll.

'Aaron,' Donal said, 'you first.'

My pick for youngest person on the crew was on his knees, taping cables to the floor. He stood up slowly, reluctantly, and mumbled something into his chest that sounded sort of like *Aaron*. He didn't give a job title and I didn't remember what Donal had said about who was doing what, but since he indeed looked like Chris Evans at the start of *Captain America*, I figured he was the general assistant guy – even though I thought that role had required driving, and there was no way this guy was old enough to get insured on a rental car. He had a flop of flat, dirty-blond hair that he kept flicking out of his eyes à la *High School Musical*-era Efron. If he'd had any confidence, he'd be boyband material, the fifth that's everyone's favourite even though he's tone-deaf.

Next up was 'Mark, sound'. His stating this was somewhat unnecessary because he was wearing an oversized pair of headphones skewed on his head and tinkering with a boom. Mid thirties, I guessed, wearing a faded Metallica T-shirt that was having to stretch across his barrelled chest. His bright red hair and thick beard were giving me serious Irish Viking vibes. He was red in the face, too, and his forehead was glistening with sweat.

Liam, second camera. Late thirties, bulging biceps, thinning hair. Attractive, but ruining it with the attitude. He didn't just look me directly in the eye when he spoke, he *glared* at me, like he was challenging me to look away. Every set seems to have at least one insecure, testosterone-poisoned roid-raging man who assumes that all women think they're better than all men and is here to tell us that we *aren't*, actually; Liam was ours.

Mick, the DOP, was the elder statesman of the group and the complete opposite to Liam. He didn't look me in the eye once. Late forties or maybe even early fifties, with salt-and-pepper hair worn a little long over the ears, wearing a plaid shirt that looked one size too small. I thought maybe Mick was shy, or perhaps he was just embarrassed – because he'd been the man that Steve had been shouting at.

And then there was only Steve left. He looked as he had in the pictures with the trophy: tall, attractive, Silver Fox, Converse'd, *cool*. He was wearing a wedding band I hadn't noticed in the photographs, and he was openly glaring at me.

I suddenly felt hot and shaky, overheating in the robe. My pulse raced uncomfortably. I took a deep breath, filling my chest with air, and smiled at Steve because despite everything, I was finally meeting my director, the man who loved *Winter Snow*, who had said that, actually, Saoirse No Last Name having to drop out might be a *good* thing, and I wanted to let him know that I understood, that I was a professional, that this was Day One and tensions were probably running high, and—

'Let's get to work,' he said flatly.

Not even to me, but to Donal.

The crew jumped into action. The room filled with the same noise I'd muted with my arrival, minus the argument. No one looked at me, let alone spoke any more to me. I stood there feeling like a prop with a pulse as a lump formed in my throat and my eyes blurred with tears.

Shit, shit, shit, shit.

No, I would *not* cry. I wouldn't.

I *couldn't*.

Donal pulled gently on my elbow, steering me towards the chairs in front of the fire.

'It's okay,' he whispered. 'It's not anything to do with you. Crew teething problems, let's just say. Steve's got a lot of noise in his head at the moment. When we've a few shots in the can and everyone's settled in a bit, it'll be different.'

I nodded like I understood, and told him I was fine.

The cameras weren't rolling on set yet, but I was already acting.

INT. LIVING SPACE - LATER SAME DAY

A bleary-eyed, dishevelled Joel sits at the dining table, staring into a mug of steaming black coffee.

Kate paces behind him, reading aloud - loudly - from a copy of *First Draft*.

> KATE
> *Her first thought was a blank pulse-beat of abject terror. Her second was how it was that something so mundane could be so monstrous. The front door of the cottage was standing open, wide enough to fill the floor in front of it with a shaft of weak sunshine.*

Joel rubs at his temples, as if the volume of Kate's voice is causing him physical pain.

> KATE (CONT'D)
> *It wasn't Jack who had done this - she could hear the rhythm of his thick snore coming from the bedroom.*

> JOEL
> (muttering)
> The rhythm of his thick snore? Jesus Christ.

> KATE
> *And the muddy footprints on the floor suggested that whoever had opened the door had come inside.*

She throws the book on the table. Joel winces
at the clatter it makes.

                    KATE
    Well?

                    JOEL
    Well … My first question is: where
    else would footprints be? On the
    ceiling?

                    KATE
    The same things that happen in the
    book are happening here.

                    JOEL
              (rolling his eyes)
    Kate, seriously.

                    KATE
    I *am* being serious. There were no
    footprints, okay, but there *was* a
    knock on the door in the middle of
    the night and then this morning, when
    I got up, the door was wide open.
    Just like in the book.

Joel drains his coffee, apparently
uninterested.

                    KATE (CONT'D)
    So you don't care? You don't think
    this is weird? You aren't worried
    for, I don't know, our personal
    safety?

                    JOEL
Oh, I'm fine, by the way. I've
already completely forgotten about
the entire implosion of my career,
thanks for asking.
          (standing up)
I need some paracetamol. I'll drive
into the village and get some.

                    KATE
Hang on. I need to have a shower
first.

                    JOEL
Don't bother.
          (pause)
I mean, stay here. I'll go alone.

                    KATE
Well, I don't want to be here alone.
Someone opened that door, Joel.
And maybe even came in while I was
asleep—

                    JOEL
          (cutting her off)
Look, I have *actual* problems, okay?
Including a splitting fucking
headache. Let me deal with them first
and then we'll start worrying about
your imaginary ones.

He grabs the car keys from the kitchen counter
and leaves, slamming the door behind him. A
stunned Kate watches him go.

INT. LIVING SPACE – LATER SAME DAY

Kate clears away the breakfast debris, rinsing
out cups, putting things back in the fridge.

First Draft is still sitting on the table.
She goes to pick it up then stops, changing
her mind. Instead she goes to the front door,
opens it and twists the deadbolt so she can
see for herself the mechanism works. She
closes it, locks it, pulls on it to make sure.

As she leaves the living space to head in the
direction of the bedroom, she looks through
the wall of glass at the trees as if scanning
them. *Checking* them.

INT. MASTER EN-SUITE BATHROOM – LATER SAME DAY

Kate exits the shower and wraps herself in
a towel. She uses a hand to wipe the fog of
condensation off the mirror above the sink and
appraises her appearance in it. Then she roots
in her make-up bag until she finds a tube of
moisturiser.

Another bag sits next to hers on the counter:
Joel's shaving kit. Something she can see
through its unzipped top makes Kate stop and
frown. She reaches in and pulls it out: a full
pack of paracetamol.

NINE

A stand-in is a person who looks like the actor in the ways that matter, i.e. height, hair, colouring. They're used to set up a shot from a technical point of view — lighting, camera angles, things like that — which can take ages, which is why the actors don't do it themselves. They're in hair and make-up while their stand-in is on set, walking where they'll walk, sitting where they'll sit and lying where they will lie. That way, when the actor arrives, they can immediately start to *act*.

On *Winter Snow*, the actors would rehearse a scene, the stand-ins would come for the set-up and then we'd return to shoot the real thing after getting our hair and make-up done in the interim. But with *Final Draft*'s skeleton crew and tight budget, I was standing in for myself. Having led me to the armchair by the fireplace, Donal furnished me with a bottle of water and a copy of *First Draft* by Gary Sheridan, the book Kate finds in the movie.

It was just a prop, of course, but it looked so good it temporarily distracted me, giving me a chance to collect myself.

If no one had told me, I would've assumed the book was the real deal. The cover image was a foggy, night-time shot of Cedarwood House, with the title overlaid in a bright red horror-movie font complete with dripping blood. There was even an author bio on the back flappy bit, under a brooding author photo: a man with enough stubble to cross the grooming line from lazy to Creative Type.

He was in profile, looking away from the lens, but I recognised him.

'Is that *Steve*?'

Donal nodded. 'I was up against it, trying to get the design to the printers on time – we literally got these done on Wednesday morning, emailed the files Wednesday afternoon, then collected them Thursday morning on our way down here. It was my first job. I didn't want to have to be in it myself but, luckily, Steve was up for doing an M. Night Shyamalan.'

'*You* did this?'

Donal laughed. 'Thanks for sounding so surprised.'

'No, it's just … It looks amazing.'

'Steve said we should just mock up something simple, but I couldn't stand to see it happen half-arsed. It's the most important prop in the movie. It's in so many scenes – and close-up, too. And I get disproportionately annoyed when books don't look like real books on screen. It's like, they can make a T-Rex look absolutely legit in 1993 but they can't mock up a realistic-looking book cover now?'

'I completely agree,' I said. 'See also: old photos.'

'God, *yes*. They're always the *worst* kind of Photoshop. Did you see that deep-fake video of Tom Cruise? I would never have guessed it wasn't him. But put him in a movie where he has to look at an old photo of himself and it's like, nope, sorry. We just can't figure out how to do *that*.'

I opened the book and saw that the dust jacket Donal had designed had been put on a novel by Harlan Coben.

'There's a different book in each one,' he said, pointing to the shelf by the fireplace stocked with additional copies of

First Draft. 'So if you get bored, just swap your copy for one you want to read.'

'Quite happy with this one. Thank you, though.'

'There's another bottle of water there' – Donal pointed now to the floor by the side of the chair – 'and I'll be close by, if you need anything.'

'What about the dress?'

I knew that if we shot anything in it, we'd have to shoot everything in it.

'Yeah, um …' Donal bit his lip. 'I'm sorry, but Steve approved it already. Neil said there's an email. He okayed all the outfits.'

'Oh.'

'I'm sorry,' Donal said again.

'It's okay.'

It wasn't, but what could I do about it? I basically *was* a prop with a pulse. I had been hired to do a job and if that job involved wearing something I personally felt was totally inappropriate for the scene in question – or, you know, common decency laws – well, them's the breaks.

Unless you were a big-name star, you didn't get a say in anything. You only got to say your lines.

'The first day is always the worst,' Donal said. 'So whatever happens, just remember: tomorrow will be better.'

I smiled. 'Let's hope.'

The last thing he said before he left me alone was, 'I know it's hot in here, but hopefully this won't take long.'

But the set-up took *for ever*. So long that I started to melt, literally. I could feel the foundation Neil had applied sliding down my temples, carried by tributaries of my own dripping sweat. The only thing worse than having to sit through Neil the Creep being inches from my face was having to sit through it twice because I'd sweated off the first make-up application.

But what could I do? I was wrapped in a robe, sitting next to a fire in full flush that was blasting a thick jet-stream of suffocating heat directly into my face. Three powerful lights shone down on me, each one feeling more like a patio heater. It seemed that Steve and Mick couldn't agree on which ones to have on and were constantly switching them on and off; whenever the closest one went dark, I luxuriated in the relatively cool reprieve. After about forty-five minutes of this sauna-torture, I finally thought to take off my wellies but doing so made very little difference. I stopped drinking water halfway down the bottle because I didn't want to have to take a toilet break.

It was clear what was causing the delay – Steve. Or to be more specific, Steve's relationship with Mick, the director of photography. They could not agree on anything. They were speaking mostly in a technical language I could only partially understand and behind the lights so I couldn't see them, but I could follow this much: Mick had set up the shot as Steve wanted it, Steve decided he didn't want it that way and set about changing everything, only to change his mind back again. The cycle repeated itself until Mick suddenly shouted, 'Like it was in the *first* place, you mean?'

Finally, Donal hurried over to them to suggest a five-minute break, and Steve barked, 'No, let's just shoot,' and then clapped his hands together.

They were, evidently, Steve's magic words. The activity throughout the room took on a sense of organisation, a purpose. Neil reappeared to touch up my face and breathe heavily enough throughout for me to feel each exhalation on my skin. Liam got behind the camera. Aaron assumed a position by its business end, ready with the slate. Donal called out, 'Okay, everyone. Settle down, please. We're about to roll on *Final Draft!*'

'Actually,' Steve said, 'I'd like to say a few words first.' A tense silence descended on the room. He cleared his throat. 'I know none of you have worked with me before, but you may have heard: I like to do things a little differently. I hired each of you because I think you're bloody good at what you do' – it took everything I had not to react at this, not to roll my eyes at the idea of that applying to Neil – 'but also because I trust you to trust me. If you trust me, I have your back. We are a team here.' If this is what being in a team felt like, I had no regrets that I'd never played a sport. 'If you *can* just trust me, I promise you, we will make something great here. Something new. Something people won't just go to see, but will experience. So I hope you can trust me, and trust the process.'

Trust the process. Those words only ever sounded like alarm bells to me, a warning that soon I was going to have reason to *distrust* it. As for making something great ... Well, I wanted to believe it. Of course I did, because if Steve Dade did make something great out of *Final Draft*, his star would rise and mine would be lifted along with it.

This could be a *Blair Witch Project*, or a *Get Out*, or even – look, you never know – a *Silence of the Lambs*. I could do better here than wallpapering over my abject failure to make it in LA and everything that had sent me running off to LA in the first place. I might have a chance here to go even further, to undo the biggest mistake I'd ever made, career-wise: leaving *These Are the Days*. I might have a chance to wipe away *all* my mistakes and take the express elevator to everything I've ever wanted.

But equally, we were about to roll camera on a cheap horror movie named for screenwriting software, with a cast and crew of just eight, that was mostly about a woman running around woods in the dark. And that woman was being played by a former soap-actress-turned-motel-receptionist who hadn't been paid to act in a year and who, not that long ago, wondered if she'd ever be paid to act again. This could just be another episode of *Delusions of Mediocre White Men* Season 481,041. But ...

It was a movie, and it was shooting now, and I was in it.

So I took a breath, pushed everything out of my mind and tried to pull Kate into the centre of it.

'Okay,' I heard Steve say. 'Let's go.'

Donal said, 'You want to do a rehearsal first or—'

'Why? She's just sitting on a couch reading a book.'

My ears pricked up at this. I'd assumed we'd do a rehearsal, or at least block out my movements during the scene, because even just *sitting on a couch reading a book* involved an array of decisions with knock-on effects further down the line. And, whenever I moved, the camera, the lights, the frame – everything pointed at me – would have to move *with* me, would have to *know* to move with me. That's why scenes were rehearsed.

For almost an hour now, I'd been me reading a Harlan Coben novel. But when the cameras rolled, I'd be Kate reading

First Draft. Those were two very different things, and the latter required me to know a number of things that only my director could tell me. Donal muttered something inaudible to Steve but, based on what Steve did next, it was something along those same lines.

'*Fine*,' Steve snapped. I lifted my eyes from the book to meet Steve's, then raised my eyebrows to let him know I was listening to him. 'She's just started reading the book,' he said to me, 'so can you go to, say, page ten, for continuity? And let me see where you're planning to hold it.' He said all this in the tone of an exasperated parent trying to direct a toddler.

I lifted the prop book from my lap, holding it with both hands in a way that looked like I was reading it but didn't block the cover details or my face.

'Good,' Steve said. 'Keep it there. We're going to roll and you're going to read. Get a few page-turns in there and watch that the book doesn't start to climb up.'

I nodded and said, 'Got it,' but Steve was already turning away, towards Donal, to mutter a sarcastic, 'Happy now?' and something else mumbled that I couldn't make out.

Then, loudly, to the room, he said, 'Let's go.'

'Right,' Donal said. 'Last looks, please.'

Neil materialised again, this time with a powder brush in his hand. He bent to tickle my T-zone with its bristles, his brow furrowed in concentration, looking and acting perfectly professional. He'd been the same earlier, in the trailer, doing my make-up while Donal hung around. He hadn't even reprimanded him for giving me a costume robe.

He was an entirely different person when we weren't one-on-one, which to me only turned his Creep Dial up even more, because I could still feel the creepiness coming off in waves.

'Robe off,' he said flatly.

Almost an entirely different person.

He stood there, looming above me, as I did my best to get out of it without something else coming out of the scraps of dress underneath. I could feel his eyes crawling all over my exposed skin. I tried not the think about the fact that behind me, at the video village, the other six men in this room could get an even better look via the monitor.

'Quiet on set, please,' Donal called. 'We're going to go for a take on this one – our first.' He paused, perhaps expecting some kind of audible excitement, but when none came he pushed on. The morale on this set was sinking like the third act of *Titanic*. 'Roll sound.'

Mark said, 'Sound speed.'

'Roll camera.'

Mick said, 'Camera speed.'

'Let's mark it.'

Aaron had the slate. Bent at the waist, he moved in close until it was directly in front of my face, inches from my nose and blocking my view of the book. He was doing this because it was going to be a tight shot, a close-up on me reading, and this meant the slate had to be closer to me than the lens or the editor wouldn't be able to read it.

But the correct way to do this was 'soft sticks', whereby the slate was held below my face and snapped gently so as not to, you know, snap something loudly and suddenly at the end of the actor's nose *right* before the take, which would not only yank them out of the moment but explode the moment and drive a bulldozer back and forth across the debris field.

But when Aaron started reading the slate, quickly—

'Scene-twelve-Charlie-take-one-mark.'

—I knew he didn't know *not* to do this, and that he was about to—

SNAP.

He did it so loud and so close to my face, I flinched, and Kate disappeared like a mirage I'd got too close to.

'Set,' Mick said and then Steve called, 'Action.'

I could've asked them to stop, reset and go again. I could've moaned about the conditions, the lack of professionalism, the chaos in this room.

But I couldn't afford to do any of that. With my past history, I *had* to be good.

So I held my breath and dived down, deep, until I was able to reach out and touch Kate, to pull on her limbs. I blocked out all the noise and focused on pushing *her* back to the surface.

When I exhaled, *she* did, too.

We put our eyes on the book and started reading.

Final Draft was, finally, rolling.

TEN

We didn't wrap at midnight as promised or planned – it took that long just for everybody to settle down and settle in, to find some sort of communal groove. This meant our midnight lunch was served closer to 2:00 a.m. and consisted of slices of reheated pizza handed out on paper plates, washed down with cans of room-temperature Coke.

Part of me was aghast. Food and drink on *set*? Eating greasy pizza, dripping cheese and tomato sauce, while in *costume*? No actual break four hours into a shoot, just a few minutes' pause to stuff some carbs into your mouth? I'd never experienced the likes of it. But a much larger part of me was starving and secretly relieved I didn't have to make small-talk with the crew over a dining table, so I ate two slices as delicately as I could and refused a Coke because there'd been nothing in the script I could remember about Kate repeatedly burping and belching.

In the end, we wrapped just after 4:00 a.m. It was just as well we'd done the reading-on-the-couch stuff first and the toasting-own-reflection-in-window stuff last because if it had been the other way around, there'd have been footage of me falling asleep. By the final 'Cut!', the adrenalin that had propelled me from LA to the West Cork countryside and through the last six hours of shooting a film in which I was the lead but didn't know existed forty-eight hours ago had all but seeped away, and it was a battle to keep my eyes open.

If our breakfast-time dinner was still being served at 7:00 a.m., I was going to skip it. All I wanted to do was go back to my cabin and fall into bed.

But first I had to return Neil's excuse for a dress to the motorhome.

Only I had been released; the crew were still working on resetting the equipment, securing whatever they needed to before they could leave it overnight. I pulled back on my robe, slipped my feet into my boots and hurried towards the door, hoping I could get in and out of the motorhome before Neil caught up with me.

No such luck.

I saw him see me, and move to follow me outside. My stomach sank. But then I heard Donal say, 'Neil, do you have a second?'

Donal had caught him by the video village and was showing him something on a copy of the script. Words were exchanged. Neil took the script, started scanning the page. Over Neil's shoulder, Donal's eyes met mine, and just in case I hadn't already got that message, he discreetly waved a hand behind Neil's back.

Donal was *detaining* him for me. What a beaut. I wondered if his coming into the motorhome earlier had really been a coincidence or if he'd offered to make me that cup of coffee for the very same reason I'd accepted it. That would make it a robe, a pair of boots *and* protecting me from our set's aspiring sex offender. He may be the least prepared assistant director I'd ever worked with, but he was steadily becoming my favourite.

I mouthed a *thank you* at him and hurried out of Cedarwood House.

*

I was exiting the motorhome a few minutes later, back in my own clothes after one of the quickest costume-changes of my professional life, when I saw that Donal and Neil had almost reached it.

'Hey,' Neil said to me, 'not so fast. We need to do some fittings.'

All three of us came to a stop a few steps from the motorhome.

'We've wrapped for the night,' Donal said, his eyes on me. 'She's free to go.'

Neil shot Donal a look. 'We've wrapped on *filming*. I need to fit the other costumes and we've got, what? Two hours until dinner? There's plenty of time and this is what that time should be used for.'

'It's been a long night,' I said. 'I was just going to go to b— sleep.' I didn't want to say anything about my being in a bed around The Creep, didn't want to fuel any wet dreams. 'Can it wait until tomorrow? Or, I guess, later today?'

Neil acted like I hadn't spoken at all and said to Donal, 'When else am I supposed to do it?'

'And the dress fit fine,' I added. 'Presumably everything is that size?' But hopefully consisted of a lot more material.

'Not tonight,' Donal said to Neil. 'Adele has come a long way on very short notice and we've already run over. She needs to rest.'

'We need—' Neil started.

'I'm releasing her,' Donal said, cutting him off. 'There'll be time for fittings before we start tomorrow. Tonight.' Then, to me, 'I'm heading up to the crew cabin, if you're ready to go?'

I nodded eagerly. 'Great.'

Neil scoffed, muttered something under his breath, and then stomped up into the motorhome, slamming its door behind him. But the door was too light to make any sort of satisfactory slamming noise or even close properly, so it clattered against the frame and then bounced back open.

'For fuck's *sake*,' we heard Neil spit from inside.

Donal and I started walking away from the motorhome, our footsteps crunching across the gravel.

'You know, don't you?' I said. 'About Neil being a creep.'

Donal raised his eyebrows, a picture of innocence.

'That's why you were in the motorhome earlier,' I said. 'Why you offered to make me a coffee. Why you gave me the robe. You were running interference.'

He smiled grimly. 'I was trying to.'

'Have you worked with him before?'

'No, but he made some … *inappropriate comments* at the meeting yesterday. We had an all-hands, once the crew were here, and let's just say he said enough to make me think I'll be reading a Twitter thread about him someday that doesn't mention him by name but doesn't have to.'

'What did he say?'

Donal shook his head. 'You don't want to know.'

'Ugh.'

'That would sum it up. Did he …?' He stopped me at the corner of the house by putting a light hand on my arm. 'He didn't, like, *do* anything, did he?'

'Just turned my stomach with his general creepiness.'

'I'm sorry about that.'

'It's not your fault.'

'It's my responsibility, though,' Donal said. 'I can talk to Steve?'

Before I'd met Steve, I knew that wasn't really an option. You couldn't fire someone because they gave someone else an icky feeling, and you certainly couldn't fire someone from the wardrobe department for looking at the body he was supposed to be dressing or the outfits he'd chosen for it. Now, after meeting Steve, I knew it *definitely* wasn't an option.

And he'd okayed that dress himself.

'No,' I said. 'Not yet, anyway. I'm a big girl. I can handle him. But I'll let you know if he kicks things up a notch.'

'You *sure*?'

I nodded. 'Yeah.'

We started walking again, down the side of the house, across the walled garden and up the stone steps.

'Thanks for walking me back,' I said as we entered the cold, damp gloom of the trees. Donal had got out his phone and was pointing its torchlight at the ground in front of our feet. 'At least there's one nice guy on this set.'

'I was just scared to walk up here alone, to be honest. It's so bloody creepy.' He grinned. 'But thank you for thinking that.'

'How do you think that went? Tonight's shoot, I mean.'

Donal didn't answer immediately and I got the impression it was because he was taking the time to come up with a diplomatic answer.

'I think it'll go better tomorrow,' he said eventually.

I didn't respond to this immediately, because I was trying to come up with a diplomatic way to say that our director seemed like a bit of a dickhead with no respect for the rules he was so intent on breaking.

'I didn't really get a chance to speak to Steve, one-on-one,' is what I went with.

'No,' Donal said. 'And I'm not sure you will. He doesn't strike me as the type to have a chummy relationship with his actors. And, ah, between you and me, I think Steve is struggling to get used to Daniel not being at his side. They usually come as a pair.'

'Is that Daniel O'Leary?'

'Do you know him?'

'No,' I said. '*Of* him, only.'

'I don't know him either. But Mick was telling me that, officially, Steve directs and Daniel produces.' Donal was keeping his voice low and occasionally glancing behind us as he said this. 'But I think in practice it's more like they both do everything together. They always have, since they were teenagers making horror shorts with Steve's dad's camcorder and bottles of Heinz ketchup. I think this might be the first week in Steve's professional life where he doesn't have Daniel by his side, so it's not entirely surprising that he's floundering a little.' He exhaled. 'I'm sure it'll be fine, though.'

'So Mick has worked with them before?'

'No, none of us have,' Donal said. 'But Mick's brother is a set designer and *he* has, so Mick has all the info.'

'Why isn't Daniel here?'

'He will be, next week, but right now he's at his sister's wedding in the south of France. Or, wait. Could be his brother's. Anyway. The original shoot – the Primal Pictures version – was scheduled to start in March. But now that we're independently financed, every cent counts, and it was cheaper to bring the shoot forward. It's January. The house was cheaper, everyone's travel cost less ... So we're going to have half the shoot with just Steve. But don't worry. I really think after a couple of days, he'll settle down. And he *is* great at what he does, even if how he does it might seem a little strange. Have you seen his work?'

I shook my head, *no*.

'You should,' Donal said. 'The short is on YouTube and I have a digital copy of *Sundown* I can send you. We can drive down to the main road tomorrow and you can download it. They're both really good, I promise you.' He smiled. 'Oh – and speaking of tomorrow, the forecast is very heavy rain during the day, tapering off in the early evening, so our schedule shouldn't be affected. But there's a raincoat in the wardrobe of your cabin, if you haven't already discovered it. I left it there for you, borrowed from the main house. Same place I got the boots, actually. Joanne – that's the owner – she must get a lot of guests who don't bring the clothes they need. There was a whole room full of that kind of stuff.'

Up ahead, a light had started filtering through the trees. The cabins were within sight. We'd be at them in a couple of minutes.

'Donal,' I said. 'Can I ask – why me?'

In the glow of what little light there was, I saw him frown at me, confused.

'For this role,' I clarified. 'I know I was, like, the ninety-ninth choice or whatever, but I'm just wondering. How did I end up on the list in the first place? I was in LA, I haven't done anything in a while ...'

I got fired from my last job for having a psychotic break.

'I don't know,' Donal said. 'But I can tell you that I never heard Steve talk about anyone else for this production. I took it that you were the first choice, after the original actress.'

'Who he didn't name.'

'Not during our conversations, no. But I got the impression he was glad to be rid of her, to be honest.' He paused. '*Please* don't quote me on that.'

'What's said in the trees stays in the trees.'

I wondered if I should tell Donal about the page of script and the earring and maybe even the weird text messages. He seemed pretty trustworthy. If I was going to, now was the time. I slipped my hand into my pocket before remembering that the script had been in the pocket of the robe and, in my rush to get out of the motorhome before Neil found me in there, I hadn't brought it with me.

'When did you get to set?' I asked instead.

'I came with Steve on Thursday morning,' Donal said, 'and by Friday lunchtime the whole crew was here.'

'And Steve hadn't been here before, earlier?'

'You mean like scouting the location?'

The light from Donal's phone landed on a huge, gnarled root in the middle of the muddy path and we both moved to make a detour around it.

'For any reason,' I said.

'I don't think so. We couldn't find the place. After an hour of driving up and down the peninsula, we had to stop and ask for directions.'

So the crew arrived after Donal did, and Steve had arrived with him. That meant there hadn't been time for there to be another, original, aborted production here, featuring a different actress who'd lost an earring, made some notes on the script and then disappeared from set.

So who *had* done it?

The thick gloom of the trees gave way to a brighter clearing. We'd reached the cabins. Donal switched off the light on his phone; the light on over the deck of mine was enough to see by. Steve's cabin was dark, as were the crew's. Neil was, presumably, still fuming in the motorhome and we'd left everybody else in the main house, shutting down the set for the night.

It was now or never.

'Donal,' I said, 'there's something I need to tell you, but I need you to promise first that you won't tell Steve.'

He frowned. 'O-*kay* ...'

'Remember the weird text messages I told you about?' I took out my phone to show them to him, even though I could've recalled them from memory. 'They were *really* weird.'

'What the hell?' he muttered as he read them.

'My thoughts exactly.'

'Did you call the number?'

'I can't. No reception.'

'We'll drive down to the main road. I would suggest we do it now, but it's approaching five o'clock in the morning. We'll do it tomorrow, okay? Or later. *Our* tomorrow.' He rolled his eyes. 'It's going to take me the entire shoot to get used to this upside-down schedule, isn't it?'

I made the sounds of agreement, even though I wasn't sure what calling the number would achieve. The anonymous texter was hardly going to pick up, say a warm hello and then explain exactly why they'd sent those messages.

The best we could hope for was an identifying voicemail greeting, and if we got that lucky, it would probably only be a first name.

'What do you think they mean?' I asked.

'I really have no idea,' Donal said. 'Who did you tell you were coming here?'

'That's the thing.' I took my phone back, slipped it into a pocket. 'I didn't tell anyone because of the NDA.'

This wasn't *strictly* true, but I'd only told Julia and Lindsey, and clearly those messages weren't from them. It wasn't relevant and I didn't want to piss off the only guy around here who was actually on my side by revealing that I'd broken the rules.

'Try not to worry about it for now,' he said. 'It's probably just someone from the first incarnation of *Final Draft* who's pissed off they didn't get rehired. Did I tell you that? Legally, Steve couldn't hire anyone who'd been offered a Primal Pictures contract. I think Steve pissed them off so much, they wanted to get their own back and piss *him* off even more. It could be that someone on the current crew had a friend on *that* crew, and everyone's numbers are on our call-sheet. They could've passed yours on. Just to, you know, mess with you. With us.'

'Yeah,' I said. 'Maybe.'

I liked this explanation. It made sense, it absolved me of all responsibility *and* it severed any possible connection the texts might have with *We Were Kings*. I liked it for all these reasons. And because it allowed me to put the texts out of my mind until tomorrow – or when our tomorrow started, at the other end of today – and get the sleep I desperately needed.

'That would violate their NDA,' Donal was saying now. 'I think it would, anyway. I could call a meeting, remind everyone that all information pertaining to this production is covered by it. Not mention you, or the texts, or anything specific. Just, you know, give a general warning.'

'Let's try the number first,' I said. 'Tomorrow. See if someone answers.'

'Whatever you think is best.'

We had stopped at the point where our paths had to diverge.

'Well,' I said, taking a step in the direction of my cabin, 'I'm exhausted. I'm going to skip dinner, if that's all right, so I'll see you in the morning? I mean, later.'

'Adele,' Donal said, stepping closer and using a tone that sounded more serious than anything that had come before. 'Look, I'm sure these texts are nothing more than some disgruntled crew member, but until we find that out for sure, I wouldn't mention it to anyone else here. Steve is *insane* about secrecy. He was pissed off that Joanne, the woman who owns the house, knew it was specifically a horror film we were shooting here. And she'd only guessed that. He *really* doesn't want anyone to know anything until that trailer drops in a few months' time. So until we know the texts are from someone who has or had a good reason to know about *Final Draft* already, I wouldn't say anything to Steve about it. Okay?'

I nodded. 'Okay.'

'But try not to worry about them. We'll sort it out. All right?'

'All right.'

'Sleep well.'

Donal turned and headed off towards the crew cabin, and I walked to the door of mine. I went inside and closed the door behind me, turning to slide the deadbolt into place, and saw, through the gauze of the privacy curtain, someone coming out of the trees.

Off the path and into the clearing, mere moments after Donal and I had parted ways. He was heading for the crew cabin, into which Donal had just disappeared.

It was so quiet around here, there was every possibility he'd heard some of our conversation, especially the bit we'd stood outside the cabins to have.

The bit about the text messages.

'Shit,' I said out loud.

Because that someone was Steve.

INT. BEDROOM - DAY

Kate finishes blow-drying her hair and changes
into a fresh outfit of casual clothes.

She sits on the edge of the bed and tries
calling Gus on her mobile, but the call won't
connect. There's no reception - the network
display on screen is showing zero bars. Kate
starts walking around the room, holding the
phone aloft, exhaling in frustration when the
situation doesn't change.

INT. LIVING SPACE - DAY

Kate repeats the process in the living room -
until, by the wall of glass, one bar finally
appears.

Kate calls Gus and puts the phone to her ear.

                    GUS (V.O.)
          Well, hello there.

                    KATE
          Why the tone of surprise?

                    GUS (V.O.)
          Just wasn't expecting to hear from
          you this weekend, that's all. I
          thought you'd be too busy with the
          Novelist. Did he run out of reviews
          to read aloud to you? He wouldn't
          have if he'd included the bad ones …

Kate sighs, long and loud.

                    GUS (V.O.)(CONT'D)
          Uh-oh. Trouble in paradise?

                         KATE
          It's just this place. It's … It's
          weird.

                       GUS (V.O.)
          Weird how?

Kate picks up the copy of *First Draft* with
her free hand. She looks at the cover as she
speaks.

                         KATE
          This is going to sound crazy.

                       GUS (V.O.)
          I'd be disappointed if it didn't.

                         KATE
          There's a book here. A novel. Self-
          published. There's, like, a dozen
          copies of it because the guy who
          wrote it wrote it here. And set it
          here. And it's about a couple who
          come and stay for a weekend. Karen
          and Jack.

                       GUS (V.O.)
          Is it any good?

                         KATE
          Karen and Jack, Gus. K and J.

                       GUS (V.O.)
          I know you think little of me but I
          can actually spell.

                    KATE

Same initials. Karen and Jack. Kate
and Joel.

                    GUS (V.O.)
So?

                    KATE
You don't think that's weird?

There is a long beat of silence on the line.

                    GUS (V.O.)
What have you guys been doing down
there? Eating special mushrooms you
found in the woods?

Kate puts the book back on the kitchen
counter.

                    KATE
Stuff happens to them, Gus. To the
couple. In the book. There's a knock
on the door in the middle of the
night, and when they wake up the next
morning, the door is open and there's
muddy footprints inside.

                    GUS (V.O.)
O-*kay* …

                    KATE
And last night, someone knocked
on the door here. At three in the
morning! And this place is *really*
secluded. I should've made him show
me pictures before I agreed to come.
I was imagining a little cottage in

a field. We're like half a mile from
the road here. And then this morning—

                    GUS (V.O.)
The door was open?

                    KATE
Yes!

                    GUS (V.O.)
                  (laughing)
I love it. Were there muddy
footprints too?

                    KATE
No, and I *don't*. It's creepy. And now
I'm stuck here by myself.

                    GUS (V.O.)
Where's Joel?

                    KATE
He went into the village for
something.

                    GUS (V.O.)
Probably to see if there's a bookshop
he can casually drop into. You know,
the one thing Joel *does* know about
writing books is that signed copies
can't be returned. I'll give him
that.
                  (pause)
What does he say about all this?

                    KATE
He says I've an overactive
imagination.

                    GUS (V.O.)
          He's just jealous that you *have* an
          imagination.

Kate smiles at this, just as a burst of static
comes down the line.

                    KATE
          Gus?
                         (pause)
          Hello?

There's no answer. Kate moves around the room,
but a low level of white noise remains on the
line.

                    KATE (CONT'D)
          Gus? Can you hear me?

Kate unlocks the front door and goes outside …

EXT. CHERRY COTTAGE - DAY [CONTINUOUS]

… crossing the gravel in front of the house
with the phone pressed to her ear. Halfway
to the treeline, the white noise on the line
disappears.

                    KATE
          Gus?

                    GUS (V.O.)
          I'm here. What was that?

                    KATE
          It's just the reception around here,
          it's terrible.

                    GUS (V.O.)
It's the trees.

                    KATE
Yeah. Them and being out in the
middle of fucking nowhere. Anyway -
what were we saying?

                    GUS (V.O.)
You were saying something about
phantom knocks and open doors.

                    KATE
You don't think it's weird?

                    GUS (V.O.)
I think it's probably *supposed* to
be weird. I bet it's some guerrilla
marketing thing. Maybe the guy who
wrote the book owns that house and
he's hoping you'll make a TikTok
about it that'll go viral.
                    (pauses)
Actually, that's not a bad idea. I
might write that one down.

                    KATE
So glad I could help you promote the
book you haven't written yet.

                    GUS (V.O.)
Great literature takes *time*, Kate.
And I need to watch all of Netflix
first. So, what did Joel say when you
told him your news?

                         KATE

Nothing, because I haven't told him
yet.

                         GUS (V.O.)

Why not?

                         KATE

It's complicated.

                         GUS (V.O.)

Is it, though?

                         KATE

I just don't know how he's going to
react.

                         GUS (V.O.)

There's only one way he *should* react
and that's to congratulate you and be
happy for you and celebrate with you.
If he does anything other than—

Gus's voice abruptly disappears. There is
nothing coming from the phone now: no static,
no white noise. Kate pulls the device from
her ear and curses. The screen is black and
lifeless. The battery has died.

                         KATE

Shit.

She turns and goes back inside.

An UNKNOWN FIGURE watches her do this from
deep inside the trees in front of the house.

INT. LIVING SPACE - DAY

A phone charger is plugged into an electrical
socket next to the microwave in the kitchen
area, the cable lying on the countertop. Kate
takes its free end and plugs it into her
phone. There is an electronic *ding* and then an
animated battery symbol appears on screen.

She walks away, leaving the phone sitting on
the countertop, charging.

A moment later, the battery symbol disappears
- the phone has died again. The digital clock
on the microwave has gone black too.

Unbeknownst to Kate, the power's gone out.

ELEVEN

My second day on the set of *Final Draft* started with noise.

It broke through my unconsciousness as a dull, gathering roar that went from background to deafening in mere seconds, and felt like it was coming from everywhere at once.

It only made sense when I opened my eyes and saw daylight filtering through the cabin's thin curtains. Then, on the window above the sink whose blind I'd neglected to pull down, an intricate network of fast-flowing tributaries making watery spiderwebs across the glass.

It was raining.

Really raining. Lashing down, in relentless torrents, hammering the roof of the cabin above my head. It was as if I'd accidentally fallen asleep inside a carwash. Donal had warned me that this was in the forecast, but also that it was due to stop before we started shooting and so wouldn't affect our schedule.

I was much more worried about the fact that I could see daylight.

I felt in the sheets for the hard smoothness of my phone, willing it to tell me I'd managed to sleep – somehow – until late afternoon and that darkness was due to fall any minute. But I hadn't even made it to the *afternoon* bit. It was 10:56 a.m.

I had to use the phone's calculator app to do the maths. If breakfast was served at 6:00 p.m. and our workday started at 7:00 p.m., waking up now was like having a job that started at 8:00 a.m. and getting up at …

Midnight the night before.

Shit.

I desperately needed to get a few more hours or I'd never make it through tonight's shoot. I rolled over, resolutely shut my eyes and tried to go back to sleep, but it was no use – because my stomach was awake too. It gave an angry gurgle. I'd skipped last night's dinner and there were still hours to go before the next catered meal.

Hadn't Donal said something about snacks in the crew cabin?

I needed to get back to sleep, so I needed to not be starving. I got out of bed, gasping in shock at the change in temperature. The cabin was *freezing*. I pulled on a pair of sweatpants and stuck my feet into the fur-lined wellies Donal had given me. The rain jacket he had left in my wardrobe was several sizes too large but that was a good thing. The hem of it was nearly at my knees and the hood completely covered my greasy hair and half of my bare face, still creased with sleep, eyes puffy and red.

I was just going to run next door, grab some stuff and run back here. Everyone else should still be asleep in bed, so no one would see me anyway.

I opened the door.

There was a curtain of rain hanging a couple of feet in front of me, from the lip of the roof's overhang. The rain was falling straight down, as if in sheets. Like movie rain, the kind they make with machines. Appropriately.

I used two hands to hold my hood in place, ducked my head and ran through the drenching curtain, out on to the soft, muddy ground and along the path to the left, to the cabin next door. By the time I made it on to *its* deck, I could feel a cold moisture gluing the jacket's lining to the skin on my arms and the back of the T-shirt I'd slept in. In mere moments, rain had managed to get in where the cuffs gaped around my wrists and somewhere else, around the back. When I reached behind my head I felt my own hair: there was a hole in the rain jacket. A line of snaps connected the hood to the body, and whoever had worn this before me hadn't done them up right. I cursed and shivered and squirmed in the clinging wetness, and hurried inside the crew cabin.

The smell smacked me in the face immediately. Spilled beer and old grease, with underlying notes of stale cigarette smoke and sweat and damp clothes and men.

Something flexed at the back of my throat and I instinctively took a step backwards, out on to the deck. The smells of the forest weren't exactly sweet either – earth and damp and mulch – but they were better than whatever was rotting inside the crew cabin. I gulped down a couple of breaths and tried again, opening the cabin's door wide, pushing it back against the interior wall.

It was no mystery why the cabin smelled the way it did. There was no bed in this one, only the built-in kitchenette, plus a larger table surrounded by stools that could seat eight if those eight didn't mind touching elbows. Every visible surface was covered in detritus from a meal – our 'dinner', served at breakfast-time this morning. The meal I'd elected to sleep through. It had, evidently, been *more* pizza, this time with beer.

Nothing looked to have been thrown away or cleaned up. I could see grease-stained pizza boxes, paper plates smeared with congealed ketchup, crumpled-up paper napkins and glassware smudged with fingerprints, empty or almost empty beer bottles. The soles of my boots made a squelching noise on the linoleum as I moved around, the floor sticky with spills. The guys had just walked out of there without any thought whatsoever about who was going to clean up after them, or under the mistaken assumption that someone else would.

I spotted a roll of black refuse bags on the counter by the sink and felt an itch. I wanted to tear one off and sweep all this mess into it, but I absolutely refused to go down that road, especially when I was the only woman on set.

I picked my way around the mess instead, breathing through my mouth while I opened cupboard doors and pulled on drawers and opened the fridge. As promised, the place was well-stocked – the fridge with eggs, milk and yogurts, and the cupboards with cereal, bread and an array of sugary snacks.

It was late morning in the real morning, but effectively the middle of the night on the set of *Final Draft*; neither my brain nor my belly knew what we were supposed to be eating right now. I hedged my bets and went for some yogurt and fruit to represent a breakfast, and a bag of crisps, a Twirl and a Coke to represent an unhealthy lunch. I stuffed everything into the pockets of the rain jacket and pulled up my hood, ready to dash through the rain again.

I left the door of the crew cabin open so the smorgasbord of disgusting smells would have a chance to waft out.

I *know* I did.

Back at my own cabin, I stepped out of my boots on the deck so as not to drag mud inside. I hung the rain jacket off the showerhead so it could drip-dry into the tray, and swapped my T-shirt for one that didn't have a big wet patch between the shoulder blades. Then I climbed into bed with a steaming cup of sweet tea, the food I'd foraged and my copy of the script for *Final Draft*.

Last night – earlier today – it had felt so good to be acting it made me a little nervous, as if I'd swallowed what I knew was a potentially lethal substance but damn it if it wasn't a great time. I'd been so focused for so long on the achievement of it, of wanting to win roles and make money and send success stories back home, and then, later, on salvaging what little career I had left, I'd forgotten just how much *I enjoyed doing it*, how much fun it was in the moment.

How good it felt to be an *actor*.

To not be in an ill-fitting poly-blend behind a reception desk, having to pretend to care about the fact that Room 22's TV wasn't working or that the rollaway bed Room 41 had booked in advance wasn't there. To not be desperately trying to keep my head above water in a drowned city of a million dreams, afraid that if someone asked, 'How are you?' with any feeling my dam would burst, but even *more* afraid that no one would ask that. To not be constantly worrying that one day I'd get an email with a link to a twenty-six-part Twitter thread that started, *Did I ever tell you about the time I got a catering gig on a movie set and I witnessed Adele Rafferty lose her goddamn MIND for no good reason? Well, buckle up!*

When the cameras rolled, all that noise disappeared.

Yes, things were a bit haphazard. Yes, this production was pushing the term *skeleton crew* to new heights. Yes, Neil would be on the evening news some day, holding a hand up to his face as cameras chased him down the steps of the Central Criminal Court. And then there was the earring and the annotated script page and the weird text messages, but there was also Donal who was going to help me get to the bottom of it.

Every set was a workplace, and no workplace was perfect. No job was. But this job was the one I loved, the lead in a movie, a sparkling opportunity that I needed to grab with both hands and then stand on with both feet so it couldn't escape me.

Starting now, I was going to give this thing my all.

First order of business: actually read the script. So far, between my properly reading the first third or so and quickly scanning the rest, what I gathered about the plot of the film was this:

In *Final Draft*: The Film, the two main characters were a couple, Kate (me) and Joel (Simon, once he got here next week). They check into a secluded country cottage in the woods in the arse-end of nowhere for what is supposed to be a romantic mini-break. But Joel is an insecure little toddler-man who can't deal with Kate being on the cusp of achieving the kind of success in novel-writing that he's thus far failed to, so things get tense instead of steamy. After Joel gets in a huff and stumbles off to bed drunk, Kate starts reading *First Draft*: The Novel. The cottage is stocked with copies of it because it's the work of a previous guest. The author wrote the book in the cottage and set it there too, a creative choice on the fictional novelist's part that struck me as a bit lazy and lacking in imagination and totally in keeping with a script named after screenwriting software.

But anyway.

In *First Draft*: The Novel — and this, I thought, was where things started to approach Christopher Nolan-esque levels of unnecessary complication — a couple called Karen and Jack (same first initials, subtle), check into a secluded country cottage in the woods in the arse-end of nowhere for what is supposed to be a romantic mini-break, but for them things get *weird* before they can get steamy. There's a knock on the door in the dead of night but Karen finds no one on the other side of it, and then, early the next morning, that same door is standing wide open with muddy footprints suggesting that whoever opened it came inside as well. But Jack doesn't believe her.

Back in *Final Draft*: The Film, *Kate* starts experiencing similar things — a knock on the door, finding the door open — and Joel doesn't believe *her*. This is the point at which I'd started to scan, but from what I'd gleaned there was a lot of running around in the woods and away from mysterious noises in the dark, and Kate freaking out because in *First Draft*: The Novel, Karen died at the end and she fears the same fate awaits her.

Reading it gave me a faint sense of déjà vu, as if I'd seen a movie like this before. I probably had. If calling a movie *Final Draft* and calling the book inside it *First Draft* was any indicator of the script's originality ... Some version of this horror film had probably already been made many, many times over.

I sipped my tea and settled in. My plan was to read it the whole way through, once, and then go back to the beginning and start again while also analysing it. I usually did this with an A4 pad by my side with a thick, vertical line drawn down the middle, dividing the page into two columns. On the left, I'd put the facts of the script. Who my character was, what they did, what happened to them. On the right, I'd put my thoughts *about* these facts. How my character felt, why she had responded to that event in this way, what she really wanted or needed in that particular moment.

I'd once heard a well-known actor describe this process as dividing a script into what it gave him to work with and what he could add to it to make it good, which sounded to me like classic Man Actor egotistical bullshit and a dig at the screenwriter. It was just close-reading. All the information I needed was already in the script. I just needed to dig it out.

That's all I ever really did in terms of preparation. I didn't go in for any of that staying-in-character-between-takes crap, or writing novel-length backstories, or prepping for the shoot by moving around in the real world pretending to be the person on the page. I'd never got over hearing about Donnie Wahlberg's antics in preparation for *The Sixth Sense*, starving himself and sleeping in city parks and jumping out of bushes to scare his friends, all for a couple of minutes on screen. Or Jim Carrey behaving like he was *actually* Andy Kaufman around the late Andy Kaufman's family. Or basically everything Daniel Day-Lewis ever did.

I sided with Laurence Olivier. On the set of *Marathon Man*, having heard that Dustin Hoffman had stayed up for three nights straight to play a character who was suffering from extreme exhaustion, Olivier reportedly said, 'My dear boy, why don't you try *acting*?'

I often wondered why all these stories always seemed to involve men. Why didn't we ever hear about Meryl Streep or

Viola Davis or Saoirse No Last Name indulging in these kinds of shenanigans? Probably because no woman's antics would ever be indulged to that degree on a set. She'd be fired first, and never hired again.

Or maybe it was because they didn't need to do it. Maybe those female actors just knew how to, you know, *act*.

I was on page seventeen of my first read-through of the script when a new noise cut through the roar of the rain: a knock. One single, hard thud, on the cabin's front door. It made me jump, then laugh – because just a page earlier, *Kate* had heard a knock on the door of Cherry Cottage.

And then I thought, *Someone* else *can't sleep either*.

I called out, 'Yeah?' because I didn't want to get out of bed and also because I didn't necessarily want whoever was out there to see the current state of me.

No response.

I tried a, 'Hello?', but still got nothing.

Maybe they couldn't hear me over the rain. Maybe *I* couldn't hear *them* over it. Resigned, I threw back the blankets and got up, doing what I could to smooth down my hair on the few steps between there and the door. I pulled it open—

There was no one outside.

The deck was empty, the scene beyond it just as before. The curtain of rain falling over the edge of the roof's overhang. The wooden slats of the deck dark with moisture, little puddles gathered in spots that couldn't absorb any more for now.

I took one step out, soaking a sock, so I could look at the deck of the crew cabin.

Its door was closed now.

I assumed that whoever had knocked had gone in there when they failed to get a response from me. But why was someone knocking on my door at this time of the day, which on the set of *Final Draft* was effectively the middle of the night? Maybe I'd left evidence of my snack retrieval in the crew cabin, thus revealing that I was awake.

I scanned the treeline for movement.

Nothing.

Was someone messing with me? In *First Draft*: The Book, Karen answered a knock on the door to find no one there and then, in *Final Draft*: The Film, *Kate* answered a knock on the door to find no one there, and now, on the *set* of *Final Draft*, the actress playing Kate had just answered a knock on the door to find no one there.

Har-dee-fucking-har-har.

Behind me, the cabin was filling up with freezing air and out of the warmth of the bed, my body temperature was plummeting. I hurried back inside, shut the door and bent to pull off my wet sock. I turned and walked to the rear of the cabin, to the bathroom, where I pulled a towel off the rack and used it to dry my foot. I hung the towel back on the rail and I took off the other sock too. I may have also paused to look in the mirror, to make faces at the state of my unwashed, bed-head hair.

At the *most*, I only had my back turned to the rest of the cabin for a few seconds.

Ten, I'd estimate. Fifteen at a push.

And yet, when I turned back around to leave the bathroom, I saw that the cabin's front door was open.

Wide open, pushed all the way in, flush against the interior wall.

TWELVE

I stood there, staring at it, while various reactions competed in my mind.

I was annoyed, because I thought that whoever had knocked on my door and run away had come back to *open* that door and run away, so I would be two for two with Kate – now we'd both heard a knock *and* found an inexplicably open door.

I was angry, because I was the only woman on set and that set was in the middle of a bloody forest, so this felt like a threat to my personal safety.

And then I was unsure how I felt because when I finally moved to close the door, I discovered that it didn't automatically lock when you closed it and you had to give it a good, firm push into place before the lock mechanism made a clicking sound.

Maybe I hadn't closed it properly. I'd swung it shut as I'd turned to head to the bathroom, but I'd been focused on getting out of my icky wet sock. The door could've bounced back off the frame, or not engaged with the lock and then been blown open by the wind, or maybe it was just one of those doors where their own weight swung them back.

Try as I might, I couldn't seem to re-enact any of these scenarios, but that didn't mean they couldn't happen.

I started wondering if there'd even been a knock on the door. Who knocked like that, once and then never again? Even if it were a prank, wouldn't they knock like a normal human person – twice, quickly – and *then* run off into the woods? Wasn't imitating the knock on the script to that level of accuracy just a bit too on the nose? Wouldn't the single knock alert me to the fact that it absolutely *was* a prank?

I decided that the door had opened by itself and that what I thought was a knock on the door was actually whoever had gone into the crew cabin banging something or dropping something or hitting something accidentally – maybe even the side wall of my cabin, OJ Simpson/Kato Kaelin-style – that I'd mistakenly interpreted to be a knock on my door. I closed it firmly now, pulling on the handle to double-check the lock had engaged, and climbed back into bed to resume reading my script.

But I struggled to stay focused on it. After a certain point it had practically no dialogue, and the dense description felt like hard work to keep wading through page after page. The upside of this was that I started feeling sleepy again, and was able to doze for another hour or so. When I woke up for a second time, I knew for sure there was no more sleep to be had this side of tonight's shoot, so I started getting ready for it.

I had a shower, washed and dried my hair. I made a coffee and ate the rest of the food I'd foraged from the crew cabin. I killed an hour lying in bed swiping through old photos on my phone, deleting ones I didn't want any more so I could free up space, ready to download Steve Dade's oeuvre when Donal drove me to the road or I happened to find one of those mysterious pockets of mobile phone service he'd talked about.

Then I started thinking that maybe I should go look for one of those mysterious pockets of mobile phone service *now*.

The rain had reduced itself to drizzle. The winter sun had started its steady descent from the sky, but it wouldn't disappear for a while yet. I had the torchlight app on my phone, if it came to it. It was 3:00 p.m. – three hours to go until evening-time breakfast. I figured a walk around outside was as good a way to kill time as any.

For the third time that day, I opened my cabin door to see no other signs of life outside. I set off, feeling the soft, sodden ground give way beneath my wellies as I made my way through the trees.

When the main house came into view, the wall of glass was dark – as was each window on its first floor.

All of them had their curtains drawn.

I picked my way through the garden gingerly, conscious of the crunch of my footsteps on the gravel while also suspecting that it wasn't anywhere near as loud as I feared it was, that there was no danger of me waking anybody, and slipped around the side of the house. As I rounded its front corner, I saw that the motorhome too was dark and silent, with a patterned curtain pulled across its back window.

I was very jealous of everyone else's ability to stay asleep.

I took my phone from my pocket. No bars. There were also no new emails or notifications, so I could be sure I hadn't accidentally wandered through a pocket of reception between my cabin and here. I decided to keep it in my hand so I could check it periodically.

I crossed the clearing in front of the house, and headed for the dirt track. As I passed through the stone pillars, I felt a prickle of something at the back of my neck.

I turned around.

The clearing, the motorhome, the house – everything was as it should be, as it had been. There was no movement and nothing had changed.

Still, I felt like …

Was someone *watching* me?

I scanned each of the house's front windows in turn, looking for a twitch of the curtain, a shadow moving in the darkness beyond, the dim glow of a low light. I held my breath and listened for a tell-tale gravel crunch, or the sound of distant voices.

Nothing.

I blamed my close-reading of the script, this place, the fact that everyone else was still asleep and so I was, effectively, alone out here. I reminded myself I was *starring* in a horror movie, not living through one.

I turned back around and continued walking.

The last time I'd been on the dirt track, I'd been in Peg's taxi as it bounced and bumped along. And no wonder it had, because now I could see that it was just two tracks in compacted dirt formed by the repeated pressure of four wheels, with a thick line of weeds sitting in the middle, dotted with potholes of various shapes and sizes. Every twenty feet or so, I met a particularly big one, usually right at the edge of the track and filled with cloudy, stagnant water. I imagined having to walk this in my battered ballet flats and said a silent prayer of thanks for thoughtful assistant directors and borrowed boots.

The track twisted and turned, refusing to stay straight for any length of time and, at the round of every blind bend, I fully expected to see the gates that attached the track to the main road. But after walking for ten minutes, there was neither sight nor sound of them or the road.

No engines roaring past, no blaring horns, no aural evidence at all that there was a road up ahead.

And *still* no bars on my phone.

How busy was that road, though? Had we passed any other cars on the way in? I couldn't remember seeing one, but then I'd only woken up for the last mile or so.

Main road could be a loose definition. *Public road* might be more in keeping with what Donal had actually meant.

Still, I hadn't realised the track between the gates and the house was quite this long. It occurred to me that no one on set knew where I was, that I'd walked down here. The darkness felt like it was falling quicker now. It was already taking root in the depths of the trees; the line where the light stopped penetrating seemed to be getting closer and closer to the road, to me. The rain had eased again so that it was now barely a drizzle, which meant there was no sound to compete with the endless rustle of the forest, the occasional shriek of what I assumed were birds, the odd crack of a branch or twig.

I picked up my pace.

And then, finally, came an electronic *ping*.

A new WhatsApp message arriving on my phone – and, when I looked at the screen, one bar of reception. I didn't want to walk any further and risk having to do some of the walk back in the actual dark. If I turned around now, I could get back to my cabin before then. One bar would do.

The *ping* was a message from Julia: *No worries, won't breathe a word. Congrats & good luck! Call if you need me.* I smiled at it and replied with a gif of Tina Fey and Amy Poehler high-fiving on stage at an awards ceremony.

I checked my email account, which told me new messages were currently downloading. While I waited for them to appear, I took a few steps further down the road – and an error message popped up on screen. The one bar of reception was back to none. I retraced my steps until the bar reappeared.

Donal wasn't exaggerating when he'd referred to them as mysterious pockets of reception.

Most of my new emails were messages from online stores, newsletters I kept meaning to unsubscribe from and casting call notification services. But there was also an email from Lindsey, in response to the thank-you note I'd sent her before I left LA.

> Thank you!! Exactly what I was hoping you'd say. Please pass on my thanks to Yvonne. It was her that gave him my number. —A

> Hey – I've been trying to call you. Can you give me a ring back ASAP? Lx

Lindsey had sent that just after ten o'clock this morning.

I found her name in my Contacts and called her phone, but after five rings it kicked me over to her voicemail.

'Hey,' I said, 'it's Adele. I got your email ... Reception here is ridiculously spotty but hopefully you'll be able to call me back. We shoot overnight and my call-time is seven, I think, so anytime before then is fine. I'll try you again if I can ... Bye.'

Around me, the dark was coming down so fast it felt like it was threatening to race me back to the main house.

I opened the one-way thread of mysterious text messages and reread them, even though I could recite them by heart. I tapped the phone number, held my finger over the little AUDIO button that, if I pressed it, would initiate a call.

But I didn't press it.

The truth was I didn't *want* to know who was sending me those texts. I didn't want any information that would prevent me from dismissing them as some crank or prank, because I wanted to stay on this set. I wanted to shoot tonight, and tomorrow night, and the night after that. I wanted to act.

Besides, there weren't any new texts. My anonymous sender must have given up.

It never occurred to me that this was because there was no point now, that my time to get away from this place had run out, that it was already too late to save me from what was coming next.

I pocketed the phone and started back the way I'd come, wondering what my former agent might want to talk to me about. I hoped it was something good.

Just as the stone pillars came back into view, I heard a man's voice.

The rain had started to pick up again, so at first, I wasn't sure I hadn't imagined it. I held my breath, strained to listen. There it was, a few decibels above the pitter-patter of the spitting rain: a man, talking loudly, somewhere up ahead.

He was standing outside the house, it sounded like to me. I couldn't discern the actual words but going by the way he was speaking them, in bursts with long pauses in between, he was talking on the phone.

I didn't recognise the voice, but I presumed it was one of the crew. Who else would it be? There was no one else here. One of them had, finally, risen from their slumber.

I was annoyed that there was evidently *another* pocket of magical mobile phone reception right by the house that I'd missed completely. There'd been no need for me to walk anyways down the track at all.

But as I went through the pillars, crossing from dirt track to crunchy gravel, there was no one there that I could see. Everything looked the same way it did when I'd left. Curtains drawn, windows dark, no movement.

And now there was nothing to *hear* either, because whoever had been talking on the phone had stopped.

Stopped and, apparently, disappeared.

INT. LIVING SPACE - DAY

Kate builds a new fire in the hearth and
lights it. She curls up on the armchair with
First Draft and continues reading.

> KATE (V.O.)
> *The morning expired. Noon came and*
> *went. But it wasn't until the sun*
> *started to sink in the sky that Karen*
> *really started to worry.*

A smattering of raindrops hit the window.

MATCH DISSOLVE TO:

INT. LIVING SPACE - LATER SAME DAY

Heavy rain pelts the same window. The fire
glows and snaps. Beyond it, the room has
become dim.

Kate continues to read, squinting now.

> KATE (V.O.)
> *It was only when she went to turn*
> *on a light that she realised the*
> *power was out. Then, suddenly, she*
> *heard a noise. A loud, dull thud.*
> *Like someone upstairs falling on the*
> *floor. Except there shouldn't be*
> *anyone upstairs. There wasn't even an*
> *upstairs, just attic space. Slowly,*
> *she raised her eyes to the ceiling.*

Absently, she reaches for the lamp on the side
table and flicks its switch.

Nothing happens.

She turns to it, frowns, tries again. An
inspection quickly reveals there is no bulb
inside the shade. With an eye-roll, Kate
throws the book on the chair and gets up to
flick the light switch on the wall.

But no light comes on.

She goes into the kitchen, checks the
appliances. All their LED screens are lifeless
and, when she opens the microwave, no light
comes on. Same for the fridge: no light, no
hum.

                    KATE
     Shit.

She roots around in the cupboard under the
sink until she finds a torch, some candles and
matches.

INT. UTILITY ROOM - DUSK

Holding the torch, Kate enters the small
utility room off the kitchen area. It has a
tiled floor, a washer-dryer and a shelving
unit filled with cleaning products. A window
overlooks the front of the house. She locates
the fuse box and tries resetting the trip-
switch but, again, nothing happens. Sighing
resignedly, she turns to return to the living
space.

Behind her back, outside, a shadowy figure
darts past the window.

THIRTEEN

I waited until ten minutes past six before I left for the crew cabin. I had planned to wait until I heard someone else go in before me, but that hadn't happened and I was too restless to wait any longer. After all, I'd slept in yesterday. I didn't want to be late two days in a row a little more than I didn't want to be the first one there.

The cabin's door was still closed. Pushing it open revealed nothing but gloom beyond. When I flipped on the lights, I was met with the same scene of abandoned greasy mess. Nothing had changed. The only difference was the smell, which was now more damp leaves than stale pizza.

Where was everyone?

I had a wild notion then that my clocks were wrong. My times were out. My phone was doing some kind of spectacular malfunctioning after its trip through multiple time-zones and my body clock, I'd already established, didn't know which way was up. But this theory was swiftly torpedoed by the digital clock on the microwave and then by the actual, analogue clock hanging on the cabin's rear wall.

It *was* well past six. Everyone should be in here, grabbing breakfast.

Unless grabbing breakfast was exactly what we were supposed to do. Maybe this wasn't a catered, sit-down meal. Yesterday's full Irish might have been a Day One treat. I'd already seen stocks of bread, milk, eggs and cereal. Could the idea be that you just popped in and grabbed what you wanted before you headed down to set? Was everyone leaving that until the last minute? Or could they have done it earlier and already be on set?

If that were the case, I wasn't going to be grabbing anything in *this* cesspit, thank you very much.

I put two slices of bread, two eggs and a knob of butter on a plate and took it back to my own cabin, back to where things were clean. I made coffee and cooked the eggs in a cereal bowl in the microwave and browned the bread under the grill. By the time I was done, it was ten minutes to seven and I still hadn't seen or heard anyone else.

They *must* be on set already.

I was done waiting. I grabbed my script, my phone and my rain jacket and headed down to the main house.

It was so cold now that I could see my breath clouding in the glow of my phone's torchlight. Without it, there was no way I'd have been able to navigate the path through the trees. The ground felt almost molten beneath my feet, my boots sinking and squelching on every step.

At one point, my foot caught in something and suddenly I was pitching forward, *flying* forward, heading for a face-first landing on the ground. I grabbed whatever I could to stop myself, which was a tree branch more than happy to scrape strips of skin off the palm of my hand. The wound immediately began to sting like crazy.

I'd stopped to point the phone at it so I could inspect the damage – it felt worse than it was – when I looked up and realised I was almost at the walled garden. I should be looking at the giant glowing window at the back of the main house already, but I wasn't because the house was shrouded in darkness.

How could they all still be asleep? And *why* were they, when we were supposed to be reporting to set in mere minutes? Didn't anyone know how to set an alarm?

I rolled my eyes as I stomped my way down the steps into the garden, planting my footsteps harder than I needed to, crunching the gravel as loudly as I could.

When I rounded the house, the motorhome came into view – and, filtering through its thin curtains, the glow of light within.

Well, *Donal* was awake.

Something tight and hot unfurled inside of me, an unexpected relief. It wasn't that I'd thought I was actually alone out here, it was just that with everyone sleeping, it had started to feel that way. After my little excursion halfway down the dirt track earlier, Cedarwood House was feeling more isolated, more secluded, than it had since I'd arrived, and the dark wasn't helping.

I didn't like the idea of having to go into the guys' rooms and wake them up – knowing my luck, I'd accidentally choose to go into Neil the Creep's room first, and he'd have chosen to sleep naked – and now, I wouldn't have to. Donal could take care of all that.

I went straight to the motorhome's door and rapped my knuckles hard on the little window, twice, and readied myself to say, *Um, where the hell is everyone? It's gone seven. I think we're the only two awake.* But Donal didn't come to the door.

I knocked again, harder this time, and called out his name, my voice sounding louder than usual above the silence.

Nothing.

Nothing at *all* – no rustling noises from within, no shadows moving behind the curtains. I couldn't hear anything except the low whistle of wind through the trees and the pulse of my own heart thundering in my ears.

I wasn't sure what to do. Could Donal have headphones on or something? Could he have fallen back asleep with the lights on?

I walked the vehicle's perimeter, stopping at each window to look through any gaps I found in the curtains, but I saw nothing that suggested anyone was inside.

Had the lights been on when I'd been here earlier, when I'd crossed the gravel to walk down the track? Or later when I'd come back to the house, when I heard the guy talking on the phone? I didn't know. I didn't remember noticing them. It hadn't been dark then. They could've been on without my realising.

I went back to the door and pulled on the handle. To my surprise, it opened.

'Donal?' This was the production office and wardrobe *and* make-up, but Donal had also referred to it as his room. I really didn't want to walk in on anything I shouldn't, especially since one of the first things I was going to say to him was that if someone *had* come and opened *my* cabin door, I was pissed about it. 'Donal? Are you awake?'

I got no response.

I went in.

The table at the rear had been completely cleared, and a pillow and a sleeping bag were rolled up neatly underneath it. Otherwise everything looked exactly as it had on my last visit just after 4:00 a.m. this morning, when I'd been rushing to change back out of my costume before Neil appeared.

Down to the fact that no one was in there, except me.

The front door of the main house was locked but when I went round the back, into the walled garden, I found that the sliding glass door opened easily.

I slipped inside and trailed the beam of my phone along the walls until it landed on a light switch. Flipping it brought on a blinding array of spotlights recessed into the ceiling. I counted twelve of them, spaced at intervals along two parallel lines. They showed me a space where all the equipment – cameras, lights, cables – was still pretty much in the same position it had been last night when we'd wrapped.

The crew hadn't been working in here today. If they had, everything would be changed, ready for whatever set-up we needed this evening, prepped for tonight's scheduled scenes.

Not that I knew what they were, seeing as I hadn't been given today's call-sheet.

The battery symbol on my phone's screen had turned red. Less than five per cent charge remained. I cursed my earlier self for not plugging it in while I'd been up in my cabin, and then failing to notice that using it as a torch was devouring what little power I had left.

As I pocketed the device, I saw myself reflected in the wall of glass, overlaid on solid dark. From the living room, you couldn't see anything outside. It crossed my mind that someone could be out there right now, watching me. They could *all* be out there, the whole crew, crouched in the trees, desperately trying to keep quiet, to stop their laughter from carrying on the wind. This could be some big joke, some ridiculous hazing ritual. A not-at-all fun game of hide-and-seek.

The front door of the main house opened easily from the inside. I stuck my head out to check if anyone had arrived since, but there was no one out there that I could see.

My eyes landed on a small white button by the door's frame: a bell. I pressed it, holding my finger down, and listened as a sustained electronic ringing reverberated loudly around the house. I went back inside, letting the door swing shut behind me, and waited to hear the sound of a mattress spring or the creak of a floorboard overhead but none came. I went to the foot of the stairs and called out, 'Hello? Anyone awake up there?'

No response.

I started up them – *clomping* up them, really, smacking each foot down with force. They were bare wood and more than willing to help me generate intrusive noise. If anyone was up there, they were definitely going to be awake by the time I got to the top.

'Hello?' I called out halfway up. 'Guys, it's gone seven.'

The upper level of the house was one long landing that ran along the front; the windows on the façade marked its length. The light from downstairs didn't reach past the top step, so I used my phone again to locate a light switch. A single, naked bulb hung from the ceiling halfway along. It illuminated four doors opening off the landing: three at the rear of the house and one directly opposite me, at the other end of the landing.

That door was open enough for me to identify it as the bathroom. Each of the other three doors were open enough for me to know, to be *sure*, that I was absolutely alone in this house. I could just feel it.

Which was to say, I couldn't feel anything. The air was dead and still. It wasn't electrified with the presence of any other ticking hearts.

The guys weren't here.

And I'd had enough of this. I decided to call Donal. I had his number on the call-sheet from yesterday, in my cabin. I'd have to go back up there anyway to charge my phone, which was now – *shit* – down to three per cent. I probably wouldn't get reception there, but once I'd got the number and let it charge for a bit, I could come back down to the spot by the stone pillars where there was evidently enough service to make a call, going by the guy I'd heard earlier.

Who was that guy? *Where* was he?

If he was a member of the crew, wouldn't he be here?

Maybe he was a neighbour, I thought, or a delivery guy – someone who had only been on the property briefly and then left again.

Who had failed to pass me on the only route in to and out of Cedarwood House.

One problem at a time. Focus on the task at hand, which was finding out where the hell everybody was, which I could do if I called Donal. But if the phone died before I got back to my cabin, it was going to be a tricky trek along the path through the trees. I might not make it at all, but end up lying on the floor of the forest with a broken leg, waiting for someone to find me.

Maybe one of the guys had the same phone as me. Or failing that, a torch. And surely there was a call-sheet lying around here somewhere? With any luck, I might not have to go back to my cabin at all.

I went to the first bedroom door, pushed it back and reached my hand around to pat the wall until my fingers felt a light switch. I refused to feel bad about snooping. Squinting in the sudden glare, I scanned the room. It didn't take long. The room was small and the furniture plain, and, to my eye, standard Swedish flatpack. There was a wardrobe standing with its back to the landing, facing two single beds with a little table between them. Both beds were unmade and strewn with clothes and other personal possessions. I spied a shaving bag, a paperback sci-fi novel, a box of protein shake sachets and a pair of well-worn running shoes.

But no phone charger or call-sheet.

I found similar scenes in the other two bedrooms: empty beds in various stages of unmade-ness, stuff scattered about, no one there. The third room had only one double bed in it and it smelled very strongly of body odour. Nice.

In the bathroom, the toilet seat was up, the sink was caked with dried toothpaste deposits and a damp towel was thrown on the floor in the corner. The shower head was leaking a slow but steady *drip-drip-drip* that stopped when I turned the tap a little further into OFF.

I went back out on to the landing and looked at each of the bedroom doors in turn. They were dark; I'd switched off the lights as I'd gone. But I felt like they were trying to tell me something, or rather that the scenes inside them were. There was something about the state of them, about the mess. It was …

Weirdly uniform.

Every bed was unmade and every crew member had, seemingly, walked out of his room having left clothes and other things strewn about. But the crew ranged in age from Aaron, barely in his twenties, to Mick, pushing fifty. Even if they were all the very *same* age, it would be odd if each of them was the exact same level of messy. With Steve in his own cabin and Donal in the motorhome, that left five guys staying here. What were the odds that not one of them was the type of person to make his own bed in the morning, or hang up his clothes, or just generally be neat and tidy?

Unless he hadn't had a *chance* to be that way.

Unless he hadn't had the time to.

That's what was odd about the mess: it didn't look like it had been made by a bunch of careless guys who all happened to be the exact same level of untidy. It looked like what might be left behind if all those guys had to leave suddenly, unexpectedly, immediately, roused from their beds at the same time.

'Shit,' I said aloud.

Because *that's* what it was. *That's* what was different. The thing that was wrong when I'd looked around the clearing earlier but that, at the time, I hadn't been able to put my finger on.

The white SUV. The Volvo. The only car I'd ever seen on set.

I ran back down the stairs, yanked open the front door, ran out into the dark—

It was gone.

FOURTEEN

It was raining again. A few moments of drizzle, then an onslaught of icy sheets. The wind whipped freezing drops against my face as I hurried back along the path to the cabins, the beam of my phone pointed at the muddy ground, hoping to get within sight of them before the battery died.

Just as the light dimmed and then disappeared in time with the chime of a sad little two-tone electronic beep – my phone's dying breath – I spotted a light up ahead: the one over my own cabin's door. I zipped the phone into my jacket pocket and kept going, stepping more carefully now, past my cabin and the crew one, and on to the deck of the third: Steve's.

It was the only place I hadn't checked yet for signs of life. I wasn't expecting to find any; the cabin was dark and still. But I didn't want to find out later that I was freaking out because I was alone out here, cursing everybody, only to find out that Steve himself had been a few feet away from me the entire time.

Unsurprisingly, my knocking on his door didn't get any response.

'Steve? You in there?'

He wasn't.

The window to the front didn't have any curtain pulled across it. I cupped my hands on the glass and pressed my face into them, trying to look inside. At first, it was impossible to separate anything from the darkness. But when my eyes adjusted, they landed on one tiny source of light, a pinprick of it, a luminous green dot. I recognised it as a charging cable for a MacBook. Plugged *into* a MacBook, sitting on Steve's dining table, lid up. I thought I could see some papers scattered around it and a coffee mug sitting nearby. Beyond that, the darkness hid whatever else was inside.

Was this another scene of interruption? Had Steve been working on his laptop, coffee by his side, when for some reason he had to leave suddenly? I tried the door handle, but it didn't give. If Steve *had* had to run off somewhere abruptly, he'd taken the time to lock up his cabin before he left.

The entire crew had squashed themselves into the Volvo and gone somewhere, on short notice, in the middle of *Final Draft*'s night. That much was becoming clear. But where had they gone and why? Why hadn't they come back in time for tonight's shoot?

And why the hell hadn't they as much as left me a note about it?

Having stopped at the crew cabin to collect a few snacks, I trudged back to my own. My wellies were so muddy now that their floral design was completely obscured from the ankle down. I stepped out of them on the deck and left them there, neatly lined up against the cabin's wall, so they wouldn't muck up the floor inside. I put the jacket back in the shower to drip-dry and dumped my haul – more sugary snacks, crisps and a bottle of beer because, why not? – on to the dining table. I caught myself thinking of it as *snackage* and gave myself a stern reprimand.

I had a clear plan now, which was to have no plan at all. If the crew of *Final Draft* wasn't bothered about coming to work on time, the cast of *Final Draft* wasn't going to be either. I was going to put on my fluffy socks, get into bed and gorge myself on high-calorie, nutrient-deficient food, and when they bothered to return from wherever the hell they were, *they* could come find *me*.

I plugged my charging cable into the socket by the microwave and my phone into its other end. I boiled the kettle to make tea. I put on my fluffy socks. I climbed back into bed and pulled the pages of my script on to my lap. I tried not to think about the fact that I was alone in a tiny cabin with one flimsy lock on its only door which could probably be forced open with a couple of swift kicks, hidden behind an empty house – which was itself hidden from the nearest road and surrounded by dense, pitch-black forest, miles from anywhere and everyone else – at night, with no mobile phone service.

If you're not, don't go. Not safe. Trust me.

I got back out of bed and did a loop of the cabin, double-checking each window was closed with its latch in the locked position and fully covered by its blind or curtain. I checked the front door yet again. I took one of the dining chairs and put it against the door, the legs tilted at an angle, the chair-back hooked under the handle.

Like I'd seen people do in the movies.

According to the clock on the microwave, it was 9:03 p.m. by then.

The rain was a thousand tiny hammers striking the roof of the cabin in every heartbeat, as heavy as it'd been since I'd arrived at Cedarwood House.

My gaze flicked to the kitchen counter, where my phone's screen was now a rectangle of blue-light glow. It had charged enough to turn itself back on, which I knew was just a few per cent. I'd need more like thirty per cent before I headed back down to the house; it would take that to make a phone call and for the phone to light my way there and back. I hadn't heard the little *beep-beep* sound that I knew it made when the phone turned itself back on. It was impossible to hear anything over the rain's endless roar.

Which made me think that maybe I'd missed *other* noises too. Like the guys walking out of the woods, laughing and back-slapping, and heading into the crew cabin next door.

The thought tugged on my mind until it dragged me out of bed.

I removed the chair from the door and turned the lock, gasping at the blast of ice-cold air that rushed in when I opened it. The deck was sopping wet now, the neat curtain of rain gone, replaced by a horizontal onslaught of freezing sheets. The roof's overhang no longer provided any protection.

I took a step forward, instantly ruining another pair of socks, to get a look at the crew cabin.

Still dark and silent. No change.

But when I turned back, I saw something *had* changed: the ground floor of the main house was now ablaze with light.

'*Finally*,' I said out loud. The crew of eejits had, at long last, come back.

I resented how relieved this made me and quickly decided that I would be *secretly* relieved. Outwardly, I would show only complete nonchalance. I wouldn't be waiting for them, hands clasped against my breastbone like some damsel in distress. I'd play it all cool and casual. I'd say I'd had my breakfast but when I didn't meet anyone else in the crew cabin, I'd assumed they'd all slept in and gone back to my own cabin to work on my script. I wouldn't even tell them I'd been inside the house or walked halfway down the dirt track trying to get a phone signal.

Oh, did you guys leave? I hadn't noticed.

I went back inside and sat on the edge of the bed to change my sodden socks. I strained to listen for sounds that weren't hammering rain. Surely the first thing they'd do is come check on me. Donal would, anyway.

The clock on the microwave said it was now 9:29 p.m.

At 9:53 p.m. I was still sitting there.

No one had come and I'd started to get paranoid that maybe they hadn't because they didn't want to disturb me, that they thought I was asleep in here. I only had one light on, the lamp beside the bed. Maybe from the outside, my cabin looked dark.

I wondered if I should be nonchalant *next door*, in the crew cabin, instead. Sit in there, prop my feet up on the table and recline with my script and a can of Diet Coke. Let them find me that way.

Yes, that's exactly what I would do.

I put on my rain jacket. I opened the front door, went to step outside—

And saw that the main house was dark again.

What the ...?

I frowned at the forest as if willing it to share an explanation. Two came to me. The guy I'd heard on the phone had returned, gone into the house, turned on the light, found he was alone, turned it off and left again. Or the crew had come back as I'd suspected and been, I don't know, swinging their dicks around for the last while, and now were on their way here, as a group, coming up the path through the trees, heading for the crew cabin.

Perhaps they could even see me now, or at least a silhouette of me, lit by the weak glow of the bedside lamp in the cabin behind me. I would make like I had been on my way out, heading next door anyway. I bent down to reach for the wellies—

They were gone.

I blinked at the spot on the decking where I knew I'd left them.

And I *did* know, for sure, because the only dry spot on the entire deck was the outline of where they'd been sitting.

Someone had *taken* my wellington boots.

Just taken them, in the last few minutes.

That's when a third explanation presented itself: the guys were messing with me. They'd come back, left the house to head up here, saw that I was in my cabin and assumed – correctly – that I'd been wondering where they were, maybe growing a little uneasy as the night drew in and the weather deteriorated, and instead of being actual adults and knocking on my door to make sure I was okay, they'd decided to have a little fun with me first.

But perhaps I wasn't giving them enough credit.

This *whole day* could've been a prank. After all, it had started with a knock on my cabin's door. A single, hard knock, but no one there to have done it, followed by that same door being inexplicably open a few minutes later.

Just like in *Final Draft*.

Just like in *First Draft*, the book in *Final Draft*.

Later in the script, Joel, the cranky toddler-man with an ego as fragile as crackle-glass, had left Kate alone in Cherry Cottage. On set, here at Cedarwood House, the entire crew had left *me*.

Maybe Steve *had* written the ending, but instead of giving me it on paper, he was planning to make me experience it in real life.

A hot, bubbly anger shot up into my jaw and made me clench my teeth. *Those absolute arseholes*. But even though it made me instantly detest myself, my overriding emotion now, my immediate reaction, was that I had to prove to those absolute arseholes that I could take the joke.

So I called out, 'Very funny, guys!' while faking a smile, making sure you could hear the good humour in my voice, directing my words at the darkness beyond the treeline, shouting them out so they might be heard over the wind and rain. 'You came back, then? Shame. I was looking forward to a night off.'

No response.

I stared into the spiky blackness of the fir trees, willing one of the guys to pop out, laughing, to point and say, 'We got you *good*!' just so I could end this charade and we could all get to work. But if there was anyone out there, they were staying hidden. No one emerged from the trees.

I did a theatrical eye-roll, amplified with a head movement so the action had a chance of being visible even at a distance and in this low light.

'I really admire your commitment, guys,' I called out. 'Maybe it's *you* who should be doing the acting?'

And then, everything fell into a darkness.

It was sudden, total and thick. A blindness. As if I had closed my eyes in an already dark room.

For a few seconds, there wasn't even a hint of light. Everything was the same flat black.

And then came a rush of panic, tightening my chest, sending a tremor into my lower jaw.

If you're not, don't go. Not safe. Trust me.

I took a step forward and looked up, searching for where the roof ended and the sky began, and then another step because the first one hadn't helped me find it, and then another, until the deck ended unexpectedly and I half-slipped, half-staggered down on to the soft, wet ground in my stockinged feet and tipped my head right back so I could look straight up—

A shade of slightly less dark, lit by some weak unseen moon and dotted with tiny, twinkling little stars.

A patch of sky, visible through the gap in the towering trees that corresponded to the little clearing the three cabins sat in.

Okay.

I took a breath.

Okay, okay.

I took another one.

You're okay. Everything's okay.

One more breath, slow and deep, holding it until my chest hurt.

The power had gone out. No, the power had been *cut off*. They had done this to me. They had heard me, shouting just now. The timing of it was too perfect to be coincidental.

Steve's crew of cretins *were* out there, hiding in the trees. I was convinced of it.

I couldn't quite believe that Donal was among them, but maybe there was some other explanation for that.

Even though I knew they couldn't possibly see me unless they'd got night-vision goggles, I held up both middle fingers and jabbed them at the treeline anyway.

INT. LIVING SPACE - DUSK

Kate re-enters the living space. She clicks
off the torch and sets it on the kitchen
counter - next to the copy of *First Draft* she
was reading.

She walks to the window over the sink and
looks out. There's nothing to see except the
treeline and a steadily thickening darkness.

                 KATE
              (muttering)
    Where the hell is he?

She picks up the torch again and goes to
leave the kitchen area - but stops dead when
she sees the book. It's lying splayed open,
facedown. There's a photo on the back cover,
upside down from Kate's perspective. She looks
from the book to the couch - *where she knows
she left it* - and then around the room.

             KATE (CONT'D)
             (uncertain)
    Joel?

She sweeps the shadowy space with the beam of
the torch.

             KATE (CONT'D)
             (uncertain)
    Joel, this isn't funny.

Fear creeps into her features: her breath
quickens, she bites her lip, her grip on
the torch tightens. The beam of the torch is

pointed towards the book, illuminating the photo on the back cover.

Tentatively, Kate turns the book over. It's open to the dedication page. *To Kate, who should never have come to Cherry Cottage.* She lets the book fall and steps back quickly, as if physically afraid of the book itself.

From directly above her head comes a loud, dull THUD.

Kate raises her eyes to the ceiling. A beat passes before there's a second, louder THUD. *Someone is up there, in the attic space.*

Kate runs to the spot where she'd left her phone charging—

It's gone, the charging cable left dangling.

                    KATE (CONT'D)
    What the …?

A third, even louder THUD.

Kate runs to the front door but, with the torch in one hand and both hands shaking, she struggles to unlock it. The beam of the torch dances crazily as she tries.

                    KATE (CONT'D)
   Come on come on come on come *on*

With a CLICK, the door - finally - unlocks. Kate pulls it open and runs outside.

FIFTEEN

I went back inside and closed the door, because leaving it open didn't allow in any more light. There was no light to let in.

I was convinced now that all this was something the crew was doing to me, some kind of Russian-doll, ego-driven creative wank that Steve Dade was having at my expense. A great story for the marketing campaign, or some kind of weird Stanley Kubrick shit where he felt the need to make me *actually* scared because he doubted my ability to act it.

Or maybe this was *it*, now. Steve could be out there in the dark, ready with a night-vision camera to capture me running scared through the woods. Maybe he'd already got me walking down the track earlier, and filmed me wandering around the main house through the wall of glass. Maybe the truth was that *Final Draft* was actually going to be a found-footage-style horror-movie, ten years too late to be relevant.

Maybe he *did* know about what happened on *We Were Kings*, had known all along, and was using it against me. Had Steve Dade cast me as Kate because he had every reason to believe that if he pushed me far enough, I'd have a freak-out?

Did this, somehow, go all the way back to Martin?

The knock on the door, the open door, being left alone and now even the power cut were all things experienced by Karen, the woman in *First Draft*: The Novel, and Kate, the woman in *Final Draft*: The Movie, and now me, the complete idiot who'd agreed to come here and play Kate because she was so damn desperate to make it as an actor. The weird texts. The lost earring in my bed. The page of script, complete with scene numbers and the annotations of – supposedly – another actor, the one who'd had this part before me but who everyone was pretending didn't exist.

Perhaps she *didn't* exist and all that was a part of this too.

When I'd first seen Donal coming out of the motorhome, he'd been putting his phone away; I'd just been sent the second weird text. There was only so much heavy lifting the word *coincidence* could carry before it completely collapsed, crushed.

Yeah, okay, I thought Donal was A Nice Guy, but I was hardly a good judge of character. I knew that much for sure. This whole thing, from the beginning, was starting to smell like a set-up. To *stink* like one. I was done playing along, but it wasn't like I could just hop in a car and drive away from here, and I couldn't confront anyone unless I found them first. I had zero interest in going looking.

I manoeuvred along the kitchenette's countertop by touch until my fingers felt my phone, and then there was light. A dim, eerie blue light coming from a device that only had ten per cent battery charge, but at least I could see around me now.

Things would be different if my phone was fully or mostly charged. I'd have light and I'd have entertainment and I'd have the reassurance of knowing that if I needed to make a call, I could. I'd have to run halfway down the track to make it, but at least I'd have the juice.

But how could I charge my phone when the cabin's power was out? I knew Steve's MacBook was fully charged next door – I could use one of its USB ports – but his door was locked. I could break a window with something but …

Well, let's call that Plan E.

Was the power gone in the house, too? What about the motorhome? I hadn't seen any cables or anything connecting it to the house. Did it run off batteries? If so, a power cut wouldn't affect it. I could go there and not only have light and heat, but whatever else I needed, too. I could even *stay* there.

I moved quickly to preserve what little battery power I had left, swapping my sweat pants for a more hardy pair of jeans and grimacing as I slipped my bare feet – I was out of dry socks – into what was left of my sodden, muddy ballet flats that were literally coming apart at the seams, ripped to shreds by the gravel. I pulled my charger from the wall socket and put it in a pocket of the jacket that zipped closed. I went to the table to grab the call-sheet with Donal's number, just in case—

But it wasn't there.

On the table was a magazine I'd taken from the Aer Lingus lounge, my A4 pad that I'd been making script notes on and the pages of my script that weren't scattered on the bed.

No call-sheet.

I pointed the beam of the phone at the floor under the table, swept it back and forth, just to make sure. There was nothing on the floor.

It hadn't slipped off the table. The call-sheet was gone.

A chill snaked up my spine.

Taking my boots from the deck was one thing, but coming inside my cabin and removing the only contact information I had for anyone else on set was something else. Coming inside my cabin to take anything *at all* was crossing a line, but the fact that it was everyone else's phone numbers – my only source of help – felt different to everything else that had happened up until now.

It felt like danger.

But still, at this point, my overriding emotion was rage. I was preparing to stomp my way back through the trees, looking and acting like I didn't give one single shit, so I could outwit these idiots by holing up in the motorhome where, once my phone was fully charged, I'd carry on down the track to call Lindsey and get her to unleash hell, preferably in the form of legal action. I would get more money – the money I'd been promised plus compensation for this. And I'd burn that NDA in a spectacular bonfire. Write a personal essay. Did the *Hollywood Reporter* take those? You say #MeToo has gone too far, but yet in 2022 a production lured a young female actor to a secluded film set where they (supposedly) abandoned and then terrorised her. A young female actor who, not that long ago, had had a breakdown. On *set*.

If that's what Steve Dade thought directing was, he didn't deserve to get to do it. He didn't deserve to direct people to their seats in the cinema. I'd make it my goal to make damn sure he'd never work in this industry again.

But then I remembered that I *did* have contact information for someone else: Peg. She'd given me her card and told me she lived nearby, just before the bridge at the bottom of the hill. I could call her and get her to come get me. I could just *leave*. Go to the nearest village or town that had a hotel or a B&B in it, check in and initiate Operation Crush Steve Dickhead Dade from there.

But I couldn't exactly haul my suitcase back down to the house in this weather in these shoes, so for now, I put my debit card and my passport into the same zipped pocket as the phone charger. I went to the wardrobe where the wool coat I'd worn here was hanging, and reached into the pocket for Peg's card—

And felt nothing but the scratchy material of the pocket's insides.

I yanked the coat towards me and put my hand in the other pocket, even though I was sure I'd had the card in my right hand. There was nothing in there either.

I pulled the coat out of the wardrobe, threw it on the bed and pointed the light from the phone directly into the pockets to make absolutely sure the card wasn't there.

What the …?

Someone had taken the boots from outside and the call-sheet off my table *and* Peg's business card from inside the pocket of a coat that was hanging in the wardrobe.

No one knew I had that card, which meant someone had come in here and *searched through my things*, my personal possessions. Looking for items I might turn to in a situation like this, so they could remove them.

So they could keep me here.

So they could *trap* me.

I was willing to ascribe all the script parallels to Steve and his band of merry manchildren, but I couldn't do the same with someone coming into my cabin and taking things I needed to have. We were all here to do a job, and any idiot who did their job like this would surely know they'd never get to work again.

And Steve Dade wasn't an idiot. He was a Bright Young Thing. He'd got a green light from Lindsey, who'd been in this business for more than two decades, which left two possibilities. Either someone on the crew was actually a psycho who had somehow engineered the departure of everyone else from set, leaving me alone with him in the middle of nowhere with no power and no reception and no numbers for the rest of the crew, or ...

Someone who wasn't on the crew *at all* had done that.

I locked my phone's screen, plunging the space back into darkness. I had to preserve every ounce of battery power I had, because I was going to need it for my new plan, the one I really should've had from the very beginning, back when there'd been that first knock on the door.

Getting the fucking hell out of here.

SIXTEEN

The rain was heavy and freezing, stinging on my skin, and the noise of it was so loud, it interfered with my trying to navigate. After just a few steps of slipping and sliding and one near-fall in the dark, I resigned myself to having to use some of my phone's battery power to light my way back to the house. I held the phone parallel to the ground, the cuff of my coat *mostly* protecting it from the rain, and hoped the moisture wouldn't make charging this thing the least of my problems. The alternative was breaking a leg, even though the screen was already showing the battery had depleted to just – *shit* – nine per cent.

But being able to see where I was going was a contaminated comfort. I was the only light in the night and the light was moving with me. If someone was out there in the dark, I may as well be wearing a flashing neon target on my back. If Steve was out there filming me, I was helpfully *lighting the scene* for him. And my having a light made the dark beyond the torchlight beam even thicker and more impenetrable to me.

If Steve *was* out there, that was best-case scenario at this point. If he wasn't, and I really was alone except for whoever was doing this to me …

A trickle of panic flowed into my chest and sped up my heart.

The dark was the thing. If I was making this journey during daylight hours, I wouldn't even be stressed, let alone scared. It wasn't like it was the middle of the night, either; it wasn't yet ten o'clock. How worried would I be about walking to the IHOP on Laurel Canyon from my place back in LA? Not at all. I had done that much later than I was doing this, more than once, and it was a much longer walk. The woods, this place – it was just a different kind of landscape, that was all. And this was a movie-*set*, not a movie. Serial killers and random violent psychos are much rarer than Hollywood would have us believe. I was almost certainly fine. There was no real danger.

That's what I kept telling myself, anyway. When it did nothing to calm me, I started counting my footsteps silently in my head.

As soon as I'd safely descended the stone steps into the walled garden, I switched off my phone, wiped its screen against the part of my jeans that my jacket had managed to keep dry, and put it in the zipped pocket.

Then I stared down the dark. For a few seconds, my vision failed to pick out anything. It was as if four solid walls had risen up around me. The darkness was so thick, it felt like something I could reach out and touch.

But, gradually, the solid shape of the house began to emerge from the black, its outline a contrast to the ever-so-slightly less dark sky.

I moved in a straight line across the walled garden, wincing as the sharp edges of the gravel path pressed into the soles of my ballet flats, heavy now with mud, slippery and loose, my toes squelching inside them.

I vowed never to travel anywhere without more robust footwear ever again.

I held my hands out at hip-level, waiting to feel the structure of the central fountain that would mark the halfway point to the house, hoping my hand wouldn't touch something else first.

Some*one* else.

Theoretically there could be a person following right behind me, unseen and – thanks to the thunderous roar of the rain – unheard.

A tremor started in one leg, then spread to another, to my hands, my jaw. I couldn't say if this was fear taking over my body or the cold, or both.

The smooth, curved stone of the fountain arrived sooner than I thought and from it, I moved as quickly as I could to the rear wall of the house, smacking both hands on the bi-fold glass doors when I reached it.

It was a relief to be at the house. Even if the power was out in there too, I'd feel safer inside than I would running around the woods. I moved to the right until I felt the shape of the handle and pulled—

But nothing happened.

My fingers were numb with the cold so, at first, I thought I was at fault. I tried again, and again, pulling harder, throwing my bodyweight into the move to help. The door wouldn't give.

Last time, it had slid open smoothly, without much effort at all. Now, it wouldn't budge.

Someone had locked it.

I tried to push down a steadily rising panic, one that was threatening to take me over, to incapacitate me.

Or worse, make me turn towards the treeline and beg Steve to show himself, to stop this. But I'd be damned if I was going to give him the satisfaction.

I cupped my hands to the glass and tried to look inside, to see if the place had electricity. All I could see beyond was uninterrupted dark – no glowing dots of light on a switch or an appliance. From memory, I knew I had a clear line of sight into the kitchen. I should be able to see a glowing microwave clock at the very least.

So the power was out in there, too.

Trailing one hand along the wall, I felt my way around the side of the house, ducking my head against the driving rain. A few steps before I reached the front corner, the light changed.

There *was* light, now.

So dim it looked more like the memory of a light, the kind you see on the back of your eyelids after staring at something bright for a while, but it was there. I picked up my pace, hurrying to reach the clearing, to see for myself—

A light was on inside the motorhome.

Pulling the door of the motorhome closed behind me was like waking up in the middle of a nightmare, right at the moment when the sleeping version of you felt sure you were about to die at the hands of whatever villain had infiltrated your dreams.

Suddenly, everything was normal. There was no threat. I was inside, out of the dark and the rain and the cold and the endless yawning abyss of the night. I was out of the trees – they surrounded the motorhome, too, but at a distance; it didn't feel as claustrophobic as the cabin did for this reason, even though it was a smaller space. The rain against the roof was even louder here, but the lights were on. There was electricity – it must run off batteries, so – and I could lock the only door with a sturdy-seeming safety chain. I removed my rain jacket and kicked off what was left of my ballet flats, luxuriating in the feel of the motorhome's carpeted flooring beneath my bare, freezing feet, and took a deep breath for the first time in what felt like hours.

The normality of the scene, the safety of it, immediately started pushing the reason I'd come here out of my mind.

Couldn't I just stay *here*? I could charge my phone. I had a bathroom of sorts. (Okay, yeah, I wasn't supposed to use it, but the more I thought about someone on this crew having to empty it after me, the more I wanted to if only out of spite.) It couldn't be that hard to figure out how to transform the table into the bed. There was hot water here, coffee and tea, and – I opened the little fridge under the kitchen counter – even some milk, too. I could just wait here, sleep here, until it got light outside. If no one reappeared by then, I'd walk out to the road with my fully charged phone and call whoever I needed to.

Peg, to come and get me. Well, if she had a website or a Facebook page or something and I could find her number online.

Lindsey, to initiate my legal action.

Julia, to tell her that her congratulations had been premature and that this *was* too soon. I should've told John no. I should've told him to fuck *right* off.

John. The guy from Cross Cut Films who'd called to offer me this part in the first place. Where was he? Was he back at the office in Dublin? I had his number in my phone, I could call him.

If I didn't get through to Donal, that's what I'd do.

I plugged in my phone and set the electric kettle to boil. I checked that the doors at the front, the ones that gave direct access to the front seats, had their locks engaged, and that all the blinds were pulled down. There were two 5L plastic bottles of water on the floor near the table, which made me try the tap over the kitchen sink: no running water, but plenty in those bottles to do me. I took the robe I'd worn earlier off its hanger and pulled it on over my clothes in an effort to get warm.

I felt in the pockets: empty. The rogue page of script had been removed.

I set about searching for socks. There were none in or around the clothing rail, but I found a bundle of brand-new men's trainer liners in a gym bag that had been stuffed in the storage cupboard. Putting one pair on felt so good, I put another pair over them for good measure and tucked a third into a pocket of the rain jacket for later.

There was no discernible difference between the motorhome's interior now and when I'd last seen it a couple of hours ago: the tabletop to the rear had nothing on it, but every other flat surface was covered in stuff. Because – of course – this was wardrobe and make-up and Donal's room and ...

The production office.

A production office had to have a call-sheet around somewhere. A call-sheet and phone numbers. Like, the one for the taxi service who'd delivered the lead actress here.

Starting at the clothing rail, I worked my way around the motorhome in a clockwise direction, going through everything quickly but thoroughly. Checking every drawer, cupboard and box. Searching through every sheaf of paper, opening notebooks and box-files. Rifling through every cubbyhole, checking every compartment on or near the dash. I even went through the pockets on the back of the front seats.

But I didn't find a single call-sheet. No leftover copies of yesterday's, no stack ready to be distributed for what should've been tonight's shoot. Moreover, there was no contact information for anyone at all. No list of phone numbers. No address book. No card for Peg's taxi company – or any other taxi company, for that matter. No number for the owner of the house.

In the *production office*.

Again, the word *coincidence* was having to do some seriously heavy lifting.

I did find something useful: a chunky yellow torch that, miraculously, came on when I pressed the power button. I set it on the kitchen counter, just in case I had to go out in the dark again.

Or if this thing's batteries die on me.

I hadn't thought about that possibility until now. The motorhome must have limited power, but I had no clue how much. How long did a motorhome battery last? I started turning things off until the only thing left on was the small light over the table, the fridge and the socket charging my phone. I shouldn't have wasted power boiling the kettle, really, but now that I had, I figured I might as well make it worth it. I made myself a cup of tea and bent to open the fridge door.

And spotted the cupboard I hadn't checked, the one I hadn't realised was there. There was built-in seating around the table, and one of the panels underneath the seats had a handle on it.

I had to crawl under the table to access it.

There were only two things inside, if you discounted dust bunnies: a heavy laptop bag and something wrapped in a plastic carrier bag that felt like a book. I unzipped the laptop bag and found an old MacBook inside. I tried powering it up, but nothing happened and there was no charging cable. I set it aside and turned my attention to the other bag, the plastic one, holding it by its end so the object inside slipped out and on to the floor.

It was indeed a book. A prop book.

It was another copy of *First Draft*.

There was a shelf full of these on set, over in the main house. Why would one copy of it be here, wrapped in a plastic bag and stuffed in a cupboard in the production office? I turned the book over, but the front and back covers were exactly the same as the one I'd held in my hands during last night's shoot. So what made this one different, if anything did? Why was this one wrapped in a plastic bag and hidden away?

Flicking through, I got my answer.

This wasn't another book with one of Donal's covers slapped on it, this was an actual copy of *First Draft* – sort of. Most of the pages were blank, but the ones that weren't had the text from the script, the extracts the audience would hear me read as Kate in voiceover. I presumed it was going to be used for close-ups, where the camera would actually pick up the words Kate was reading. It even had a proper title page, *First Draft: A Novel by Gary Sheridan*, and a dedication—

The book slid from my hands and landed on the floor, open to it.

To Adele, who should never have come to Cedarwood House.

What the actual—

I touched my fingertips to the words, trying to smudge them, trying to reveal the ones I knew should be there instead. I blinked rapidly to clear whatever hallucinatory fog was responsible for this mirage. I closed my eyes, shut the book, waited. Opened the book and my eyes again.

But the words remained.

To Adele, who should never have come to Cedarwood House.

I stood up quickly, backing away from it, as if the object itself presented a threat.

Something flickered in my peripheral vision: a little red indicator light, on a console just above the door.

Beneath a label that said, LEISURE BATTERY CHARGE.

Then the same console started beeping.

Shit shit shit.

The power was going. I grabbed my phone, bringing its screen to life. Eleven per cent charge and—

A little red circle with a '1' in it, telling me I had an unread text. My eyes immediately went to where I'd expect bars of service to be, but there were none.

How had I got a text?

I hadn't checked for any when I'd first come in; I'd only plugged in the phone and waited for the electronic *ding* that confirmed it was charging. If I'd heard the beep of the battery warning, I would definitely have heard a new text alert. That meant that somewhere between the cabin and here, unbeknownst to me, I'd met a mysterious reception pocket and this new text had made its way on to my phone.

My anonymous friend was back. This time, they'd sent a command, and typed it in all caps.

GET OUT OF THERE NOW.

EXT. CHERRY COTTAGE - DUSK

Darkness is falling fast; the forest is
already thick with it. Rain makes a PITTER-
PATTER sound on the leaves and the ground.

Kate takes off running across the gravel, each
step CRUNCHING, the beam of her torch sweeping
back and forth across the ground.

EXT. DIRT TRACK - NIGHT

Kate reaches the muddy, uneven ground of the
dirt track, muting her footsteps. She stumbles
and trips, but doesn't fall. A dense forest
looms on either side of the track, pitch black
beyond the narrow beam of her torch.

The rain and wind worsen. Drenching sheets
whip against Kate's face, get into her eyes,
flattening her hair. She slows, her breathing
more laboured, her gait increasingly flailing
and desperate, until suddenly—

Kate falls face-first on to the ground and,
simultaneously, the torchlight disappears.

A beat passes.

We see Kate then, lit only by moonlight, lying
on the ground, submerged from the knees down
in a pothole filled with cloudy water. She
winces and groans as she pulls herself up on
to her knees and out of the water. She looks
for the torch—

                              KATE
                           (mutters)
        Fuck.

-and finds it lying in pieces a few feet away,
useless and broken.

Kate gingerly gets to her feet. Everything
that has been on the ground - one cheek,
her hands, the front of her clothing - is
thick with mud and her jeans are soaked and
clinging. Tears threaten, then come.

Something SNAPS in the trees to Kate's left.

Her head turns towards the sound, her eyes
wide with fear. At the sound of a second SNAP,
Kate - as best she can - takes off running
again. She doesn't look back.

EXT. MAIN ROAD - NIGHT

The ground beneath Kate's feet changes from
muddy dirt to slick tarmac; she has made it to
the main road.

She stops, bent at the waist, winded. She
gulps down a couple of deep breaths, then
straightens up to survey the scene. Kate looks
to her right. There are no cars, no lights,
no signs of life. She looks to her left, the
direction from which she and Joel arrived
earlier, and finds a similar scene. She turns
to look behind her, at the track that leads
back to the house.

Resignedly, she turns right and starts
walking.

EXT. MAIN ROAD - LATER SAME NIGHT

Kate limps along a road so dark that we can't
really see her - only hear her. Shuffling,
irregular footsteps. Shallow breaths.
Whimpering.

>   KATE
>   (whispering)
>   You're okay. You're okay.
>   (voice breaking)
>   You'll be okay.

And then—

A pinprick of white light appears in the
distance.

Kate stops. She blinks, squints.

We see the light from her POV, her vision
blurred by tears and rain - and watch as the
light comes into focus, splits into two, each
orb growing brighter, bigger—

Kate, lit now by the approaching white light,
raises a hand to shield her eyes from it.

And now we *hear* something too: an ENGINE. A
car is coming up the road. Kate runs towards
it, into the middle of the road, waving her
arms.

>   KATE (CONT'D)
>   (shouting)
>   Hey! Hey! Stop, please!

The car SCREECHES to a stop just feet from
Kate, its engine idling.

> KATE (CONT'D)
> (quietly)
> Please … Please be help … Please.

A long beat passes.

The driver's door opens slowly. A booted foot
steps on to the road.

From behind the driver's shoulder, we see Kate
stare at him, open-mouthed.

Then we see the driver staring at Kate, pale-
faced, features twisted with confusion.

It's Joel.

SEVENTEEN

Stay or go? Stay or go? Stay or go?

I stood stock-still in the motorhome, staring at the text, paralysed by indecision. The dedication in the prop book ... I couldn't even begin to make sense of that. More mind games? Another way to try to scare me? But if so, why hide it away?

No one could've predicted I'd even come in here, let alone search the place – and I'd only found that cupboard by chance.

Stay.

But I'd come in here because it was the only place with a light on, so maybe it wasn't entirely unpredictable.

Did they leave a light on *so that* I'd come in here?

Go.

Was I really expected to take that text seriously, though? I mean, come on. It was straight out of Horror Movie Tropes 101. Presumably I was supposed to get the text message outside, with a hidden camera on me, and my seeing it would be accompanied by a beat of ominous, stomach-dropping percussion in the score – in the alternate fantasy universe where actors were secretly filmed and still agreed, after the fact, to sign the release, which was the one in which Steve Dade apparently operated.

If I'd had any service, I'd have texted back, *How?? In THIS weather?*

I'd been right the first time: the texts had come from someone on the production. Hadn't I seen Donal come out of the motorhome, when I'd arrived, with a phone in his hand?

Hadn't I just got the second text then, the one that warned me this wasn't safe? There'd probably been a modem or something in here then that had been removed since.

Stay.

This was all just a bunch of bullshit that a gang of idiots had mistaken for talent and creativity and art. But how far were they prepared to go? I suspected that *Final Draft* was really *Secretly Filmed Footage Lawsuit*, but I *knew* that I was effectively alone at a house in the middle of nowhere with terrible mobile phone service and no power, and that no one not associated with the production knew exactly where I was.

Go.

What if something went wrong? *More* wrong? What if something happened to me? What if whoever was out there in the woods was under strict instructions to *National Geographic* this and not interfere even if I needed help?

Go.

My phone had ten per cent battery unless the power came back on. The only place I knew for sure I could make a call was halfway down the dirt track. If I went and did that now, I could. I would have enough power. But if I didn't, and I stayed in here, and later the situation changed …

I might not be able to make any calls at all.

Go.

Outside was dark and cold and wet and hiding an untold number of other people whose plans and intentions I didn't fully know. In here, it was dry and warm, there was a bed, and I was alone with a locked door between me and everyone else.

Stay.

My eyes strayed to the front of the motorhome, to the passenger and driver doors. I'd checked their locks were engaged. But this was a vehicle. It had keys, and those keys undoubtedly unlocked those doors from the other side. I hadn't come across them in my search of the motorhome. Someone else must have them.

Go.

A dull pounding was building at my temples. It was proving impossible to untangle this shit, to get a grip on it. In the end, I didn't know which was the better option, what I should do. I couldn't decide.

I could only identify what I *wanted* to do.

And I knew that I wanted to not be in this situation. I wanted to not be here. I wanted to get the fuck away from Cedarwood House, *Final Draft*, Steve Dickhead Dade and this whole entire awful mess. So ...

Go. Right now. GO.

Shoes. Rain jacket. Torch. Phone. Deep breaths.

I unlocked the motorhome's door and pushed it open. Instantaneously, the wind caught it and smacked it against the motorhome's body with such force that it bounced back and I had to push it open for a second time. I took another deep breath and forced myself to step out and down, on to the gravel.

And into what felt like a cyclone.

The rain wasn't falling any more, but whipping in every direction, a tumult of driving, drenching sheets that were instantaneously hitting the ground *and* coming up from it, so dipping my head and pulling the hood of the rain jacket tight around my face was no protection. The wind was blowing against me, trying to stop my forward motion and forcing my breath back into my lungs. The cold was biting and I'd come outside wearing ridiculous shoes that were already wet over socks that were quickly becoming that; within moments, my feet were painfully numb with the cold. Then there was the noise, the constant, thunderous roar of rain and wind and the things the rain and wind were hitting that made it impossible to hear anything else.

And all of this was happening in a dark so deep that when I lifted what I knew to be a bright yellow torch in front of my face, I couldn't pick out its paint colour. I felt for the switch on the handle and turned it on. The beam was narrow and weak and only willing to show me four, maybe five feet in front.

It made the dark beyond the light seem even denser than before.

I thought, *I can't do this*. I couldn't walk halfway down the track in these conditions and there was no way I'd make it to the road. I was already out of breath, I was trembling with the cold and I could hardly see where I was going.

And then I thought, *Perhaps I don't have to do it*.

The man I'd overheard earlier – I didn't know who he was, but I was sure what I'd heard was him talking on the phone. I'd just been about to walk through the stone pillars; he must have been standing at or near the far corner of the house. I pushed my way through the wind and rain to cross the clearing and position myself in the same spot.

I turned off the torch and tucked it under my arm, then I took out my phone. In the moment it took to bring it to life, a spray of droplets spread across the screen. If I drowned the thing, I was in a real trouble. I unzipped my jacket and held the phone inside it, to my chest, wincing as an icy wind forced its way in there too.

I was going to have to be methodical about this; I didn't have infinite time to wander around out here looking for a signal. I mentally marked out a path from the front door of the house to just past its far corner, by the hedge that had taken over the job of marking a boundary from the crumbling stone wall, and walked its length, counting to five between my steps, watching my phone's screen for signs of service. When none appeared, I repeated the walk in the opposite direction, having moved a few feet further away from the house.

I managed to do this five times before I had moved far enough away that I was now back within touching distance of the motorhome and I *still* hadn't found a mysterious pocket of service. While I'd been looking, the phone's battery had dropped to eight per cent and I'd started to feel overwhelmed with a sudden, debilitating exhaustion. I knew what it was, and it wasn't anything to do with jet-lag, my weird sleep schedule over the last forty-eight hours or exertion. It was my wanting to give up.

To give in.

To stop fighting this, whatever *this* was.

I looked longingly at the motorhome, which still had a light on inside. Its batteries might be about to die, but the motorhome was still (relatively) warm and dry. I wanted to be back in there and not out here, in the rain and the dark.

Well, if we were wanting things, I'd go for being magically teleported away from here, back to civilisation, to somewhere where there were other people.

And if we had magic at our disposal, I'd use it to turn back time and never come to this godforsaken place at all. I'd tell John to take his offer and his NDA and his business-class flight and shove them all up his arse.

The light inside the motorhome flickered and went out.

I put away my phone, zipped up my rain jacket and turned the torch back on. I thought about how good it would feel to open the door to a luxury hotel room right now – one with a Jacuzzi tub, complimentary robe and slippers, a mammoth club sandwich on the room-service menu and Egyptian-cotton sheets. I thought about burrowing down inside those sheets after a warm bath, in a carb coma.

I told myself that that's what I was walking to, and then I set off down the dirt track.

It was impossible to accurately judge the passage of time or the distance walked when I could only see the dim beam of the torch ahead of me and hear nothing but the indiscernible roar of the rain and the wind.

I didn't think it would do me any good to know. The cold was becoming a distraction, a painful numbness in my extremities, a burning on my tongue, a stinging on my exposed skin. My legs were growing heavy – literally, because of the moisture and mud my inappropriate footwear was collecting with each step, and figuratively because I was steadily losing the motivation to keep moving them. I had never walked the full length of the track and was worried that I was misremembering the car journey along it, that it was far longer than my time in Peg's taxi might have led me to believe. I thought repeatedly about stopping, finding some shelter among the trees and waiting there, sitting in the mud, for someone else to appear and take me away from this.

When I wasn't thinking that, I was wondering how on earth I had ended up in this situation.

How had it come to this?

And then, eventually, I was too tired and cold and wet to think about anything, so I just concentrated on putting one foot in front of the other and zoned out.

And then the wind eased and the rain stopped.

I thought I was imagining it at first. I stopped, pulled down my hood, listened. No roaring wind, no whipping rain. But it wasn't quiet. It was a *kind* of quiet, but not silent. The fury of the weather had been replaced by a new soundtrack: the indeterminate noises of the natural world at night. Rustling leaves. A snapping branch. The ungodly shriek of some unidentifiable bird.

A trickle of running water.

When I swept the beam of the torch to the side of the track I saw that this was rainwater, running in a little natural gutter. There was something shiny glinting in the stream. A coin, maybe. I stepped closer and stopped, pointing the torch at it, bending to look.

But the slap of my footsteps didn't stop.

I frowned, confused, and then realising, I froze.

What I was hearing weren't *my* footsteps. Not only was I standing still, but even when I had been walking, I couldn't have made the noise I was hearing now. I was in disintegrating ballet flats that hadn't had much of a sole to begin with – if I made any sound when my feet touched the ground, it was a squelch in the mud.

The steps I could hear now were dull thuds, as if the walker was in a pair of heavy-duty boots.

They were behind me, at a distance, and apparently had been masked by the noise of my moving – my breaths, the *whooshing* sound of my rain jacket as I pumped my arms, the thunderous beat of my pulse in my ears.

Until now.

Someone had followed me down the track. *Was* following me. Present tense.

With a shaking hand, I switched off the torch.

The darkness rushed in at me from all sides, cloaking me. *Choking* me. It was so thick, I couldn't see my hand in front of my face. I couldn't see anything. I couldn't even tell the forest from the track.

I hadn't moved, but I was struck by a sudden uncertainty about which way I was facing. What was down the track now? Right or left? Where was the house? Behind me?

My heartbeat thundered in my chest, reacting to a rising panic that was threatening to overtake me. I gulped down a few deep breaths, forced the icy air deep into my lungs, closing my eyes and making myself count slowly – silently – as I exhaled it. I thought about the imaginary hotel room I'd told myself I was walking to, how relaxed I'd feel once I got there. I told myself that nothing was wrong, that I wasn't in danger. At the very worst, I was at risk for exposure to assholery, thanks to Steve Dickhead Dade and his crew.

After about thirty seconds of this, the thunderous noise of my own beating heart subsided.

I held my next breath and listened. As far as I could tell, the footsteps had stopped.

I could hear the little trickle of water again. I knew that was to the right of the track and I knew it followed alongside it, so all I had to do was keep it close to me and keep it on my right and I'd be moving in the right direction, even if I couldn't see a thing.

Tentatively, I put one foot in front of the other. Solid, relatively smooth ground. I took another step, feeling the surface with what remained of the sole of my shoe before risking putting my weight on it. It was the only way to avoid tripping or falling, or stepping into a massive pothole that would *cause* me to trip or fall.

In practice, it was more like sliding along the path than walking along it, but it was forward motion and that's what mattered. I set off again, moving as carefully as I could while still maintaining a decent pace, careful not to move away from the trickling water sound.

And then—

SNAP.

A branch or a twig, breaking in the trees to my right.

Immediately to my right.

With a dawning horror, I realised that whoever's footsteps I'd heard hadn't stopped following me somewhere back along the path. They'd simply moved into the treeline, where the soft forest floor masked the sound.

And now, I could *hear* something else belonging to them.

Their breathing.

Not as close to me as the trickling water, but not too far away from it.

Someone was standing to my right, in the trees, *breathing*.

Hiding.

Waiting.

I could feel them. Sense them. It was the opposite of the feeling in the house earlier, when I'd gone upstairs hoping to find a sleeping crew but knew, once I'd reached the landing, that I wouldn't. That air was dead and still.

This air was alive and electric and pulsing with not one but two beating hearts, and it wasn't bloody wildlife that was responsible.

There was another person out here, hiding in the dark.

I didn't know what else to do except take the advice of my anonymous text-message sender. I sucked in a breath and then I took off running.

For three, maybe four strides.

Then it happened.

Nothing was there, and then something was. Something hard and horizontal, thicker than my arm, just below my knee.

A branch.

Sticking out into the middle of the track, maybe a foot off the ground.

I wasn't expecting it and ran right into it, at full tilt, exploding a pain so intense in my right leg that it felt like a nuclear detonation, a blinding flash that instantly vaporised everything else, reducing the world to nothing except the dark and white-hot pain.

I cried out.

My heart beat and the pain changed, retracting, racing in from its edges to its epicentre: a line across the middle of my right shin.

And then I was falling, flying, forwards through the air.

Tripping over the branch.

My right hand hit the ground first, my wrist twisting, another, smaller mushroom cloud exploding. My left hit second, hurting too but in a different way. As I landed I felt something protest in the depths of my right ankle, and then it sent a burning flare all the way up my leg and into my hip joint.

And then I was flat on the cold, wet ground; my cheek in water; limbs at angles they shouldn't be.

In the next heart beat the mushroom cloud of pain bloomed again, pulling in more power, billowing and growing, pulsing in fire at the points of injury, and I couldn't breathe, I couldn't breathe, I couldn't take a breath—

I closed my eyes and watched real darkness fall.

EIGHTEEN

Pain was the next thing I knew, swiftly followed by cold and wet.

I had never been so aware of my body. I could feel *everything*. Every bruise busy forming beneath my skin; every wet, groaning, swelling limb; the dark pebble digging into my right cheek and the muddy rainwater that had pooled in dark depressions in the dirt; and the hard and sharp thing digging into my ribs that I hoped wasn't one of my actual ribs, broken. It was as if every last cell was sending a full status update.

I was lying on my stomach on the ground and had no idea if I'd been out for moments, minutes or hours, but seeing as I hadn't frozen to death yet, I figured the answer had to be on the shorter end of the scale.

What the fuck had just happened?

I had tripped over a fallen branch in the dark. Or …

I had tripped over a branch that had felt like it had been hovering above the ground, like it was *being held there*.

Which wasn't as insane as it sounded, seeing as, moments before I fell, I'd heard a twig snap and what sounded like someone hiding in the trees to my right.

And moments before *that*, footsteps, following me down the track.

Or had I?

Could I say for sure that's what I'd heard? It was so dark out here, and the forest so noisy – it could've been something else that I mistook for that. A snapping twig on a forest floor was hardly an isolated event, and the branch I'd tripped over could've just fallen into the track, been blown down there by the wind.

Because why on earth would someone trip me, try to hurt me, on purpose? Freaking me out in the name of *Final Draft* was one thing, but *physically assaulting me* was a crime.

And an accident made what I had to do next easier, because I didn't really have time for abject, in-fear-for-my-life terror right now. I had to get up, get down the track and on to the main road so I could call someone.

Imagined footsteps and bad weather blowing down the branch it was then.

I gritted my teeth and exhaled hard, trying to breathe through the pain. It was difficult to tell what was stinging cold, what was cramping limbs and what, if anything, was actual injury.

I tested each extremity in turn, checking I could move it. Right arm: check. Left arm: check. Left leg: check. Right leg—

Shit.

Something was wrong with my right ankle. I could move it but it hurt like hell. If I'd done something to it that meant I couldn't get up and walk, then I was all out of ideas. I had a vision of my dragging myself back up the track and across the gravel to the motorhome, skin scraping into bloody ribbons, and I thought, *Even if I manage that, how will I get myself inside?*

Hopelessness tightened my chest, threatening to overwhelm me, and I felt a new heat on my face: tears. All I wanted to do was surrender, to give up, to close my eyes and let whatever would happen happen. I wanted someone to come and help me, to solve this for me.

I couldn't do this by myself.

As if on cue, rain started spitting again. It sounded louder than ever, a sustained cacophony of drops hitting leaves all around me. My teeth were chattering now, the cold feeling like it had penetrated my bone marrow. I couldn't stay here. I couldn't wait for someone to come save me.

I had no other choice: I *had* to save myself.

I didn't know exactly how far down the track I'd walked, but it felt like going back to the motorhome would be a longer journey than continuing down to the road where I could make a call—

My phone. Was it still working?

Needing to check was a great motivator. Breathing hard through the rolling waves of aches and pains, I managed to bring my hands up to my chest and then gingerly push myself up on to my knees. I didn't have the sharp pain in my ribs any more – that had been my phone. It was zipped into my jacket pocket and I'd fallen on top of it. That part of the jacket was wet to the touch, though, miraculously, the phone inside wasn't even damp – and it was, crucially, still working.

A small, spiderweb crack had appeared on the screen's bottom-right corner, but otherwise the glass was intact. I brought the screen to life, not caring about the light because *what had just happened was an accident.*

No service. Battery down to six per cent.

I surveyed the scene using only the light from the phone's home screen. The treeline was still to my right. One of my ballet flats had come off and was lying a couple of feet away; I reached to pick it up. The torch was lying in several pieces

237

off to my left, shards of its broken bulb reflecting the light back to me like little stars deep in a dirt sky.

I couldn't see any branch on the road now but I told myself that was because it was outside the reach of the phone's dim light, or because I'd landed several feet past it in a sort of flying fall, or a combination of both.

Because *what had just happened was an accident.*

I switched off the phone and put it back in my pocket – I needed the battery to last until I got to the road.

And I *had* to get to the road.

The headlines were that everything hurt like hell, but still worked. Nothing seemed broken; I'd watched enough episodes of *Grey's Anatomy* to know that if I could move something, the bone connecting it must be intact. I could wiggle the foot below the searing pain of whatever was going on with my ankle, so at worst it was a sprain.

But could I actually walk on it? Slowly, gradually, carefully, I brought one knee up until I was in the world's most awkward, painful lunge. Then, hands out ready to brace myself in case of a total collapse, I tested my other ankle's reaction to my weight in tiny increments until I found myself upright, balanced precariously and unsteady on my feet, but standing.

Just about.

The ballet flat had come off my bad ankle, so I stood on one leg and, after a couple of failed tries, managed to slip it back on just before I would've toppled over completely.

I tried putting all my weight on the bad ankle, as a test. *Fail.* Fresh pain shot up my leg, making me cry out.

Nope, not doing that again.

I took one tentative step forward with my good leg, followed by the quickest step possible with my bad one. There was a sharp twinge of painful protest, but I managed to take a step. If I limped and moved quickly and ignored the pain, I could, theoretically, walk to the main road.

And then I'd put a stop to this, whatever this was. For once and for all. I was injured now and even though *what happened was an accident*, this much was clear: I needed to get the hell out of here. This wasn't about *Final Draft* or Steve Dade or even trying to get Peg to come and get me, not any more. I was done with all that.

When I got to the main road, I was going to make one phone call, and it was going to be to the Gardaí.

I walked until I was sure I couldn't physically do it any more, until taking another step may as well have been the effort required to summit Everest, but I didn't stop. I kept putting one foot in front of the other, telling myself I'd take just one more step, one more, one more.

Whatever adrenalin I'd had in my veins had long seeped away, leaving my muscles screaming in protest and my breath feeling like it couldn't penetrate my lungs. My chest burned. My lower right leg felt like one big bruise. My ankle screamed. I was newly aware of the elasticated cuff of the sock and wondered if maybe that was because the ankle was swelling. I tried to remember what life had been like when I didn't feel these things, when I'd been blissfully unaware of my own body, but I couldn't.

When I searched for forms in the dark, I could just about make out a stretch of road ahead of me. I'd been in the dark so long, my vision could finally differentiate it from the walls of dark on either side. That was progress.

I'd stuck to the treeline on the road's right-hand side, hobbling alongside the little gutter, listening in case the trickle of rainwater started to sound further away. The forest felt alive with sound and movement. I occasionally patted my coat pocket, feeling for the reassuring shape of my phone zipped safely inside there.

Maintaining a steady rhythm was my only painkiller. I reduced the entire world to the pinprick focus of my own footsteps. Normal step, quick step, normal step. One foot in front of the other, braced for the bad one, luxuriating in the one that didn't hurt.

And then, finally – it could have been minutes or hours or an eternity later – I rounded a bend and saw gates.

The gates.

I'd made it to the road.

I'd made it to the road and I could *see something*. Not the actual moon, but what must be moonlight, finding enough of a gap in the forest to actually reach the ground.

I wanted to cry with relief. The last time I'd seen the gates, Peg and her *Jurassic Park* sweatshirt were nosing her cab through. How was it that that was just a day ago? It felt like a scene from another life. But I hadn't *seen* the gates then, actually. Because they'd been standing open, pushed all the way back.

Now they were not only closed, but a thick, industrial-looking chain looped around the place where they met had locked them that way.

I put that in a box and put the box in the back of my mind to worry about later. Right now, I just needed to get past them and on to the road. The railings were horizontal and spaced well apart – a person could easily climb over them, although not a person who was doing well just to remain upright and didn't know how much longer she could stand the pain that was the price of doing that. But the moonlight was as good as floodlight to someone who'd spent the length of a dirt track in the relentless dark. I scanned the stretch of hedge on either side of the gates that joined it to the treeline, and spotted a thinning area to the left that I could push through.

It meant scratches and more mud, and a misstep on soft ground which made my bad ankle feel like it was cracking open for a brief moment, but this was immediately followed by my first step with my good leg on to smooth, hard tarmacadam.

The actual road.

There was a part of me that had started to wonder if I'd dreamed it up, if the world beyond the grounds of Cedarwood House and the forest that surrounded it was just a figment of my imagination. Standing on its solid, even surface in my sodden ballet flats may as well have been standing barefoot on the thick, plush carpet in the imaginary hotel room of my mind.

Now I *did* cry with relief.

But although I was on the main road, the night was still intact. I made my way into the middle of it and looked to my left, the way I'd come in Peg's cab, but saw no lights that might indicate houses. No approaching vehicles, no sounds that might be an engine. The forest still loomed over me from both sides of the road, preventing me from seeing anyways into the distance. I turned to look for lights in the other direction and caught a flicker of something reflective, sitting on the ground outside the gates.

A small, square ... box? A couple of foot high. I strained to make out more detail in the unhelpful dark, then decided it was worth a moment's phone battery to check to see what it was.

I moved closer, turned on the phone.

Banishing the dark only made things more mysterious. The box wasn't a box, but a bright green cooler bag, the kind my weekly meal-prep supplies had been delivered to my apartment in when I was trying to lose weight for a role that I ended up doing at the exact same weight I'd been when I'd auditioned because I didn't have any weight to lose. This one didn't have any logo or some awful company name that included words that should never be used to describe food – the company I'd used had managed to incorporate the top-three offenders, *Clean Power Fuel*, ugh – but I couldn't imagine it was designed to do anything except transport fresh food.

I unzipped its top flap and pulled it back.

The cooler bag was filled with a neat stack of foil trays whose white paper lids were marked in Sharpie with various elements of breakfast. *Sausages*, read one. *Rashers*, read another. I counted six large foil trays and two sliced pans – one brown, one white – wedged down the side, the bread squeezed and malformed by the tight space. I put a palm flat on the top tray: cold. I reached down to the bottom of the bag to see if I could detect any heat at all, if I could determine how long this had been sitting out here, when my fingers touched something else: a folded piece of paper.

I pulled it out, opened it and held it in the beam of my phone's light.

It was a note, apparently hastily written in a biro that was giving up the ghost.

This was our breakfast, the one we should've had as a cast and crew hours ago, that the catering service couldn't deliver because someone had locked the gates. I was trying to figure out what to do with this information when the battery notification on my screen dropped to five per cent.

I switched off the torchlight. In the trees, on the other side of the locked gates, just at the end of the dirt track, I *saw* a light.

A red light.

A pinprick of it, dancing in the dark at about head-height.

The afterglow of the light from my phone's screen was still fading from my vision, an overlay floating in front of me in the dark. I tried to blink it away, to get a better look at the light – which then split, separating into two parts.

Like *eyes*.

When I blinked again, it disappeared.

Someone – or something – was *in the trees*.

And then, if I had any doubt, a sound cracked like a gunshot through the night: the *snap* of a twig underfoot, just like before, coming from the same direction.

I lurched away from the gates and into the cover of the treeline alongside them, my back to the road, and limped away as fast as I could, down the road in the direction Peg had brought me, back towards civilisation, towards people, towards help—

Beep.

A single electronic note, as loud as a foghorn in the otherwise silent dark.

Beep. Beep. Beep. Beep. Beep.

Coming from me, somehow …

My phone!

I had finally found some mobile phone service at the absolute worst possible moment, and now a string of text messages was flooding in. It was giving me away, betraying me, pinpointing my location for whoever – whatever? – was coming down the track.

In a blind panic, I tried to flip the switch at the side that would silence it but my hands were shaking and I fumbled, dropping the phone on to the ground, generating *more* noise, a sickening *crack* of glass – if I couldn't use the phone, what would I do then? – and bending down to retrieve it sent a new, boiling wave of pain through my right leg. I swallowed the cry it wanted me to make and tried again with the switch.

Second time lucky. The phone was on silent, but it had already given me away.

Now I had to *get* away.

I didn't know what else to do then, but run.

INT. LIVING SPACE - NIGHT

Back inside the empty cottage, lamplights glow
warmly. A healthy fire burns in the hearth.
The fridge hums. The front door is securely
closed. Kate's charging cable no longer
dangles off the edge of the console table -
because it's plugged into her phone.

Headlights sweep across the windows. Car doors
slam. Keys clink in the front door's lock
before it opens, and Joel helps a shivering,
unsteady Kate inside. She is soaking wet,
covered in mud and has angry red scratches on
her face and hands. She looks around the room,
confused.

                    KATE
     The power's back on.

Joel nods towards the phone on the console
table.

                    JOEL
     And your phone is here.

                    KATE
     But I … It *wasn't* there. Before. It
     was gone, Joel. I swear. Whoever was
     in the attic must have put it back.

                    JOEL
               (dismissively)
     Okay.

                    KATE
     Don't you believe me?

                    JOEL
          Let's just get you warmed up, okay?

He helps her down the hall towards the
bedroom.

INT. BEDROOM - NIGHT

Joel flips on the lights, revealing that
the blinds on the floor-to-ceiling windows
overlooking the trees at the rear of the house
have been retracted once again.

Kate stares at the glass - at their
reflections in it, and then through them, into
the dark.

                    KATE
     I put those down earlier. Did you put
     them up?

                    JOEL
     I don't know. Maybe I did.

                    KATE
     You don't remember?

                    JOEL
     Do you want to talk about the
     curtains or do you want to get
     pneumonia?

Kate relents and sits on the bed. Joel peels
her wet, muddy clothes from her skin.

                    KATE
                (to herself)
     I know I put them down.

Joel reaches out to press the button by the
window and the blinds begin to descend.

INT. LIVING SPACE - LATER SAME NIGHT

Kate sits on the armchair in front of the
fire. Her face is clean, her hair is tied back
and she is bundled up in dry, warm clothes.
She stares glassy-eyed into the flames.

                    JOEL
          Here. Drink this.

Joel hands her a glass of amber liquid.

                    KATE
          What is it?

                    JOEL
          Whiskey. I bought a bottle in town.

                    KATE
          I hate whiskey.

                    JOEL
          Just have a few sips. It'll warm you
          up.

Kate takes the glass, sniffs, makes a face.
She takes a small, tentative sip.

Joel sits down on the other chair.

                    KATE
          Aren't you going to check upstairs?

                    JOEL
          There is no upstairs.

                    KATE
The attic, then.

                    JOEL
Check it for what, Kate? The power's
on and your phone is here. And I bet
...

He gets up and goes to the kitchen counter to
flip through the copy of *First Draft* Kate was
reading.

                JOEL (CONT'D)
Yeah. Look.

He brings the book back to the armchairs and
thrusts it towards Kate, who takes it from
him. It's open to the dedication page, which
now reads, *To Karen, my muse, for coming to
Cherry Cottage.*

                JOEL (CONT'D)
Look, I don't know how to say this so
I'm just going to come out with it,
okay? Are you ...?
        (takes a deep breath)
Kate, are you on any medication? Or
should you be?

                    KATE
Yeah, I am actually. It's called Fuck
You. 100 milligrams twice a day, but
I'm really feeling like I should up
my dosage.

                    JOEL
That's not funny.

                    KATE
     None of this is.

A beat passes.

                 KATE (CONT'D)
     Where were you, Joel? *All day*?

                    JOEL
     I told you.

                    KATE
     No, you didn't.

                    JOEL
     Didn't you get my messages?

Kate looks at him blankly. Joel gets up again,
this time to retrieve Kate's phone.

                 JOEL (CONT'D)
     They're all here. See for yourself.

He hands her the device. New notifications
crowd the screen.

                    KATE
     The phone was off. It died while I
     was on the phone to Gus.

                    JOEL
     I called Belinda and we ended up
     chatting for … I don't know, but it
     must have been two hours at least.
     Then I went to get some wine for us
     and came back to a flat tyre. And no
     fucking spare. Bloody rental company.
     The nearest garage is in the next

town, so I had to get a lift from the
guy who owns the shop …

As he speaks, Kate scrolls through the texts.
They are effectively a real-time, blow-by-blow
of Joel's story.

                    KATE
          So, what? You think I imagined it?

                    JOEL
          I don't know what happened, but
          everything's fine now.

                    KATE
          I don't like it here.

                    JOEL
          Well, maybe you should be more
          discerning in your choice of reading
          material.

                    KATE
          What did Belinda say?

                    JOEL
                 (sighing)
          That I completely overreacted and
          that I should apologise to her.

He moves to sit next to Kate, pulling her in
for an embrace.

                  JOEL(CONT'D)
          And I know I need to apologise to
          you, too.

                    KATE

You do.

                    JOEL

I'm sorry.

                    KATE

You should be.

                    JOEL

I am. I'll make it up to you.
Starting with my making dinner.
                 (pauses)
And then you can tell me your news.

                    KATE
                 (surprised)
What?

                    JOEL

Last night. You said something about
having news?

                    KATE

Oh. Yeah. No.
                 (waves a hand)
It wasn't anything important.

Joel kisses her before heading into the
kitchen.

Kate pulls the copy of *First Draft* into her
lap and stares at it, lost in thought.

NINETEEN

And now I *could* run. Adrenalin, it turns out, is a truly wonderful thing.

I ran until I ran out of forest.

One moment it was there, on my left, and then in the next it was gone, replaced with nothing but clear air under sky and over a field. I could see it was a field because I could also see the moon for the first time all night, hanging low on the horizon.

The more I looked, the more I saw. The road was about to drop down over the brow of a hill. The forest next to me had ended but the forest on the opposite side, to my right, hadn't yet. The edge of the field that buttressed the forestry was protected with what might be a barbed-wire fence strung between a series of evenly spaced, elbow-high cement poles. In the distance, far down below, I could see clusters of tiny, pinprick lights linked by glowing amber tubes. Houses. Roads. Civilisation. There but miles away, beyond my reach.

If I could see around me, that meant whoever was following me would soon see *me*. I ducked in among the last of the trees, pressing myself into the tickle of their leaves and the scratch of their branches, manoeuvring until I could feel the uneven hardness of the trunk against my back. Everything smelled of pine and damp and earth.

I could still see the road, but now I was hidden from it.

I held my breath, waited.

I needed to call the guards, and soon. I needed my faceless follower to pass me by, to keep going, to assume I'd carried on down the road. And luckily, I'd watched enough TV to know exactly what to do to make them think that. I bent down, wincing as something sharp scratched a stinging welt across my cheek on the way, and felt on the ground for anything resembling a stone or a pebble. My fingers touched a loose rock about the size of a golf ball.

I straightened back up, steeled myself and then lobbed it as hard as I could out on to the road. It landed with a satisfyingly loud *thud* at least ten or fifteen feet further down the hill from where I was hiding and then kept rolling for another few feet more.

With any luck, any moment now, I'd see the shape of my attacker hurry towards it, past me, thinking that sound was my footsteps or, failing that, me accidentally kicking a rock on a road. After they'd been gone a reassuring amount of time, I'd make my phone call.

If I *could*. I hadn't dared to examine my phone post-fall yet.

One problem at a time.

But no one came. I waited and waited, for so long that I started to lose track of how long it'd been. I strained my eyes trying to find shapes or movement in the dark, but found none that shouldn't be there. Moreover, I couldn't hear anything that suggested the other person was still out there. No footsteps, no cracking twigs.

The rain was quieter now without the canopy of the forest to catch it above me, diminished to a low level of white noise. If there was someone else out here, on the road, I felt confident that I'd be able to detect them.

If there had ever been someone out there at all.

The dark, the isolation, everything that had happened – it made certainty illusive, a moving target. Had I *really* heard footsteps? Didn't twigs snap in the woods all the time? It could've been an animal. A fox, for instance. Wasn't that far more likely an event than some crazed stranger following me, or Steve Dade pushing this ridiculousness into the realm of criminal activity? I could be out here waiting for a phantom while my phone battery drained away.

Fuck it.

I unzipped my raincoat and held my phone up inside it, more of a shield from the rain than anything else – I knew, out here, I couldn't entirely hide its blue glow. My stomach sank when I saw the thick, decisive crack that went right across the screen in a diagonal, bottom left to top right. Shards of the screen were missing at the edges.

The crack went right through the battery status, so now I couldn't even tell how much power I had left.

But I could just about see that I had two bars of reception.

It *was* the trees that had been blocking it, just like Gus had suggested to Kate in the script. I tapped 9-9-9 on the screen, grateful that that digit was away from the damage, and put the phone to my ear with a shaking hand.

One ring. I'd never been so happy to hear a sound in my life. Two.

'Emergency,' a male voice said then, quickly knocking the sound of an electronic ring into the runner-up spot of my all-time most welcome sounds. 'Which service do you require?'

'G—Gardaí,' I said. It came out as more of a whispered croak.

'Say again? The line isn't every clear—'

'Gardaí,' I said, firmer, shouting a little.

'One moment please.'

There was a *click* and then a new voice, a female one. 'Gardaí, what's your emergency?'

'I ...'

But now I faltered. What was I supposed to say? There was so much, and so little time. The phone could die any second. I needed short, declarative sentences. No pauses, no time for a back-and-forth. These calls were recorded. They were trained to deal with people who didn't have much time.

'I need help,' I said. 'I'm at a house in West Cork, near Bantry. Cedarwood House. I'm supposed to be shooting a film. I'm an actor. But everyone left and the power's gone out and I've no transport and I'm alone out here and ...' I'd been about to say *someone might have attacked me*, but that sounded like something I could get in trouble for saying if it wasn't true. 'And I fell.'

'What's your name?'

'Adele. Adele Rafferty.'

'And this is your phone number?'

'Yes, but my battery's low and the power's out at the house so I don't—'

'What's the address?'

'I–I don't know. Cedarwood House.' My voice was rising, turning shrill, filling with panic. Any moment now, I expected to hear a sad beep and dead air.

'You said Bantry is the nearest town?'

'I think so.' An image of Peg's business card flashed in my mind. 'Sheep's Head! Is that a place? I think it's near Sheep's Head.'

'You're on the Sheep's Head peninsula?'

'Uh …' That sounded right. 'Yeah. Yes.'

'One moment, please.'

'*No*,' I said desperately, 'please don't—'

But I was already on hold.

I wanted to cry.

I *was* crying, already. I could taste the salt on my lips.

Then, a new voice. Male. Older. Gruff. 'Bantry,' he said, sounding bored.

I tried to explain for a second time, but only got as far as Cedarwood House. At that point, he said, 'Hang on there one second for me now,' and then put me on a hold *again*.

I wanted to scream.

I had to bite down on my bottom lip to stop myself from actually doing it.

'Yeah?' a new voice said.

The fourth voice I'd heard on this call and the third male.

'I need help,' I said. 'I'm at a place called Cedarwood House and—'

'Yep, we know all about it.'

My brain tried to find a way to make this true, but the pieces wouldn't fit. How could they know? *What* did they know? Who would've called them?

What the hell did they *say*?

'It's nothing to worry about,' the man said. I could hear a rustle of papers on the line; he was talking to me *and* doing something else. 'They're making a film there.' *Fill-um.* 'Some kind of horror job. So don't worry. That's all it is.'

'No,' I said. 'I know about that. But that's not—'

'You heard some screams or something, is it? That'll just be them, acting, you see. Nothing to worry about, like I said.'

'I *know* that,' I said desperately. 'I'm part of it. I'm the actor. But the power's gone out, everyone's gone, I'm alone out here, and I'm hurt.'

'Hurt how?'

'I hurt my ankle.'

He scoffed. 'Your *ankle*?'

'Yes, and I really need—'

'Look, love. I'm guessing you're not from around here, but in this part of the world, ambulances take hours, not minutes. They don't bring you to Bantry General, they bring you to the CUH in Cork City. That's fifty miles. And they have to *get* here from the CUH first. So we don't call them out for *hurt ankles*. Elevate your leg, stick some ice on it and take two Panadol. Visit your GP tomorrow if it's still at you then.'

'*You* look,' I said, getting angry now. 'My phone is about to die and the power's out so I can't charge it. I'm out here, all alone, and I'm hurt, and I have no means of transport—'

'*Transport*?' A derisive snort. 'You've called the Gardaí, not West Cork feckin' Taxis.' In the background, I heard someone laughing. 'Keep your dramatics for the camera, love. It's an offence, you know, to make a hoax call to 999. Punishable by fines of up to a thousand euro.'

'This isn't a joke, I'm—'

'You're right there. There could be someone in real trouble trying to get through.'

'I *am* in—'

Click. He'd hung up on me.

I allowed myself one moment of absolute fury and then, mindful of my dwindling battery, moved on to the question of who else I could call.

The battery symbol was obscured by the crack; I might have one per cent left, for all I knew. This could be my last chance to let someone know where I was and what was happening. If my phone died first, my options would be reduced to hiding out in the woods all night where hypothermia might prove to be the least of my worries, or trying to make my way down the hill and into the town, which could take hours and would definitely involve a fuckload of physical pain. I wasn't sure I had the stamina for it, and I was already freezing ... Whoever I called would have to be someone who would instantly understand what I was saying, to whom I wouldn't have to explain every last little thing, someone who would believe me.

Julia.

She was hundreds of miles away, in Dublin, but she knew about *Final Draft* and would know what to do, who to call.

'Hey,' she said. 'What's up? I can't exactly talk right now—'

'Jules, I'm in trouble and I need your help. It's an emergency.'

I told her I'd been abandoned on set, that the power was gone so I couldn't charge my phone, and that I'd tripped and fallen and hurt my ankle. I said I wasn't sure what was going on but that I thought maybe the crew were doing this to me, that Steve Dade was, but also that it was possible I hadn't tripped by accident and maybe all this had gone too far. I told her I'd run off the property and on to the road, but there seemed to be no other houses around and the nearest village or town looked to be miles away. I told her I'd called the Gardaí but they didn't believe that I warranted assistance, and now I didn't know what else to do.

'My phone is about to die,' I said. 'So look, it's *Final Draft*, Steve Dade, Cedarwood House, owned by a woman named

Joanne, just past Bantry. There's a taxi driver, Peg, Sheep's Head Transport, she lives nearby, if you get her number somehow you could send her to come get me.'

'Got all that,' Julia said. 'Where are you now? Are you safe?'

'On the road outside the house. And ...' I scanned the darkness. 'Honestly, I don't know.'

'Can you see any lights at all?'

'I think so, but miles away.'

'Stay on the road but walk towards them, if you can. Okay?'

'Okay.'

'I'll call—'

The end of her sentence disappeared into the wind.

I pulled the phone from my ear just in time to see the screen go black. I jabbed the screen, pressed buttons, shook the thing, but it was no use.

The device was dead.

Panic surged up through my body, flooding my cells, tightening my throat. I wanted to scream. I wanted to cry – more. I said a silent prayer to the universe for this to all be some kind of horrible, lucid nightmare that I was about to wake up from.

And then I heard a new noise.

Not the rain or a sound of my own making. But something I'd never heard before: a god-awful, inhuman shriek. A wail.

The kind I'd always imagined the banshee made.

Growing louder, getting more high-pitched. Coming towards me.

It is *the banshee*, I thought.

And then I heard – and felt, a little – a loud *whoosh* as something flew directly over my head. I looked up just in time to see its silhouette against the night sky: a bird with an impressive wingspan.

An owl, maybe.

But definitely just a bird.

And then I was laughing, and then doing it hysterically, and crying too, unhinged from every last thread of normality, of *reality*. What was even real any more? How could I tell? Everything was too ridiculous and nothing made any sense.

I should never have left LA.

No, I should never have *gone* to LA.

Hell, if we're doing do-overs, I should never have gone to that *These Are the Days* audition. I wanted a time machine, I *needed* one, because I had to go back and start unpicking all the threads of my life, every link in the chain that had led me to here, because something had gone bloody badly wrong somewhere.

And then I saw a light.

Two lights, tiny and white, in the distance.

I stumbled out of the trees and into the middle of the road so I could see them better, but when I stared at them they blurred and merged and then separated again, transforming like the shapes in a kaleidoscope. I wiped the moisture from my eyes. Tears or rain or both, I didn't know. I didn't care. When I looked again, I saw the light merge into one and stay that way, growing solid and defined.

There was a single, round light, soundless and small, floating towards me, maybe three or four feet above the ground, a ways down the road.

Moving but not making any sound, because it was ...

A bicycle.

I was looking at the lamp on the front of a bicycle, coming towards me.

Someone was out here, cycling. Coming this way.

A local. It had to be.

Which meant that wherever they were going – a house, their home, a place with a phone and other people – had to be near here. They could bring me to it. This was, *finally*, help.

I lifted my arm and started waving it madly.

'Hey!' I shouted. 'Hey!'

There was a beat before the light in the dark answered back.

'Adele?'

The light stopped, suspended in place, then fell to the ground in a perfect arc.

Footsteps, running to me.

'Adele? Jesus Christ. Are you all right? What the ...?'

I recognised the voice just as a shape emerged from the dark.

It was Donal.

TWENTY

'Adele? Jesus Christ. Are you all right? What's happened?'

I could hear the words. I understood the questions. But I couldn't understand how Donal could be here, standing in front of me, asking them.

'What happened to your face?' He was coming towards me now, reaching for me. 'Your cheek ... It's bleeding. Did you know that?'

I held up my hand in a *stop* gesture to tell him to come no closer, to stop the barrage of questions. I needed to think. Everything I wanted to say to him was bubbling up in my throat – *Where the hell were you? Where did everyone go? What the fuck* is *this shit?* – creating a bottleneck, so that when I did open my mouth, nothing came out.

I didn't know where to start.

I didn't know if he was rescue or danger.

'W–where were you?' I asked, my jaw trembling with the cold.

That was the most important question. But instead of answering, he asked me if I was all right again. That brought the words in my throat to a boil of red-hot anger and before I knew what I was doing, I was lifting my hand and smacking Donal hard across the face while screaming, 'Where the fuck *were you?*' at a volume that surprised us both.

Stunned, Donal took an uncertain step backwards, tripping a little before regaining his balance. His hand went to his cheek, palm pressed flat against it, as if to check it was still there. He looked at me in horror.

'What the …?'

'Shit,' I said. 'Sorry.' But I wasn't really. My hand was stinging like crazy but I felt better for it. 'Where were you? Where is everyone? Where the hell did you all *go*?'

'I can explain,' Donal said.

'Then *do*.'

He shook his head a little and muttered, 'I *knew* you weren't getting my texts,' in a tone that made it sound like he was addressing an invisible person who had been arguing the opposite.

'Your *texts*?' I spat. 'What texts?'

'I sent you messages. Or tried to. I wasn't sure you'd got them. I wasn't even sure I was sending them. I didn't get any delivery confirmation on my phone.'

'*You* were the one who told me about the reception around here,' I shouted, jabbing a finger on my non-hurting hand at him. 'About the complete *lack of it*. But then you *send me texts*? Are you actually *serious*?'

Donal held up both his hands and then slowly reached into the windbreaker-style jacket he was wearing with one of them, in the style of a cop being held at gunpoint who swears he's just going for his ID. The hand withdrew a phone. He turned it on and looked at it, then turned it to me so I could see the screen.

There were three text messages on it, a one-way conversation from him to me.

I was more interested in the fact that Donal's phone had about a quarter battery and full service.

'Look,' he said. 'See?'

He pushed the phone at me and I took it from him.

4:15 p.m. – Just FYI we're in town. Back soon. If you want anything from the shop let me know by 5. Hope you had a good day's sleep! Donal ☺

5:55 p.m. – Weather causing problems. Looks like bridge back is flooded, can't cross. We'll be delayed and Steve has CXL tonight's shoot. Hope you're ok? Donal

7:34 p.m. – Worried you're not getting my texts. Can you reply if you are? D

'I didn't get these,' I said.

'That's what I suspected,' he said. 'That's why I came back.'

I stared at him, waiting, but he didn't say any more.

'From fucking *where*?' I shouted, infuriated. 'This isn't a cross-examination, Donal. Feel free to explain to me what the hell is going on, now, in full.'

'Okay, okay.' He held up his hands. 'Sorry. Yeah. You know the bridge, the one that connects the peninsula to the mainland? You drove over it on your way here?'

I just glared at him. I was done talking.

'It's, ah, flooded,' he went on. 'Impassable. A combination of high tide and all the rain we've had today. Or it was. They had it closed off all afternoon, waiting for the water to recede. They told us this happens every now and then and that it would be a couple of hours. A delay but no big deal. I texted you to let you know. But you didn't respond, and it was taking for ever. So I left the guys in the pub in the village – that's where we'd parked, waiting until we could drive back up here – and I walked up to the bridge to see if there'd been any progress. They were letting one of the local farmers across in his tractor, they figured that was safe ... So I asked him if I could hitch a lift as far as his farm, and he said yes.' He pointed over his shoulder. 'It's just down the hill. When I told him where I was going, he offered me his son's bike … And when we crossed the bridge, it seemed like there really wasn't much water left on it at all. I texted Steve to tell him.' He glanced behind him. 'I bet the guys will be here any minute.'

It was an explanation, okay, but it didn't answer the obvious question.

'What were you *doing* on the other side of the bridge,' I said, 'when, according to *your* shooting schedule, everyone should've been asleep in their beds?'

'We're all struggling a bit with that. I woke up early, just before ten, and couldn't get back to sleep, so I thought I'd drive down to the village and grab a coffee at the pub. They have good wifi there, I could do some work. But it turned out Steve was awake as well, and Liam, and they wanted to come too, and I guess us talking outside woke the others up and then everyone wanted to come. Just to have something to do. So off we went. But then the rain started, and we heard they were closing the bridge—'

'And when you left here, you didn't think to as much as leave me a *note*?'

'I thought we'd be back by the time you woke up.' Donal exhaled hard. 'Look, I get that you're mad. You have every right to be. But why are you out here in the road, bleeding and …? Are you injured?' He stepped closer to me again, lowered his voice. 'Can you please just tell me what's going on? What happened? Are you okay?'

What a stupid question.

'I'm clearly *not* okay,' I spat at him.

'Can you tell me what happened?'

I didn't like the way his voice sounded now. There'd been a gearshift. His tone was more gentle, placating, kind. *Condescending.* Like he was talking to a child, or someone holding a loaded weapon that was pointed at him. Like he was afraid of me. No sudden moves.

'Who went into town?' I asked.

'All of us did.'

So the guy I'd heard talking on the phone wasn't a member of the crew.

'Did you lock the gates when you left?'

Donal nodded. 'Steve thought we should lock them up just to discourage anyone from driving in. When you were, you know ...' He cleared his throat. 'There on your own.'

'I found a book. A copy of *Final Draft*. With my name on it. The dedication was to me. It said, *To Adele*—'

'*Who should never have come to Cedarwood House*,' Donal finished. 'Yeah. Wait, you found that? What were you doing—'

'*Why* is there a book that says that?'

'It's a wrap gift. I had it made specially. To give to you on the last day of filming. It's just like it is in the script. You know, "To Kate, who should never have come to Cherry Cottage"?'

A gift. A weird, somewhat disconcerting choice of gift, but when he explained it like that, it made sense. One by one, every strange thing I'd thought was inexplicable was being felled by the mundane.

Or, Donal had an answer ready for everything.

'The power went out,' I said.

'Did it? Shit. Must have been the weather. For how long?'

'It's still out.'

In what little light there was, I saw Donal frown. Then he raised an arm to point over my shoulder, in the direction of the house. When I turned to look, I saw yellow light filtering through the trees.

The power at Cedarwood House was back on. How very fucking convenient.

'I wanted to call you,' I said, turning back to him. 'But I couldn't find my call-sheet. Someone took it from my cabin.'

'Ah, yeah. *I* took it. But from the house. You left it on set, last night. Or this morning, I suppose. I threw it out at the end of last night's shoot, along with the rest of them, so no one would get it mixed up with today's.'

I tried to picture the call-sheet on the table in my cabin where I had been so sure I'd left it, but my mind's eye wouldn't cooperate. It would only show me my accidentally collecting it from the tabletop when I picked up my script and my notes, and then doing the same thing in reverse when I left the couch on set hours later: getting up and taking my script, but leaving the call-sheet behind. I could've done that. It was possible.

But *had* I?

'Where are today's, then?'

'Not printed yet,' Donal said. 'I was planning on doing that when I got back – which I thought would be lunchtime, mid-afternoon at the very latest. I thought there'd be plenty of time, but obviously ...'

'Someone took my boots.'

As soon as I said it aloud, I realised how insane it sounded.

'What?'

'My boots,' I repeated. 'The wellies you gave me. They were on my deck earlier, around dinnertime – breakfast-time, whatever – and then they weren't. But there was a dry patch where they had been, so I know it happened then. Or just before then. It could've have been sooner.' The words were tumbling out now, making sense on my tongue but sounding strange and mixed-up and messy once they left it.

Donal looked confused.

No – worse, *concerned*.

'And there was a man on the phone,' I said. 'Outside the house. So there was a man at the house who wasn't the crew if they were with you. On set. I heard him, but then he was gone.' I waved a hand, as if I could delete that jumble of words and start again. I tried to focus, tried to clear a pathway through all this, trying to find something that felt like sense.

'It could've been a neighbour,' Donal said. 'Or someone who works for Joanne, coming to look for us. The catering service, even. There were supposed to deliver—'

'They put it by the gates.' My voice was rising. 'You said everyone went to town, but there was a man by the stone pillars. But when I went to see who it was, he wasn't there. And the gates are locked, so how would a car come in? And there wasn't a car.' I took a breath. 'Look, I know I'm not making sense. But something is … Something is *happening*.'

A beat passed before Donal spoke.

'Adele,' he said quietly, 'you're shaking. We should get back to the house.' He unzipped his jacket, pulled it off, held it out to me. 'Here. Put this on. It's relatively dry and it's got a fleece lining. I'll take your one.'

I let him help me swap our jackets because it was easier than arguing, and because I was more than cold. I was absolutely *freezing*.

'I'm not going back there,' I said. 'You said the other guys would be back soon. I'll just wait here and when they come, someone can drive me to Bantry. I'll find somewhere there to stay for the night.'

'Adele—'

'I am *not* going back to that house.'

'Why not?'

I opened my mouth to respond, but all of a sudden, I was stumped. Why *didn't* I want to go back to the house, exactly? A few minutes ago, before I had seen the light of Donal's borrowed bicycle appear on the horizon, the answer seemed obvious – *so* obvious, just asking the question was ridiculous. But now everything I thought I was sure of was disintegrating in my grasp, like I'd tried to grab hold of a cloud. Donal had efficiently vanquished most of the mystery that had grown over the course of the day.

I woke up alone on set because everyone else had woken up earlier than me and gone into town. They couldn't return because of the rain, coupled with a high tide that had flooded the bridge I'd driven over yesterday, the same one that had made me feel like the car was driving on the surface of the water, so high was the waterline even then. The weather was also why the power must have gone out, because it was back on now, and I didn't get Donal's texts because this whole area was, evidently, a black hole of reception and they hadn't managed to leave *his* phone yet, let alone find their way to mine. The man on the phone could've been a wandering neighbour. The book with my name in it was a gift.

I'd just tripped over a fallen branch, just imagined that I could hear footsteps. Like how, for one brief moment, I thought I was hearing the wail of a banshee.

But what about the anonymous texts? The knock on my door? That door then being open? The lights in the house going on and off, the sliding door getting locked, the earring, the page of script stuffed in the robe, someone taking Peg's business card from my coat pocket while that coat was hanging in the wardrobe in the cabin …

I didn't have explanations for those things, but now that everything else had, seemingly, been explained away, it felt like they were ready to follow them. Like they were just awaiting *their* perfectly ordinary, logical, mundane explanations, too.

The book, for instance. The one with my name on it. It had terrified me, made me bolt, sent me running down the dirt track in the dark and the wind and the rain. But it had just been an off-kilter present that, actually, wasn't really off-kilter at all when you considered the script.

Wasn't it just as likely there was an ordinary explanation for everything else?

'Adele,' Donal said again, 'we need to get inside, get warm. Please.'

Whatever adrenalin had got me to this point, the fight-or-flight instinct that had pushed me up off the ground and down the track and out on to the road dissipated in an instant, letting in the pain and the cold. Everything hurt. The scratch on my cheek stung. My jaw had started to tremble uncontrollably and I couldn't feel my feet.

I didn't want to go back to the house. I wanted to leave. But if what Donal said was true, we really couldn't leave, not until the bridge reopened.

If what he said was true, I didn't *need* to.

'*Adele*,' he said again.

I rubbed my temples as if that would help get my thoughts in order. I was so tired. Tired and cold and hurting and wet and now, confused as well. When I looked back over the last few hours, I didn't know what to think. The things that were real and the things that might have only felt that way were helplessly intertwined, like several sets of Christmas lights that are so tangled up, you take one look at them and decide to buy all new ones. I couldn't pull them apart, couldn't separate them.

I didn't trust myself to.

The cold wasn't helping. If I was somewhere warm and I was dry, maybe I could figure this out, find some solid ground again. Charge my phone, call the people I needed to. Standing on a dark country road in the rain with a dead phone was not the place to get my head straight.

'Okay,' I said. 'I'll go back to the house.'

Donal looked relieved. 'Good.'

'But I need to use your phone first.'

I only knew one number off by heart, besides my own: Julia's. She'd had the same number since we were teenagers. I tapped it into Donal's phone – which he'd handed over immediately, no reluctance – and pressed CALL, then put the device on speaker.

'Hello?'

'Jules, it's me.'

'Jesus fucking Christ. *Adele*. Are you okay? What's going on? Whose phone is this? Where are you? I've been calling—'

'It's okay,' I said. 'I'm okay. I'm still at the house. Well, on the road outside it.' I looked at Donal, his face eerily lit by the

271

blue-glow of the phone. He was frowning slightly, probably wondering why Julia was sounding so freaked out. 'The AD has come back.'

'From *where*?'

'It's a long story. But I still want to leave, so—'

'I found Peg,' Julia said. 'Well, I found this other company online, out of Bantry, but they told me to try her, that she was closer. She said she knew you, that she'd dropped you there? She's on her way, but she said something about a flooded bridge, and how it might be an hour.' A pause. 'I didn't call the guards, but I—'

'No, no,' I said quickly, as Donal's eyes widened so much I thought his eyeballs might fall out. 'Don't. I'll go with Peg when she gets here. My phone is dead but the power's back on, so I'm going to charge it as soon as I can. I'm heading back to the house. I'll wait there for Peg. If you need me in the meantime, you can call me on this number, okay?'

'Can you tell me what's going on?'

'Not right now, but I will. It's a long story.'

'Is it …?' Julia paused. 'Is it like before?'

I dared glance at Donal. He was watching me.

'No,' I said quickly. 'I have to go, Jules.'

'It's just that … Well, your voice. Your voice sounds like it did that day.'

'I'll call you later, okay?'

'Adele—'

I ended the call and handed the phone back to Donal who took it silently.

I'd done all that over speakerphone so he would hear Julia say that she knew where I was. But it turned out even better than that, because he'd heard her say that Peg was on her way here to get me – or would be once that bridge was passable again.

Donal picked up the bike and walked it back to where I stood. I positioned myself on its opposite side with one hand resting on the handlebars, using the bike as a sort of mobile crutch.

'Ready?' he asked me.

I nodded. 'Yeah.'

'Then let's go.'

And off we went, back to Cedarwood House.

INT. LIVING SPACE - NIGHT

Kate sits in front of the fire while, behind
her back, Joel potters in the kitchen.

                    JOEL
     I'm just going to hop in the shower.
     You okay?

                    KATE
                 (absently)
     Yeah. Fine.

                    JOEL
     I'll be out before it's done.

Over Kate's shoulder, we watch Joel disappear
down the hall into the bedroom, closing the
door behind him but not shutting it.

INT. MASTER EN-SUITE BATHROOM - NIGHT

Joel reaches into the shower to switch on
the water. He stands in front of the sink and
meets his own eyes in the mirror above it. He
shakes his head.

                    JOEL
     What a fucking shitshow.

Behind him, through the open door to the
bedroom, we see an UNKNOWN FIGURE dart past.

INT. LIVING SPACE - NIGHT

Kate, still in front of the fire, tilts her
head back to drain the last of the whiskey in
her glass. The HISS of the shower is audible.

Over her shoulder, we see the shadowy blur of an UNKNOWN FIGURE slip from the bedroom to the utility room.

                                        CUT TO:

INT. MASTER EN-SUITE BATHROOM - NIGHT

Joel undresses and gets into the shower, which is starting to fill with steam.

                                        CUT TO:

INT. LIVING SPACE - NIGHT

Kate stands up, holding her empty glass, and turns towards the kitchen.

But then she stops, turns back. Her eyes go to the shelf full of copies of *First Draft*. She glances back towards the bedroom. The shower continues to HISS. Moving quickly, she pulls out each individual copy of *First Draft*, one at a time, checking the dedication page. Each one reads as it should: *To Karen, my muse, for coming to Cherry Cottage*. She throws the final copy to the floor in frustration.

Kate turns towards the kitchen, brow furrowed, thinking.

She starts down the hall to the bedroom. As she passes the door to the utility room, we see that it's about a third of the way ajar. The room beyond is dark.

We watch as some unseen force slowly and silently closes it.

INT. BEDROOM – NIGHT

Joel's backpack is sitting on the floor beside the bed. Kate, glancing towards the bathroom door, retrieves a laptop from it.

She sits on the bed with the machine on her knees and boots it up. Quickly, she conducts a number of Google searches. *Cherry Cottage Cork. Cherry Cottage West Cork. Cherry Cottage Maggie.* The search returns numerous listings for homes for sale and holiday lets to rent, but none are a match for the cottage they're in. She searches for *First Draft Gary Sheridan* and *Gary Sheridan writer* and *Gary Sheridan writer Cork*, but none of the results turn up anything that suggests they're linked to the novel she's been reading or its author.

Frustrated, Kate goes to close the laptop's lid – but stops when she spots one of the icons on the desktop is a Word document labelled 'FIRST DRAFT'. She glances towards the bathroom. The shower continues to HISS. She looks back at the screen, biting her lip, hesitating. And then she clicks on the icon.

A virtual document opens onscreen, thick with text. It has a heading: *CHAPTER ONE*. And beneath it, lines she has read before. *The dense fir forest loomed above the car, growing darker with every twist and turn of the narrow, crumbling road …*

She doesn't see Joel emerge from the bathroom, a towel wrapped around his waist.

                    JOEL
          What the hell are you doing?

                                        CUT TO:

INT. LIVING SPACE - NIGHT

Kate storms out of the bedroom, coat and boots
on now, carrying her weekender bag. As she
passes the console table, she yanks the phone
charger out of the wall socket. She goes to
the armchair and starts upending cushions.

                    KATE
                 (muttering)
          Where is that goddamn phone *now*?

Joel, in sweatpants and hurriedly pulling on a
T-shirt, comes out of the bedroom.

                    JOEL
          Kate, what the *fuck*?

She reels on him.

                    KATE
          You tell me, Joel. You tell me.
          It's on your laptop. I saw it, okay?
          The jig is up.

                    JOEL
          What is? What brand of crazy are you
          on now?

                    KATE
          Oh, that's the plan, is it? To
          gaslight me?

                    JOEL

To gas … *What*?

                    KATE

Where are the car keys? I'm leaving.

                    JOEL

You can't drive. You've been
drinking.

                    KATE

I'm fine.

                    JOEL

I don't know what's going on here,
Kate, but I know *that's* not true.

Kate starts for the front door.

                    KATE

I'll just walk out of here then.

Joel starts after her.

                    JOEL

Can you just calm the fuck down for a
second?

                    KATE

Don't you *dare* tell me to calm down!

Seeing that he's following her, Kate grabs
the bottle of whiskey off the kitchen counter
and hurls it at Joel. He ducks. The bottle
narrowly misses him and hits the wall behind
him instead, bursting open, sending shattered
glass and liquid everywhere.

Joel looks from the debris to Kate, flabbergasted.

                    JOEL
    What the …?

                    KATE
    It's you! This is *all* you. *You're*
    doing this!

Joel throws up his hands, frustrated.

                    JOEL
    Doing *what*? What the hell are you
    talking about, Kate? Who even *are*
    you? You sound *insane*.

                    KATE
    That's what you want, isn't it?
    That's why you brought me here.

                    JOEL
    I brought you here for a romantic
    weekend. To make up for me being so
    consumed with work lately. More fool
    me.

                    KATE
    I thought I was losing my mind
    but actually, no, it was just my
    boyfriend with the fragile ego
    fucking with it. What is this, Joel?
    Some weird meta-fiction thing? Is
    this what you have to do to have
    something to write about now? You
    can't just make it up like everyone
    else?

A beat passes.

Joel sighs, letting his shoulders drop. He takes a step towards her, holding out his hands as if to say, *I come in peace*. When he speaks, it's in a softer tone than before.

                    JOEL
        Look, I don't know what's going on
        here, but let's just sit down, take a
        breath, take a minute …

                    KATE
               (voice breaking)
        Are you punishing me? Is that it?

                    JOEL
               (confused)
        Punishing you?

                    KATE
        For signing with Siobhán O'Sullivan.

                    JOEL
        You signed with Siobhán O'Sullivan?
        What? When?

                    KATE
        It's on your *laptop*, Joel. The book.
        I saw it.

                    JOEL
        My book? Yeah, I know. Where else
        would it—

                    KATE
        No. *The* book.

(pointing to the bookshelf)
First Draft. It's on *your* fucking
laptop. Explain that.

TWENTY-ONE

We didn't talk much at all on the way back.

Donal had the combination for the padlock on the gates, and opened them. He collected the cooler bag and hung it from the bike. He lit our path with his phone. I kept an eye out for the branch that had tripped me but didn't see any candidates.

I couldn't tell you how long it took to walk back to the house, but it felt like only a fraction of the time it had taken me earlier to get from the house to the road.

When we got to the front door, Donal opened it with a key. Inside, everything looked as it should.

'I'll light the fire,' he said.

A neat pyramid of logs was already sitting in the hearth, ready for what should've been tonight's shoot. He lit them with a box of matches he'd got from a kitchen drawer. I stood in the middle of the space and stared into the red-yellow flickering flames as they took hold, curling up around the pile of logs, spreading until the wood began to snap and crack and hiss.

I was so cold now, it felt as if my brain had been locked in a steel box, too thick for signals to penetrate, and then put in a chiller to freeze over with a layer of ice. I could only think about cold, know cold, feel cold. There was no room for anything else. So when Donal took charge of things, I was happy to let him.

I went where he directed me: the armchair in front of the fireplace, the one I'd filmed in last night. I obeyed his instructions, which were all delivered in a quiet, soothing voice. 'Lean back. Sit forward. Arms up, please.' I let him undress me to my underwear, appreciating his not looking directly at me as he peeled cold, wet layers from my stinging pink skin as I sat and then stood and then sat again, rigid but shivering.

He disappeared upstairs briefly and returned with a pair of sweat pants and a sweatshirt, soft and smelling of detergent, and helped me pull them on. He gently put white sport socks on my feet, scratchy ones, threadbare in places, that must have been washed many, many times. Everything may as well have been the most luxurious cashmere, it felt so good on my skin.

'I'm going to clean up that cut on your face now,' he said. 'Okay?'

He dabbed near my hairline with a piece of damp cotton wool which came away red, and then gently touched it with another piece that had been covered in an antiseptic. When I winced in pain at the sudden stinging sensation, Donal winced too, and apologised. He sat me back into the chair closest to the fire, applied a plaster and then placed a steaming cup of sweet tea into my hands which I held tightly, willing the warmth to spread from my fingers to the rest of the body, to make me feel normal again.

Donal pushed another chair close to the fire and sat across from me, holding his own cup of tea.

'How are you feeling now?' he asked.

'Better.'

'Do you want me to go and pack your things?'

I was confused by the question for a second, but then I remembered that Peg and her taxi were on their way here.

'No,' I said. 'Not yet.' I'd get him to do that when she arrived, while she waited, so I wouldn't have to be by myself.

I was done being by myself at Cedarwood House.

'What are you going to say to Steve?' Donal asked.

'What are *you* going to say to him?'

'I need to know what happened here, Adele.'

I studied his face. Donal looked the same as he had when I'd arrived here yesterday, only the flush on his cheeks was from the fire now. Open. Friendly. Nice. He'd been the only one who was any of those things on this set, the only one who'd done anything to welcome me or look after me, or even just treat me professionally. He was here now because he'd come back out of concern, because he knew I was alone and suspected I wasn't getting his messages – and, again, he'd been the only one to.

'Why were you down on the road?' Donal asked. 'What happened to your face? Why were you …?' He hesitated. 'When I first got to you, you seemed sort of … scared.'

'Nothing happened.' I turned my gaze to the fire. 'I'm fine.'

It was less complicated than saying that everything I thought had happened wasn't really happening at all.

Ever since I'd met Donal on the road, the events of the last few hours were becoming increasingly slippery, escaping my grasp whenever I tried to pin them down, and now there were almost no solid parts left to them at all. It felt like the hangover after the very drunk night before – when I tried to play things back in my head, I only got glimpses. And it was like I was watching them happen under metres of murky water.

'I just needed to use my phone,' I said, 'and that's where you said we could get reception.' I turned back at him. 'Where did you put my raincoat? My phone was in the pocket.'

Donal hopped up immediately and went into the kitchen, opening the door next to the fridge and disappearing into whatever room was on the other side. Perhaps a utility room. There was a rustling noise and then he emerged, holding the phone aloft triumphantly – along with my charger. I'd forgotten that I'd put that in the pocket too.

'Will I plug it in for you?'

'Please,' I said. 'Thanks.'

I watched him push the plug into a socket on the wall next to the microwave, listened for the little *ding* that signalled charging had begun. So easy now, such a simple act. A short time ago, it had felt like an insurmountable obstacle. Nearly a matter of life or death.

Donal returned to his seat by the fire, by me, and we spent an awkward half-minute sitting in silence, staring into the flames.

Then he said, 'I don't know how to say this, but ... Your friend. The one you called on the phone ... I can't pretend I didn't hear what she said to you.'

I took a sip of my tea, waited for more.

'I'm responsible for your health and well-being,' he said, 'while you're on this set. If there's something ...' He hesitated. 'If there's something I should know about, if there's something that my knowing will help me to help you, then ... Look, Adele, I don't want to pry, and you can tell me to shut up and piss off if you want, but I want you to know that you can trust me. If there's something you want to say, I can promise you, it won't go any further. I don't have to tell Steve, if that's what—'

'There is something,' I said, my voice practically a whisper. Because it was just easier now to tell him. To come clean.

And because it *was* something that his knowing would help him to help me.

Really, I should've told him as soon as I'd arrived. I could've done it discreetly. *He* would've been discreet about it, I was sure.

'I didn't really read the script,' I said, 'before I got here. Not properly, anyway. There wasn't really time. To be honest, I didn't even know I didn't have the ending. This morning was the first chance I had to actually go through it properly, to take the story in rather than just looking for my lines, and when I did, I thought there was something about it that was weirdly familiar. I couldn't put my finger on it, but I assumed it was just that it reminded me of some other film I'd seen, or a book I'd read or whatever.' I paused. 'But that wasn't it.'

A log cracked loudly in the fire.

'Kate is experiencing all these weird things,' I continued. 'The knock on the door, the door being open in the morning, the power going out – which are all things that are also happening in the book she's reading, but no one believes her. Joel doesn't believe her. Same with Karen and Jack, in the book Kate is reading.'

'Yeah …'

'You must have read the ending,' I said. 'The original one.'

'Once,' Donal said. 'Quickly.'

'Do you remember it?'

'Where does your one end? Isn't it Joel, dead in the back seat of the car?'

I nodded. 'Yeah.'

'I think after that Kate legs it into the woods. Finds another house. A cabin or something.'

286

'And then what? Does she make it to the end credits?'

'Yeah,' Donal said. 'The final scene is, like, a year later, and it's her in a bookshop.' He gave a small smile. 'Don't worry, I'm sure Kate will survive Steve's version, too. You don't kill off your hero. As much as Steve loves breaking rules, even *he* knows that.'

It struck me as a weird thing to say, under the circumstances.

'What does this have to do with what you need to tell me?' he asked.

'So far today, there's been a knock on my cabin door, and then I found that door open, and then I found the book with the dedication—'

'I explained that—' he started.

'I know.' I held my hand up to say, *Wait, let me finish*. 'I know that. But I did find a book with my name in the dedication, and the power went out, and then I walked down the road. Or fled down it, just like Kate did. And then I met you out there, just like she met Joel. And then we came back here, and you explained everything away, and now we're sitting here in front of the fire – again, just like Kate and Joel.'

'I'm not entirely sure that I'm ...' Donal cleared his throat. 'I'm not quite following.'

'There were other things, too,' I went on. 'A lost earring in my bed, even though you said that we were the first people to stay here, in the cabins. And last night, when you gave me the robe? There was a page of the script folded up in the pocket. But from a version that had scene numbers, and someone had written some notes on it. A woman, I'd guess from the handwriting style. And the notes were for Kate's character.'

For the first time, Donal looked surprised.

'I've worked in hospitality,' I said, 'so I know you can accidentally lose things when you're making beds. Jewellery. Fake nails. Hairs from your head. So if I needed to, I suppose I could explain the earring away too. And I'm sure you're about to tell me that there were original versions of the script floating around here, and they had scene numbers on them, and anyone could've made notes on a page of it. And once you establish that, it's not a giant leap for it to end up in an item from the wardrobe department.'

'Yeah,' Donal said absently.

'The thing is, I know now why the script felt so weirdly familiar. It wasn't because it reminded me of some other film. It was because it reminded me of *me*, six months ago, on the set of another film. A time when strange things were happening, and I was telling people about them, but nobody believed me. But I knew they were. Or at least ...' I could feel a lump forming in my throat, the threat of emotion spilling into my voice. 'Or at least I think I knew they were. That's the problem really. I don't know, do I? If you're having a mental breakdown of some sort, some kind of psychotic break, you don't think that at the time, do you? You don't think to yourself, *Oh, I'm definitely just imagining this*. You think it's happening. It *feels* like it's happening. And it's only then, when someone else says it isn't, that you realise something's wrong.'

I searched Donal's face for anything that looked like pretending, but it really seemed as if he didn't know, as if he hadn't heard about what happened on the set of *We Were Kings*.

So I took a deep breath.

And then, I told him everything.

TWENTY-TWO

That audition was on a cold, wet January day, almost exactly a year ago.

The first in-person one in the process, which I suppose was technically a call-back. There'd already been two rounds: a self-tape and, a week after that, a ten-minute Zoom. Now a shortlist had been compiled, an unusually short one so as to minimise the risk – after what the government called 'a meaningful Christmas', Ireland was practically back to square one – and everyone on it was to report to a hotel in Dublin city centre, individually, where a Trestle Table Quartet awaited in a basement-level room.

I was still high on the success of *Winter Snow* and I'd just told my agent I wanted to start extricating myself from *These Are the Days*. I thought I was about to get everything I'd ever wanted: all the offers *and* all the time to accept them. I was deliriously happy and ridiculously naïve, and more confident than I'd ever been in my entire life.

I absolutely nailed the audition.

We Were Kings was a World War II drama with Danish money behind it that was shooting in Ireland with a cast who would be expected to speak like they were on-air talent at the BBC. The sides were all from the first twenty pages of the screenplay but, going by them, I could guess the rest. Boys off to war, coming back as men – which I think, when it came to WWII dramas, was practically a legal requirement, thematically speaking.

The biggest female role, the one I was auditioning for, was Wife Waiting Fretfully for News at Home. She featured only in the connective tissue of the movie, the cutaways that would give the audience a breather from all the fighting at the Front. Classic scenes such as Wife at Washing Line Stares into the Middle Distance While Sheets Blow in the Wind Behind Her, Wife Puts On Brave Face for Kids Then Cries Self to Sleep, and Wife Catches Glimpse of Own Future When Neighbouring Wife Waiting Fretfully for News at Home Gets It and It's Bad.

Yes, the script was clichéd and bloated and every character had at least one speech that sounded like it had been written by inspirational fridge magnets, but I didn't care. It was a feature film, only my second ever, with no chance whatsoever – as far as I was concerned – of it being my last. If I'm being honest, what I thought at the time was that *We Were Kings* was going to get lucky by casting me. Right now, it was destined for the odd late-night, midweek TV showing, but if they gave *me* the gig, all the major streamers would be scrambling for it when my next movie affixed a jet-pack to my rising star.

Whatever *that* movie turned out to be.

It went so well in the audition room that the actor waiting in the corridor, the woman scheduled to go next, openly glowered at me when I came out. I could still hear voices through the door I'd just closed behind me, so she'd almost certainly heard my entire audition, including all the excessive laughter, friendly chat and effusive praise.

She looked like me. Or I looked like her. Because both of us looked like Caroline, the role we were auditioning for. Same age, same size, same shoulder-length blonde hair.

'Good luck,' I told her as pleasantly as I could, determinedly ignoring her expression. 'They're really nice in there.'

She said, 'Fuck you.'

'Oh.'

I actually said that. *Oh.* Like she'd said something else to me entirely. Like she'd said, 'Actually, I'm not auditioning. I'm just waiting here. I like it, it's quiet.' *Oh.*

I turned and hurried down the hall, worried that at any moment I was going to feel a knife in my back, and escaped up the marble stairs to the lobby. On the top step, I heard a man calling my name. When I turned, the director was on the stairs behind me. He'd left the audition room to try to catch me.

'Could you stick around?' he asked. 'Just for, say, a half-hour? We weren't planning on doing this, but ...' He smiled conspiratorially. 'The part is yours, Adele – if you want it. And we want to make sure you want it. We know Caroline is a little light on the page right now. But we have this new screenwriter coming in, and he's going to beef her up a bit. We don't have much time, but we've enough to make some significant changes. We'd *really* like to bring you back in for a more expansive chat, before you go.'

'Oh,' I said again.

'Can you give us, say, fifteen minutes?'

I nodded like that was totally normal and not a scenario outside the parameters of even my wildest dreams, and went to wait in the lobby. It was dotted with plush armchairs. I picked one by the window which gave me a view of the street, but hid me from anyone else who would come up the stairs.

Like other actors, leaving after their auditions.

Like Ms Fuck You, who arrived moments later.

I heard her before I saw her, heels smacking angrily across the lobby's marble floor. She pushed through the hotel's doors and stormed across the street, her body rigid with fury, not bothering to look left or right. When a taxi had to stop suddenly to avoid running her over, she responded to the driver's annoyed horn-blowing with an obscene gesture.

When she turned to do that, I saw that she was crying.

There hadn't been enough time for her to audition, so they must have told her there was no point, that the part had already been cast. Sent her straight home, or maybe invited her back another day to read for another role. Whatever they'd said to her, this was not the way to react to it. I watched her through the window, feeling pity (a little) and superiority (a lot), transfixed by her behaviour.

And then someone else ran out on to the street after her: the director.

She walked away from him at first, but in that half-hearted way that promised she'd stop so he could catch up. He pulled her into a doorway and she let him. He bent his head to talk to her and she listened. And then he cupped her chin with his hand and used his other arm to pull her close to him.

Watching this, I thought, *They're together*.

They were together, the director of this movie and this actor auditioning for it, and he'd just had to tell her that she wasn't getting the part because they'd already chosen *me*, and she was – quite understandably – reacting to this with upset. It wasn't just the rejection, I had to imagine, but the fact that some of it was *his*.

I was mildly surprised, a little scandalised, mostly impressed. By him. By how fair and professional he was being, doing everything by the book. Setting his personal relationships aside. Giving the part to the best actor for the job over the woman that was sleeping in his bed.

When I returned to the audition room a little while later, I was properly introduced to everyone at the table for the first time, and that's when I found out that the producer, Sandra, was the director's wife.

I should've thought more about the kind of person who would tell a stranger who was trying to be nice to fuck off, and why she might have done that. Why the married man she was seeing might have started to worry about her ability to be discreet, and why that might have made him question the wisdom of her working closely with him, for weeks on end, in the same place where his wife worked too. How he might have seen me in the role of a solution to all his personal problems long before he ever saw me in the role of Caroline.

But I didn't. Because right after that, he said, 'So? What do you think? Will you be our Caroline?'

And I wanted the role, the glory, the next phase of my career to begin.

So I smiled and told Martin Clarke that my answer was yes.

Pre-production was uneventful. I spent most of it distracted, tangled up in talks with the bosses at *These*. Lindsey mediating, trying to placate both sides; me just wanting to quit the talking and strut away while things exploded behind me. She thought it would be wise to push for a break, a sabbatical of sorts. Keep the door open in case I ever wanted to come back. But that would take longer and require more finesse, and I had absolutely no interest in diplomacy. I wanted it done *now*. I told her I wouldn't need to go back. 'Let's just set a date for Wendy Morgan's demise,' I said. 'Get me out of there and nail that bloody door shut. Then glue it shut with some kind of non-dissolvable sealant.'

I had got my way by the time principal photography commenced on *Kings* in early July, at Ardmore Studios in Wicklow. They were starting with the small scenes, the wife-at-the-washing-line stuff. The war re-enactments were scheduled for fields and beaches in neighbouring Wexford in the autumn, by which time I'd be busy sorting through all the offers that had come in for my next role (I presumed). A production assistant checked me into an apartment with a view of the back of the DART station – fitting, I thought, considering how Wendy had met her death – and the next morning, I reported to set.

As soon as I set foot on it, I knew something was off.

This was Martin and Sandra Clarke's fifth production in eight years and they worked with the same people each time, so the crew all knew each other well and were tight-knit. Moreover, the shoot had actually started a week before, with scenes Caroline wasn't waiting fretfully in, so the other actors had already had a chance to bond. If I felt like a bit of an outsider, like the new kid with the wrong clothes who arrives at an incredibly clique-y school after moving house halfway through the academic year, I put it down to that.

But it didn't really explain why, every single time I walked into a room or the catering tent or on to a sound stage, I got the impression that everyone already there had just, at that *very* moment, stopped talking about me.

294

More than once, it was more than a mere impression. I'd hear my name muttered behind my back, or catch someone whispering in someone else's ear with their eyes on me, or join a group laughing and joking in a corner who, as soon as they saw me, fell silent and turned stony-faced.

It was weird, but it also felt like a weird thing to complain about. No one was being outright rude to me, or ignoring me, or worse. They just weren't *liking me* very much. But then this was a job, not a popularity contest. I tried not to worry about it and focused on my scenes.

This proved impossible to do when, at the end of the first week, things escalated from frosty atmosphere to outright animosity.

My copy of the script went missing from my dressing room, the one in which I'd made all my notes. When I started asking around if anyone had seen it, someone suggested that one of the cleaners may have accidentally thrown it away, so I – *very nicely* – asked one of the PAs if they could check where the rubbish went. I thought maybe it was sitting in a bag of paper in a recycling bin round the back somewhere and although I didn't relish the thought, I could go and have a dig for it. The next thing I knew, Lindsey was calling me to ask in her We Might Have A Problem voice if it were true that I'd been complaining about the janitorial staff ...?

The following morning, I walked into my dressing room and saw the script on the coffee table, its long edge neatly aligned with the edge of the table.

Three days in a row, my call-sheet was wrong. I was given one with the wrong start-time (so I reported to set an hour late), then one with the wrong list of scenes we were due to shoot that day (so I was unprepared) and then one intended for a shooting day a week in the future, on which I was off (so I failed to show and got a call asking where the hell I was, because everyone was waiting on me). Sure, yeah, mix-ups happen, but I seemed to be the only actor on set this had happened to, on those particular days or any others. What was weird was that on *Kings*, the call-sheets were distributed by email and physical print-outs, and when I went back to check the emailed versions – which I wasn't in the habit of checking, until then – they were correct.

From then on, I ignored the print-outs.

Late one evening, I was called to the wardrobe department to ask if I knew how I'd managed to get a bleach stain on the skirt I'd been wearing in scenes shot earlier that day. I didn't, and neither did the wardrobe department, because to their knowledge there wasn't even bleach on set. The garment had been specially made and was needed for the first shot tomorrow morning, and the seamstress who had to stay late to fix it was, understandably, unimpressed with me, even though she said, 'Look, accidents happen. Just try to be more careful going forward, okay?'

And then, all of a sudden, everyone seemed very interested in whether or not I was on Twitter.

It was a former *These Are the Days* cast member who first alerted me to the anonymous account, sending me screenshots with a string of 'eyes' emoji. Someone purporting to be a cast member on *We Were Kings* had set up a profile under the username @WWKActress and had, for weeks, been posting daily updates, supposedly all dispatches from the set. Every single tweet was a cutting insult, complaint or potentially libellous gossip-mongering. If you went by them alone, you'd think Martin Clarke was spending every waking minute mauling every female on set, that no one wanted to be there and that *We Were Kings* was going to be to critically acclaimed war movies what *Scary Movie 4* was to *Psycho*.

I sent Julia a link to the account along with a string of question marks.

She texted back: *WTAF? Who do you think it is? They sound LOVELY.*

Me: *No idea.*

Julia: *No mention of you at least.*

Me: *Thank fuck.*

Me: *Yet!*

Me: *Martin had a special friend who auditioned after me. Left crying. Could be her gone a bit Anti-Rabbit Glenn Close ...?*

Julia: *WHAAAAAT?! Spill.*

It was only later that night, lying in bed utterly exhausted but way too wired to sleep – my permanent state, since I'd started on *Kings* – that I remembered everyone's new interest in my social media habits. And there'd been no mention of me in the tweets, as Julia had pointed out. If you were trying to identify an anonymous tweeter from among a group of people, the person the tweeter *didn't* post any crap about would be the logical place to start, wouldn't it?

It's hard to explain how the day-in, day-out of this made me feel. Imagine you get a new job and, from the first moment you arrive in the office, you get the vibe that no one likes you. You've never met these people before, so you can't imagine why that could be, but logic dictates it's because of something they've heard about you, or were told you'd said, or were told you'd done. There's no obvious candidate for this in your mind, so you spend all your time racking your brain trying to come up with one, because if it *is* something you actually did or said, and you don't know what that is, you feel as if you're in constant danger of accidentally and unintentionally doing it again.

It's an unease that becomes a stress, and then that stress starts to solidify, and with the pressure of enough days that feel that way, it takes the form of a worm, a parasite, that burrows its way deep down into your psyche, infecting and affecting your every waking thought.

Julia said I should just come out and ask someone about it, or talk to Martin, or even Sandra, but every time I played out that scenario in my head, I ended up in a worse place than I was in now.

And there was no *way* I was telling Lindsey that I wasn't happy on the first feature film I'd done post-blowing up my TV career.

With a week left to go on set, I was only a shadow of the actor Martin had hired, utterly obsessed with trying to figure out what was happening on set, and *why* it was happening. I'd lie awake for hours at night, replaying every moment of the day, scrutinising it for clues. I wasn't eating as much as I should have been. My concentration started darting away from me without warning, so I began forgetting lines and making mistakes and, once, completely zoned out while the cameras were rolling, so now the invisible enemy on set had something new to whisper about me: I couldn't act, either. I was coming undone. I couldn't even be myself, let alone pretend to be Caroline.

Throughout this, Martin had been nothing but nice to me. Whatever was going on, I had the sense that it was happening below him, that he wasn't involved and probably wasn't even aware. So when I heard him say that an actor in one of the smaller parts had had to drop out because she'd got a better offer, I suggested that he hire Julia to fill in. She had just come off a weeks-long run in the West End and was back in Dublin, unpacking and recovering; I knew she was free and that she'd be willing.

This was no selfless act, of course. Having Julia on set, even if it were just for the last few days, promised not just a friendly face but also a witness. After weeks of obsessively telling her every little thing that had been going on, she'd finally get to see it for herself – and understand. Sympathise. *Believe.*

But it just made everything worse. In hindsight, I suppose it must have looked like some brand of nepotism. I'd robbed some jobbing actor of a few days' work because I'd whispered in the director's ear about *my* best friend, the actor. Or maybe whoever or whatever was behind all this just wanted to negate the effects of my having a friend on set.

A rotten stench in my dressing room was traced to a bag of soft, blackened apples on their way to putrefaction that someone had left in the bin. The hair stylist, while setting my hair in curlers, told me briskly, 'In future, if you have a problem with your hair, I'd appreciate it if you come to me directly.' I nodded and smiled and said of course before realising that her *in future* meant *if it happens again*, and so it had already happened, but I hadn't had any problem and hadn't complained, so had someone *else* said that I did?

And then, with only three days left to go, I got sick.

I hadn't eaten or drunk anything all day except for a few gulps of water from a bottle in my dressing room, one of those uber-fancy glass-tube bottles that cost more than a haircut and look like something geologists might use to store a core sample in a Hollywood movie about an impending natural disaster that no one outside of science is even remotely interested in reacting to.

The kind where it's almost impossible to tell whether they've been opened already or not.

Now I was doubled over, feeling a sudden, intense pain in my side, as something rushed up from my insides and forced itself out of my mouth. A stringy, brownish bile. While I was standing, dressed as Caroline, in the middle of a set built to look like Caroline's kitchen.

While we were *rolling*.

Cue a stunned silence, broken only by a couple of shocked gasps. Martin yelled, 'Cut!' and rushed towards me. Others rushed away, worried about getting what was coming out of me on to their costumes (cast) or equipment (crew). Most just stood there, watching me. Julia appeared, dressed in her own clothes but with her make-up still on from the scenes she'd shot before lunch, a half-eaten protein bar in her hand. Someone had run and got her from the cafeteria.

I felt so sick, and I was already so exhausted, and now I was also scared. Stealing a script or staining a skirt was one thing, but *poisoning me* was quite another. It was clearly time to stop worrying about the consequences.

So while I sat with my head between my legs on Caroline's battered couch, with Julia and Martin crouched beside me, I decided to finally let it all out. I told them everything.

Well, I told *Martin* everything, because of course Julia already knew.

And whoever was standing in the darkness beyond the lights got to hear everything, too.

It all came out in a rush, jumbled and sounding silly and occasionally incoherent, from my feeling that no one liked me to the missing script to the weird bleach stain to how you couldn't tell whether those glass water bottles had already been opened or not and we should find it? Because, you know, it was evidence.

While I spoke, Julia's eyes were wide with the effort of trying to desperately communicate to me that I should stop talking, that by telling Martin – and everybody on set – that I was singlehandedly ruining my own career before it had even had a chance to get going. Martin's brow was furrowed, like he was listening intently, but I couldn't tell what he made of any of it. In hindsight I was probably lucky I couldn't see the faces of the cast and crew standing in the shadows – although maybe it would've been a good thing if I could, because then I might have stopped sooner.

I knew it even as I was saying it: I sounded deranged. It must have sounded like I was alleging that a mix-up with a call-sheet, a wayward bleach stain and not everyone wanting to be best friends with me was hard evidence of some kind of hate campaign. But it was only after I ran out of steam and saw the look on Martin's face – incredulity, tinged with annoyance – that I realised what *else* I sounded like: an egomaniac. A no-name actor in a supporting role having a complete emotional breakdown, at work, because she was convinced that she was at the centre of some grand conspiracy, that people cared about her enough to conduct it, that the women and men who Martin and Sandra had worked with for years and years had decided, on this project, that taunting me, a woman they didn't know, was far more important than doing their actual jobs. That I was in the centre of this part of the universe, that this world had been revolving around me.

They called a doctor, and then they fired me.

INT. BEDROOM - NIGHT

Joel enters and goes straight to the laptop, which has been discarded on the bed. He powers it on and scans the desktop until he sees the 'FIRST DRAFT' Word document. He opens it and scrolls down a few virtual pages, quickly, shaking his head in apparent confusion.

He picks up the laptop and carries it out of the room …

INT. LIVING SPACE - NIGHT [CONTINUOUS]

… and into the kitchen, where he sets the laptop down on the counter.

Kate is standing with her back to the front door, leaning against it, arms wrapped around herself. Her eyes glisten with tears.

                    JOEL
You're saying you think that this document is that book?

                    KATE
It *is* that book. The text is an exact match.

                    JOEL
I didn't write this. I've never even seen it before.

                    KATE
                (sarcastically)
Sure.

                    JOEL
And I would *never* write anything in
Arial.

Kate glares coldly at him.

                 JOEL (CONT'D)
That was a joke, by the way.

Kate's expression doesn't change.

                 JOEL (CONT'D)
Look, I teach workshops, Kate.
Three different ones, at the moment.
Everyone in them has to send me stuff
in advance. That's, what? Nearly
forty different Word documents of
overwritten, semi-autobiographical
novels that have no hope of ever
seeing the light of day. I save them
all to my desktop, for ease. This
must be one of them. I can check my
emails, find out who sent it. But I
know it's not mine.

                    KATE
I searched for this place online.
Cherry Cottage. There was nothing.
Nothing at all.

                    JOEL
So when I have an explanation for
something, you just ignore it and
throw something else at me, is that
it? And you accuse *me* of gaslighting
you?

                    KATE
How did you book it?

                    JOEL
                 (exasperated)
I *told* you. A friend recommended it
to me. He's come here to write, in
the past. He gave me Maggie's number,
I called her, we did the credit card
thing over the phone. Why?

                    KATE
How do you know your friend didn't
write that book? It's set here. It
describes a cottage just like this.
And the couple in it, Karen and Jack
- they have our initials.

                    JOEL
Our …?
        (shaking head in disbelief)
Fucking hell, Kate.

                    KATE
How do you *know*?

                    JOEL
Know what?

                    KATE
That he didn't write it?

                    JOEL
Because he's never written *anything*,
okay? And he never will. He just
likes to tell people that he's going
to.

                    (to himself)
Jesus Christ.

                    KATE
You've lied to me.

                    JOEL
No, I haven't. Not once. But you've
lied to *me*, by omission. Why didn't
you tell me you'd signed with an
agent?

                    KATE
When would I have done that, exactly?
Last night when you were telling me
I didn't know what I was talking
about, or today when you abandoned me
because you were in a sulk, or since
we got back here and you've been
trying to convince me that I'm going
mad?

Joel looks down at his feet. Kate wipes away
tears.

                    JOEL
                    (softly)
What happened to us here?

                    KATE
I don't know.
                    (pauses)
I hate this place.

                    JOEL
Then let's leave.

Kate looks surprised at this suggestion.

                    JOEL (CONT'D)
Let's just go. If we don't find a B&B
or something, we'll just keep driving
until we hit the city. Check in
somewhere nice. The Imperial, maybe.
Or the Hayfield.

                    KATE
                (brightening)
Really?

                    JOEL
Really. Needless to say I'll be
calling them first to check no hack
wrote a terrible book in one of their
rooms *about* one of their rooms and
then self-published it and delivered
loads of copies to them …

                    KATE
You better.

She manages a smile.

                    JOEL
And we need to celebrate your news. I
want to hear all about it.

                    KATE
                (sceptical)
Do you?

                    JOEL
Of course I do.

He goes to her, pulls her to him and they
embrace.

JOEL (CONT'D)
I'm proud of you. You deserve every
success. And something good happening
to a writer I know is good gives me
hope.

They kiss.

KATE
But, Joel, I *did* hear something.
Someone. In the attic space. And
the power went out, and my phone
disappeared … I wasn't imagining all
that.

JOEL
You said you spoke to Gus earlier?

KATE
Yeah.

JOEL
Did you tell him about any of that
stuff?

KATE
I told him about the knock on the
door and it being open this morning,
but the other stuff hadn't happened
yet so, no. Why?

JOEL
Did he know I was gone? That you were
alone?

KATE
Yeah …?

JOEL

The friend who recommended the
cottage wasn't *my* friend, Kate. He
was yours.

KATE

What? Are you saying *Gus* recommended
this place?

JOEL

It's owned by his aunt or something.
I called him to ask what you'd got
on this weekend - I wanted to make
sure my surprise wouldn't mess up
other plans. I thought maybe that
concert you were going to with Gus
was this weekend … I told him what I
was planning and he recommended this
place.

KATE
(confused)
He didn't say anything to me.

JOEL

And he asked me not to say anything
to you. Until afterwards.

KATE

But why?

JOEL

I don't know. Maybe he thought it
wouldn't be very romantic if you knew
you were staying in a house belonging
to the guy who hates me and secretly
loves you.

                    KATE

He doesn't secretly love me.

                    JOEL

You're right - it's not a secret.

                    KATE

But that explains the trees.

                    JOEL

What?

                    KATE

When I called him, I complained about
the reception and he said it was
the trees. But I hadn't mentioned
anything about trees … That explains
how he knew.

                    JOEL

Could *he* have written that book?

                    KATE

And, what? Emailed it to you and then
come here to freak me out?

                    JOEL

To ruin *our* romantic weekend. To
drive a wedge between us.

                    KATE

Now *you're* sounding like the crazy
one. And overestimating Gus's
imagination. *And* work ethic.

Joel holds up his hands as if to signal that
he only speaks the truth.

                    KATE (CONT'D)
Let's just get out of here.

                    JOEL
Agreed. Can you pack up my stuff
while I clear up the kitchen?

                    KATE
Yeah.

                    JOEL
Do you want to eat dinner before we
go or …?

Kate shakes her head.

                    JOEL (CONT'D)
Me neither. We can stop somewhere on
the way.

Kate nods and then disappears down the hall,
to the bedroom.

Joel busies himself with the kitchen. Behind
his back, the door to the utility room starts
to open, slowly.

TWENTY-THREE

'Jesus,' Donal breathed, his gaze fixed on something invisible hanging in the air between us.

'Martin thought I was the anonymous tweeter,' I said. 'And that I'd done the other things myself. A drama queen, desperate for attention. And I couldn't disprove it. Nothing else happened after I left and the Twitter account disappeared, so ... All the weird stuff that happened here today, the parallels to the script – Kate experiencing all these things and Joel dismissing her – that's what it reminded me of. Not some other movie, but what happened to me on *We Were Kings*. Whatever *that* was.'

And if it did actually happen.

'What do you think was going on?'

'My best theory,' I said, 'was that someone who knew Sandra saw Martin on the street with Ms Fuck You the day of the audition and told her about it. They assumed it was me – we looked similar, Martin had just followed me out of the audition room *and* I ended up getting the part. The crew were the same people they always worked with, so they must have had friends on it, and maybe Sandra whispered it to one of them or they heard it from somewhere else ... I arrive on set as the mistress and everyone hates me for it.'

Donal frowned.

'I know,' I said. 'It needs a lot of very professional, experienced people to choose to behave like tweens in a schoolyard because of something that's happening in someone else's marriage, and Sandra herself was always super nice to me. And it doesn't really explain everything.' I sighed. 'A therapist I went to – once, only – said it was most likely a build-up of stress and anxiety. That I was experiencing a time of great upheaval in my life and this was how it manifested itself. That nothing was ever going on, really. Just me ascribing meaning and intent to random, disconnected things because I felt like my world was out of control. Which is often why people subscribe to conspiracy theories. That's what I was doing, in effect, according to this therapist: building my own personal conspiracy theory.'

The fire in the hearth was now a crackling bouquet of flames, having engulfed the logs. I could feel the heat of it on my hands, the skin on my face. It was welcome, warming me back up after my stint out in the cold, but hot enough for me to know that if I stayed here, I'd soon be sticky and sweating.

'Did Steve ever mention anything about it to you?' I asked. 'Do you think he knows? Or that any of the crew do?'

Donal shook his head. 'No, never. I never heard about any of this. I mean, I'm not exactly in any loops, but ... Is it, you know, *public*?'

'That's the million-dollar question. Lindsey and Martin had a chat, and I don't know what she told him – well, I can guess what she told him – but it was agreed that it was a private medical event that unfortunately happened in public, and that it should be kept under wraps. Now maybe, in addition to that, Martin did his own investigation and found out that people thought I was his mistress, and since he really did have one, figured it was in his best interests to keep it quiet. I don't know.' I shrugged. 'I've never been confronted with it, but the risk of it coming out is always there. Every time I walk into an audition room or even meet someone else in the industry ... I started making excuses not to see my friends, because they're all actors or associated with acting in some way, and I became paranoid that they knew. It's why, in the end, I went to LA.'

A beat passed.

'And it's why,' I said, 'I thought this job was so perfect, because there was no time for Martin to ring up Steve and warn him that I'm trouble. It was secret, and last-minute, and filming out in the middle of nowhere in a place where our *phones wouldn't even work*, for God's sake. I could just skip straight to the bit where I'm in a movie that's coming out. And that's all I need, you know? A success that gives me some power back. Some confidence. I need to be able to walk into rooms and know that *that's* what people are thinking about, that great thing I was in that everyone loved, and not, *Isn't that the actor who thought she was too good for a soap, who went crazy, vomited in the middle of a scene and then started ranting about being poisoned by the crew on the first job she did after she left it?'*

'Okay, *but* ...' Donal started. 'The situations aren't the same, though. On *We Were Kings* you thought stuff was happening that, um ...' He glanced at me, uncertain.

'Go on. You can say it.'

'Well, maybe they weren't.'

'They *probably* weren't,' I said. 'Being realistic about it.'

'But the stuff that happened here, today, *did* happen – but we have explanations for them.'

'Not all of them,' I said.

I told him about the lights in the house coming back on, then going off again, when the power in my cabin was unaffected. The sliding glass door being open, then locked, even though I was supposed to be the only person on set. Peg's business card going missing from my coat pocket.

Donal only reacted to the last one.

'What?' he said, straightening up. 'Where was the coat?'

'In the wardrobe. In my cabin.'

'And the card was definitely in the pocket? Are you sure you didn't, you know, accidentally drop it somewhere?'

'But that's just it, isn't it? How can I be sure I didn't? I might have pulled it out by accident when I took my hand out of the pocket. I have to allow for that. Therefore, I can't be sure someone took the card. But what if someone *did* take the card and they're relying on me thinking this way?' I rubbed at my temples. 'Honestly, this whole thing ... I need a drink.'

'What did you say Martin's last name was?'

'Clarke,' I said. 'With an "e".' It struck me as a strange detail to pull out of everything I'd told him about *We Were Kings*. 'Why? Do you know him?'

'No, never heard of him.'

But that came out sounding different to everything else Donal had said to me since I'd first met him, coming out of the motorhome.

That sounded like a lie.

'Donal—' I started.

Abruptly, he stood up. 'I need the bathroom.'

I looked at his face, held his gaze, searched for something I could rely on, something that would give me some certainty either way.

Could I trust him? Or was he in on this too?

Was there a *this*?

Or did Donal just need to go to the bathroom?

'I'll be back in a sec.'

'Actually,' I said, 'before you go — is there a copy of the script here? The original one, I mean. With the ending.'

I knew this much for sure: I wanted to read it. Because if something *was* going on, there were undeniable parallels. Kate and I were having a shared experience, all the way from the knock on the door to this, now, here, sitting in front of a roaring fire with a seemingly trustworthy man who had an explanation for everything.

But my copy of the script wasn't the whole story. Steve was — supposedly — reworking the ending on the fly, and so the ending in mine was actually just the Act II break.

I didn't know Kate's fate.

I'd left her at her lowest point, the last few moments she'd spend in the upside-down world the events of Act II had landed her in, feeling defeated, like all was lost, about to give up and give in, to succumb. But the night is darkest just before the dawn and, if Steve and Daniel had stuck to the principles of storytelling that had served humankind for millennia, Kate was about to have an a-ha moment that would change everything. The path forward would crystallise, the way through would be revealed, and she'd realise that whatever she needed to get to the other side had been right in front of her or lying dormant inside of her, or both, all along. Armed with this new knowledge, Act III, the climax, could commence.

I had barely scanned the pages that far into my copy of the script, and the last time I'd done that had been somewhere over the Atlantic. But from what I could remember, Kate's lowest point had been her discovering Joel's body in the back seat of their car.

The one phrase I knew for sure I'd read was *slashed to the bone*.

Donal didn't respond immediately and I thought for a second he was going to come up with an excuse. But then he said, 'Of course, yeah,' and crossed the room to a pile of boxes stacked in the corner. 'I think I saw one in here yesterday.'

I turned back to the fire and listened to him digging around, wondering how far to push this, what I would say if he claimed he'd been mistaken, that there was no original script in there, no original script around at all.

One of the boxes fell over, spilling its contents on to the hardwood floor with a series of clatters, and Donal swore loudly.

Then he said, 'Here it is.'

He handed me a well-thumbed script, pages curling at the edges, bound with brass tacks. It was missing its title page but, when I flicked to the final one, the last line on it indeed read *FADE TO BLACK*.

This version also had scene numbers, like the page I'd found in the pocket of my robe. I wondered if that page would be missing from this, but I found the corresponding scene quickly. It was there, intact.

'Do you need anything else?' Donal asked. 'Anything I can grab from upstairs? Are you warm enough? I could get a blanket?'

I waved him away, said I was fine.

He told me he'd be back in a minute.

TWENTY-FOUR

THUD.

A sudden, loud bang from directly above my head.

I jerked with the fright of it, then lifted my eyes to the ceiling. It had sounded like something heavy, falling on the floor.

Some*one* falling.

I waited for more, for the sounds of that someone getting up again, for Donal's voice calling out, 'Don't worry, I'm all right!'

But none came.

I'd been engrossed in the script and hadn't noticed how much time had passed, but now I saw that, according to the clock on the mantelpiece, Donal had been gone for the bones of fifteen minutes.

The only sound was the crackling of the fire in front of me. I didn't think that, actually, I'd heard anything since he'd disappeared upstairs. Not him walking around, or closing a door, or the flush of the toilet.

'Donal?' I called out.

No response.

I set the script aside and stood up, testing my ankle. It wasn't as bad as it had been; I could walk on it, although not without a bit of a limp.

I made my way to the bottom of the stairs.

'Donal? Are you all right?'

Still nothing. No noise at all. I had been upstairs – there was no way a person could be up there, even at the other end of the landing, in the bathroom, not even with the door closed, and not hear my voice shouting at them from here.

And what had that bang been?

I lifted a foot on to the bottom step, then thought better of it. Cherry Cottage, the house in *Final Draft*, was a bungalow. Everything was on the one level. I suspected this was the only reason there wasn't a scene where Kate ran up a set of stairs like an idiot, towards obvious danger, while the audience rolled their eyes. I wasn't about to add one to this shoot.

Not without getting some kind of weapon first.

I cast about the room looking for something suitable. The space was filled with equipment – cameras and lights and cabling and rigs, Mark's boom – but nothing that was both light enough and heavy enough for my needs. I turned towards the kitchen. There were probably knives in the drawers but ...

Knives? Really? In *real life*? What was I going to do with one of those, exactly? Push it into someone's actual flesh? Cause them physical injury or, you know, *death*? Was I really prepared to *commit murder* because someone had gone to the bathroom and then didn't answer me after I heard a noise?

And what if he actually had fallen, or had some kind of medical event, and I was wasting precious time down here acting like I was in a horror movie?

I turned towards the stairs, ready to start up them, but then I thought of the way Donal's voice had sounded, the lie I was sure he'd told.

What had he *really* gone upstairs for? And why wasn't he answering now?

'*Donal!*' I barked.

No answer.

Maybe I *was* ready to commit murder.

There wasn't anything else of potential use to me in the kitchen that I could see, so I pushed open the door next to the fridge, the one Donal had disappeared into earlier and emerged from with my phone.

It was a little utility room. There was a washing machine, open shelves filled with cleaning products, and a coat rack affixed to the wall from which the raincoat I'd had on earlier was hanging, right next to the one Donal had had on when I met him on the road.

And another door.

It wasn't closed fully and, behind it, a light was on, so I knew what it was going to reveal to me before I pushed it all the way open: a bathroom. A little WC, just big enough for a commode and the tiniest sink I'd ever seen, so small that I doubted you could actually do your business *and* close the door at the same time.

Donal hadn't needed to go upstairs at all.

I went back out to the kitchen. I wasn't going to bother calling his name any more. I was going to find out what the fuck was going on here, once and for all.

My phone was still sitting, charging, on the counter. I pulled it off the cable and watched the screen come to life. The crack was still through the battery symbol, but I thought I could see a hint of green. Still no service, *quelle surprise*. I put it in the pocket of my sweatpants and did one last scan of the downstairs space.

My eyes landed on the corner diagonally across from me, the one between the fireplace and the sliding glass door. There was a little wrought-iron rack there, about two feet high, holding a half-dozen wooden logs. What I hadn't noticed until right now was that hanging off both sides of it was a set of matching accessories: a shovel, a brush, a pair of tongs and a poker. The items weren't particularly large and, when I picked up the first one – the tongs – I discovered that they weren't very heavy either.

But they were something. I could at least whack someone in the lower leg with the shovel, make them fall or trip.

Like someone had done to me earlier, with the branch, out on the road.

Or might have.

I looked at the front door. I could go, walk out of it right now, leave this place. I *should*. My phone had charge. I could run down the road, wait for Peg down there. Well, I could *limp quickly* down the road and wait for Peg down there. Call Julia and get Peg's number, then call Peg and tell her I really needed to go, like, *now*.

But hadn't I tried that exact thing already? And look how well that had turned out.

Here I was, once again, right back where I started, alone at Cedarwood House. Wondering what the fuck was going on. Scared that it was something more than the filming of some shitty horror movie.

Enough was enough. Bring on Act III.

Gripping the shovel, I started up the stairs.

My stockinged feet made no noise on the bare wooden stairs, but they creaked with every change in weight, giving me away. Mine was a slow ascent, seeing as the least painful way for my injured ankle was to get both feet on a step before advancing to the next one. I also accidentally banged the shovel off the banister halfway up, revealing that I wasn't just coming up the stairs, but bringing something I could hit someone with, too.

Great work, Adele. Maybe I was more suited for Lead Female Actor in a Horror Movie than I knew.

Since stealth was no longer an option, I called out Donal's name again when I reached the top. No response. I strained to hear something – anything – in the silence, but all I got was a faint rustling noise whose origin I couldn't detect.

Where the hell had he gone?

It was dim on the landing and when I turned around, I saw why: the only light was the one on inside the bathroom, and the door to it was only a foot or so ajar. Either Donal wasn't in the bathroom or he was a lot more open about his bodily functions than me.

I lifted a hand to feel for the light switch I'd flipped on the last time I was up here, but only felt smooth wall. And I felt something else, in the air: the presence of another person, the beating pulse of some other heart.

Donal was here, somewhere. I could feel it.

Or *someone* was.

But where the hell were they? Hiding in one of the bedrooms? Why would they do that? What the hell was going on?

And with that – with my having to ask myself that for the umpteenth time since I'd come to this godforsaken place – I snapped and shouted, '*Donal!*'

Screamed it, really.

'Where the fuck are you? I'm warning you *right now*, if you don't answer me in the next five seconds, I'm holding a shovel and I *will* drive one of its corners straight into your *balls.*'

Nothing.

'*Repeatedly*. I mean it. Because I am *so* fucking done with this s—'

A number of things happened then in quick succession, none of which, in isolation, made any sense.

There was a rumbling noise, directly above my head, even though all that was above my head was attic.

There was a loud but abrupt yelp.

A pair of legs appeared in front of me.

Dangling, at eye-level. *Hanging* in front of me. From the ceiling.

Men's legs, in jeans and muddy Nikes.

I looked up just in time to see that they belonged to the man who was hanging out of an open square in the ceiling – the attic's access hatch was open – and then the legs fell, followed by the rest of the body attached to them, dropping from the ceiling in a crumpled heap on the floor at my feet, moaning loudly in pain as it landed.

Someone had just *fallen out of the attic.*

That someone wasn't Donal, because a ladder was unfolding now, extending down from the open hatch, and another pair of jeans-wearing legs were coming down them, and those legs belonged to him.

Hiking boots, neon laces.

Donal stepped off the ladder, reached out a hand and flipped a light switch between two of the bedroom doors I hadn't noticed before. The landing was suddenly bright –

bright enough to identify the crumpled heap on the floor at my feet as it rolled over, towards me.

The face was red and angry and scrunched up in apparent pain, but I recognised it. It was the DOP, Mick.

I said, 'What the hell?'

Mick said the same thing to Donal, but louder and angrier and with an extra swear word.

'I'm sorry,' Donal said to him. 'I was trying to get the hatch closed before she came up the stairs.'

'You *knocked me out of the ceiling,*' Mick spat at him. 'I think I just broke a feckin' *rib.*'

'It was an accident.'

'Oh, was it? Great.' Mick rolled his eyes. 'That's me healed, then.'

'What did you want me to do?'

'She *knew* you were up here, you moron. What was closing the hatch going to do? What were you going to tell her afterwards – that you'd jumped out the window?'

Neither of them had yet acknowledged that I was standing there, inches from them, or that I was holding a shovel. I watched Mick pull himself into a sitting position, his back against the banister, and Donal lean against one of the closed bedroom doors. I looked from Donal to Mick, from Mick to the open attic hatch, and then back to Donal again.

'You said everyone.'

They both turned towards the sound of my voice.

'You said *everyone,*' I said again, to Donal. 'You said everyone went into town this morning. The whole crew. I asked you that specifically because if I was alone here, I couldn't explain anything that had happened.' The volume of my voice was steadily rising. 'But Mick didn't go, did he? He was here.' I pointed. 'Up there. And you *knew* that. You came up here to, what? Check on him? Get him? *Warn* him?'

'Adele,' Donal said, holding his hands up, 'I can explain.'

'No,' Mick said to him. 'You *can't*.'

'Mick, come on. She's not stupid. She *knows*.'

'Then we don't need to explain it to her, do we?'

'Yes,' I said, my grip tightening on the shovel. 'Yes, you do.'

'Steve will be here any second,' Mick said to Donal. 'Let *him* explain it to her. Let's not get ourselves in more trouble than we're already in.' He turned to me. 'Please don't put the shovel in my balls for saying this, love, but it's nothing personal. I needed the money. You probably did too. So let's not turn this into a whole *thing*, okay?'

My knuckles were white on the shovel's handle.

'Adele—' Donal started.

'Both of you,' I said, 'really need to just shut the fuck up.'

I stepped over Mick, pressing the shovel against Donal as I pushed past him, forcing him to take it from me, and stood at the bottom of the ladder. When I looked up, through the open hatch, I saw dark.

No, *mostly* dark. Something up there was emitting a blue light.

I knew what it was, but I needed to see it for myself. I needed evidence. No ambiguity. No more second-guessing myself, no more wondering, no more weirdness that could be explained away. No more worrying that I couldn't even identify reality any more, that I might be losing my mind.

I reached out, gripped the sides of the ladder and started up it, ignoring the protests of my bad ankle.

'Adele,' Donal said. 'Wait, no—'

I felt his arms on my legs and kicked out my good one with as much force as I could muster. My heel connected with something soft, and Donal squealed at a pitch the banshee would be proud of.

Free of his grasp, I hurried up the rest of the way, not stopping until my head and shoulders were through the hatch, my injured ankle was burning and I had a clear, unobstructed view into the attic space.

What I saw rendered me speechless.

Kate gathers Joel's clothing and personal
items and throws them indiscriminately into
his suitcase, lying open on the bed.

> KATE
> (calling out)
> Should we call the owner, tell her
> we're leaving?

There's no response.

> KATE (CONT'D)
> Joel?

She stops packing.

> KATE (CONT'D)
> Did you hear me?

Kate turns and goes to the bedroom door, which
is standing open.

> KATE (CONT'D)
> Joel?

There is no response - or noise of any
description. The rest of the house is
completely silent.

CUT TO:

51   INT. LIVING SPACE - NIGHT   51

A close-up of a hand in a leather glove,
pressing a button on a small remote control.

52   INT. BEDROOM - NIGHT   52

The silence is broken by a sustained
ELECTRONIC HUM.

Kate frowns. Over her shoulder, we can see
movement, the source of the hum: the blinds on
the floor-to-ceiling window are retracting.

Now she turns and sees it too. She stares at
it, then turns back towards the door.

                    KATE
                (uncertain)
        Joel?

53   INT. LIVING SPACE - NIGHT   53

Kate slowly advances down the hall, nervous.
As the kitchen area comes into view to Kate's
left, we see that Joel isn't there.

And then that the front door is open.

Kate goes to it …

54   EXT. CHERRY COTTAGE - NIGHT [CONTINUOUS]   54

…and stands in the open doorway, looking out
into the night.

There is a small puddle of light on the
gravel: the light that is escaping from the
house through the open door. The front half
of the rental car sits inside it. Beyond the

puddle's perimeter, everything is cloaked in a
thick, inky darkness.

Kate scans the scene, but doesn't find Joel.

It is still wet and windy, and now thunder
roars in the distance.

55   INT. LIVING SPACE - NIGHT   55

Kate re-enters the house just as the oven
emits an electronic BEEP. She hurries to find
an oven glove, pulls it on and removes the
dish inside. A cloud of smoke comes with it.

She turns to set it on the counter behind her
and sees—

BLOOD.

All over the counter, an area of the kitchen
hidden from her line of sight when she checked
for Joel before. Splattered all over the
marble. Dripping down the white cabinets.
Pooling on the wooden floor.

Kate SCREAMS and drops the dish, which
SMASHES. She shakes her head in utterly
contemptuous disgust.

                    KATE
         This is fucking sick, Joel.
                 (louder)
         You are fucking *sick*!

She sees the car keys further down the counter
and grabs them.

> KATE (CONT'D)
> Oh, and by the way, I hated *Inside*.
> And just FYI, women do *not* go around
> all day thinking about how good their
> bras feel. That reviewer was *right*.

She collects her bag - by the door since
she threatened to leave - and strides back
outside, slamming the door behind her.

56 EXT. CHERRY COTTAGE/INT. CAR - NIGHT   56

Kate unlocks the rental car with the fob
and gets into the driver's seat. But when
she turns the key in the ignition, nothing
happens. She tries again, and then again, all
to no avail.

> KATE
> (muttering)
> For fuck's sake.

Frustrated, Kate leans back against her seat -
which is when she sees, reflected in the rear-
view mirror—

JOEL'S DEAD BODY.

Propped up on the back seat. His eyes are open
and glassy, and his throat is slashed to the
bone.

Kate SCREAMS.

TWENTY-FIVE

The attic space was just that: space in the attic. It hadn't been converted. A single bulb with a string hung from the ceiling; I pulled it, turning on a dim light. The joists in the floor were exposed, as were the rafters and the shiny insulation packed tightly under the eaves of the roof. What looked like MDF sheeting had been layered as a makeshift floor. The pitch of the roof was at a height that I didn't think would give me enough vertical inches to stand up straight anywhere. Most of the space was taken up with dusty cardboard boxes and clear plastic bins filled with what looked like Christmas decorations, but at the far end, against the gable wall, was what had just made my breath catch in my throat.

Two plastic bins full of red and green baubles had been pushed end-to-end to form a sort of makeshift desk, and serving as a chair was a saggy, grey beanbag. Empty Coke cans and foil food wrappers littered the floor around the beanbag, forming a circle with a radius of an arm's length.

On top of the 'desk' were two widescreen computer monitors. Both displays were divided into six smaller screens and each of those was currently showing a familiar scene from an unfamiliar angle, all of which were from the ground floor of Cedarwood House.

'What is this?' I asked no one in particular.

But I already knew.

I climbed off the ladder and crawled on my hands and knees to the screens to get a better look.

'Adele?' Donal's voice called from below.

Then Mick's, muttering, 'Just leave her.'

'We need to explain.'

'We need to get ourselves feckin' solicitors is what we need.'

One of the boxes on the left screen showed a view from the kitchen area towards the fireplace, taking in the armchairs and some of the sliding glass door, captured by a camera up high but not quite at ceiling level. If I'd had to guess, I would've said it was fixed to the top of the kitchen cabinets, or hiding in plain sight on one of the open shelves.

Another showed the reverse, looking at the kitchen from the corner where I'd got the shovel. That lens was much lower – hiding in something sitting on the fireplace. The clock I'd seen there, probably.

On the screen to the right, there was a view looking straight down on to the foot of the stairs. Another was of the kitchen, from above the window there. Another camera appeared to have been placed in the utility room.

At least two were attached to the exterior wall of the house: one at the front, looking down at the front door from the left, and one at the rear that would capture anyone coming in through or leaving via the sliding glass door.

Me, earlier, desperately trying to open it.

One camera appeared to be mounted on the roof of the motorhome, capturing Cedarwood House from the front. That image was mostly dark, the lit windows glowing white on screen.

A little red dot was flashing in the upper left corner of every box: these feeds were recording.

And they were live. I could see the fire flickering. The charging cable on the kitchen counter was in the exact position I'd left it just a couple of minutes ago. I heard footsteps going down the stairs and then, on screen, saw a figure stop on the bottom step.

Mick looked up, directly into the lens. We stared at each other for a long moment. Then he held up his hands and made a shrugging motion before walking out of the shot, shaking his head.

My eyes went back to the feed transmitting from the mantel above the fireplace. The lens was facing the armchair I'd been sitting on. I would've been right in the middle of the shot, up close, when I'd changed out of my wet clothes earlier. When Donal had *directed me* to change out of my wet clothes, knowing full well that that camera was there.

Donal, the only one on this crew who'd been in any way nice to me. Who'd brought me room-service breakfast. Who'd run interference with Neil.

Whom I'd trusted.

To whom I'd just told the whole story of what happened to me on *We Were Kings*, the thing that had nearly derailed me entirely, that had pushed me to my lowest ebb.

Who'd lied to me.

A mouthful of bile pushed its way up my throat, and I heaved.

'Adele?'

Donal's voice came from right behind me. He'd come up the ladder and was on his knees just inside the hatch.

I jumped and scrambled away in a panic, into the far corner, feeling a sting in my ankle. I pressed my back up against the wall, ready to kick out my good leg if he came any closer.

'Get away from me,' I spat.

Even though I wanted him to come closer because I suspected that hurting him right now would feel so good.

'It's okay,' he said gently, holding up both hands as if to assure me that he had come in peace. 'But Steve will be here any second so let me tell you now, all right? Let me tell you everything. Or at least, what I know – what I know now, because I swear – Adele, I *swear* – I didn't know about any of this until today.'

I shook my head, disbelieving.

As if I was going to believe anything he ever said again.

'As far as I knew,' Donal said, 'this was a normal production. I really did wake up early this morning and I really did just want to go into town to get a coffee and check my emails, kill some time, and then everybody else wanted to come with me …' He stopped, swallowed. 'Well, everybody except Mick. So we all go in, and we have some breakfast, and a few of the guys go to the shop or whatever, and I check my emails as planned … And then Steve's like, let's stay and watch the match. We have time. But then the weather started getting bad, and then it was getting dark, and, well, time was ticking on. And as far as I knew, Mick was still asleep in bed. I hoped you were too, but I thought there was a good chance you'd woken up, and soon it'd be time for dinner – breakfast – and you'd be wondering where we were. So I start pushing Steve, saying we need to get back, and …' Donal cleared his throat. 'That's when he told me that he didn't want us to go back, that this was great, actually – for him – because he was, ah … He was filming you.'

I was all but curled up in a ball in the corner of the attic space now, arms wrapped around myself, trying not to throw up, trying not to cry.

'Mick,' I said. 'He wasn't asleep at all, was he? He was up here all day.'

Donal nodded. 'And everyone else already knew. Steve told them last night, after I'd gone to bed. Apparently he was planning on telling me then too, but he overheard us chatting on the path back to the cabins last night and thought I might have been too chummy with you, that I would've told you or, you know, refused to go along with it.'

I rolled my eyes. 'Well, he didn't need to worry about *that*, did he?'

'I'm telling you now,' Donal said in a small voice.

'Oh, fuck off.' I could feel a white-hot fury bubbling in my gut. 'The time to tell me was the moment you came back, when we met out on the road. It should've been the first thing out of your mouth. Actually, no. Scrap that. You should've come back the moment he told you.'

'I tried to,' Donal said. 'But the bridge—'

'So everything was Mick, was it? The knock, the lights?'

'And it was him you heard talking on the phone, too. Although that wasn't supposed to happen. You'd gone off down the track, and Mick didn't know what to do, so he called Steve to ask.'

'How do you know this? Were you in contact with him?'

'No, he just told me now. When I was up here.'

'And what?' I said. 'Steve told him to trip me? To follow me down the road and physically hurt me? To scare the shite out of me?'

'Trip you? What are you …?' Donal blinked at me. 'You didn't say anything about anyone tripping you before. And Mick didn't go anywhere. He came back up here. No one followed you down the track, Adele.'

'Oh, and I'm just supposed to believe you now, am I? Everything up until now has been a lie but *this* is the truth?'

'He didn't go down the track,' Donal said. 'That's all I know. And he didn't take Peg's card out of your pocket either. That's what I came up here to ask him, to check. Because that had nothing to do with the stuff that happened in the script, so I knew it wasn't a part of it. The idea was to create parallels with the script, so … I was worried Mick had, I don't know, gone rogue, and if he had, then—'

'What?' I said mockingly. 'You'd have put a stop to that, would you?'

'I was trying to protect you,' Donal said to the makeshift floor.

'Oh, come *on*.' I pointed at the computers. 'You made me *undress*. Right in front of that camera. That's *recording*.'

Donal's face started flooding with the colour of beetroot.

'Look, I *tried*,' he said. 'I stood between you and the camera as best as I could.'

'What a saint you are.'

'What else could I do?'

'Um, how about *tell me*?'

'Look.' Donal threw up his hands, suddenly frustrated. 'I really wanted this *job*, okay? I'm sorry but I did. I wanted the opportunity to work with Steve Dade. I'm sorry I took the best offer I'd ever got in my career. I'm sorry I didn't want to be unemployed.'

Our eyes met and I sensed him sensing my resignation, his knowing that I couldn't argue with that because *I* had wanted the same things and, despite what I should've identified as a *carpet* of red flags leading me all the way to the door of Cedarwood House, I had still come here.

Stayed here, despite everything. And I still hadn't left.

'So what is this? What is actually going on here? The *truth*, this time.'

'Well ...' Donal paused to take a deep breath. 'I don't have all the details. Trying to get straight answers out of Steve is like trying to get blood from a stone. But from what I can gather, there *is* no *Final Draft*. No production that's going to film the movie as it's written, anyway. Instead, Steve wants to make the script happen for real. Not literally, not with a couple checking into a cottage and all that, but the, ah, thematic premise of it.'

I fucking knew it. *Trust the process.* Alarm bells, every time.

'You probably didn't get time to read this far,' Donal went on, 'but the ending is that the author of *First Draft,* the book they find in the cottage, says something like, "True-crime sells better than crime fiction, so I've written a true-crime book, and now all I have to do is make it come true." He wrote about a couple staying at the cottage being attacked, and then he attacked a couple staying at the cottage to make what he'd written real. So Steve has a script about that, and an actress—'

'Actor,' I muttered, as if that's what mattered now.

'An actor who's at the cottage to play the role, and I guess he's thinking if you have the same experience, if you're here at the cottage and weird shit is happening to you, too, that's *another* layer of fiction becoming true. Or something.' He swallowed. 'I don't know exactly, but he used the word *meta* a lot. That's what this is all about.'

'What this is all about,' I said evenly, '*all* this is about, is Steve being a fucking reckless lunatic who's never going to get to work in this industry ever again.'

'I think this is why it didn't work out with Primal,' Donal said. 'They must have found out his real intentions and told him to forget it. It's not just ethically questionable; I think it's probably illegal, too. And that would also explain why he didn't rehire anyone who'd been hired by the original production. And why he *did* hire me, who'd never done this job before. There probably never was an original AD. He just wanted a crew who didn't know, wouldn't figure it out by themselves and—'

'Wouldn't do anything about it,' I said, 'if they *did* find out.'

'Adele,' Donal started, 'I was just—'

'Following orders, is it?' And then I thought of something else. 'The text messages,' I said. 'The weird ones I got, just as I arrived. And the one I got while you were gone. Were they all a part of this too?'

'I really don't know. Steve didn't say anything about texts, and Mick didn't seem to know about them.'

'And I suppose the bridge is fine?'

'No, the bridge really is flooded,' Donal said. 'But it almost always happens whenever exceptionally heavy rainfall meets a high tide, and Steve knew the forecast. That's why there was this big rush to get you here. It's supposed to be dry from midweek on. He said what happened today was a lucky break, that he only needed the rain, really. If the bridge *didn't* flood, he was just going to tell you it had.'

'What about Simon Pearse?' I asked. 'My co-star who is supposedly arriving next week?'

'Steve told me this afternoon that the email he gave me for the guy's agent was a Gmail account he'd signed up for himself. I've been sending travel arrangements to no one.'

'But this is all so ...' I closed my eyes, rubbed at them, trying to find a term that would encapsulate the full scope of this shit-show. *Preposterous? Ludicrous? Certifiably insane?* There wasn't one. I opened them again. 'How could he even be sure he could *control* this? The cameras are only in the main house. How did he know I'd even come in here? And how did he know I wouldn't leave? I could've done anything, gone anywhere. I could've just sat in my—' I stopped, having thought of a new horror. '*Please* tell me there isn't a camera in my cabin, or I swear—'

'The only cameras are these,' Donal said, pointing at the screen. 'I promise you that's true.'

This felt true, but I couldn't trust anything he said any more.

'And you didn't,' he said quietly. 'Stay in your cabin, I mean.'

'No, I didn't. I went to the road, where *you* convinced me to come back. And what the hell happens next? I say, *Oh fine, yeah, genius at work, please continue, where's the release so I can sign?* That's *never* going to happen. And it never *was*. This is all for nothing. Steve Dade just ended his career and he probably took the careers of everyone on this crew with him.'

Donal let a beat pass before he said, 'I think he must know what happened on *We Were Kings*.'

'What? You *just* told me—'

'And that was *true*,' he protested. 'He didn't say anything to me and I hadn't heard anything about it. But now, having heard it from you, my guess would be that someone told him. And are you working in some kind of motel? In LA? Because Steve knows about that, too. And that you don't have an agent, and that you haven't really been working since you, um ...' Donal was blushing again. Ironic, since he was listing reasons *I* should be embarrassed. 'I think maybe he offered the part to you because he thought that ... Well, that you'd be ...' He cleared his throat. 'That you'd—'

'Be so desperate for the gig that I'd go along with it,' I finished.

'Something like that, yeah.'

A beat passed.

'I really am sorry, Adele.' Donal wouldn't meet my eye.

'Those are just words, aren't they?'

'I'm still sorry.'

'Honestly, Donal ... I don't give a fuck if you are.'

Something on the screens caught his attention then. I looked too, just in time to see one of the feeds go completely white.

But then the white moved off, out of the shot, and I realised that what I'd seen was a pair of headlights sweeping past the camera.

A car had just pulled up outside Cedarwood House.

Now that I listened for it, I could hear the crunch of gravel under the wheels, the low hum of the engine.

'Is it Peg?' I asked, moving to go.

'Ah …' Donal squinted at the screen. 'No. It's Steve and the guys.' He moved towards the hatch, positioned himself to start climbing back down it. 'I'll go down and talk to him first, okay? Stay up here until I call you.'

'Why?'

But Donal didn't answer me.

He'd already disappeared down the ladder.

TWENTY-SIX

I swore under my breath. I didn't want to stay in the attic. I wanted to get down there and confront Steve. The only thing that made me feel any better about this situation was imagining that. *But …*

Neil the Aspiring Sex Offender would be there, too. And Liam, the women-hating roid-rager. And Aaron, who didn't look like he could stand up to a breeze. Mark had seemed okay, but then so had Mick.

So had Donal.

The reality was, if I *did* go down there and confront Steve, I didn't know what else would happen. I didn't know who'd be on my side. I couldn't guarantee anyone would be.

And if Steve was willing to risk his entire career to do this, what *else* was he willing to do?

A car door slammed outside, but wherever the car was parked, it wasn't in sight of any of the cameras. Instead, I watched Donal on one of them hurrying down the stairs and then out the front door, into the dark.

I took my phone out of my pocket and saw that the screen was crowded with notifications. New texts, missed calls, unread emails. *How have I …?* When I looked at the top left-hand corner, I saw a beautiful sight: three whole bars of reception.

It must be the height: three floors up.

For some reason, the device was on silent – I didn't remember doing that, but perhaps Donal had when he'd plugged it in for me downstairs, the little shit − so I hadn't heard any of this stuff come in. I put the volume back on and started flicking through it.

The text messages Donal had claimed to have sent were there now.

4:15 p.m. − Just FYI we're in town. Back soon. If you want anything from the shop let me know by 5. Hope you had a good day's sleep! Donal ☺

5:55pm − Weather causing problems. Looks like bridge back is flooded, can't cross. We'll be delayed and Steve has CXL tonight's shoot. Hope you're ok? Donal

7:34 p.m. − Worried you're not getting my texts. Can you reply if you are? D

Nearly everything else was from Lindsey.

Missed calls. Texts asking, *Where are you?* Texts from other people telling me Lindsey was trying to reach me, her asking them to ask me to call her back.

I did so, now.

She answered right away.

'Thank *God*,' she said. 'Talk to me. Where are you? Are you okay?'

At the sound of a familiar, trustworthy voice, a huge lump suddenly bloomed at the back of my throat and my bottom lip began to tremble. I hadn't realised how tense I'd been all day, how much energy it took to keep yourself in a constant state of *braced*.

All I wanted to do now was crumple and cry.

But I couldn't. Not yet. Instead, I took a deep breath and answered the question it was easiest to answer.

343

'I'm in West Cork,' I said. 'On set. With Steve.'

Lindsey exhaled, a harsh whistling in my ear. 'That's what I was afraid you were going to say. Is he there with you now? Can you talk?'

'I'm alone, but …' I glanced at the monitors. 'I might have to go soon. Why? What's wrong?'

'To be honest, I'm not exactly sure.'

Welcome to the club.

'Where is this set,' she asked, 'exactly?'

'A place called Cedarwood House. Near Bantry.'

I heard the click of a pen on Lindsey's end. She was writing that down.

'Listen,' she said then. 'When you emailed me first, I thought you were talking about *A Wound of Words*. It's this famine thing Steve's been trying to drag up the hill for ever. Terrible title, but anyway. I heard a couple of weeks ago he finally got funding for it, so I thought that's the project you meant. But then when you mentioned Yvonne in your second message …'

I got your number from Yvonne – Yvonne Stokes? At the Lindsey Ryan Agency?

'Adele, Yvonne hasn't worked for me for six months.'

But that was how John, the guy at Cross Cut who'd called me about the part, had said he'd got my US number.

'And then in your voicemail,' Lindsey went on, 'you said you were shooting at night, and I realised you weren't talking about some future production, but something that was happening right now. But I was *so sure* this week was Conor's wedding. That's Steve's brother. He's getting married in the south of France. *Did* get married there, yesterday. So I called Adam Dunne – he's a screenwriter friend of ours, the mutual I mentioned – and Adam was actually *in* France, at the wedding. *With Steve.'*

'What do you mean?'

Because I had no idea. My brain was flashing an error code.

'Steve is in France, Adele. I spoke to him. Adam put him on the phone. And he doesn't know anything about any shoot that's happening in West Cork.'

Blood rushed in my ears, pushing Lindsey's voice into the background, so when she said, 'Is there someone there *saying* he's Steve? Or did I just pick this all up wrong?' it sounded like it was coming from very, very far away.

Steve wasn't Steve.

Steve wasn't *Steve*?

How could that be? The crew called him by that name. I'd looked him up online, found his picture. This production was legit. I'd signed a contract. They'd flown me over.

Steve *had* to be Steve.

But how could Steve be Steve *and* be at a wedding in France?

Something new, on one of the screens. The camera mounted on top of the motorhome was pointed towards the house, but also took in the stone pillars that marked the start of the dirt track. A light had just appeared between them, a few feet above the ground, bouncing a little, swinging back and forth in an arc.

I thought, *Torch.*

Someone holding a torch had just arrived at Cedarwood House, having – presumably – walked down the track.

'Adele?'

I put my phone down and crawled to the screens to get a better look.

'*Adele, are you still there?*' Lindsey's voice was tinny now, coming from my phone on the floor behind me somewhere.

It was a man. Dressed in jeans and a wool coat, it looked like. Not exactly something you'd wear for a walk in a forest in the middle of nowhere in the middle of a wet night. I watched him walk into the centre of the clearing, look towards the house, and then to something I couldn't see, something below the camera.

There was something weirdly familiar about him.

'*Hello? Can you hear me?*'

If Steve wasn't Steve, then Donal might not be Donal, and really, I didn't have any idea *who* was here with me at Cedarwood House. I couldn't trust that any of them were who they said they were. Hell, Peg might not even be Peg – who hasn't heard of *Jurassic Park*?

But I *did* know who this new man was.

I knew it because I knew *him*. I'd met him before, in a basement room in a hotel on Drury Street, and then every day I'd reported to the set of *We Were Kings*.

I knew him, even if his being here made absolutely no sense to me at all.

Martin Clarke.

Kate, panicked and crying, stumbles out of the
car and back to the front door of the cottage
- but it's locked. She looks back towards the
car, swallowing hard. She attempts to lift one
of the sash windows and then bangs her fists
on another one - to no avail.

She looks at the car again. Resigned, she
reluctantly returns to it.

We get a better, longer look now at Joel's
body. There's time to take in the depth of
the gash on his neck. How it gapes, revealing
tissue and bone. Blood, everywhere, wet
and glossy. His lifeless eyes, as glassy as
marbles, which - as we watch him from Kate's
POV as she reaches into the front seat to pull
the keys from the ignition - seem to make eye
contact.

Whimpering, Kate grabs the keys and runs back
to the front door. She unlocks it and runs
inside.

58   INT. LIVING SPACE - NIGHT [CONTINUOUS]   58

Kate runs to the armchairs and starts tossing
their cushions until—

                    KATE
                (to herself)
      I know it was here, I had it— Ah!

—she finds her phone. With shaking hands, she
dials 999 but when she puts the device to her
ear, she hears nothing.

KATE (CONT'D)
Come on. Come on, come on.

She repeats the process at various points
around the room, growing increasingly panicked
and desperate, all to no avail.

Kate pockets the phone and runs into the
kitchen. She pulls the largest knife from
the knife block on the counter. She grips it
blade-down in her right hand, ready to strike.

For a beat, she stands there, paralysed,
breathing rapidly.

Her eyes land on the welcome basket and,
sitting beside it, the ring binder with the
picture of the cottage on the front.

KATE (CONT'D)
(whispering)
Maggie.

She rushes to open the binder and starts
flipping through its contents. She stops at a
hand-drawn map that shows a property marked
Cherry Cottage (*You are here!*) – and, via
a winding path through the trees behind it,
Cherry Lodge (*My house!*). Kate rips out the
map.

As she does this, a FLASH OF LIGHTNING reveals
an UNKNOWN FIGURE standing outside the sliding
glass door to the rear, just as it turns to
go.

Kate stuffs the map in a pocket. She hurries to the sliding glass door, opens it and slips out into the night.

59   EXT. FOREST - NIGHT   59

Kate slips and stumbles her way through the trees, across the uneven forest floor. The forest is thick with dark. The wind and rain whip against her. Lightning flashes, thunder rolls.

We watch from behind Kate's back as she darts between the trees, occasionally casting a nervous glance back over her shoulder, until—

Kate vanishes.

60   EXT. FOREST GULLY - NIGHT   60

Kate tumbles uncontrollably down a steep incline. She lands in a heap in a stream, bloodied and bruised and wet.

Groaning in pain, she pulls herself to her knees, then her feet. She shivers, her teeth chattering. She assesses her surroundings: she's at the bottom of a gully with steep, 15-foot-high sides.

                         KATE
          The knife … Where's the …?

She looks around, feels around - but doesn't locate the knife. Kate deflates. She collapses against the wall of the gully and puts her head in her hands. She starts to cry.

Lightning flashes again. The rain gets heavier, its volume significantly louder.

A beat passes.

Kate reaches into her pocket and takes out her phone. Still working, but no service. She takes the map out too and points the light of the phone at it. It's already wet, the paper soft and dissolving. The gully is marked on the map and it appears to be only metres from the other house.

Kate grits her teeth, takes a deep breath. She sweeps the phone's light along the side of the gully until she finds a large, exposed root.

She puts the phone back in her pocket. She steels herself, takes another deep breath and grips the root with both hands. She climbs her way out of the gully, using the root as a rope.

61   EXT. FOREST/CHERRY LODGE - NIGHT   61

Kate's head appears above the lip of the gully's edge. Her face is illuminated by a source of light. What she sees makes her cry out in relief.

From Kate's POV, we see the edge of the forest is only feet away. In a clearing beyond it sits a small stone LODGE. Lights glow from inside and smoke billows from its chimney.

Kate hoists herself out of the gully and on to her feet, then runs towards it. She goes

directly to its front door and starts banging
on it with her fists.

> KATE
> (shouting)
> Help me! Please! Help me! I need
> help!

CUT TO:

62 INT/EXT. HALLWAY, CHERRY LODGE/CHERRY LODGE - NIGHT   62

On the other side of the door, Kate's
fists make a louder noise but her voice is
muffled. A MAN walks down the hall, pulling a
sweatshirt over his head. His hair is wet.

> MAN
> (cautiously)
> Hello?

He puts his eye to the peephole - and then
hurries to open the door.

Over his shoulder, we see Kate's mouth fall
open.

63 EXT/INT. CHERRY LODGE/HALLWAY, CHERRY LODGE - NIGHT   63

Over Kate's shoulder, we see who it is: Gus.

ACT III

TWENTY-SEVEN

Martin Clarke, the director of *We Were Kings*, the feature that had nearly ended my career, had just walked on to the grounds of Cedarwood House, on to the set of *Final Draft*, the film a man who wasn't really Steve Dade was directing but it wasn't really that film he was making at all. None of it made any sense. It was like trying to solve a word puzzle written in code.

'*Adele? Hello?*'

I picked up my phone and ended the call with a shaking hand, before slipping the phone into a pocket. I couldn't deal with Lindsey right now. I couldn't deal with anything; I needed to figure this out. Until I did, I couldn't trust anyone. For all I knew, Lindsey was a part of this too. Maybe Steve *was* Steve and her telling me otherwise was just another ploy to freak me out. For now, everything was suspect. Every*one* was.

I scanned the monitors, but not a single feed currently had a person in it. I couldn't hear any noise downstairs, so they must be out there, in the clearing, but standing out of shot. Standing where they knew I couldn't see them, because they knew exactly where I was: up here, watching these screens.

Movement, in my peripheral vision.

On one of the monitors, Martin had walked into view again. His back was to me, but then he suddenly swung around and shouted something at someone in the motorhome or standing right outside it, someone beyond what the angle of the camera could capture. Then he took a phone out of his pocket, tapped the screen and put it to his ear.

And in *my* pocket, *my* phone began to ring.

I scrambled to dig it out, to flip the switch on the side that would silence it. I thought it was Lindsey, trying to get me back, but it wasn't her name on screen. There wasn't anyone's name on screen.

Only an Irish mobile number. A number I'd seen flash up on screen before.

Are you in Cork yet?

If you're not, don't go. Trust me. Not safe.

GET OUT OF THERE NOW.

I lifted my eyes to the monitor. Martin still had his phone to his ear. I watched as he waited a few seconds, then shook his head a little, frustrated, brought the phone down and jabbed with a finger.

A moment later, *my* phone stopped buzzing.

Which meant ...

Martin Clarke is my anonymous texter.

If Steve wasn't Steve, could *Martin* be the real director?

On the monitor, he moved again, walking out of the frame of one camera and into another, the one that was mounted on the front wall of the house. The front door was open, light was spilling out on to the gravel from inside. He stood talking animatedly to someone I couldn't see but then, one by one, more figures came and joined him.

Steve – or Not Steve. Mick. Neil. *Donal.*

Donal had said he'd talk to Steve, then come get me. But he didn't appear to be in any rush to do that. The men were standing with their arms folded or hands in their pockets, some rocking a little on their heels, not looking in any way anxious or hurried.

Even though they must know I was up here, and that I knew the truth.

Or at least, knew what the truth *wasn't*.

I was so sick of navigating this mess in the literal and figurative dark. I needed to know what was going on down there, what was being said.

I secured my phone in a pocket and made my way back to the hatch. Cautiously, I lowered my face over the opening, half-expecting to see some cretin on the ladder staring back up at me, waiting to pounce, to pull me down.

But there was no one there.

As quietly as I could, I climbed down the ladder and on to the landing.

There was a window at the top of the stairs. From what I had seen on the monitor, I knew the men were standing almost directly below it. It might be too high up, and they might be talking too low, but it was worth a shot.

Cedarwood House had what looked like its original sash windows, but the lower sash slid up easily and without making much noise. I knelt on the floor – wincing on the way down as my injured ankle sent up a flare of pain – and put my face into the cold air. As long as the men stayed standing close to the house, they shouldn't be able to see me.

But I could hear them.

'Where *is* she?' one of them demanded.

It sounded like Martin and like it was a question he wasn't asking for the first time.

'We can explain, okay?'

Steve. Or Not Steve.

'How about everyone just calms the fuck down for a second?'

Mick.

'*Calm down?*' Martin again, angrier now. 'You want me to *calm down?*' He muttered something under his breath. 'One more time and this is the *last* time I ask this question. Where *is* she?'

'Adele is in her cabin.'

Donal, his voice oddly loud and clear.

'Which is *where*?'

'Round the back, through the trees. She ran up there when she heard the car coming in. I can bring you there, now. If you want.'

'How about,' Martin said, '*you* go and get her, and I wait here?'

Someone else said something then, something said too quiet for me to make out the individual words, but it had the timbre of a retort, and it was the last thing said before the sounds of a scuffle broke out: swearing and shouting and grunting and gravel crunching underfoot.

When that noise died down, Steve – Not Steve – said, 'What the *fuck*? Did you actually just *punch* me? What a fucking *psycho*,' but in a wet, nasally way that suggested that that punch had landed on his nose.

'We're *all* going to the cabin,' Martin said then. He sounded a little breathless, which made me think he was the punching psycho Not Steve had been referring to. 'Right now. Come on. You – what did you say your name was? Donal? You're going to show us the way. Let's go.'

Donal's voice, oddly loud again: 'The quickest way is around the side.'

Was he doing that for my benefit? Talking loud? Was he telling me where everyone was going so I could escape in the other direction?

Did I *need* to *escape*?

Or was this just more *Final Draft* bullshit? Had I just been treated to a performance that was supposed to make me want to run away, to take off down the track? Were their cameras down there now, waiting to capture me? Was this just an attempt to flush me out of the house and back into the night?

There were no answers, no certainties, nothing that made any sense. But if I was outside, I would at least have options. That felt like a better idea in the short term than remaining here, hidden inside the house.

Trapped inside it.

The gravel helped me track the men's footsteps as they moved away. I waited until I couldn't hear anything except my own breaths, and then I started down the stairs.

TWENTY-EIGHT

The front door was ajar, but I couldn't see anyone in the sliver of night showing through the gap. I couldn't hear anyone either. It seemed like a safe bet that they'd all headed off around the back, to the cabins. But I couldn't just run out the door. I was in socks, and it was freezing. I needed shoes and something warmer to wear, or I wouldn't get very far.

I needed to get to the utility room.

It was only a few feet away, but the lights were on and there was an enormous wall-to-wall, floor-to-ceiling window on the other side of the living space. On the other side of *that* was the crew – and Martin Clarke – somewhere between crossing the walled garden and following the path through the trees. It was bright in here and pitch black out there. If any of them happened to turn and look behind them, they'd see me.

Unless I kept low.

I dropped to the floor and half-crawled, half-slithered my way across it, only getting to my knees when I was safely behind the kitchen cabinets, and only getting to my feet when I reached the door to the utility room.

'Interesting technique.'

A male voice, to my immediate left. With a smarmy tone and now, wafting into the air around me, the smell of stale cigarette breath.

Neil stepped out of the shadows.

I froze, my hand in mid-air above the door handle.

He must have been standing there the whole time. He had seen me creeping down the stairs, crossing the floor.

Crawling across it.

Not everyone had gone to the cabins, but if everyone *else* had, that meant I was alone in here with him.

And he definitely *was* a threat.

'Oh, hey,' I said as casually as I could. 'Where is everyone? I thought I heard them come back.'

Neil shook his head, just twice, slowly.

'Oh no, no.' He pushed himself off the wall and came to stand right in front of me, close enough for me to feel his breaths as well as smell them. 'I just watched you cross that floor on your *belly*.' He licked his lips, a cartoon villain. 'You're not looking for anyone. You're *hiding* from them.'

He was taller than me, bigger than me, physically stronger than me.

But I had to get away from him somehow, and I had to do it now.

'Okay, fine,' I said, rolling my eyes. 'You can be in on it too, I suppose. If you want to be.'

I looked at him from beneath my lashes; I'd read enough scripts written by men to know that that was something they considered alluring and thought happened all the time. If that didn't work, I still had talking about being able to feel my breasts moving whenever I moved, how they were always entering rooms ahead of me and bouncing up and down stairs.

'In on what?'

'Donal just told me everything. I know what's really going on.'

Neil raised a single eyebrow. 'Oh you *do*, do you?'

'I do. And I think it's quite exciting, actually.' I took a step closer to him, close enough now to move in for a kiss. I tried not to think about that, or I'd lose it completely. 'Don't *you* think it's' – I licked my lips, bit down my lower one – 'quite exciting?'

Neil glanced away, shifted his weight. *I* was making *him* uncomfortable. Ha! It felt like unlocking a superpower and I really had to focus to stop smugness from seeping into my performance.

'Steve is basically reinventing the genre,' I went on, my voice breathy and low. There was no flicker of anything on Neil's face when I said the name Steve. If our director wasn't who he said he was, was it possible the crew didn't know?

'Is he now?'

'He is.' I moved closer again, as close as I could get without actually touching him. 'People will go nuts for it.'

The air pulsed between us, but I was willing to bet that it was for two very different reasons.

He thought I was coming on to him. I was gearing up to *destroy him.*

'That's not what Donal told us,' Neil said. 'He said you freaked out, that you were crying, that you were refusing to come down.'

'Because I *told* him to say that.' I rolled my eyes again and almost let out a *duh.* 'I mean, come on. Do I look like I've been crying?'

I stared as hard as I could into Neil's eyes until he looked away again.

'I don't want to ruin it,' I said. '*Final Draft*: the Steve Dade version. I want to be a part of it. But yeah, I'm a little pissed off about being kept out of the loop so I'm going to get my own back first. I'll hide in here' – I pointed at the utility room – 'and when Donal brings the guys back in, I'll spring out. That's our plan. Well, my plan that I'm making him carry out. A little jump-scare.' I winked. 'A *real* one.'

I took his hand, but not in an Adele way. In a *Neil* way. With both of mine. Gentle, caressing, disgusting.

Neil's hand was clammy, and as I held it, he swallowed hard.

I leaned in and whispered to his neck, 'Wanna hide with me?'

It truly was the performance of a lifetime. In a way, I was glad there was a hidden camera somewhere behind me, capturing this. Someone *should* be recording it, for posterity. I might even have to get myself a copy of the footage afterwards, stick this scene on my goddamn show reel.

'I, ah, I should get back to Steve,' Neil said, glancing towards the front door. I told him—'

'Come *on*,' I purred, reaching out to open the utility-room door. 'Just come inside with me for a sec ...'

I was already scanning the space on the other side, taking an inventory. Jackets were hanging from hooks on the wall: bright yellow rain jacket, red puffa, green wax. The yellow would be too visible and the puffa too warm, so I'd grab the green. One pair of boots on the floor, men's wellingtons. Too big for me, but better than stockinged feet. They'd do. A large golf umbrella with what looked like a dangerously pointy end was propped against the wall outside the little toilet—

Whose door opened outwards, because there was so little space.

I hadn't really known what I was going to do if and when I got Neil into the utility room, other than a vague plan with the working title of *Try To Lock Him In There Somehow*, but now one crystallised.

I knew exactly what I needed to do.

There was no key in the lock of the door to the toilet, but the handle was a loop. If I got it closed, I could slot the umbrella through it. It wouldn't hold for long, but it would be long enough for me to grab what I needed, and there *was* a key in the lock of the utility room, on the outside. So: get Neil in the toilet, close door, jam umbrella, grab and go.

I pulled on Neil's hand, teasing him inside.

'The only thing is,' I said, making a show of looking around. 'This is a bit obvious, isn't it? They'll expect to find me in here if I'm not upstairs. I want this to be a real fright— *Oh.*' As if the idea had just occurred to me. 'I know! Let's hide in the toilet. Both of us. They'll never suspect.'

'The toilet?' Neil made a face. 'But it's tiny. We won't even get *in* there.'

'Sure we will.' I gave him my best suggestive look. 'I can sit on your lap.'

This part of the plan didn't require any persuasion. Neil nodded eagerly.

The absolute cretin.

I pulled open the toilet door with my free hand. 'You'll have to go in first.'

Neil did what he was told – and I sprang into action.

The element of surprise was my main advantage, I *had* to move fast.

I pushed the door shut. Grabbed the umbrella. Jammed it through the handle. I heard Neil say, 'What the …' and then, 'What the fuck!' and then there was a bang as the toilet door burst open – but only a couple of inches, pressing against the umbrella. It could snap any second, but I only needed a few. I grabbed the jacket, boots, and ran back out into the kitchen, slamming the utility door behind me, turning the key in its lock just as I heard a crack that must have been the umbrella, and then Neil's fists behind me, on the other side of the utility-room door.

'You fucking *bitch*,' he spat.

'That's Best Bitch in a Leading Role to you, you fucking pervert.' I took the key out of the utility-room lock and threw it in a high arc into the room behind me, where it landed on the wooden floor with a satisfying clatter. 'See you on the news, Neil.'

Then I stuck my feet into the boots, pulled on the jacket, hurried out of the kitchen and over to the front door, yanked it back—

And found myself face to face with Steve Dade.

Or Not Steve Dade, as the case may be. And not quite face to face, because I was standing and he was slumped on the ground with his back against the passenger door of the Volvo, legs straight out in front of him, covered in a spill of blood from the nose down. His eyes were closed and his head was lolling to one side. I thought he was asleep. Or unconscious. He didn't feel like a physical threat.

But the shock of seeing him there – the unexpectedness of *so much blood* – made me gasp, and that gasping made him open his eyes and look straight at me, and I froze.

'*There* you are.' A weak smile, a woozy expression. 'Where's Neil? He was supposed to be getting me a towel.'

I scanned the clearing, listened for any other sounds. There was a dull banging coming from the direction of the utility room, but other than that, nothing. We seemed to be alone. Whatever was going on, I didn't think that our director getting punched in the nose by the last director I'd worked for was something either of them wanted to capture on camera and put in a movie so, for the first time in what felt like for ever, I was in a situation that felt *real*.

I might be able to get some answers.

'You ruined it,' he muttered. 'Dumb bitch.'

'I see your insults are as original as your script.'

'It's not my script.' He smiled, revealing teeth grotesquely stained with blood. 'See? Like I said.' He pointed a finger at me. 'Dumb.'

'Not that dumb,' I said. 'I know you're not really Steve Dade.'

'You what?' This had woken him up a little. 'Did he call you? He's being trying to ... To call me. All fucking day. What did you tell him? You weren't supposed to ... You shouldn't have told anyone.'

'Did *who* call me?' I took a beat to try to pull some sense out of the mess of facts in my head. 'Do you mean the real Steve? Are you saying you *know* Steve, the real one?'

'*Know* him?' Another bloodstained smile, a lazy laugh. 'He's like a brother to me.'

And with that, an asteroid-sized chunk of the puzzle fell into place.

Steve Dade and Daniel O'Leary, partners in movie-making since they were teens and, as adults, in Cross Cut Films. They did everything together, so much so that the only photos of them I'd found online were of both of them, standing together. That's how Steve could be at a wedding in France while the guy I'd thought was Steve was here, at Cedarwood House, on the set of *Final Draft*.

Because *this* Steve was actually Daniel O'Leary.

'What *is* this?' I asked.

'It was going to be something amazing.' Daniel dabbed at his nose with the cuff of his jacket, frowned at whatever came away on the fabric. 'It still could be.'

A voice – a shout – from somewhere behind the house.

Definitely not far away enough to be coming from the cabins. The guys were on their way back here.

I had to get going.

'Just tell me this,' I said. 'Why is Martin Clarke here?'

'This was all ...' Daniel's eyes closed momentarily. 'It was all Martin's idea. He wrote the script. With his little ... With his actress friend.' A pause. 'Who's a total bitch, by the way.'

There came another shout then, so close I could hear what the person was saying: Steve's name.

Someone was coming this way, calling out for Steve.

Which made me think, in this order:

The guys will reappear any second.

The rest of the Final Draft *crew don't know this isn't really Steve.*

RUN.

TWENTY-NINE

And then I was running, blindly, around the nearest stone pillar, on to the track and then off it again, into the wilds of the woods.

The terrain was uneven, a minefield of gnarled roots, soft mud and trip-hazard protrusions. Branches and leaves whipped relentlessly at my face, scratching my skin, cutting and stinging. It only took a few strides for my injured ankle to start burning with pain again. But I didn't think, I just ran.

I didn't care about the direction, once it was *away*.

From Daniel. From Martin. From Neil.

From Cedarwood House.

From *Final Draft*.

The forest was pitch black, the ground slippery, the trees alive and rustling with noise. It had started raining again, not heavy but persistent. I was taking a chance, running in the opposite direction to certain civilisation, keeping the main road to my left instead of my right. I'd already tried right, when I'd met Donal coming up the hill, so I knew there were no houses anywhere near in that direction.

I was hoping I'd find something sooner going the opposite way.

I quickly discovered that whenever I moved fast, everything hurt, and whenever I moved slow, I became convinced that someone was following me, that they were right behind, within touching distance, and that any moment now I'd feel the brush of outstretched fingers catch on the ends of my hair, and that fear would make me move fast again.

Fear and adrenalin.

I kept going, pushing hard, until I felt something rushing up from my insides, blocking my next breath: I was going to be sick.

I stopped and bent over and vomited something up and on to the ground. It was too dark to see but I could taste the remnants of a meal I didn't remember eating, followed by a sour, acidic bile. After a bout of dry heaves and painful coughs, I felt empty and like something inside me was burning, and knew there was nothing else to come up.

I wiped the tears from my eyes and straightened up – and knew instantly that I was lost. I had no idea now which way I was facing. I'd lost track of the road, if I'd even been right about where it was in relation to me before I'd stopped.

Should I just run on, straight, or had I got myself turned around, and running on straight would bring me back to the house?

There'd been a storyline on *These Are the Days* years ago that had captivated viewers for months: the Morgan clan, of which my character Wendy was the youngest daughter, had had their car break down on a lonely country road in the middle of the night and then been chased through the woods by a convicted killer who'd escaped from a nearby psychiatric hospital – because that was just the kind of thing people wanted to watch right after their dinner of a weekday evening, the bosses said. There were limited funds for filming outside of the *These* studio in north Dublin, so the chase through the woods was done in a thin patch of trees that separated the staff car park there from the motorway, overnight, from creative angles that hid the sweeping high-beams and brake lights of the real-life passing traffic, and with the sound guys stopping us every other minute because of the background noise. What was funny to me at the time was that this patch of pretend forest was only about the size of a tennis court and yet when seen on screen, you'd never know.

Even *I* was convinced that the Morgans were running through an expanse and not just back and forth across the same fifteen feet.

It was as though the director had somehow managed to take that patch of trees and stretch it and reshape it, repeatedly, to change its dimensions, enough to disconnect what I saw on TV from what I remembered from that night. The experience left me feeling discombobulated, disorientated – and I felt like that now, again. It seemed impossible to get the lay of this land. The forest had shed all its compass points.

Panic started to rise in my chest.

I pushed it down and then pushed the rain, sweat, tears – whatever it was now – out of my eyes, the strands of sopping-wet hair out of my face, and forced myself to gulp down several deep, burning breaths.

And then I heard voices.

From somewhere behind me. Calling my name.

I didn't want to run any more. I was tired and cold and wet and my ankle was hurting and I was out in a forest, in the middle of nowhere, by myself, running towards God knows what in the dead of night.

But *why* was I was doing it? What exactly was I running from? Donal maintained that no one had followed me down the track earlier, so in all likelihood I had just tripped over a branch. No one had tried to hurt me, they'd just secretly filmed me. Did that warrant my running off into the night? Or was I just doing exactly what I'd done on *We Were Kings*: inflating small events with my own imagination, using them as building blocks for my own paranoid conspiracy theory, convincing myself once again that the universe revolved around me, and – *for the second time* – having some kind of mental breakdown on a set?

I took a step in the direction of the voices.

But if everything that had happened on *We Were Kings* had really only happened that way inside my own head ...

Why was Martin here, now?

It was all Martin's idea. He wrote the script. With his little actress friend.

And Donal, so loudly announcing the path they'd take to the cabins. It had to have been him telling me where they were going so that I could use the opportunity to get away.

He would only do that if he thought I *needed* to get away, surely.

And he knew more about this than me.

No, I'd been right the first time. I *should* run. I had to get away from these men, this place. So long as I didn't know exactly what was going on or why, anything could be. It wasn't safe to stay and find out.

In the distance, I heard my name being called. The voices were getting closer. But they were, inadvertently, pinpointing the direction of the house.

I took off again, in the opposite direction to the voices, darting through the trees, studiously ignoring the pain in my ankle at first and then delighting in it, *welcoming* it even, because it getting worse signalled speed.

Pain meant I was going fast. Worse pain meant I was going faster.

I ran and ran and didn't look back, until I put my foot down and found there was no solid ground there to meet it. I swung wildly, half of my body hanging in mid-air, threatening to fall, until I reached out and grabbed something, anything – a branch. A thin one, which snapped almost immediately.

But it was enough to slow my momentum, and I managed to lunge towards the tree the branch had come off of, putting all my weight on the lone foot that remained on solid ground, and then I *did* fall but backwards, into some mud.

What the hell?

I stared into the dark, waiting for the shapes to reveal themselves.

There was a giant hole in the ground in front of me. Running lengthways, across my path. It was hard to be sure with the sound of the rain, but I thought there might be some kind of water at the bottom of it, running.

A stream, maybe.

And then the word for what it was floated up out of my memory: *gully.*

I knew it because I'd just read it earlier this evening, just after Donal had disappeared upstairs, in the original script for *Final Draft.* Kate had run into the forest and fallen into one and, metaphorically, into her lowest moment. But she'd dug deep and found the grit and determination she needed to climb back out of it, and just moments later—

She found the lodge.

I'd been so focused on life on set mirroring the events of *Final Draft*, it hadn't occurred to me that maybe some real-life was already in there.

Like the location.

Cedarwood House had a second storey, but the ground floor was identical to the one described in the script. As was the clearing the house sat in. The dirt track that led to it. The road up a forested hill that got you to it in the first place. Whoever had written it – I didn't have the bandwidth to puzzle out how it could be Martin right now – hadn't just pulled this location out of their arse. They were basing it on something real, somewhere real. Here. Cedarwood House, with its dirt track and its forest and its gully and its *other house*.

I took off again, moving faster now.

64   INT. HALLWAY, CHERRY LODGE – NIGHT   64

Kate falls into Gus with relief.

                         GUS
                    (whispering)
          Kate, what the …?

Kate starts sobbing noisily against his chest.

Gus hurriedly pushes the front door closed
with a kick and then ushers Kate into a door
off the hallway, and into …

65   INT. LIVING ROOM, CHERRY LODGE – NIGHT [CONTINUOUS]   65

… a cosy if outdated living room. The
upholstery boasts a swirling print and has a
fringed edge. An old television is tuned to
something black-and-white, on mute. A fire
glows warmly in the hearth.

He helps Kate to the couch and then goes to
gently close the living-room door behind them.

                         GUS
          My aunt's already asleep. Or she was.
          You could've texted me, you know. Or
          knocked once. You didn't really need
          to bang down the door.

                         KATE
                    (confused)
          What?

Gus waves a hand dismissively. He perches on
the arm of a chair across from Kate.

GUS

It doesn't matter. She sleeps like
the dead. So … how's it going down
there? Not good, I'm guessing, if
you're up here and crying about it.

KATE

I don't … Gus—

GUS

Good old Joel let the cat out of the
bag, then?
        (looks Kate up and down)
Why are you so wet? Did you *walk*
here? Is that …?
        (frowning)
Is that blood? Did you fall?

KATE

Gus, listen. Joel is dead. Someone
killed him.

GUS
        (laughing nervously)
What are you …? What?

KATE

Why are you here?

GUS

I'm staying with my aunt for the
weekend. She owns both places. I
thought you'd like it in the cottage,
and I was trying to send Mags some
business in the off-season, but I
thought it'd be weird for you if you
knew I was here at the same time.

Joel was originally talking about
last weekend … Where is Joel?

                    KATE
I told you. Joel is dead.

For the first time, Gus looks genuinely
concerned. He stands up again.

                    GUS
Did something happen? Was there an
accident?

Kate shakes her head.

               GUS (CONT'D)
Where is Joel now, Kate?

                    KATE
In the car. The back seat.

                    GUS
Here?

Gus moves to look out the window until Kate
says—

                    KATE
No. Outside the other house.

                    GUS
Is he hurt?

                    KATE
I think so, seeing as he's dead.

She mimes a throat-slashing.

Gus's eyes widen. He swallows hard.

                    GUS
     Um, okay. Look, I'm going to go get
     the car keys off my aunt, and we'll
     drive down there.

                    KATE
     You have a car?

                    GUS
     We have two, hers and mine, but hers
     is a Jeep. Better around here in this
     weather. They're parked round the
     back. You stay put, okay? I'll only
     be a minute.

                    KATE
     I need a phone. We need to call the
     guards.

                    GUS
     What happened to *your* phone?

                    KATE
     There's no reception around here,
     although maybe there is now …

She reaches for her pocket.

                    GUS
     No, there's none here either. You
     have to be out on the road.

Gus points to an old-fashioned rotary-style
phone on an end-table next to the couch.

                    GUS (CONT'D)
You can use that.
                    (pause)
What are you going to tell them?

                    KATE
That someone killed Joel.

                    GUS
Are you sure?

                    KATE
What else would I say?

                    GUS
I mean, are you sure he's dead?

                    KATE
                  (looking away)
Yes. And you would be too if you'd
seen him.

Gus exhales loudly.

                    GUS
Okay, look …

A number of small items - pieces of paper, a
lighter, a pair of reading glasses - sit in a
ceramic bowl on the coffee table. Gus pulls
what looks like a utility bill from it and
hands it to Kate.

                    GUS (CONT'D)
That's the address of the cottage.
Tell them we'll meet them there.

The bill is addressed to Margaret Doherty,
Cherry Cottage, Dooleen Woods, Co. Cork.

                    GUS (CONT'D)
     I'll just be a sec.

                    KATE
     Okay.

She looks at him, her lip trembling.

                    GUS
     We'll sort this all out, all right?
     Don't worry.

                    KATE
                 (unconvincingly)
     Yeah.

Gus leaves.

Kate wipes her tears, then gets up and goes to
the phone. But when she puts the receiver to
her ear, there's NO DIAL TONE.

She presses the button on top a couple of
times, to no avail. She frowns. She replaces
the receiver and bends to follow the telephone
cord off the edge of the table and …

It's DANGLING. It's not plugged in.

This angle reveals the corner of a cardboard
box, sticking out from behind the couch. A
swatch of a familiar book cover peeks out
between the not-quite-closed flaps.

Kate pulls the box out and opens it.

THIRTY

And then something unexpected happened: it became easier to run.

At first I thought it was because the rain had eased again, or because there was so much adrenalin coursing through my veins, I felt like I was practically levitating above the ground, but no – it was because, beneath me, the forest floor was changing. Smoothing out. The gnarled roots, fallen branches and sudden troughs were starting to thin. Then they disappeared altogether and my calf muscles told me that the forest's gentle rise had fallen into a flat, even surface. The trees were thinning out too, letting in more light, enabling me to see better.

And then I saw light.

Shining from behind the window of a house. A miniature version of the main one, with the same style roof-tiles and window frames. The front door was even painted the same bright red.

I'd found the lodge.

I stopped at the edge of the treeline, just before the forest floor would switch to gravel beneath my feet, and surveyed the scene up ahead. A car was parked outside the lodge and smoke was wafting from the chimney.

Someone was in there.

The car parked outside was new and had a Dublin registration plate on it, but that didn't tell me much. It could be a rental.

I was desperate to go straight to the door, to bang on it with my fists, to scream and call out and get whoever was inside to bring me into the light and the warmth and the safety, to lock me in with them on the *other* side of that door ...

But there could be anyone in there.

I elected to proceed with caution and walk around the lodge first, to see if I could find out who or what was inside before I made my presence known.

The light from the house was bright enough to illuminate the immediate area. I started my reconnaissance at the corner where the car was parked. It was a blue Ford Fiesta, shiny and clean. There was nothing on the back seat or between the front two that might give any clue to who'd been driving it – in fact, there was nothing inside the car at all except a couple of empty water bottles and a copy of the *Examiner* newspaper from a few days ago.

I kept going, moving along the side of the lodge.

There were three windows there. One was narrow and frosted, suggesting a bathroom, dimly lit as if the light wasn't on in the room itself but filtering into it from beyond, from a hallway. One was dark but with its curtains open. The third was bright and large, revealing a sliver of interior in the gap where the two curtains didn't quite meet.

I risked stepping up to the sill to get a better look.

I could see a fire glowing in the hearth, a large mirror on a wallpapered chimney breast and a mantelpiece on which a cluster of dried flowers sat in a vase next to a flickering candle. The mirror reflected nothing back to me but a blank, magnolia wall.

I moved on.

Rounding the rear corner, a ramshackle lean-to came into view. It had been tacked on to the back of the building, presumably around the lodge's rear door. What counted for windows in it were made of sheets of opaque, corrugated plastic; I couldn't see inside. The door to the lean-to had a big, rusted padlock looped through the handle.

Outside it, on the ground, were two pairs of wellington boots, neatly lined up, toes out. One was a pair of women's that could easily be by the same brand that made the ones I had been wearing until they were stolen from my cabin's deck, only these were navy and white polka-dot instead of a floral design. Next to them was a plain, black pair, larger and muddier, potentially belonging to a man. The mud was dry but it didn't look like the boots had been sitting out here for too long.

There could be a couple in there.

I looked back towards the trees. Re-entering the forest was not an option and I had to assume this lodge had a similarly long and winding track connecting it to the road, which I didn't fancy having to walk down either.

To hell with it.

I was going to knock.

I picked up my pace, hurrying to complete my loop around the house, and rounded the last corner just in time to see the light by the front door change. A narrow, bright column had appeared, falling across the gravel clearing, forming a path between the lodge and the treeline. As I watched, it yawned open, expanding.

Someone had opened the front door.

A woman stepped into view. She had her back to me, looking towards the treeline.

I froze in place, unsure what to do. I didn't want to frighten her.

She was dressed in jeans and a chunky cardigan, arms wrapped around herself for warmth, hair piled on top of her head in a messy bun. Her breath billowed like smoke in the freezing air. A set of car keys dangled from a ring around her right forefinger.

She turned and saw me, and both our mouths fell open at the same time.

Julia.

THIRTY-ONE

We stood staring at each other, dumbstruck, until I said, 'What are you doing here?' at the exact same moment she said, 'Where the hell have you *been*?'

Before I could answer, she ran to me and pulled me to her in a tight hug. She was warm and smelled soapy, with a hint of the floral perfume she always wore.

I was stiff with cold and shock and confusion.

Julia, *my* Julia, was here?

'Are you okay?' She pulled back, held me at arm's length to evaluate me. 'What happened to your face?' She scanned the length of my body, frowning at my footwear. 'Where did you come from? Were you …? Were you walking in the *woods*?'

'What are you doing here?' I asked again.

'Looking for you, obviously. *Waiting* for you. I kept trying your phone but the reception out here seems to be non-existent. Where have you been?'

'At the house. Cedarwood House.'

Julia frowned. 'I thought *this* was Cedarwood House.'

'This is the lodge.'

'You didn't say anything about a lodge.'

'No, I … I know I didn't.' A thick cloud of confusion had settled into the middle of my brain and I was struggling to find a way around it. 'Why are you *here*?'

'I came to get you,' Julia said, slowly and distinctly, as if English wasn't my native language. 'You called me and said you needed help, so I came.'

I didn't remember Julia saying anything about coming here herself, but so much had happened tonight …

And she'd been cut off mid-sentence, hadn't she? The first time we spoke. When my phone had died. Maybe she *had* said that, and I'd missed it.

But still—

'How did you get here?' I asked.

Julia jangled the car keys. 'I borrowed Paul's car.'

'Who's Paul?'

'He's in the play. The one I'm in rehearsals for.'

'In Dublin.'

Over two hundred miles away. Four hours' drive from here, at least.

'In *Cork*,' Julia corrected. 'Remember? That's why I suggested we meet at the airport before you go back.'

'I was going back from *Dublin* Airport. Same place I flew into.'

'Oh, really? I thought they'd fly you into London, then onwards to—'

'When did you leave Cork?' I said. 'What time?'

'Straight after you called me.'

'*Which* time?'

Julia was looking at me now like I was speaking in tongues.

'Adele,' she said gently, 'are you all right? You don't seem like yourself. And where's everyone else? You said the AD came back. Where is he? Is he with you?'

I looked towards the treeline, over Julia's shoulder.

'No,' I said. 'But Martin is here.'

'Martin who?'

'*Martin.*' There was only one in either of our lives. 'Martin

Clarke. He's here, and Steve isn't Steve, and I don't know what's going on but I want to leave. We need to leave. Right now. I need to be in a place with people and phone service and no bloody *trees* so I can figure out what the hell is going on.'

The expression on Julia's face was one I'd only seen once before, on the set of *We Were Kings*.

'O-*kay*,' she said in a tone that implied nothing was. 'Look, why don't we just go inside? The fire is lighting and I have some nice wine. Have you eaten? Let's get you warmed up and then we can talk about all this, all right?'

She moved to stand by my side, a hand in the small of my back, and began gently steering me towards the front of the lodge.

'Wait,' I said. 'You're *staying* here?'

'Where else was I going to stay? I could hardly drive back up to Cork at this hour and I didn't know how long it'd take to find you. And I assumed ...' Julia bit her lip, ultimately thinking better of saying whatever the end of that sentence was supposed to be. 'Joanne was lovely about it. She basically threw me the keys and said we could sort out payment in the morning. Fierce apologetic that she hadn't a chance to clean it since the last guests left, but it's—'

'Joanne owns both houses?'

'Uh-huh.'

'How did you find her?'

An impatient sigh. 'The *internet*, Adele. How else?'

But if Julia had spoken to Joanne, and Joanne owned both houses, the subject of *Final Draft* would've surely come up in conversation.

So why was Julia waiting at the wrong house?

And how had she got here so quickly?

'Let's just get inside,' Julia said, as we rounded the corner and the front door of the lodge came into view.

It was ajar, allowing me to see a slice of perfectly welcoming hallway. The decor was a little outdated, but it looked homely and warm. *Safe*. And it was my best friend who was leading me in there, having driven down from Cork City to come to my rescue.

But an alarm in the back of my head was flashing, *WRONG WRONG WRONG*.

'No.' I stopped, dug my heels into the gravel. 'I'm not going in. I don't want to. I need to leave here, Julia. You're not listening. You don't understand.'

'Adele, listen to *me*.' She moved in front of me, looked me in the eye. 'This comes from a place of love. You know it does. But you need to trust me. You need to trust me, because you can't trust whatever it is your brain is telling you right now. This is just like that day on *Kings*, when you were sick. You look just like you did then – your pupils are like saucers. And your voice is the same. Different to how it normally is. Quicker and higher, and you're saying things that I'm sure make sense in your head, but—'

'But Martin is *here*,' I protested. 'Don't you get that? He's *here*. So something *was* happening on *We Were Kings*! I didn't imagine it. There has to be a connection. It's too much of a coincidence otherwise. Don't you see?' I heard my voice waver; tears were threatening. 'Please, Julia, can't we just go? Please?'

Something over my shoulder caught her attention then, but when I turned to look at the treeline, all I saw was dark.

I turned back to her. 'I'm *not* crazy.'

'I never said you were.'

'You think I am. It's all over your face. In your tone.'

'I think you've been under a huge amount of stress,' she said, 'and your body clock is all messed up with this last-minute trip from LA – when did you last sleep? And this is not an I-told-you-so, I promise it's not, but you really should've seen someone after what happened, someone you could talk to, a professional. Regularly. Not just once. Because this kind of thing, it doesn't resolve itself. It just lies in wait, waiting to strike again.'

I shook my head, even though I wasn't exactly sure which part of what she'd said I was disagreeing with.

'Why … why are you here?' I asked again. '*How* are you here?'

I felt like if I could just get a handle on how and why Julia had appeared in West Cork, I could start to make some sense of all this.

'*Because*,' she said impatiently, 'you called me and said you needed help.'

'But not long ago enough. There wasn't time.'

'It's gone midnight. We spoke hours ago.'

'No …' But it must be at least past midnight by now – and when *had* I spoken to Julia, exactly?

'The first thing I did,' she said, 'was call Paul's phone to ask about the car. I was on the road within half an hour. I found Joanne and called her on the way, so she gave me directions and I was able to drive straight here. Probably took me, what? An hour and a half? Two hours max, all in. I can show you the times of the calls on my phone if you like. And think about it.

What the hell *else* would I be doing here?' Julia sighed. 'Look, I really don't want to have to have this conversation now, like this. This isn't the place for it. Let's go in—'

'What conversation?'

She hesitated. 'It's just that ... Well, this is what you did the last time, too. I don't think you're doing it on purpose. I *know* you're not. But you ... I don't know what the right way to say it is ...' A deep breath. 'Adele, you create this big drama – that revolves entirely around you – and then you refuse to accept anything that doesn't, you know ... *reinforce* it.'

Something in the trees caught the attention of us both then: a voice, in the distance, calling my name.

'We should go inside,' Julia said. 'You should.'

'I don't understand,' I said. I had never meant it more.

'This isn't the time or place. We—'

'*Tell me,* Julia. What are you talking about?'

She looked at me with what I could only describe as pity.

'Other people got sick that day,' she said. 'They weren't all projectile vomiting in the middle of shooting a scene, but there were, I think, four other people who had some kind of stomach upset too? They thought it was the chicken casserole the cafeteria had served the night before. It wasn't just you.'

I didn't remember that.

More than that, I was sure I'd never even known it. I searched and searched for something, any vague memory, any sense at all that this was something I'd once known, but there was nothing.

'The thing with the hairstylist,' Julia went on. 'Do you remember her apologising to you? The next day? She'd got her wires crossed. It was actually Rebecca Long who'd been complaining. Not just about her, as it turned out, but make-up and wardrobe too.'

I didn't even remember there being anyone called Rebecca Long.

'And the call-sheets were right, Adele. You'd just read them wrong.'

'No ... I ... I ...'

I didn't know what to say.

Reality was falling away from beneath my feet like some cracking Arctic ice sheet. There were words waiting on my tongue – *Are you a part of this too?* – but something told me I shouldn't say them, that my saying them would be proof of what *Julia* was saying.

Suddenly the terrifying thing was not what had happened here, but the possibility that nothing much had happened at all. That I had invented this. Created an elaborate drama that revolved entirely around me, and then refused to accept anything that didn't reinforce it. A self-confirming delusion.

That possibility was the most horrific one of all.

Even just my being here, at the lodge, now ... Why had I taken off running through the trees when every weird thing from the day had already been explained away, by Donal and the cameras and Steve not being Steve?

What was I running *from*?

A new feeling of complete and utter helplessness threatened to overwhelm me.

I looked to Julia, who nodded and put an arm around my shoulders, and started leading me gently towards the front door of the lodge. I let her.

And then Martin Clarke walked out of the woods.

He stopped short when he saw us, just a couple of steps on to the gravel, leaving him probably forty or fifty feet away.

We both stared at him, stock-still, until Julia moved her body in front of mine.

'Go inside,' she told me over her shoulder, at a volume too quiet for Martin to hear. 'Lock the door. Let me talk to him. I'll sort this out, okay?'

'Julia?' Martin called across the space between us. He took a couple of steps forward. 'What's going on? What is this?'

'That's what I'd like to know,' she shouted back at him. Then, to me, 'Get inside. Now.'

But I didn't want to leave Julia out here alone with Martin. She didn't know about the hidden cameras, or about him punching Steve – Daniel – in the nose, or him demanding that Donal go to the cabins and get me.

And those things definitely *had* happened.

Hadn't they?

'Julia, *please*.' I tugged on her arm. 'Let's just go. I really want to leave.'

Martin called out my name.

'Don't talk to her,' Julia snapped at him. To me, 'I said, *get inside*.'

'Let's just have a conversation,' Martin said, taking another step towards us. 'Before you do something you'll come to regret.' Another step. 'Adele? Adele, I need you to come with me.'

I wasn't sure of much, but I was sure I wasn't going to do *that*.

'Julia,' he said, 'this has gone far enough. It needs to stop.'

He took another step forward.

'Please,' I whispered. '*Please.*' I moved the hand I had on Julia's arm down to her hand, closing my fingers around hers and the car keys they were holding. 'Let's *go.*'

'What's your plan here?' Martin called out. 'What's the endgame? Because we can all come back from this now, as it stands. But if anyone gets hurt …'

His voice trailed off and for one, interminable moment of tension, everyone just held their position, silently, waiting one another out.

Then Julia's hand moved in mine, pressing the end of a key into my palm.

'It's open,' she whispered to me. 'You ready?'

I glanced towards the car, only a few feet away on the other side of the lodge's front door. It was parked facing the lodge, the passenger-side door closest to me.

'Yes,' I said. 'Yes.'

'*Go!*'

I ran.

Julia ran.

Martin ran after us.

I was at the car in five strides, four of them on a protesting ankle. I threw myself towards the door on the last one, pulling on the handle, yanking the door open, jumping in—

I got my door closed just as Martin reached out, his hand and the door *just* missing each other in mid-air.

I fumbled, desperately looking for a lock.

Martin reached for the handle again—

Clunk.

—but when he pulled on it, it didn't open.

In the meantime, Julia had got inside the car, scrambling

into the back on the passenger side directly behind me, and she'd just reached between the front seats to press what must have been a central-locking button.

Martin started banging on my window with his fists.

'Julia, for fuck's sake,' he shouted, his voice muffled through the glass. 'Stop this. Stop this *now.*'

She was climbing into the driver's seat, keys in hand, ignoring him.

Martin bent down to look at us through my window, to look at me, and I saw something unexpected in his eyes.

It looked almost like—

The engine roared to life.

—*fear.*

'Okay,' Julia said, a hand on the gearstick. 'Let's do this your way.'

Tyres squealed and gravel chipped against the wheel-wells as she reversed the car in an aggressive arc that forced Martin to jump out of its path.

Before he had even fully regained his balance, we were speeding away.

THIRTY-TWO

I leaned back against the headrest, exhaled, closed my eyes.

But the incessant beeping of the seat-belt sensor forced me to open them again. I reached for the belt, stretched it across me and clicked it into place. Julia already had hers on. The car was jerking and rocking its way over the potholes on a muddy track that seemed to be in even worse condition than the one connecting the main road to the main house.

'So what now?'

'We get out of here,' Julia said, keeping her eyes on the road. 'Like you wanted.'

As the car swerved around a bend in the track, something heavy rolled out from beneath my seat and hit against my boot. I reached into the footwell to pick it up.

'What's that?' Julia said, glancing over.

'A torch.'

A heavy-duty one, with a lens the size of a dessert plate and a handle on top.

'Huh,' she said. 'Must be Paul's.'

'Is he an astronomer?'

'What?' Julia made a face. 'No. Just a terrible actor. Why?'

'Because this has been modified.' The lens had what looked like black electrical tape almost all over it, except for two vaguely circular spots in the middle which had clear adhesive tape on them instead. The tape had been coloured red with a marker. 'To emit red light. Good for seeing things in the dark without actually banishing the dark. If you're out in a field at night trying to see through a telescope, this is what you want.' I reached to put the torch on the floor behind my seat. 'Wendy Morgan had an astronomer boyfriend for a while – who, it turned out, was just trying to get her into a lonely field in the middle of the night. We got in trouble with the broadcasting authority over the watershed. Do you remember that?'

We rounded another bend and met a pair of wrought-iron gates, only one of which was standing open. The end of the track, the start of the road.

Julia nosed the car through and then swung right.

'It's the other way,' I said. 'Bantry is to the left.'

All that was in this direction was the peninsula, jutting out into the Atlantic, and this road bringing us closer and closer to its edge.

'I have a better idea,' Julia said. 'We're going to Joanne's house.'

'Where's that?'

'Just down here.'

All I could see in front of us were the twin beams of the headlights on the surface of the road and a dense, matte darkness.

'How do you know where her house is?'

'I met her there earlier,' Julia said. 'To get the keys.'

'I thought you said you met her at the lodge.'

'No.' She glanced over at me. 'I wouldn't have said that, because I didn't.'

'How far away is it? Are you sure she'll be home? Maybe it'd be better if we just drove straight into Bantry, rather than further away from—'

'Let me worry about that, okay?' Julia said. She took a deep breath, exhaled loudly. 'Why don't you tell me what happened? Today. On the set.'

I didn't even know where to start, and I told her so.

'Try the beginning.'

'Well, that's just it,' I said. 'I don't actually know where the beginning of this is. I thought, if Martin's here, it must go back to *We Were Kings*, but now you're telling me ...' I swallowed, trying to push back the lump I could feel in my throat. If what Julia was saying was true, what I thought had happened on *Kings* was just a story I'd been telling myself. 'I don't really know what's true and what's just ...'

All in my head.

But I couldn't seem to say those words. Didn't *want* to say them.

'Just tell me what happened,' Julia said. 'From your point of view.'

So I did.

As quickly as I could, in the broadest of strokes, I told her about the phone call offering me the job, my checking with Lindsey. The weird text messages coinciding with my arriving on set. Finding the lost earring, the page of annotated script. Waking up to find myself alone on set. Then the weird, script-parallels stuff: the knock, the open door, the power going out. But other stuff, too, that wasn't in the script: someone taking my boots, lights going on and off, Peg's card gone from my pocket. The book with my name on it. Someone following me down the path, tripping me, maybe.

Me thinking I was going insane, calling the guards, calling Julia.

Donal coming back, explaining things away, and then me discovering the cameras in the attic.

'It was all a set-up,' I said. 'There *was* no *Final Draft*. At least, not an actual, proper production based off the script. They were trying to make the events in the script come true, to me, so I'd be scared, like her. Like Kate. Like *The Blair Witch Project*, if the actors were really lost in the woods, thinking their co-stars are really going missing and that an actual witch was to blame.'

'That's nuts,' Julia said.

There was still nothing visible on the dark road ahead of us except more road and more dark.

'Could you have passed Joanne's by mistake?' I asked. The car was accelerating, picking up speed. Everything rushing into the beam of the headlights – road, hedgerow, treeline – felt like it was doing so very fast. 'Maybe we should slow down a bit.'

'What I don't get,' Julia said, ignoring me, 'is how the hell Daniel thought he was going to get away with it. I mean, yeah okay, the crew didn't know – or seem to care – but he hardly thought *Steve* was going to be so blasé about it? It's his reputation. His company. They could've been sued. They still might be. And what about, you know, actually *releasing* the film? How did he think that was going to happen, legally, with footage captured without consent based on a script he didn't own the rights to?'

'No, I know. That's what I—' But then I stopped, confused. Because that alarm in the back of my brain had just started flashing again.

WRONG WRONG WRONG.

'What?' Julia said, glancing over at me.

I turned to look at her.

'I didn't say anything about Daniel,' I said. 'That was the next part.'

'You told me back at the house.' Her eyes were on the road. 'When you first came out of the woods. Steve isn't Steve. That's what you said.'

'But I didn't say he was Daniel.'

A deep sigh. 'Adele, who do you think is a more reliable source on what has and hasn't happened here tonight? You just told me that you thought ... I don't even know *what* you thought, but you saw your *name* in a *book* and freaked the fuck out. Took off running. What kind of person does that? You're obviously not well. The sooner you accept that, the better.'

She took us around a sharp corner at such speed that my upper body slid towards the door.

In the footwell behind me, I heard the torch roll.

The red-light torch.

That thing that might look like a pair of demonic eyes in the dark, hiding just beyond the treeline.

Julia's hair was pulled into a bun, exposing her ears. The one closest to me had no earring in it. I leaned forward to try to see her other ear, reflected in the side-mirror. I *thought* I could see something glinting in her other lobe, but the mirror was too far away for me to be sure.

Maybe this did go all the way back to *We Were Kings*, but not at all in the way that I'd thought.

Maybe it went back much further than that.

'Julia,' I said, 'when did you come to West Cork?'

She didn't respond. She was staring straight ahead, both hands gripping the wheel.

'Where are we going, really?'

'I don't know,' she said in an odd voice. 'It's not like I had a plan.'

'Is it you, Julia? Is all this you?'

Quietly: 'Who the hell else would it be?'

The road was rushing into our headlights at such speed, I was braced at every bend for the sensation of the wheels leaving it. It felt like we were in a video game – and about to crash out of this level. I double-checked my seatbelt was secure, covered the mechanism with my hand. Used the other one to grip the interior door handle.

'Let's be clear about one thing,' Julia said. The rear wheels slid a little as she took a corner. 'I didn't do this to you. *You* did this to *me.*'

'Can you slow down? Or better yet, stop. Pull in and let's talk about this.'

'It's always about *you*, isn't it? What you want. Which we all know is just whatever I might get. You've been doing it to me for years. Taking everything for yourself, ruining every single fucking chance I get. It started at that goddamn casting call for *These* and it never, *ever* stopped.'

A blur of lights flashed by on the left. It looked like we'd just passed a cluster of houses or a farm.

Julia, this has gone far enough. That's what Martin had said. But he wasn't just addressing her, he was telling her.

That *she* had taken things far enough.

'Do you ... do you *know* Martin? Like, outside of *Kings*?'

Julia rolled her eyes.

'You truly *are* oblivious,' she said. 'So wrapped up in yourself, so self-obsessed, you don't even see what's right in front of you. Step off Planet Adele for a second, why don't you? Open your eyes, look around.'

I was trying to, but I couldn't identify what I was seeing.

Julia suddenly slammed on the brakes, bringing the car to a screeching, skidding stop right in the middle of the road – right in the middle of a crossroads.

I pulled on the passenger-door's handle, but it wouldn't give.

The door was locked.

'That girl,' she said, 'the crying crazy one that day at the *Kings* audition. Her and Martin weren't together. She was some unhinged drama-school dropout who he'd worked with once who was obsessed with him, that's all. Martin was with *me*.' She paused. '*Is* with me. *Was* probably, after all this. After *you*.'

I didn't know what to say to this, so I opted for nothing.

'We were happy,' she went on. 'His marriage was just a business arrangement by then – to him, anyway. He didn't love her, he loved me. And we were going to be together. Build a life together. *Careers* together. And then, just like she always does, Adele Rafferty waltzes in and destroys everything.'

I had no idea what she was talking about, or *when* she was.

'Do you mean on *Final Draft*?'

'On *We Were Kings*! That bloody audition that you' – Julia put on sing-sing voice, apparently mocking mine – '*absolutely nailed*.' Another eye-roll. 'Martin came to my place that night, lay in my bed, and went on and on and on about how great you were. About what a star you'd be some day. About how they were going to change the script for you. Clearly, he didn't know we were friends.' She paused. 'If that's what we even were. I don't think friends make it their mission to take everything that matters from each other.'

'I never took anything from you,' I said.

But that wasn't true, though, was it? I had taken the role of Wendy Morgan in *These Are the Days*, at that open casting call, back when we were kids – and with it, the career that Julia should've had.

But this was the first I was hearing of her *wanting* it. She had trained and gone into theatre and was hugely in demand. As far as I knew, she looked down her nose at TV. I had always thought I was the discount-store version of the kind of actor she wanted to be, that she was glad she'd dodged the bullet that had lodged in me.

Unless this wasn't about acting.

'Julia,' I said, 'please believe me when I say I had absolutely no interest in Martin. *Have* no interest in him.'

'But he had it in *you*.'

'That's not my fault.'

'Nothing ever is, is it? And yet, here we are again, with you in a role meant for me. And this time, you came *all the way back* from LA to steal it from me.'

'What are you— Did you audition for this?'

'*Audition* for it?' Julia spat. 'I bloody *wrote it*.'

Whatever parts of the jigsaw puzzle I'd thus far managed to assemble slid off the tabletop and smashed back into their constituent pieces.

'We wrote it together,' she said. 'Martin was going to direct, I was going to play Kate – and those were our terms, we weren't interested in selling it unless that was the agreement. So we've been shopping it around, we brought it to Cross Cut at some point – months ago – but Steve Dade passed. Which was fine, he was way down our list anyway. I mean, one incomprehensible short and one miserable feature? Big whoop. We moved on. But then, the next thing I know, *you're* calling me from LA to tell me that you've just been *offered the lead* in it.'

My phone call, the one I'd made overlooking the radioactive pool.

'I knew as soon as you said about the book and the woods,' she said. 'And Steve Dade was too much of a coincidence. He'd either stolen our script or stolen our idea.' Julia turned to glare at me. 'Why did you even call me? Really? Because it was hardly to ask about a guy who had directed one episode of a thing I was in for five minutes years ago, when we both know you'd already decided to take the part. Let me help you out: because you *had* to tell me. You just couldn't resist shoving it in my face, like every other thing you got that I was supposed to have.'

A beat passed.

'And then?' I asked. 'What happened then? What did you do?'

Julia sighed. 'Look, it wasn't like I had a plan, okay? I just, I don't know … *reacted.*'

'How?'

She looked out at the road. 'I actually was in rehearsals when you called me. Afterwards, I just walked out. Called Martin. He freaked, because of course Cross Cut hadn't bought our script. No one had, so how the hell could it be in production? We spent a couple of hours trying to get a hold of Steve, and then of Daniel, but neither of them were answering. In the end, I persuaded Martin to just get in the car and come here. We made some calls on the way down, to various rental properties that would be big enough, and eventually we made contact with Joanne. She not only confirmed the location for us, but she had another house we could book into ourselves. We checked in, thinking we'd stay for a night, have a snoop around the set, figure out what the fuck was happening. Confront Steve, Martin thought – until Daniel knocked on our door.'

'You met Daniel?'

'And the AD, the wimpy guy. They came to warn us about the shoot – the noise, at night. Daniel hadn't met us before, but of course we'd met Steve, so we knew it wasn't him. Martin was all riled up – we'd just had a fight – and wanted to punch the guy in the face there and then, but I thought it was better to try to collect some intel before we went storming in. So we decided to stick around, to see what was happening. We were there, you know, when you got out of the taxi. In the trees. It was easy to walk between the houses – during the day, anyway.'

'What were you fighting about?'

Julia hesitated. 'Well ... You.'

'*Me?*'

'I'd only just told him you were playing Kate. Prior to that I'd just said it was some actor I knew. He got upset.'

'Was he worried I'd have another breakdown?'

Julia laughed darkly. 'Seriously?'

'What?'

'Can you even conceive of something not being about you?'

'But you just said—'

'He was worried about *me*. About why I'd really wanted to come down to the set.' And then, in a whisper, she added, 'What I might be planning to do.'

Julia's eyes were unfocused now, staring into space.

I looked in the direction she seemed to be looking in and saw, for the first time, a signpost attached to a telephone pole at the corner nearest to us. A sign pointing to the road on our left promised a PIER. It occurred to me that we had been stopped in the middle of the crossroads for at least five minutes now and had yet to meet another car.

'What does that mean,' I said, 'what you might do?'

'I didn't want to hurt you, Adele. Of course I didn't. I just needed you to not get this bloody thing too, you know? *I needed to not be hurting.*'

'What did you do?'

'I didn't know about the cameras, and Daniel making stuff from the script happen.'

'What did you *do*?'

'The earring,' Julia said. 'The script page. The ...' She swallowed. 'Tripping you, on the track. They had no security and there wasn't even a fence. They didn't even lock all the doors. When you ... when you called me from the road, I was only a little ways away. That's how I knew about the flooded bridge – because I overheard Donal telling you about it.'

'But *why*?'

She hesitated. 'You know why.'

And I did.

Finally, pieces were falling into place.

'So I'd freak out,' I said. 'Like I did on *Kings*.'

An almost imperceptible nod.

'Because you did all that, too. Didn't you?'

Julia was crying now, which I took as my answer.

'And Martin *knew*? He knew it was you and he fired *me*?'

'No,' she said, wiping at her eyes with a sleeve. 'He never knew, and he only started to suspect after the fact. I always denied it. And I didn't plan that either, Adele. I *swear*. It just *happened*, okay? It was self-preservation. There was a rumour going around that Martin was seeing someone behind Sandra's back, and I knew that would just cause loads of trouble – and he'd already been saying we should end things, pause them until he could get out of his marriage – so I needed them to go away. I just whispered to a few people that it was you.'

'But how did that help?'

'I didn't tell anyone you were *seeing him*,' Julia said, as if that would've been preposterous. 'I said that you wanted people to *think* you were, so you'd get like, special treatment on set or whatever. That *you* were the source of the rumours. Martin found out, eventually, and then when you had your little breakdown ... Well, he thought maybe I had something to do with that. That I was doing the things you said were happening. And that I'd started that stupid Twitter account. Because I was jealous, and I wanted you gone.'

'*Were* you?'

'How could I not be jealous?'

'I meant, were you doing those things?'

In a near-whisper, Julia said the most unconvincing, 'No.'

'What you told me back at the lodge, about other people getting sick, and the hairstylist, and the call-sheets ...'

'I made that up,' she said miserably.

A few more disparate pieces came together, slipped into place.

'Martin was coming to get me,' I said. 'To get me away from Daniel and whatever else was going on. What you were doing, or what he feared you'd do. He'd been warning me when he sent those texts.'

'On your side, even then. His precious Adele.' Julia rolled her eyes. 'Well, the first two were from him. The third one was from me. I sent it after I found the first two.'

We sat in silence for a beat.

'I'm not a bad person,' she said then. 'You just don't know what it's like. What it feels like. To want something so badly that your life is just a shadow of the life you're supposed to have. Where every morning, you wake up and wonder, will today be the day? Is this where my actual life begins? Or is this another one where I don't get to live it, where I'm still cold in the shadows? It just … over time … It takes you over. Completely.' Julia's voice cracked. 'I can't do it any more, Adele. Really. I *can't.*'

'I get it,' I said, putting a hand on her arm. 'I really do. The wanting. How awful it is. Not being able to turn it off. It's like that therapist said to me – it's a stress, and over time, that kind of stress can mess with your head.' I couldn't imagine a scenario where that stress pushed me to behave like Julia had, but my main priority now was getting out of this car, to somewhere other people were and she wasn't. 'Let's turn around, and go to Bantry, find a hotel room for the night. Get some sleep and sort all this out tomorrow.'

Julia shook her head. 'We can't sort this out.'

'Of course we can.'

'No.'

She released the handbrake, put the car in gear and swung its wheels to the left.

On to the road that promised a PIER.

'Julia,' I said.

The engine roared as she pushed the accelerator.

'Julia,' I said again. 'Please.'

'It'll just be easier this way.'

'*What* will? What the hell are you doing?'

'I don't want to want it any more, Adele. I can't.'

The surface of the road was falling away beneath us, leading down to something – sea level, I'd guess – while the car was speeding up.

'We can just go home,' I said. 'We can still turn around and go home.'

But Julia wasn't listening to me any more.

She was going to drive us into water. She was going to drive us into water and there was nothing I could do. There wasn't even time to panic, I had to think. Even if I could somehow get my door open, what was I supposed to do then? Jump out? At this speed? Or drown in this car after we went in?

I can roll down my window.

If I could roll down the window, at least I might have a chance of getting out.

I felt for the controls on the door, pressing them at random, trying to find the one that would start the window rolling down.

And then the thing flew out of the dark.

A blur of movement. Something winged and feathered,

detaching itself from the dark and diving – it seemed – straight for our windshield.

A flash of glowing red eyes.

A high-pitched, otherworldly, demonic screech.

I thought, *Barn owl.*

I don't know what Julia thought, but she screamed and swerved to avoid it, and then the tyres were screeching too, and there was no room left on the road, no road left for the car to turn on—

It's not like it is in the movies. Nothing happened in slow-motion. It was all over in what felt like a single heartbeat.

The back wheels locked, sending the rear of the car ahead of the front of it, spinning violently – screaming, things flying around inside the car, headlights sweeping so fast my brain couldn't keep up with the view speeding by – and then—

Impact.

The driver's side of the car slammed into something.

But the rest of the car kept going, lifting off the road on the passenger side, underneath me, and then the world was topsy-turvy, and nothing was where it should've been, and I was sliding, falling, towards Julia—

Screaming.

Breaking glass.

And then, darkness.

The box is filled with COPIES OF *FIRST DRAFT*.

Kate blinks at them in confusion.

> GUS (O.S.)
> You understand why I did it, right?

Kate freezes.

> GUS (O.S.) (CONT'D)
> Why don't you come out from under
> there?

Gus has a knife - small, jagged edge, perhaps
for hunting - and he uses it to lift the leg
of Kate's jeans, exposing flesh. He presses
the tip of the knife into it until a spot of
blood appears.

> GUS (CONT'D)
> I'm not asking.

Slowly, Kate gets to her feet and turns to
face him.

> KATE
> (confused)
> Gus?

> GUS
> (pointing)
> Sit down.

> KATE
> But I—

                    GUS
                 (shouting)
     I said *sit down*.

Kate obeys.

                    KATE
     Did you …? Did you hurt Joel?

                    GUS
     Well, I think so, seeing as he's
     dead.

Kate starts to cry again.

                    KATE
     But … why?

                    GUS
     Oh, no. We're not doing that. We're
     not doing the thing where the villain
     gets distracted explaining his whole
     evil plan so that the final girl can
     kill him.

Kate glances towards the phone. It's at the
end of the couch, on her right. She's sitting
in the middle of it.

                GUS (CONT'D)
     You know what *I* want to read? A
     thriller where the bad guy dies
     before anyone finds out what the hell
     was going on.

She edges towards it, barely a couple of
inches. Gus doesn't see this.

GUS (CONT'D)
Before he has a chance to explain.
More true to life, that way. Leave
'em hanging, I say.

KATE
Then you should write it. Write the
book you want to read. You know who
said that?

GUS
The dead guy? I'm not sure we should
be taking *his* advice, to be honest.
That's the thing about this business.
So many people telling you what you
should do and so few people actually
knowing what the fuck they're on
about.

KATE
Is this some kind of joke? A prank?
Are you and Joel in on this?

GUS
(sarcastically)
Oh babes, no. That would be a good
twist but I don't think poor Joel is
in on anything any more.

KATE
You're scaring me, Gus.

GUS
Well, mission accomplished. It
wouldn't be very dramatic if you
weren't scared, now would it?

Kate edges closer again to the phone.

                    GUS (CONT'D)
Did you like it, by the way? *First
Draft*? Please don't let the sharp
knife influence you in any way. I
want the truth. I *like* feedback.

                    KATE
I didn't get to the end.

                    GUS
Oh, but you *did*. This is it. Right
here. The real ending. And trust me,
you won't see the twist coming.

                    KATE
What are you talking about?

                    GUS
To be fair, it's more of a reveal.
I hate when people use those words
interchangeably. Don't you?

                    KATE
Gus, please. Tell me what's happening
here.

                    GUS
Come on, Kate. Just think about it
for a minute. Memoir is so much
easier to sell than fiction. Just ask
James Frey.

Kate starts to inch her hand under a throw
cushion. She's doing this behind her back, her
eyes on Gus; he doesn't see.

GUS (CONT'D)

He couldn't get his novel published
until he pretended it was all true
and then, bingo, Oprah's on the
phone.

KATE

That didn't work out so well for him,
from what I've read.

GUS

Because he lied. It wasn't true and
he got found out. But *I* won't be
making the same mistake.

KATE

What?

GUS

I've written my novel, and now I'm
going to make it come true.

Kate's hand is now within reach of the phone.

GUS (CONT'D)

Look, I'm not saying I *wanted* to do
this. Joel was annoying as fuck,
yeah, but you've been a good friend.
I just want the getting published
thing so much more than I want
friends, you know? I want it so much
that sometimes … Sometimes it scares
me how much I want it. I have to have
it, Kate. There's no other option.

KATE

You lured us here.

                              GUS
          Ooh, *lured*. Good word. I should write
          that down.

                              KATE
          Your aunt isn't here, is she?

                              GUS
          No. So …
                    (raising the knife)
          Feel free to scream.

Kate lunges to grab the phone with her right
hand.

The knife comes down on her left arm, slashing
the skin open, but she still manages to whip
the phone up and - with a scream - into the
side of Gus's head with force.

He falls to the ground.

Kate runs—

66 INT. HALLWAY, CHERRY LODGE - NIGHT [CONTINUOUS]   66

—to the front door.

But it won't open. It's locked.

                              KATE
          Fuck fuck fuck

She turns back around. The hallway is a tunnel
of closed doors.

Kate checks each door in turn, pulling
desperately on their handles, pushing the

doors themselves, but each one appears to be
locked.

>   GUS (O.S.)
>   Kate?

She freezes.

>   GUS (O.S.) (CONT'D)
>   Where'd you go, Kate?

Kate has one more door to check. Frantic now,
she pushes it—

And it opens. She slips inside.

67   INT. STUDY, CHERRY LODGE – NIGHT [CONTINUOUS]   67

The room is dark, but has a window with no
curtains. Kate waits for her eyes to adjust to
the dim.

It's an office. Bookshelves, a messy desk,
half a dozen open boxes of what looks like
more copies of *First Draft*.

Sitting among the debris on the desk is a
VINTAGE TYPEWRITER.

Kate grabs it with both hands and then hurries
to hide behind the door.

A shadow appears beneath the door: two feet.

>   GUS (O.S.)
>   You're in the office? I love it.

The door knob begins to turn.

Kate raises the typewriter—

The door starts to open—

The knife enters first. Gus pauses, as if expecting a blow to come.

But Kate doesn't move.

He steps inside, looks around. Relaxes slightly. Turns to go—

Kate brings the typewriter CRASHING down on his head.

Gus falls to the floor and drops the knife for the second time.

Kate picks up the typewriter and stands with it over his body, holding the machine above his head.

A halo of blood is already seeping out from behind Gus. His eyes are closing, his skin turning pale.

                    GUS (CONT'D)
                    (weakly)
          Death by typewriter? Come on. That's
          so unoriginal.

                    KATE
          It doesn't matter how much you want
          it, Gus. No one wants to read *your*
          fucking book.

She drops the typewriter. Its mechanism makes a satisfying DING on impact.

Kate limps along the main road in the dark.
There is no sound except for her footsteps.

Suddenly, a blue-tinged light illuminates her
face, showing us that she's bruised, bloodied
and red-eyed from crying. The light starts
to flicker. In the distance: SIRENS. They're
getting louder, coming closer.

From behind Kate's back, we see emergency
vehicles approach. One of them stops in the
road. A uniformed garda gets out and starts
running towards her.

Before the garda reaches Kate, she collapses
on the ground.

DISSOLVE TO:

THE NEXT MORNING

Opening my eyes didn't turn off the dark.

For one heartbeat of total panic, I didn't know what was happening or where I was. But then a shape started to take form in the depths of the darkness: a rectangle of not-quite-as-dark. As my eyes adjusted, I put a name to it. *Window.* In this ... *Bedroom.* In a hotel in Bantry, half an hour's drive from the set of *Final Draft.*

'Thank fuck for that,' I said out loud.

There was no one to hear me; I was alone in the room. Donal had brought me here from Bantry General, where they'd stitched the wound on my forehead, X-rayed my limbs and set one of them – my left arm – in a plaster cast that prevented me from bending it at the elbow. Everything else was stiff and sore, but in the scheme of things, I'd got away lightly.

The ambulance Julia had needed had taken her all the way to Cork University Hospital, nearly fifty miles up the road.

I had no idea what time it was, whether the light creeping around the edges of the black-out curtains was from the moon or the sun. I swung my legs out of the bed and made my way to the window, pushing back the heavy material—

You have got *to be kidding me.*

The view out of the floor-to-ceiling window was entirely of trees.

When I pressed my nose to the glass and looked straight down, I could just about see some machinery that might be a ventilation system for the hotel, but that was the only thing I could see that wasn't branches.

Until I looked up and saw blue sky.

Day, then. Morning time, it felt like. I couldn't have slept very long, seeing as I'd only checked into this room around 4:30 a.m.

Behind me, the phone on the desk began to ring.

It made me think of my own phone, and how I had no clue where it was. I didn't know where any of my stuff was. The only thing I had with me that I wasn't currently wearing was the pair of boots I'd taken from the house last night, and what I was wearing was a pair of too-big sweatpants and a too-big sweatshirt that Donal had brought to the hospital for me. I didn't even have a toothbrush.

'Hello?'

'Good morning, Ms Rafferty,' a female voice said smoothly. 'This is Aisling on reception. I have a gentleman here who'd like to speak to you. Can I put him on the phone?'

We got two takeaway coffees from the hotel bar and walked outside, into chilly morning sunshine. There were a couple of picnic tables directly across the road, by the water's edge. We went to the furthest one and sat side by side facing the grey-blue waters of Bantry Bay, with Whiddy Island and the Beara Peninsula in the distance. The surface was so still it looked like glass in places. The view extended for miles and miles.

'It's beautiful, isn't it?' Steve said.

The *real* Steve, newly arrived from France on the first flight he could get out of there.

'To be honest,' I said, 'I'm just happy it's not trees. I never realised how much I like to be able to see, you know, *distance.*'

'I feel like I should show you some ID.'

I took a sip of my coffee. 'If only I'd asked Daniel for his.'

'That's not what happens, though, is it? You don't go for a job interview and ask the interviewer to prove who they are.'

'I think I will from now on.'

Steve smiled at this.

'Is Dade your real last name?' I asked.

'Legally, now, yeah, but it's adopted. Did you ever see the movie *Hackers*?'

I shook my head, *no*. 'I've never heard of it.'

'Before your time, I'd say. Jonny Lee Miller and Angelina Jolie are in it, looking like neither of them can legally drink. I was obsessed with it, and Miller's character was called Dade. I thought it sounded cool. Way cooler than Murphy.'

'How was your brother's wedding?'

'Great – until my phone started exploding.' Steve pointed at my cast. 'How's this?'

'It's all right.' I lifted it a little, as if to test it. 'More awkward than painful. Six weeks, they said I'll be in it.' I paused. 'So go on, then. Let's hear it.'

Steve took a sip of his coffee before starting.

'Daniel and I have been best friends since we were kids. Very different people, though. I'm very risk-averse, methodical, by the book, and Daniel is … Well, he's *not* those things. That's why we work so well together, and have for so long. We balance each other out. He pushes me to take chances and I stop him from … Well, I stop him from trying to do fucked-up shit like this.'

'Not this time,' I said.

'No, not this time.'

'So what happened?'

'I *vaguely* remember that script crossing my desk a few months ago. I remember because of the title – it's the same as the software screenwriters use. Struck me as a bit stupid to call your screenplay that. It's a bit like writing a novel and calling it *Microsoft Word.*'

I laughed at this, but only until I felt a twinge in my side as my ribs let me know that they didn't like the movement.

'I don't think I even read the whole thing through,' he said. 'We passed, I got a nice email from Martin thanking me for considering it, all was good – and then the next thing I hear, it's months later, and he's left me a voicemail during my brother's wedding to accuse me of going into production with a script I never bought. Then a friend of mine at the wedding comes up to me with your agent on his phone, asking me about the same thing. But it's because her client is already, somehow, on set – of a Cross Cut production that I know nothing about.'

'So what had happened?'

'Apart from Daniel losing the plot?'

'I meant more like the logistics of the thing,' I said.

'I'm hoping to find out for sure when I get back to the office, but from what I can tell, I got in a taxi to the airport and Daniel set about making this movie. Just like he would any other production of ours – a real one – except for it being a skeleton crew and low budget. He used our corporate cards, suppliers – even an unsuspecting intern who helped him book the travel. I was going to Italy after France, he wasn't expecting me back for another week.'

'I was told it had been with another company,' I said. 'Primal something? But that that had fallen through due to *creative differences'* – I made a face as I said this – 'so now you were doing it your way, the way you'd made movies back when you were in college.'

'It's a good excuse to justify why everyone was being hired for a production that was starting almost immediately, but that's it.'

'So that was more bullshit?'

Steve nodded. 'Yeah.'

'Is there a John at your company? Who would've rang me to offer me the part?'

'No ...'

I was starting to think that that had been Daniel, too.

'So,' Steve went on, 'he hires the smallest possible crew, none of whom have ever worked with me, and really, who haven't done much work at all. Inexperienced, so they won't realise their director doesn't know how to direct, and probably in need of the work, so they won't run off when he tells them the truth.'

'Why pretend to be you, though? Why not just be Daniel?'

'So he could do all those things,' Steve said. 'Sign my name. Use my credit card. Get equipment from our usual suppliers. Add legitimacy. Convince you.' He sipped more coffee. 'And, I suppose, feel like the big man on campus for a minute. The one everyone listens to, rather than the one everyone goes to with their problems.'

'But what then? What did he think was going to happen when you found out? That you'd be all, *Wow, genius, let's release this thing?*'

'He's refusing to speak to me now, so I can't say for sure. But there's been tension. Since we started Cross Cut. If I was risk-averse before, imagine me now when I have employees to think about ... Daniel lives in a dream world where he thinks all we have to think about is what we'd like to watch. That's not how it works. It's called the film *industry* for a reason. I've had to shoot him down a lot lately, and I guess it was getting to him. Something must have just snapped and he ran off and did this, to prove something to me. Easier to ask for forgiveness than permission. Isn't that what they say?'

'Did Donal fill you in on ...?'

'Julia?' Steve nodded. 'Yeah. Martin, too. Who would like to talk to you, by the way, when you're feeling up to it.'

'They were both doing the same thing,' I said. 'Julia and Daniel. Messing with my head, just for different reasons.'

'And unwittingly amplifying each other's efforts.' Steve paused. 'Why did *she* do it, do you think?'

'Jealousy. She says. Although I've felt jealous and I've never done anything like this ... But it's been building up. It goes back a long way – I have her to thank for my career, you see. I tagged along with her to an open casting call when we were kids, and they gave the part to me. I ended up on a soap opera for fourteen years, and then that led to *Winter Snow.*'

'I loved that movie,' Steve said. 'Did I—'

'Before you ask,' I said, 'I don't give a shit about any sequel.'

He blinked at me.

'Sorry,' I said, colouring. 'I just get asked that all the time, and I died in the first one.'

I took a sip of my coffee, discovered it was nearly cold.

'You know,' Steve said then, 'when I think about it, I could say something similar about Daniel. A lot of what happened in my career might not have happened if it wasn't for him, but I get the glory. Or, look, maybe it would've, it's hard to know. They blame us for being more successful than them, but not everyone gets what they want. Not everyone *can*. That's not how the world works. Some of us are just more talented than others.'

'But some of us get a lot more luck than our talent deserves,' I said. 'Julia is a much better actor than me. Always has been. But when it came to TV and film, I was the one who got the breaks.'

'How is Julia?'

'Awake, last I heard. On lots of painkillers. And going to be setting off metal detectors for the rest of her life – they had to put some pins in her lower legs. They took the brunt of the impact, they said.'

'Ouch.'

'They said she'll make a full recovery.'

'And she wrote *Final Draft*?'

'With Martin, yeah. But the story was all hers.' I paused. 'I don't know if she realises, but she kind of wrote herself into it, didn't she? She's Gus. She wanted something way, *way* too much.'

'What's the alternative, though? To wanting something? Lie down and wait for death to come?'

'How about relax and enjoy life a bit?'

'I do enjoy my life,' Steve said. 'And my work. Maybe problems arise when you're just too focused on the results. The joy is in the process, the trying. The pursuit.'

I threw him a look. 'If you say anything about it being the journey, not the destination, I *will* risk injury to my other hand.'

Steve laughed, held up both of his in a surrender gesture.

'Okay, okay. I'm just saying, there *is* a way to chase your dreams without sacrificing everything else in your universe. There has to be. People do it. *I* do it.'

'Steve, no offence, but your best friend since childhood just impersonated you, stole from you, risked your business and reputation, *and* broke every employment law in the land. And what if you *don't* get them, after everything? After all the chasing, what if your dreams remain out of reach? What then?'

We fell into an uncomfortable silence.

'How is Daniel?' I asked – to break it, not because I particularly cared.

'Well, we really only talked on the phone long enough for him to tell me he didn't want to talk to me, but during that conversation he said, "Nobody died," at least three times, so ... I'm guessing he's fine. Annoyed, I think, more than anything, that his directorial debut was cut short.'

'And disappointed, probably. I mean, who'd want to watch a horror movie where nobody dies?'

'Hey,' Steve said, turning up his palms. 'At least it'd be original.'

A small fishing boat was gliding across the water, approaching the pier.

'It's such a crazy coincidence,' I said. 'Julia wrote this script – news to me she was writing anything – and then her and Martin – who I didn't know she was involved with – take it to Cross Cut, where Daniel dreams up this ridiculous scheme and decides to cast *me* in it? Julia's best friend and the actor who had a freak-out on Martin's last set?'

Steve shifted in his seat. 'Ah, no,' he said. 'Not exactly.'

'Not exactly what?'

'It's not exactly a coincidence.' He paused. 'I'm sorry, Adele, but everyone's heard about what happened. It's common knowledge. This country is a village, and this industry is so small … Word got around. So Daniel knew. And he was looking for someone he knew could act, who fit the part, but who would also agree to something extremely last-minute, who wouldn't have an agent who'd raise any concerns, and who … you know …' Steve trailed off.

'Who was primed for maximum freak-out, to make the footage as good as it could be?' I shook my head, disgusted. 'So glad I could be of service.'

'I'll make sure all the footage is destroyed.'

'Please do.'

'And Cross Cut will cover all your costs.'

'Thank you.'

We fell into another silence then.

'So,' I said, 'to recap. Your best friend was frustrated, and my best friend was jealous. Doesn't that make you feel a little …?' I didn't want to say the word that was on my tongue, but there was no other word for it. '*Disappointed*?'

Steve frowned. 'How so?'

'I just thought … When all the weird stuff started happening, when I woke up alone on set, when I found the book … It just felt like something bigger was going on, you know? A genuine mystery. The explanation is actually … Well, it's pretty mundane, don't you think?'

'That's the problem with mysteries,' Steve said. 'They only exist because you don't have the answers. When you get them' – he clicked his fingers – 'all the mystery gets vaporised. This is a big part of why I don't make horror movies, to be honest. Or even watch them. Whenever the explanation comes, whatever it is, it can't live up to those "What the hell is going on here?" moments at the start.'

I shrugged. 'Depends how it's done, I suppose.'

'If this was a movie,' Steve said, 'we'd need another twist.'

'Or *a* twist, since Julia as villain was pretty obvious, in hindsight.'

'Maybe this isn't the end. Maybe there'll be a sequel.'

'Julia's mother,' I suggested, 'doing a Mrs Voorhees. She never liked me. Not after the audition.'

'Or something jumping up out of the water. Some kind of mythical creature. A paddling Mothman.'

'A *drowning barn owl*, you mean.'

Steve raised an eyebrow. 'That's not what my taxi driver would say.'

'Let me guess: was her name Peg?'

'No, it was a man. A local. Michael something. Who already knew all about the accident and *Final Draft*, of course.'

I rolled my eyes. 'But of course.'

'He said that there's hardly any barn owls around these parts any more. Especially not enough to account for two sightings in the space of a few days.'

'*Two?*' I hadn't told him about the owl I'd seen when I was down by the road. I hadn't told anybody about that.

'Donal said they saw something when they were in the car the other night,' Steve explained. 'Him and Daniel. So maybe there is *some* mystery, lingering still.'

'Or just a few noisy owls.'

Steve laughed.

'So,' he said, 'what are you going to do now?'

'Right now? Find a toothbrush. And then the rest of my stuff.'

'I think Donal might be up at the house, getting it for you, as we speak.'

'And then I'm going to go back to LA—'

'Good for you.'

'—pack up my stuff and come home.'

'Oh.'

'I'm done with this,' I said. 'Acting, I mean. *Really* done this time. I want to do something normal for a living, something I can actually control.'

'I'd understand, but ...' He smiled. 'Never say never.'

'*Never*,' I said, firmly and distinctly.

'Well, I'm going to head up to Cedarwood House, talk to the crew. You have my number, if you need me, and like I said, I think Donal's getting your things. Are you staying long or—'

'My parents are on their way down,' I said. 'They'll be here by lunch.'

'I'm sorry this happened.'

I nodded. 'Me too.'

'If you ever change your mind about the acting thing—'

'I won't.'

'—call me.' Steve stood up. I stood up too. 'Failing that, I hope you find something else to want.'

'Hopefully *not*.' I looked out at the calm surface of the water. 'I never want to want anything, ever again.'

Super: One year later

An expansive bookstore, filled with nooks and crannies. The customers browse quietly, as if in a library.

Kate browses the Fiction A-Z, searching until she lands on *Inside* by Joel Jackson. She runs her fingers tenderly down the spine of the book, lost in thought.

A FEMALE BOOKSELLER approaches.

                    FEMALE BOOKSELLER
         We're ready for you.

                         KATE
         Great. Thanks.

Kate looks back at the book one more time, then turns to follow the bookseller through the store …

70   INT. BOOKSHOP, EVENT SPACE - DAY [CONTINUOUS]   70

… to steps leading up on to a small stage.

                    MODERATOR (O.S.)
         And here she is. Please welcome Kate
         Hegarty!

An audience of two dozen people applaud enthusiastically as Kate walks onstage, smiling and waving but looking a little nervous. There are two seats, facing each other across a small table. Several copies of the same book are stacked on the coffee table in between them: *Final Draft* by Kate Hegarty.

The MODERATOR (40s, blonde, way too glam for a book event) is standing by one of the seats. She motions for Kate to take the other one. They both sit down.

>   KATE
>   (to the audience)
>   Thank you for that generous welcome.

>   MODERATOR
>   They're excited to see you – and
>   so am I. In fact, I can't wait to
>   talk about this book. There's so
>   much I want to ask you. I've so many
>   questions!

The audience laughs a little; a few heads nod.

>   KATE
>   Yes, well …
>   (smiling tightly)
>   Great.

>   MODERATOR
>   I'm going to start with something
>   that *isn't* in the book. I've a
>   quote here from an interview you
>   did recently with the *Sunday Times*.
>   You said, *Instagram mantras tell us
>   to do whatever it takes to achieve
>   our dreams, but there's an inherent
>   danger in that.* Can you explain what
>   you mean by that?

KATE
(scanning the audience)
Well, I just meant—

She stops abruptly. She's seen something.
Someone, in the audience. Someone who
shouldn't be there.

Gus.

Sitting in the last row, holding a copy of her
book. He grins manically at her.

MODERATOR
Is … Is everything okay?

Kate blinks - and Gus is replaced by a
frowning elderly man.

KATE
Yes. Sorry. Just thought I saw
someone I knew.
(clears throat)
But, ah, yeah. It's dangerous to want
something at the cost of everything
else. So much that you can't imagine
reaching the end of your life without
having got it. You don't want to
imagine it. That kind of wanting …
It becomes a problem. The not-having
starts to corrode, and the wanting
starts to change you. So much so
that, eventually, you get to a point
where even if you have the thing …

Kate's eyes move to the stack of her books on
the coffee table.

                    KATE (CONT'D)
Where even if you have the thing,
it's cost you so much, you're left
asking yourself: Was it worth it? And
the answer is, honestly, no.

A beat passes.

                    MODERATOR
Which is, essentially, what happened
at Cherry Cottage.

                    KATE
I don't talk about that.

                    MODERATOR
But clearly, the book is about—

                    KATE
It's a novel.

                    MODERATOR
But obviously there are parallels
with what you experienced at Cherry
Cottage—

                    KATE
                  (firmly)
It's a *novel*.

The moderator bites her lip, shifts awkwardly
in her seat.

71 INT. BOOKSHOP, EVENT SPACE - LATER SAME DAY   71

Kate sits behind a table, signing books. A
long line of audience members clutching their
copies of *Final Draft* await their turn.

A YOUNG WOMAN approaches (20s, giddy with
excitement).

                    KATE
     What's the name?

                    YOUNG WOMAN
     Clare. With no 'i'. Please.

Kate signs the book.

                    YOUNG WOMAN
     I loved it *so much*. I've read it
     twice already!

Kate hands the book back with a tight smile.

                    KATE
     Thank you. And thank you for coming.

                    YOUNG WOMAN
     Can I ask you a question?

                    KATE
     Sure.

                    YOUNG WOMAN
     What's the best writing advice you
     ever got?

                    KATE
     Ah …

                         FADE TO BLACK.

'FINAL DRAFT' PROVES STRANGER THAN NON-FICTION

Real-life horror show to be made into real-life horror movie

Steve Dade's Cross Cut Films has optioned the screen rights to *Winter Snow* star Adele Rafferty's upcoming memoir, *Run Time*.

The former *These Are the Days* regular hit the headlines earlier this year when she signed on for a starring role in an independent horror film, *Final Draft*, with Dade at the helm. But the shoot was hijacked by Daniel O'Leary, Dade's former business partner, who impersonated him on set and filmed Rafferty using hidden cameras in a bid to make a found-footage-style feature starring a cast who would be scared for real. A number of crew members suffered injuries including Rafferty's friend, the actor Julia McLoughlin, who was hospitalised. Civil proceedings are pending and Gardaí say criminal charges may yet be brought.

Now the real Steve Dade looks set to direct a real movie about the fake movie that someone pretending to be him pretended to make. Screenwriter Sheena Lambert will pen the adaptation while Rafferty will executive produce. *Beyond the Woods* star John Ryan Howard has also signed on for an as yet unspecified role.

Production is slated to begin early next year. Thoughts and prayers with whoever has the job of writing the Netflix description.

Rafferty's *Run Time* will be published in August.

AUDREY COUGHLAN

ACKNOWLEDGEMENTS:

Thank you to Jane Gregory, Stephanie Glencross and everyone at David Higham Associates; editor extraordinaire Sarah Hodgson, Will Atkinson and everyone at Corvus/Atlantic Books; everyone at Blackstone Publishing; the team at Gill Hess Ltd; Michael Signorelli; Alison Tulett; Caroline Grace-Cassidy; Sheena Lambert; Hazel Gaynor; Carmel Harrington; Mum, Dad and Claire (and Dexter!).

My brother John gets his own sentence because it was his role in the independent Irish horror movie *Beyond the Woods* (2016) that led to my having the idea for this book, and he also helpfully told me everything I needed to know in order to write it.

To all the incredible booksellers at home and abroad who have been so supportive of me and my work: extra special thanks to you.

Forgive me, West Cork, for messing with your geography for my own gains, but there's a reason they call it fiction.

Thank *you*, most of all, for reading.